SWEET VALLEY

Twins

BEST FRIENDS

Also by Francine Pascal

Sweet Valley Twins

Sweet Valley High

Sweet Valley University

Sweet Valley Confidential

Fearless

My First Love and Other Disasters

Save Johanna!

Little Crew of Butchers

La Villa

Also by Nicole Andelfinger

Power Rangers Universe with Simone Ragazzoni

The Dragon Prince: Bloodmoon Huntress with Felia Hanakata

A Thief Among the Trees: An Ember in the Ashes Graphic Novel with Sabaa Tahir & Sonia Liao

A Spark Within the Forge: An Ember in the Ashes Graphic Novel with Sabaa Tahir & Sonia Liao

Also by Claudia Aguirre

Hotel Dare with Terry Blas

Lifetime Passes with Terry Blas

SWEET VALLEY Twins

BEST FRIENDS

Created and story by
Francine Pascal

Adaptation written by
Nicole Andelfinger

Illustrated by
Claudia Aguirre

Colors by
Sara Hagstrom
Andrea Bell

Letters by
Warren Montgomery

RH
GRAPHIC

NEW YORK

Text copyright © 2022 by Francine Pascal
Cover art and interior illustrations copyright © 2022 by Claudia Aguirre

Visit us on the web! RHKidsGraphic.com • @RHKidsGraphic

Educators and librarians, for a variety of teaching tools, visit us at RHTeachersLibrarians.com

Library of Congress Cataloging-in-Publication Data is available upon request.
ISBN 978-0-593-37647-8 (hardcover) — ISBN 978-0-593-37646-1 (paperback)
ISBN 978-0-593-37648-5 (library binding) — ISBN 978-0-593-37649-2 (ebook)

Designed by Patrick Crotty

MANUFACTURED IN CHINA
10 9 8 7 6 5 4 3 2
First Edition

A comic on every bookshelf.

To my daughters, Jamie, Laurie, and Susan

–F.P.

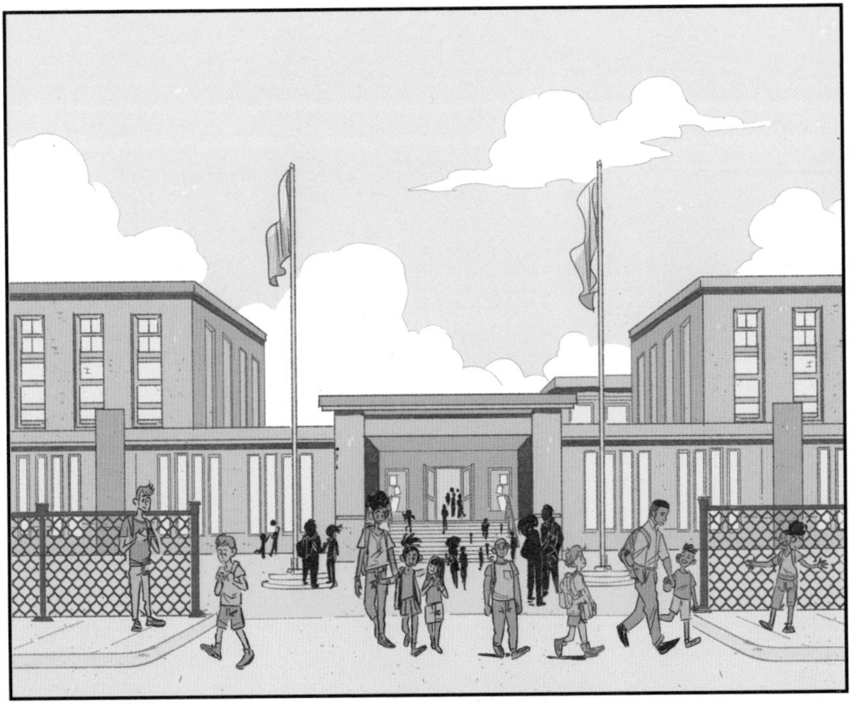

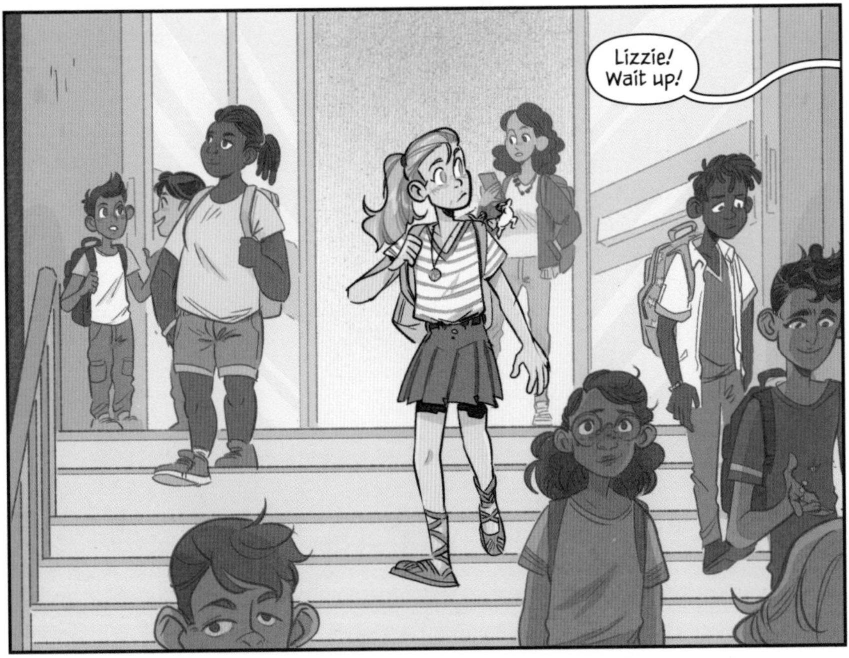
Lizzie!
Wait up!

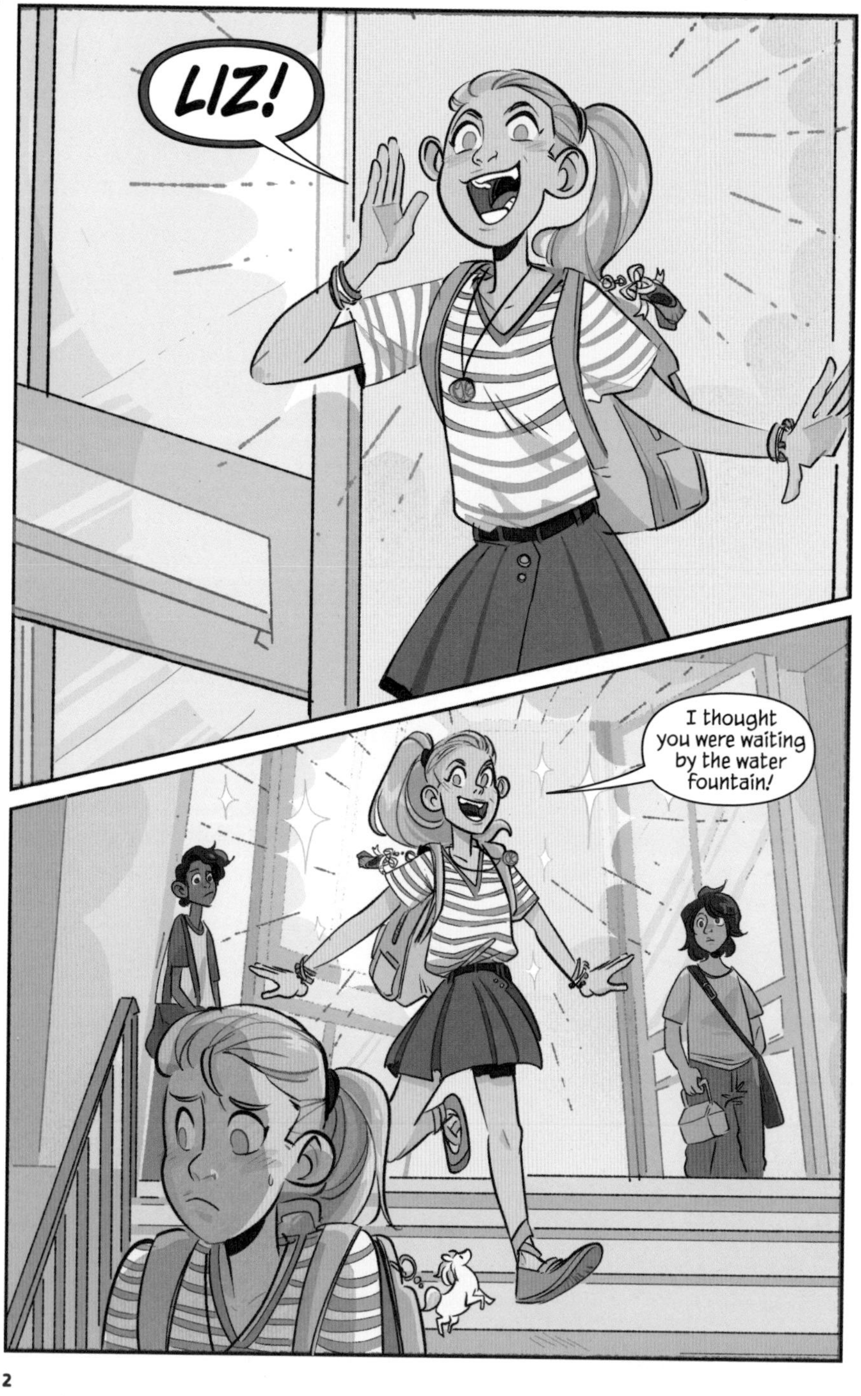
LIZ!
I thought you were waiting by the water fountain!

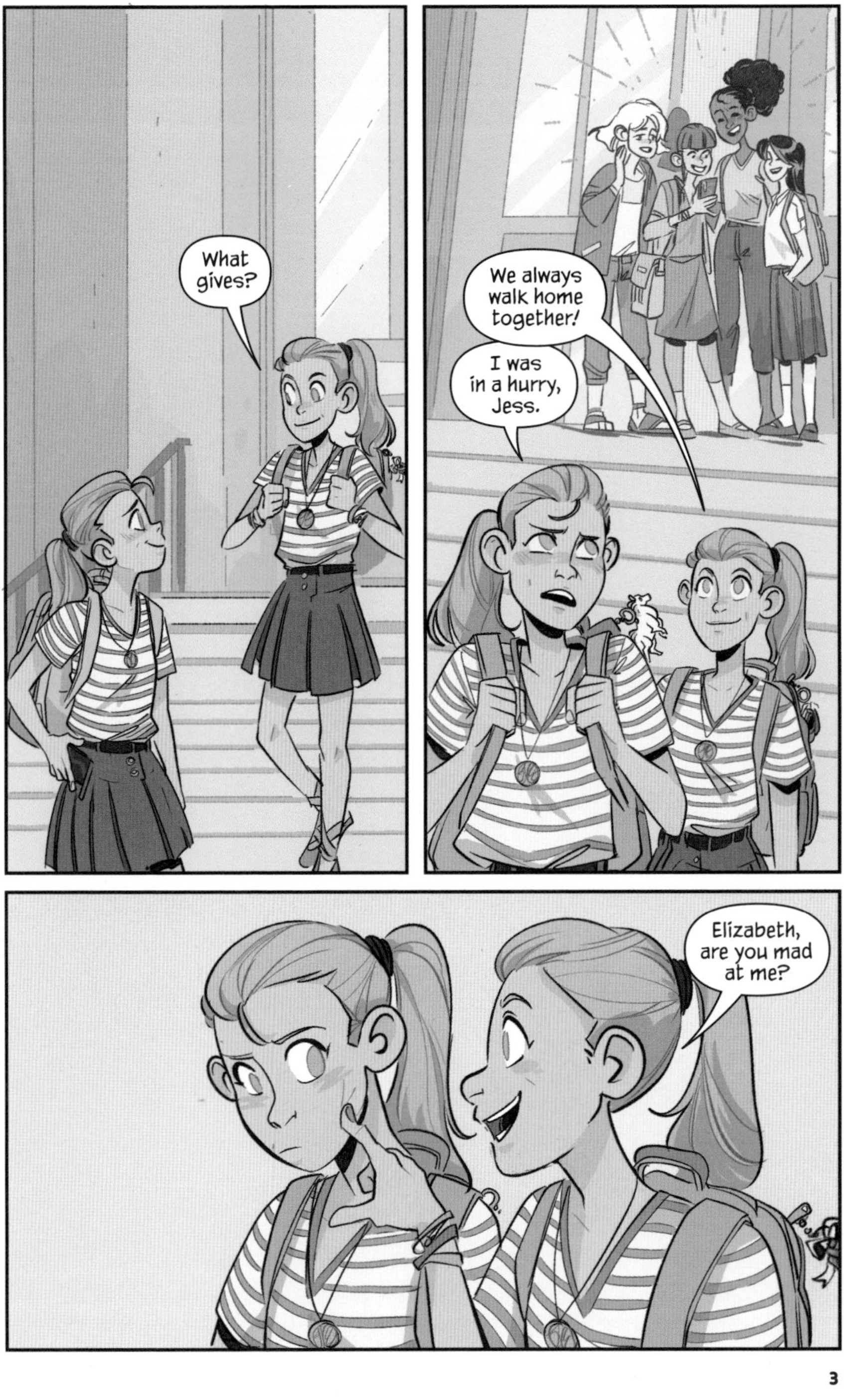
What gives?
We always walk home together!
I was in a hurry, Jess.
Elizabeth, are you mad at me?

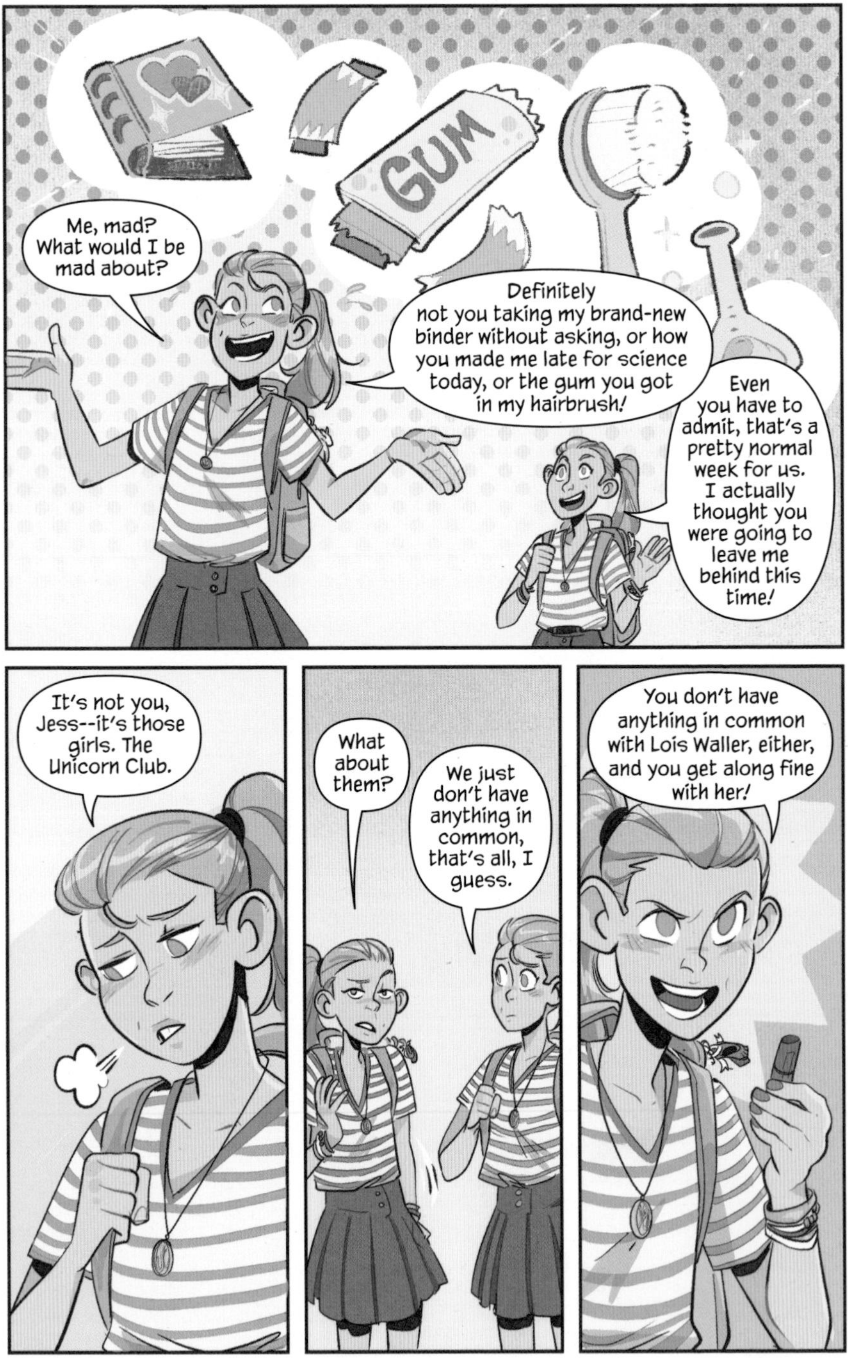

GUM
Me, mad? What would I be mad about?
Definitely not you taking my brand-new binder without asking, or how you made me late for science today, or the gum you got in my hairbrush!
Even you have to admit, that's a pretty normal week for us. I actually thought you were going to leave me behind this time!
It's not you, Jess--it's those girls. The Unicorn Club.
What about them?
We just don't have anything in common, that's all, I guess.
You don't have anything in common with Lois Waller, either, and you get along fine with her!

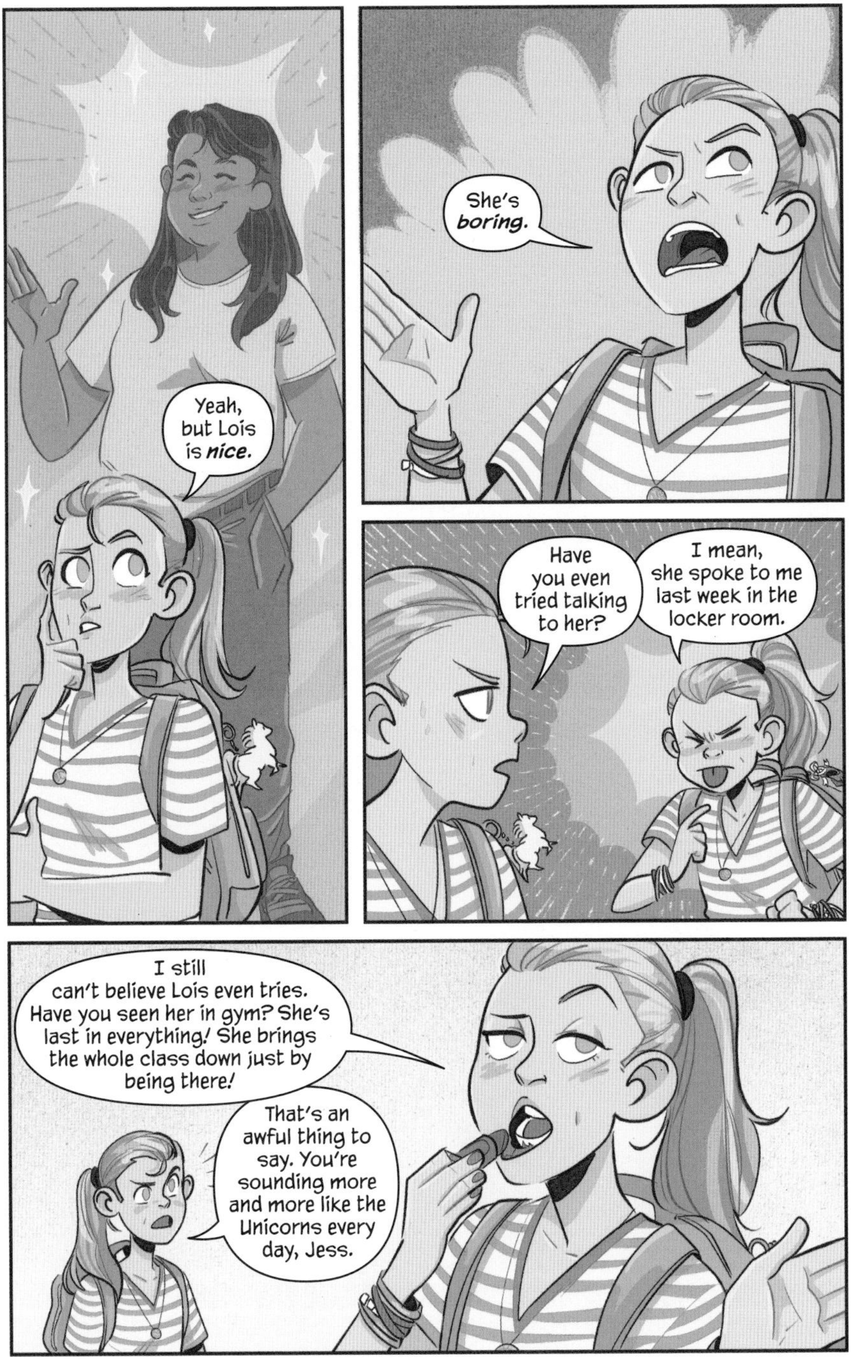
Yeah, but Lois is *nice.*
She's *boring.*
Have you even tried talking to her?
I mean, she spoke to me last week in the locker room.
I still can't believe Lois even tries. Have you seen her in gym? She's last in everything! She brings the whole class down just by being there!
That's an awful thing to say. You're sounding more and more like the Unicorns every day, Jess.

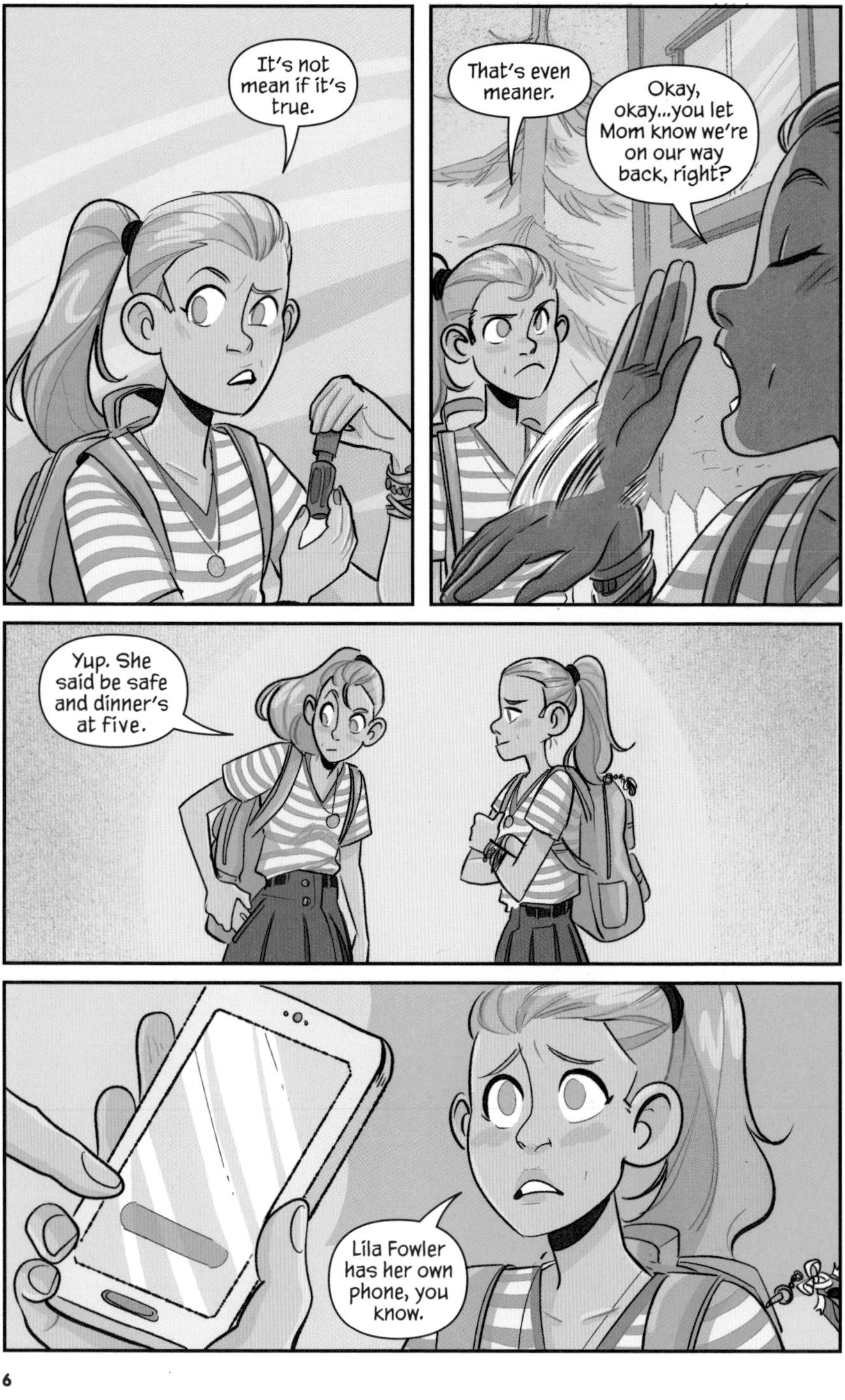
It's not mean if it's true.
That's even meaner.
Okay, okay...you let Mom know we're on our way back, right?
Yup. She said be safe and dinner's at five.
Lila Fowler has her own phone, you know.

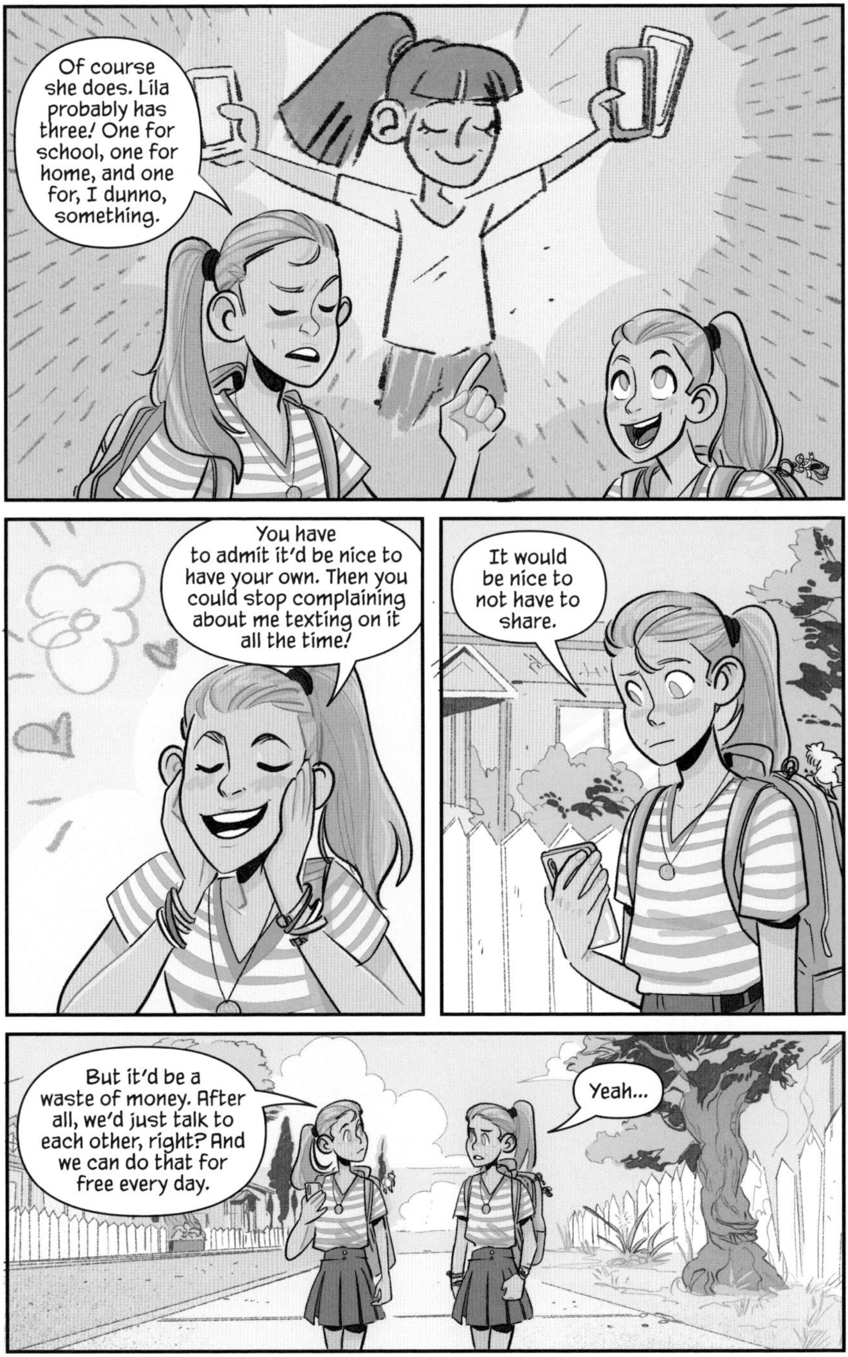
Of course she does. Lila probably has three! One for school, one for home, and one for, I dunno, something.
You have to admit it'd be nice to have your own. Then you could stop complaining about me texting on it all the time!
It would be nice to not have to share.
But it'd be a waste of money. After all, we'd just talk to each other, right? And we can do that for free every day.
Yeah...

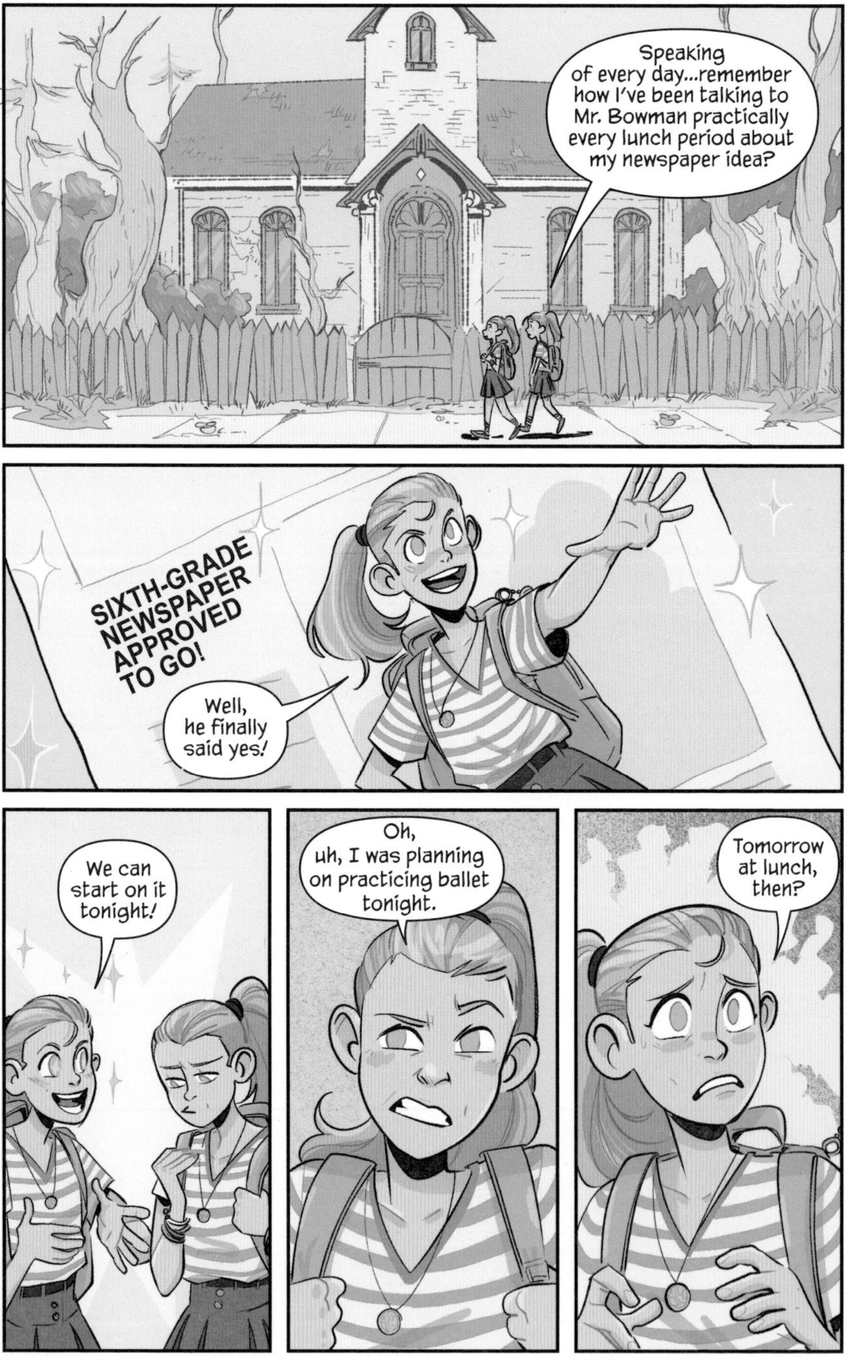
Speaking of every day...remember how I've been talking to Mr. Bowman practically every lunch period about my newspaper idea?
SIXTH-GRADE NEWSPAPER APPROVED TO GO!
Well, he finally said yes!
We can start on it tonight!
Oh, uh, I was planning on practicing ballet tonight.
Tomorrow at lunch, then?

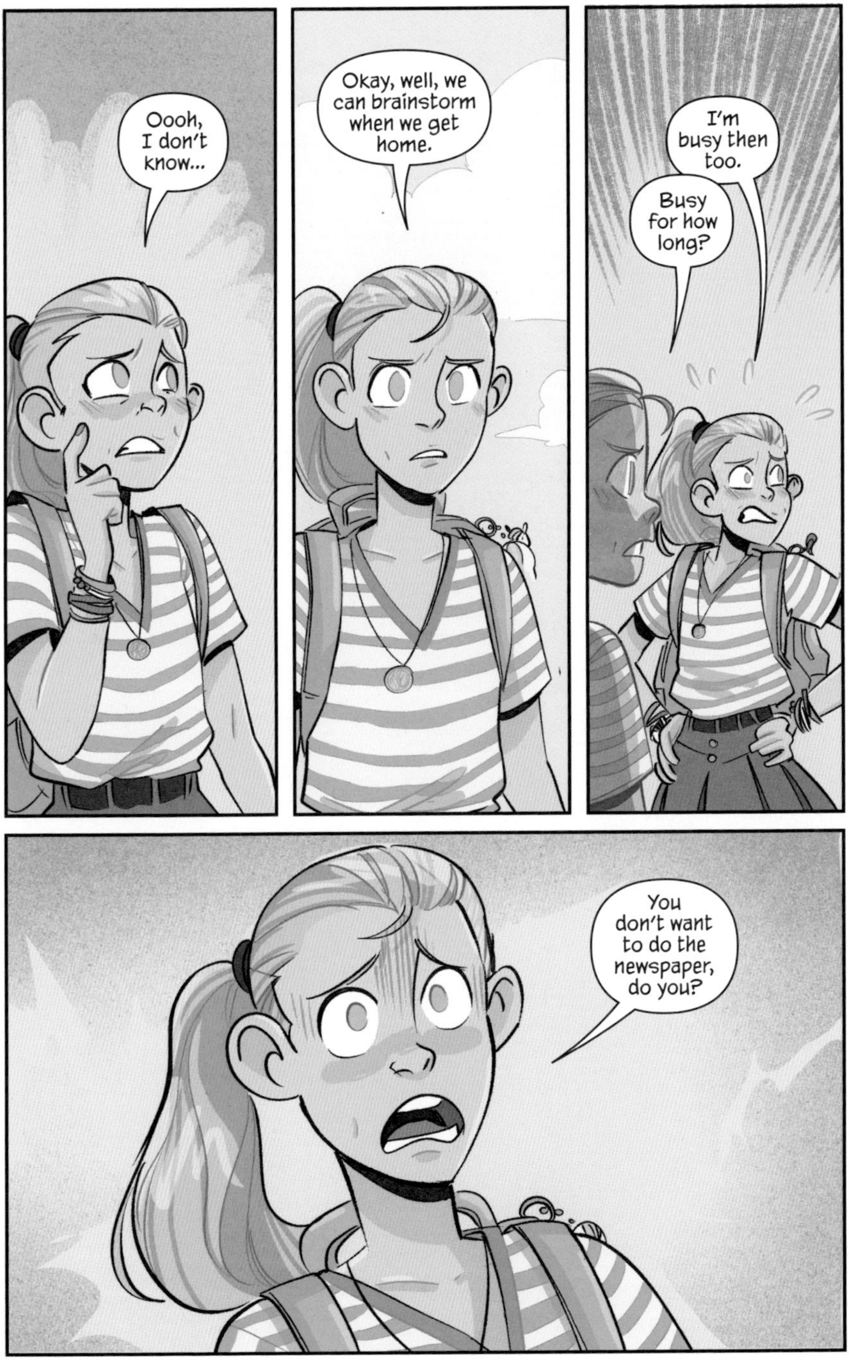
Oooh, I don't know...
Okay, well, we can brainstorm when we get home.
I'm busy then too.
Busy for how long?
You don't want to do the newspaper, do you?

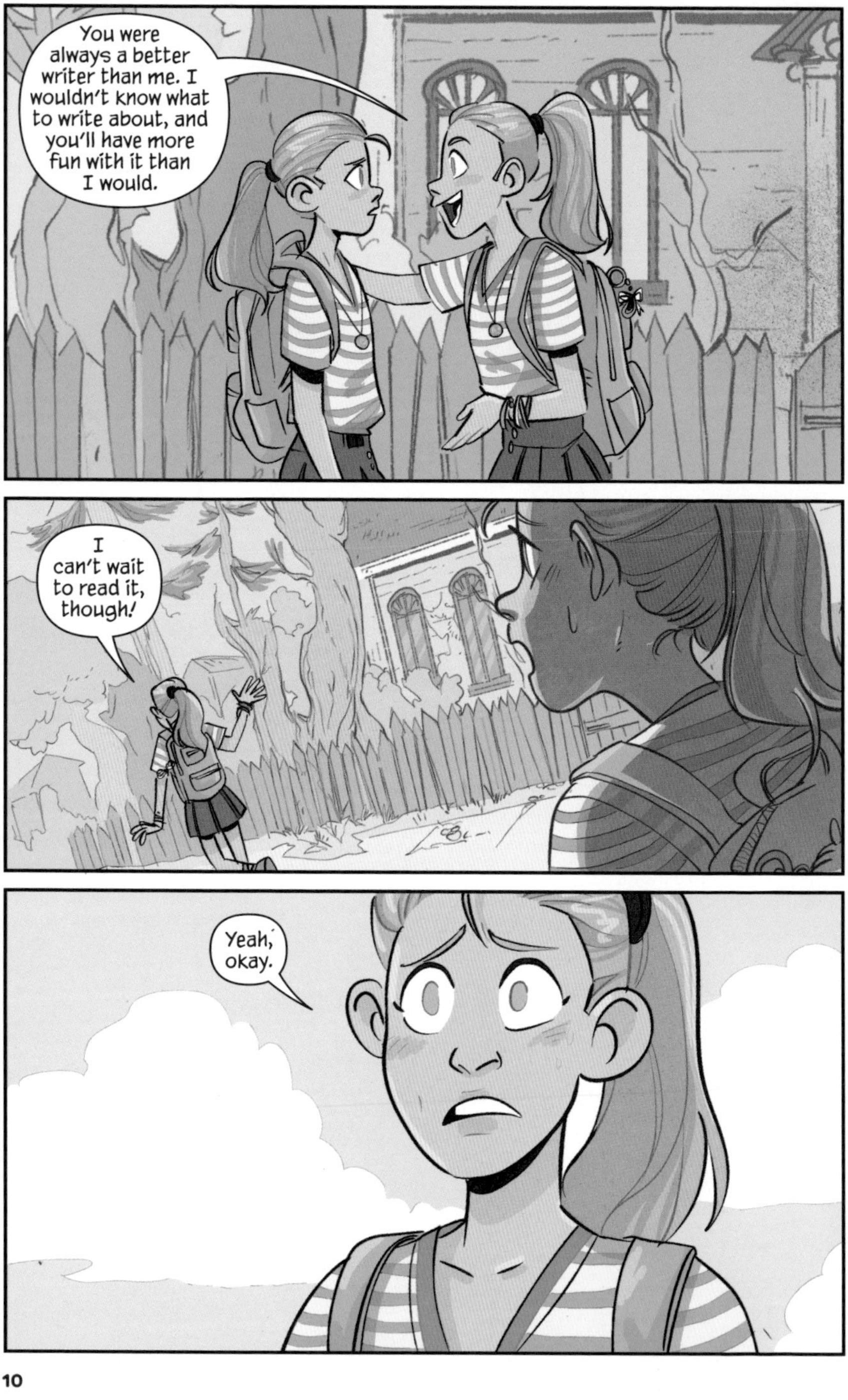
You were always a better writer than me. I wouldn't know what to write about, and you'll have more fun with it than I would.
I can't wait to read it, though!
Yeah, okay.

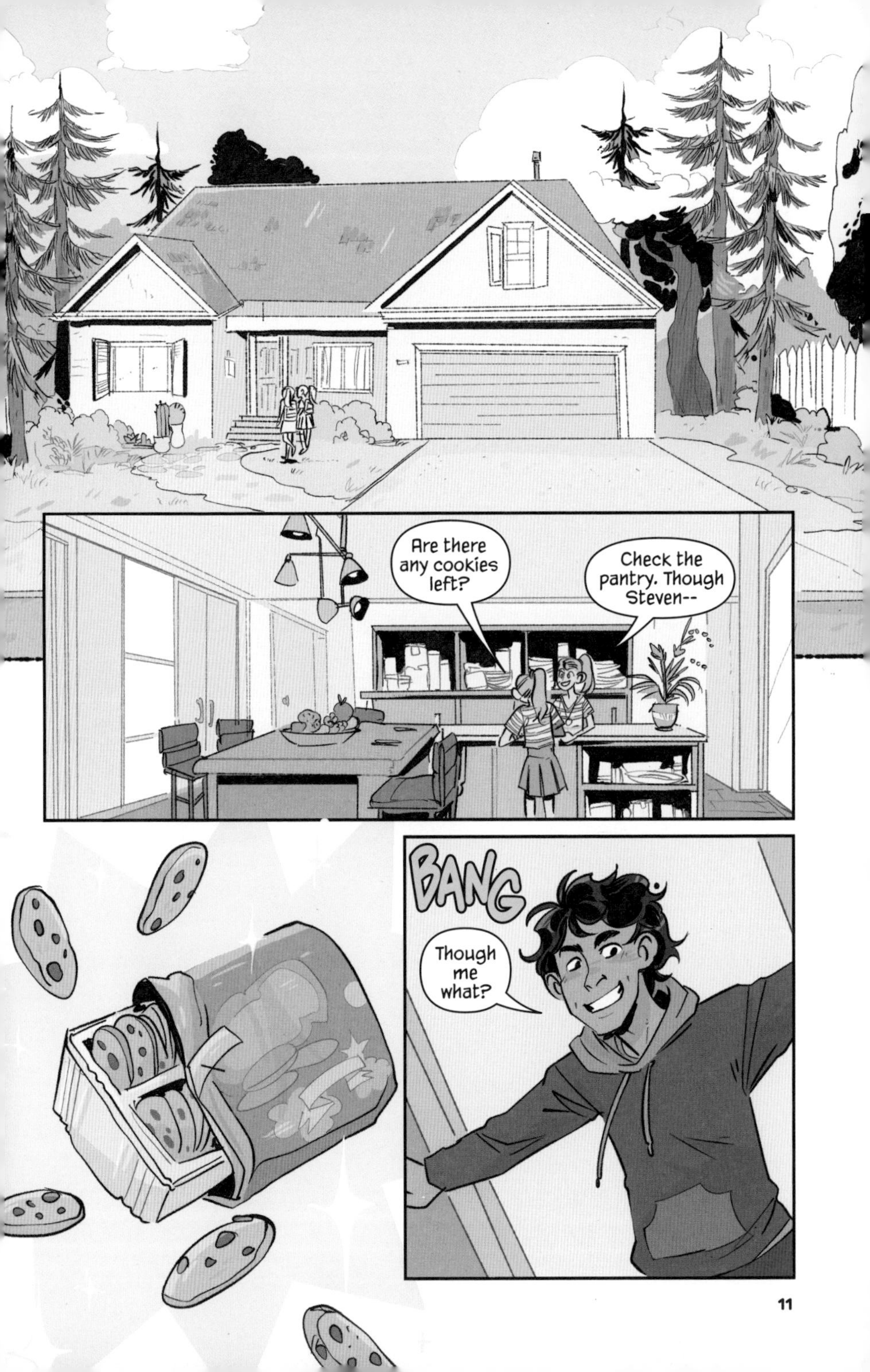
Are there any cookies left?
Check the pantry. Though Steven--
BANG
Though me what?

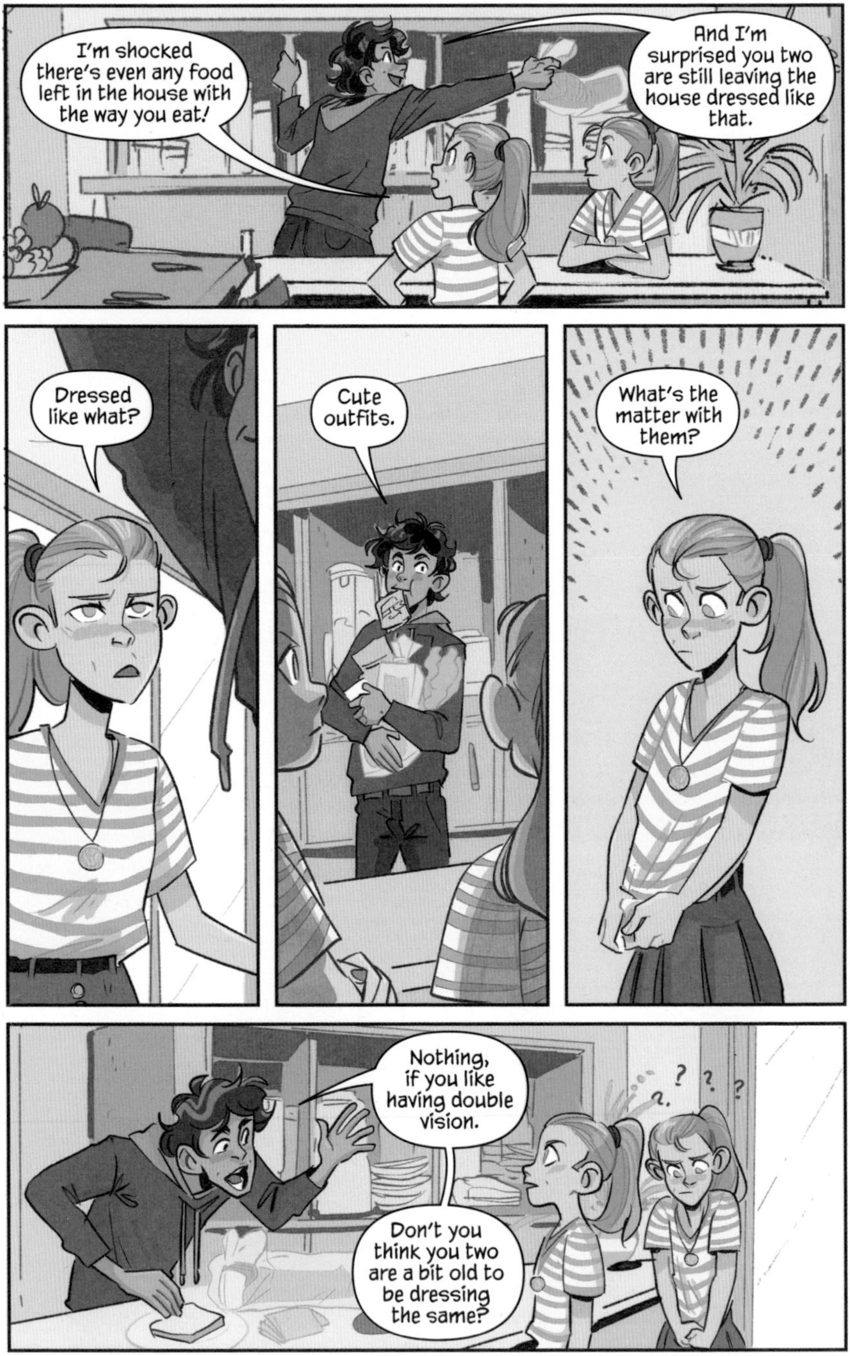
I'm shocked there's even any food left in the house with the way you eat!
And I'm surprised you two are still leaving the house dressed like that.
Dressed like what?
Cute outfits.
What's the matter with them?
Nothing, if you like having double vision.
Don't you think you two are a bit old to be dressing the same?
? ? ?

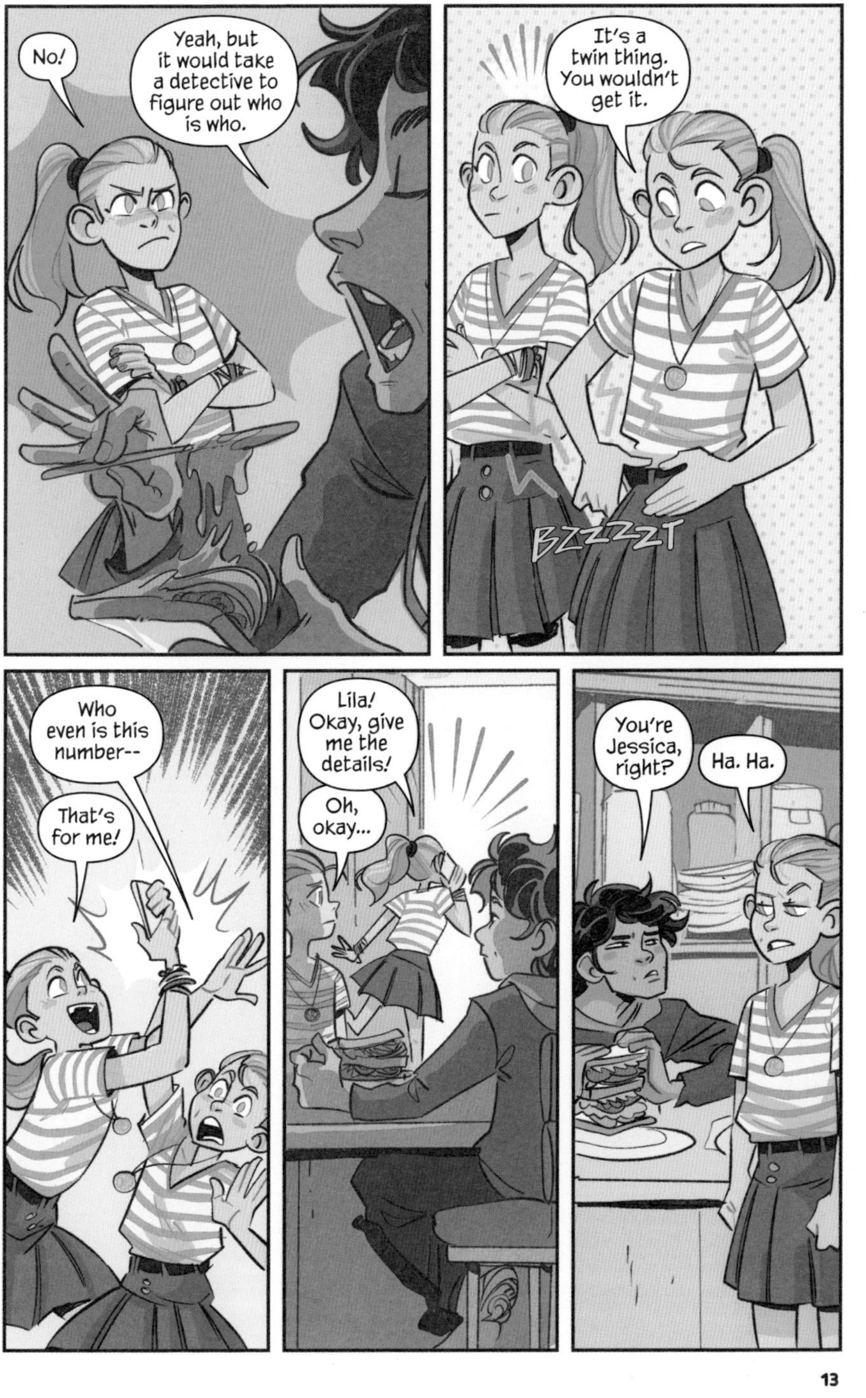
No!
Yeah, but it would take a detective to figure out who is who.
It's a twin thing. You wouldn't get it.
BZZZZT
Who even is this number--
That's for me!
Lila! Okay, give me the details!
Oh, okay...
You're Jessica, right?
Ha. Ha.

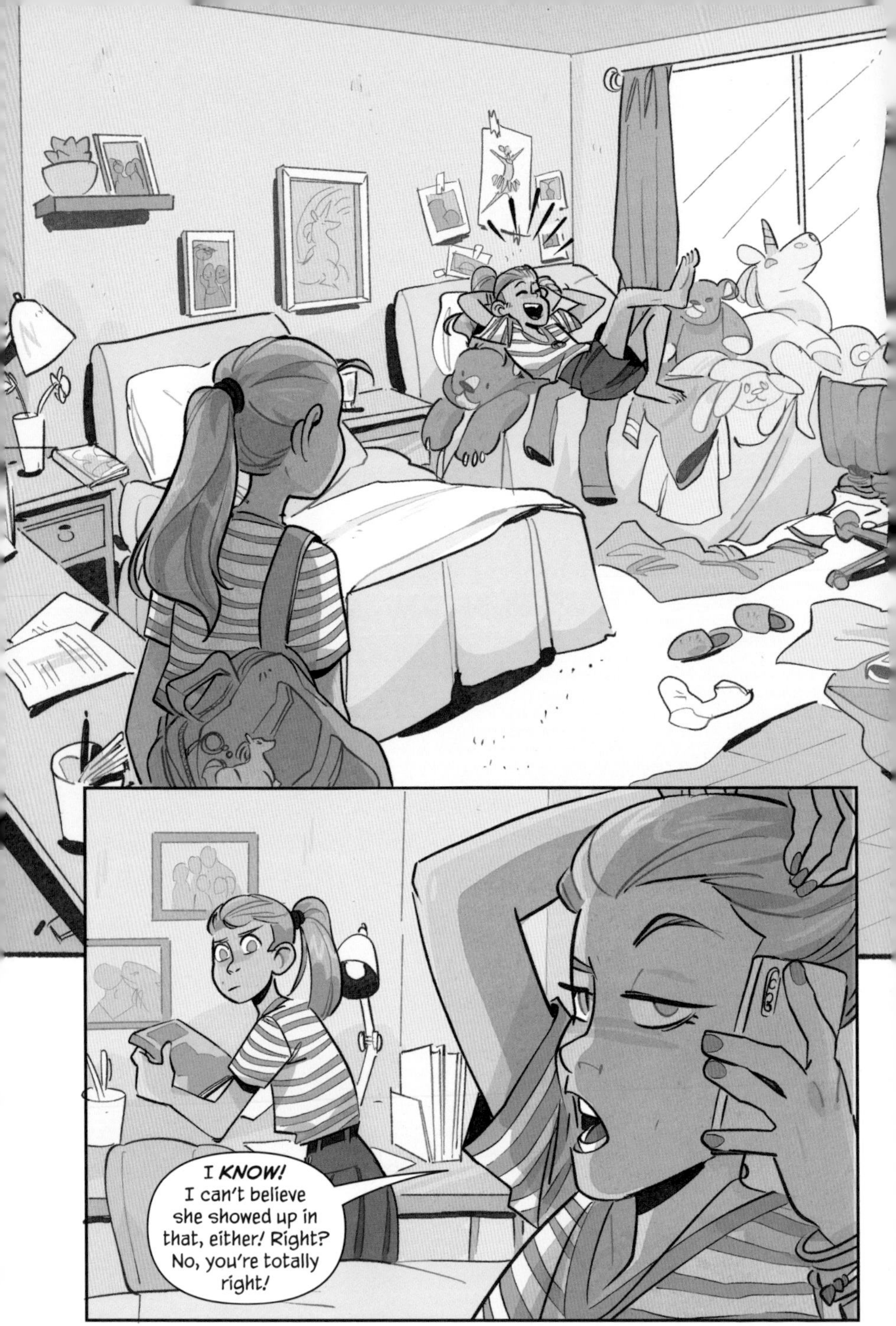
I KNOW!
I can't believe
she showed up in
that, either! Right?
No, you're totally
right!

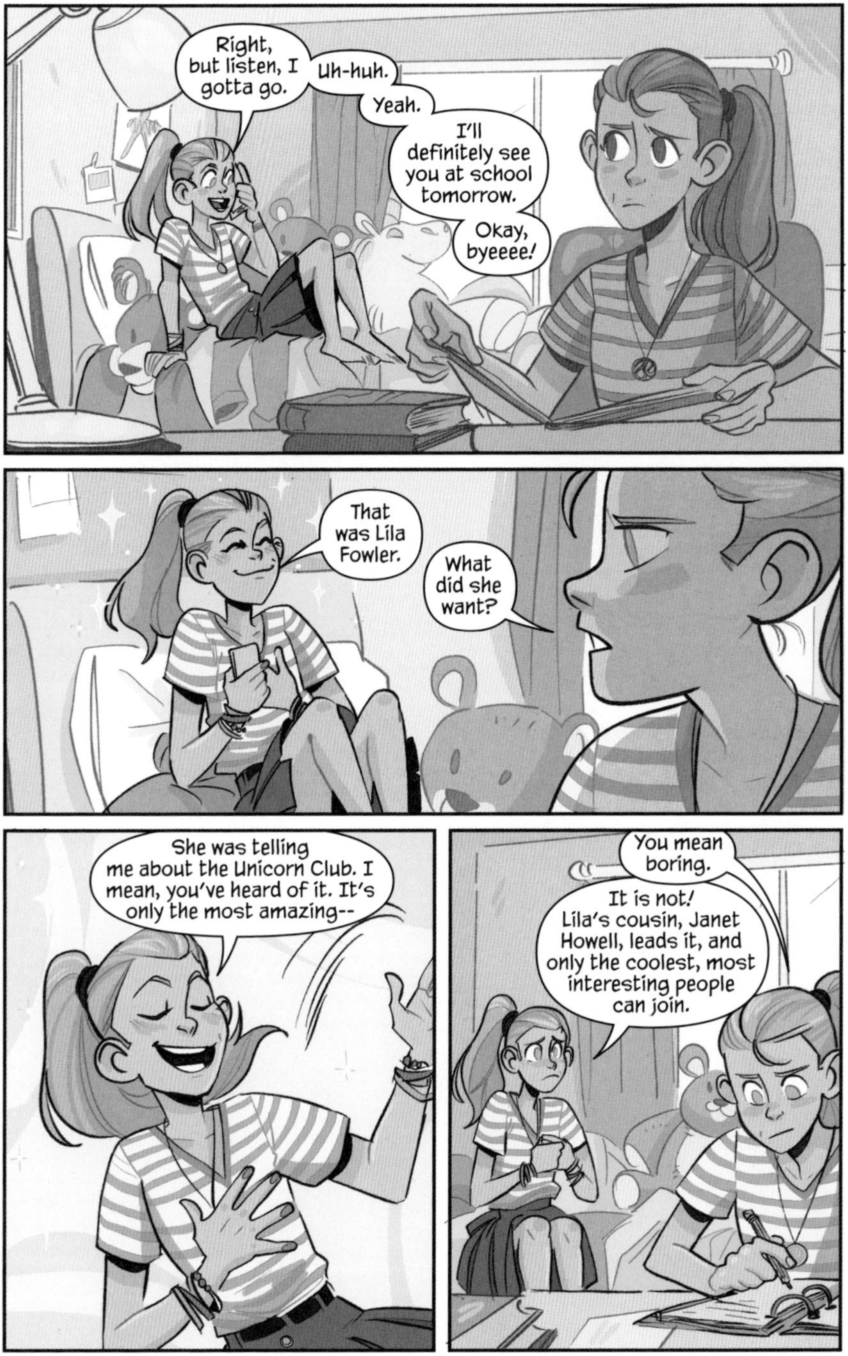
Right, but listen, I gotta go.
Uh-huh.
Yeah.
I'll definitely see you at school tomorrow.
Okay, byeeee!
That was Lila Fowler.
What did she want?
She was telling me about the Unicorn Club. I mean, you've heard of it. It's only the most amazing--
You mean boring.
It is not! Lila's cousin, Janet Howell, leads it, and only the coolest, most interesting people can join.

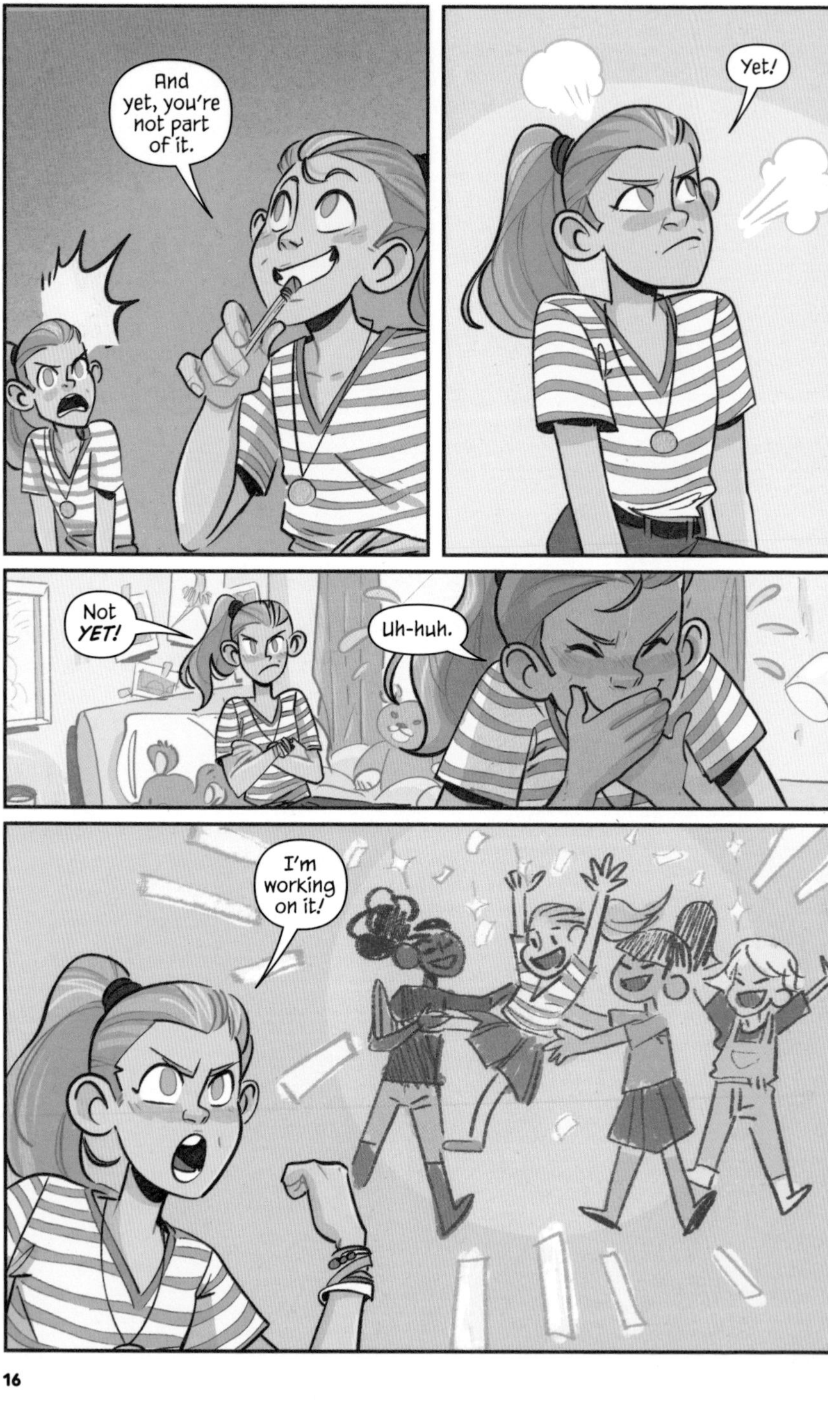
And yet, you're not part of it.
Yet!
Not YET!
Uh-huh.
I'm working on it!

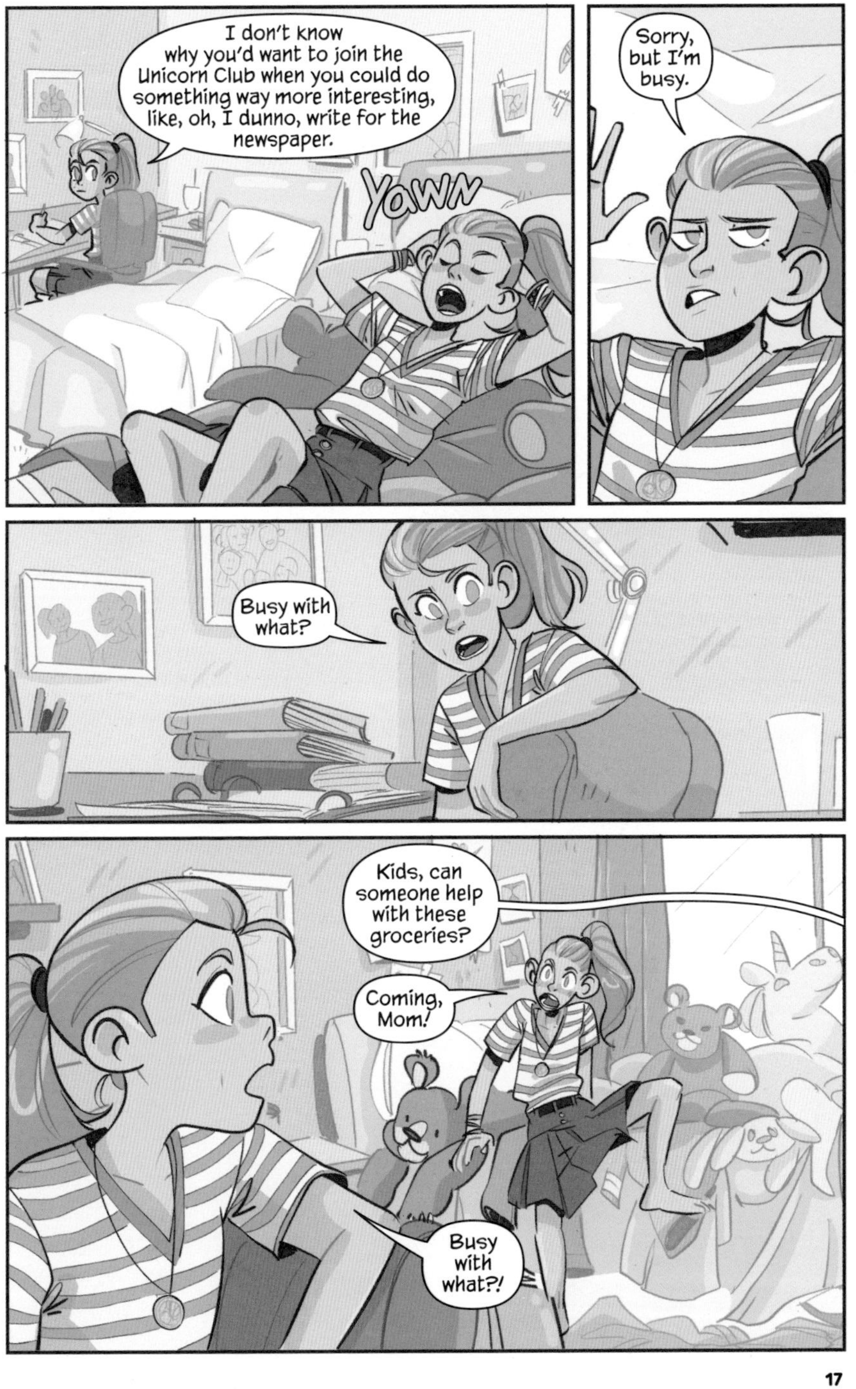
I don't know why you'd want to join the Unicorn Club when you could do something way more interesting, like, oh, I dunno, write for the newspaper.
YAWN
Sorry, but I'm busy.
Busy with what?
Kids, can someone help with these groceries?
Coming, Mom!
Busy with what?!

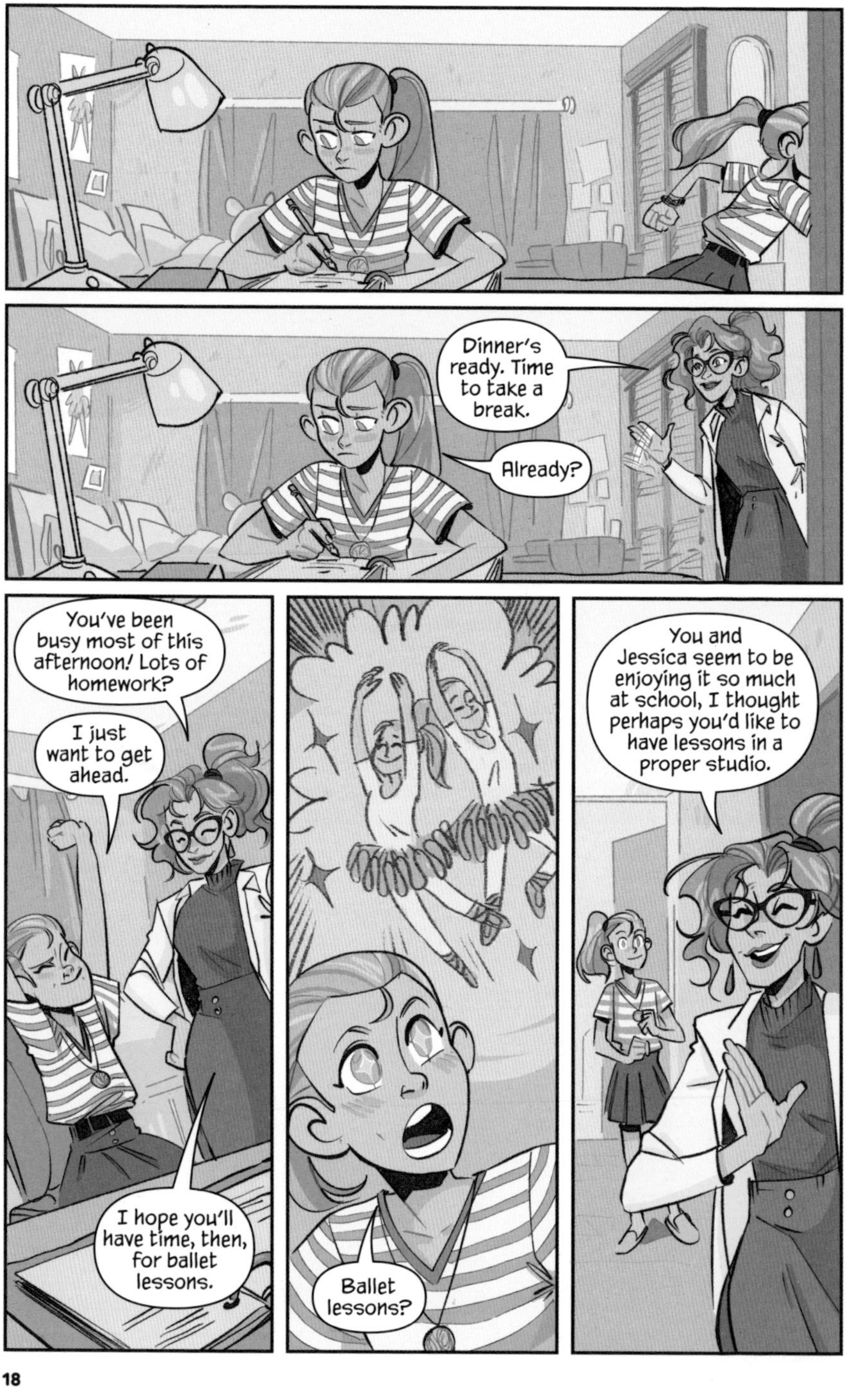
Dinner's ready. Time to take a break.
Already?
You've been busy most of this afternoon! Lots of homework?
I just want to get ahead.
I hope you'll have time, then, for ballet lessons.
Ballet lessons?
You and Jessica seem to be enjoying it so much at school, I thought perhaps you'd like to have lessons in a proper studio.

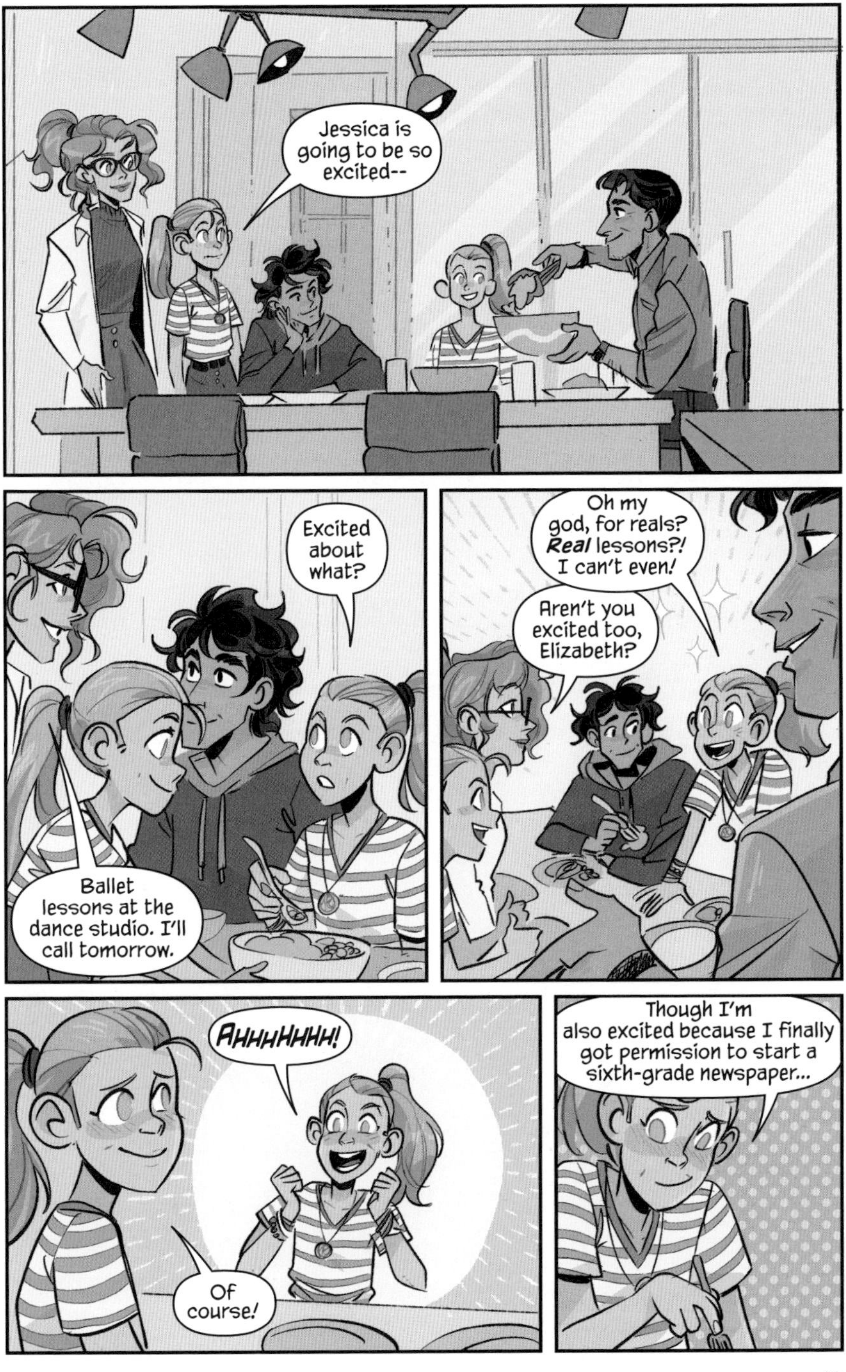
Jessica is going to be so excited--
Excited about what?
Ballet lessons at the dance studio. I'll call tomorrow.
Oh my god, for reals? *Real* lessons?! I can't even!
Aren't you excited too, Elizabeth?
AHHHHHHH!
Of course!
Though I'm also excited because I finally got permission to start a sixth-grade newspaper...

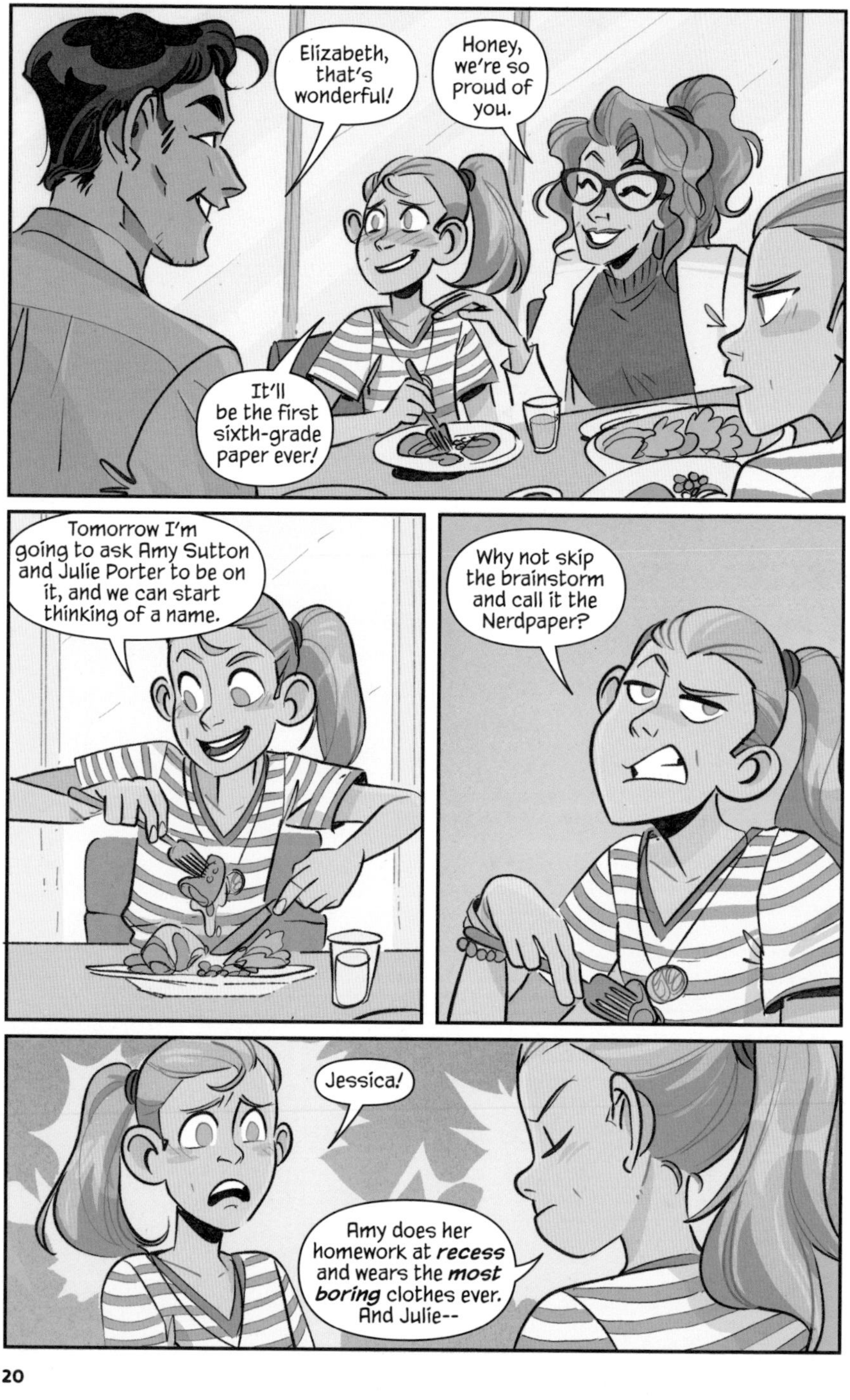
Elizabeth, that's wonderful!
Honey, we're so proud of you.
It'll be the first sixth-grade paper ever!
Tomorrow I'm going to ask Amy Sutton and Julie Porter to be on it, and we can start thinking of a name.
Why not skip the brainstorm and call it the Nerdpaper?
Jessica!
Amy does her homework at *recess* and wears the *most boring* clothes ever. And Julie--

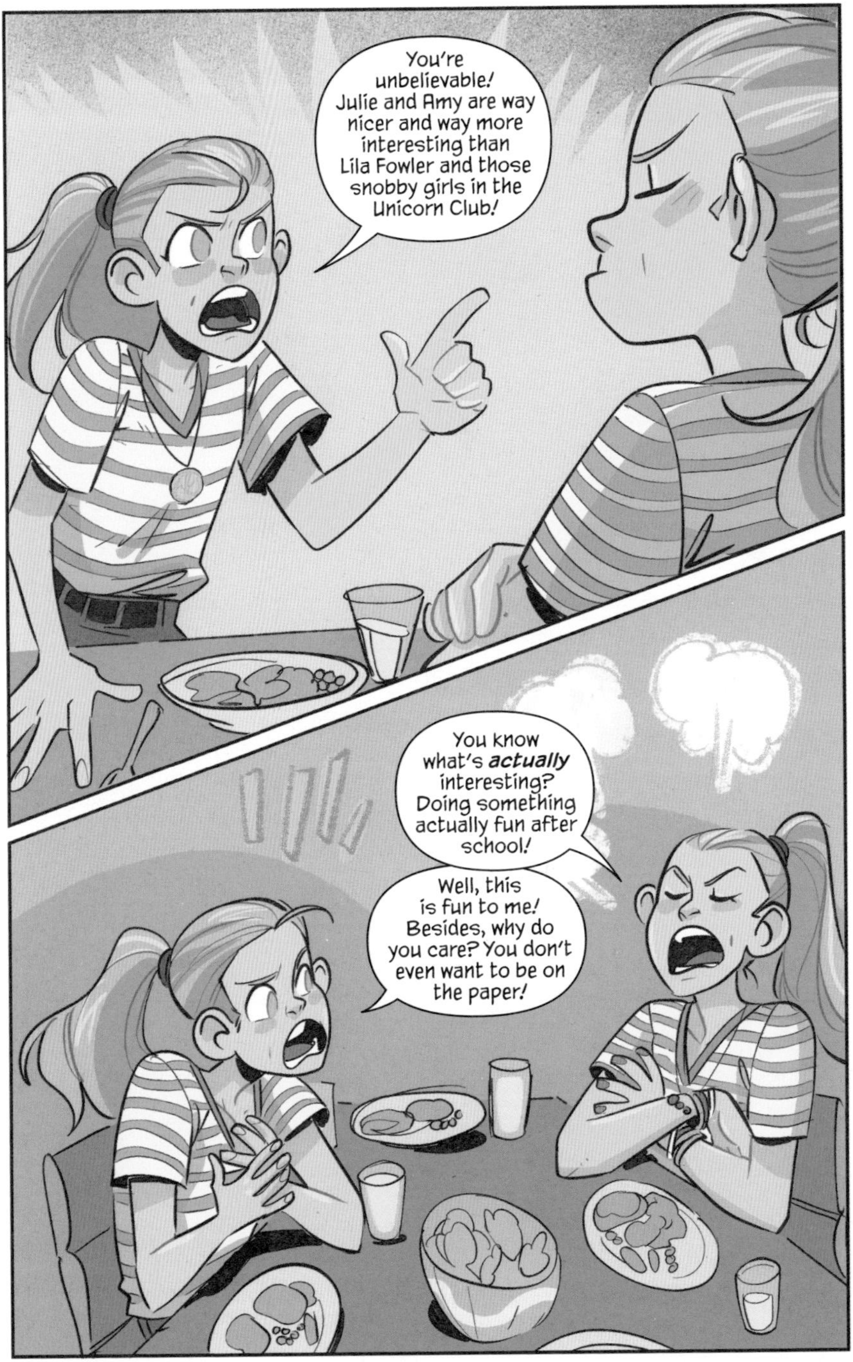
You're unbelievable! Julie and Amy are way nicer and way more interesting than Lila Fowler and those snobby girls in the Unicorn Club!
You know what's ***actually*** interesting? Doing something actually fun after school!
Well, this is fun to me! Besides, why do you care? You don't even want to be on the paper!

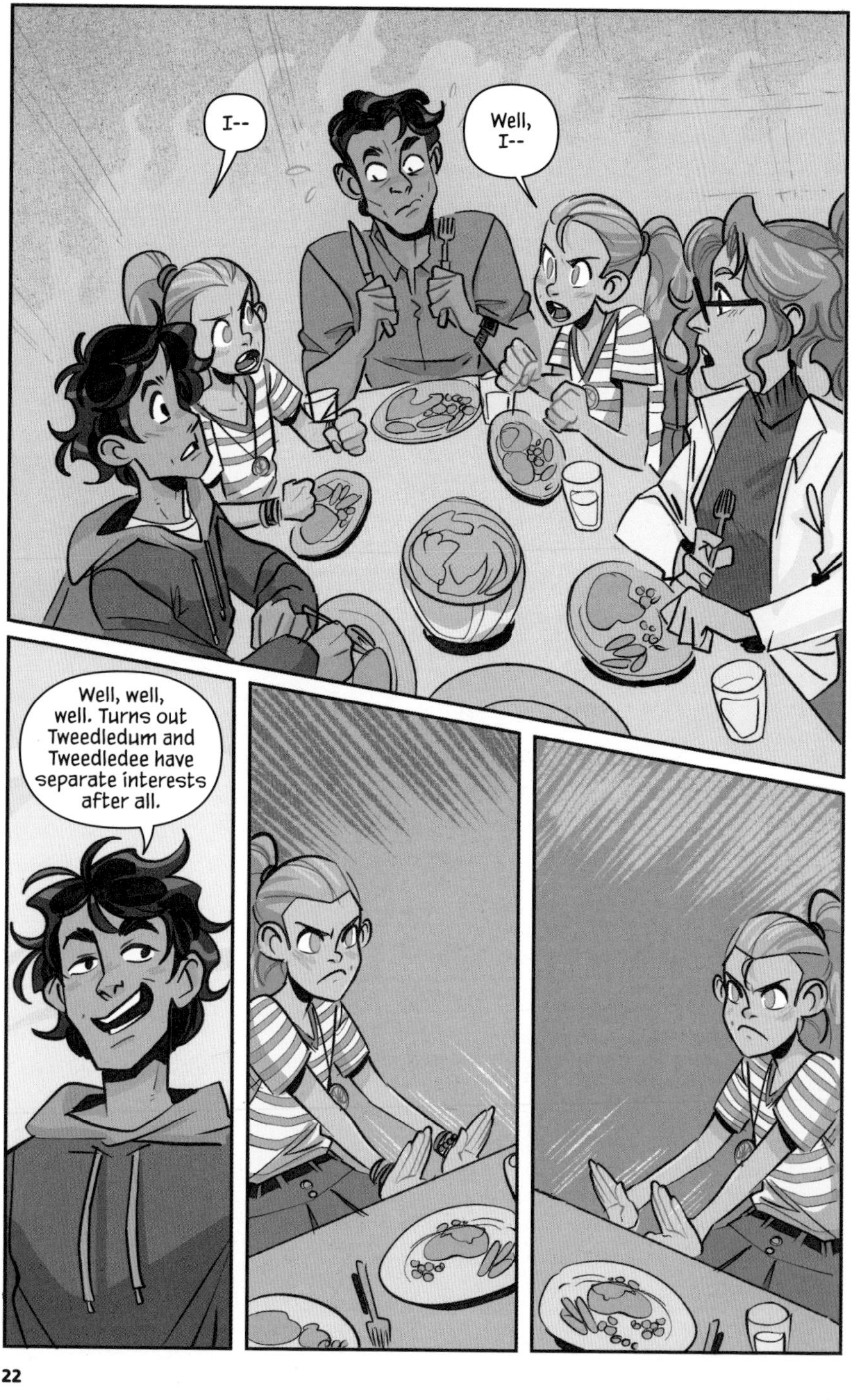
I--
Well, I--
Well, well, well. Turns out Tweedledum and Tweedledee have separate interests after all.

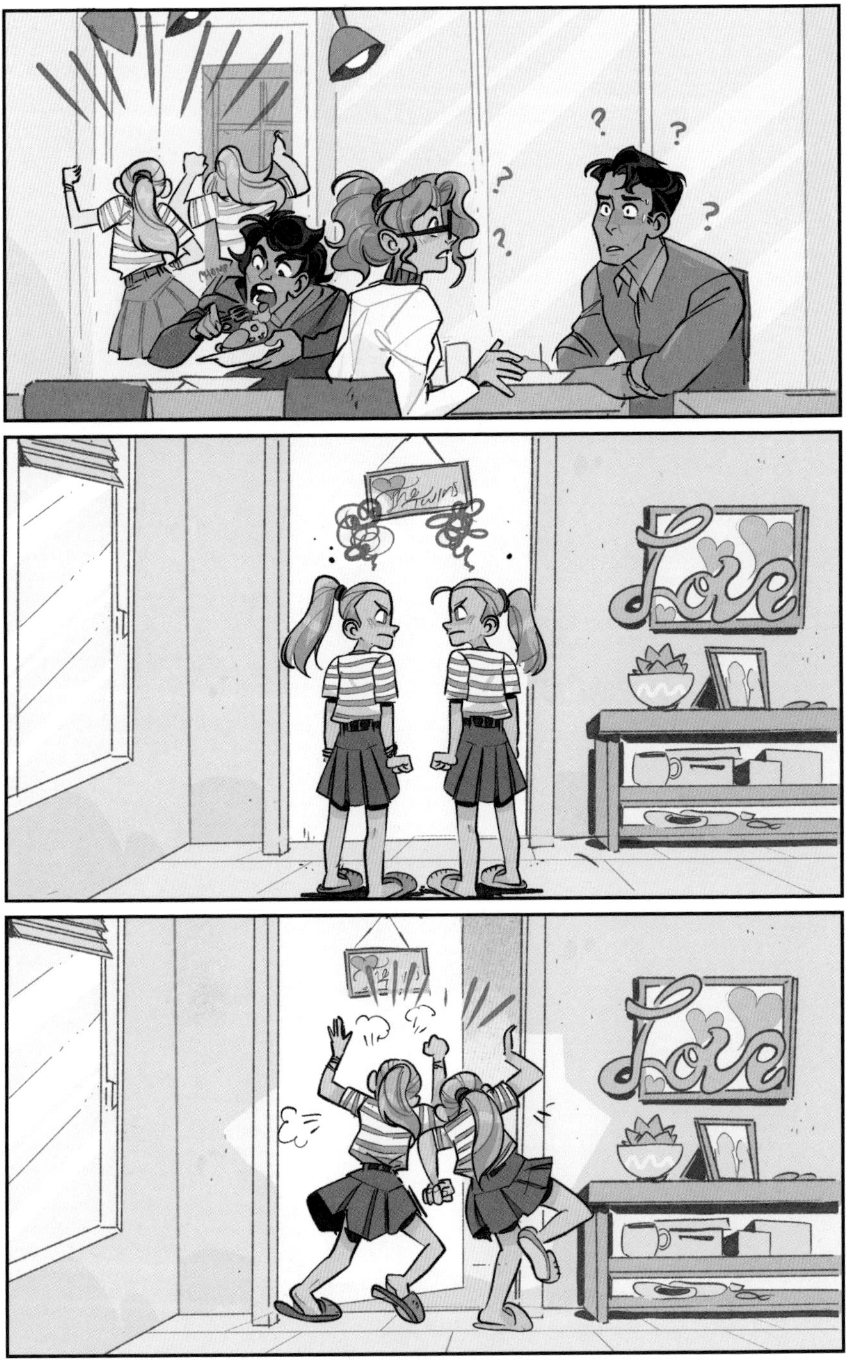
CHOMP
The Twins
Love
Love

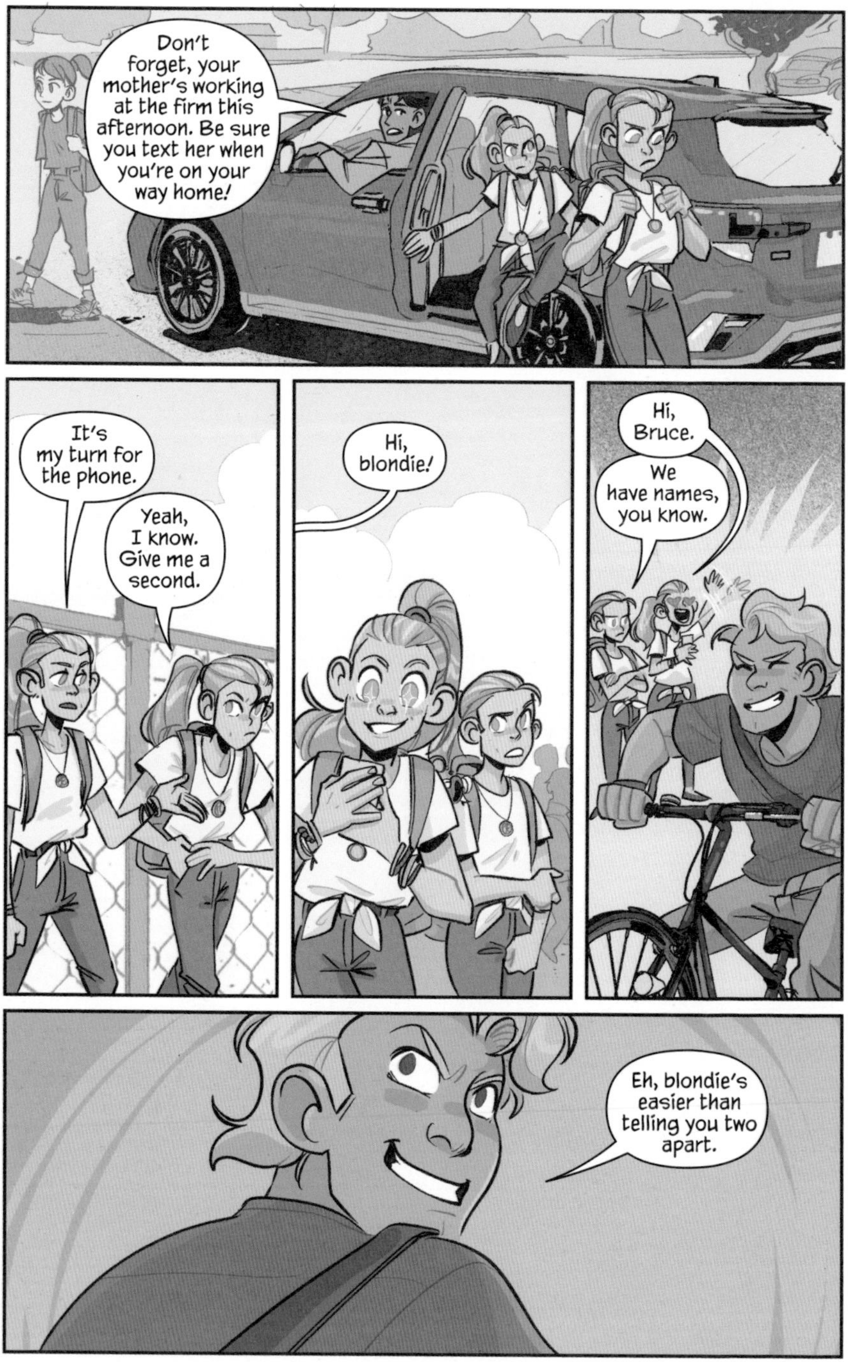

Don't forget, your mother's working at the firm this afternoon. Be sure you text her when you're on your way home!
It's my turn for the phone.
Yeah, I know. Give me a second.
Hi, blondie!
Hi, Bruce.
We have names, you know.
Eh, blondie's easier than telling you two apart.

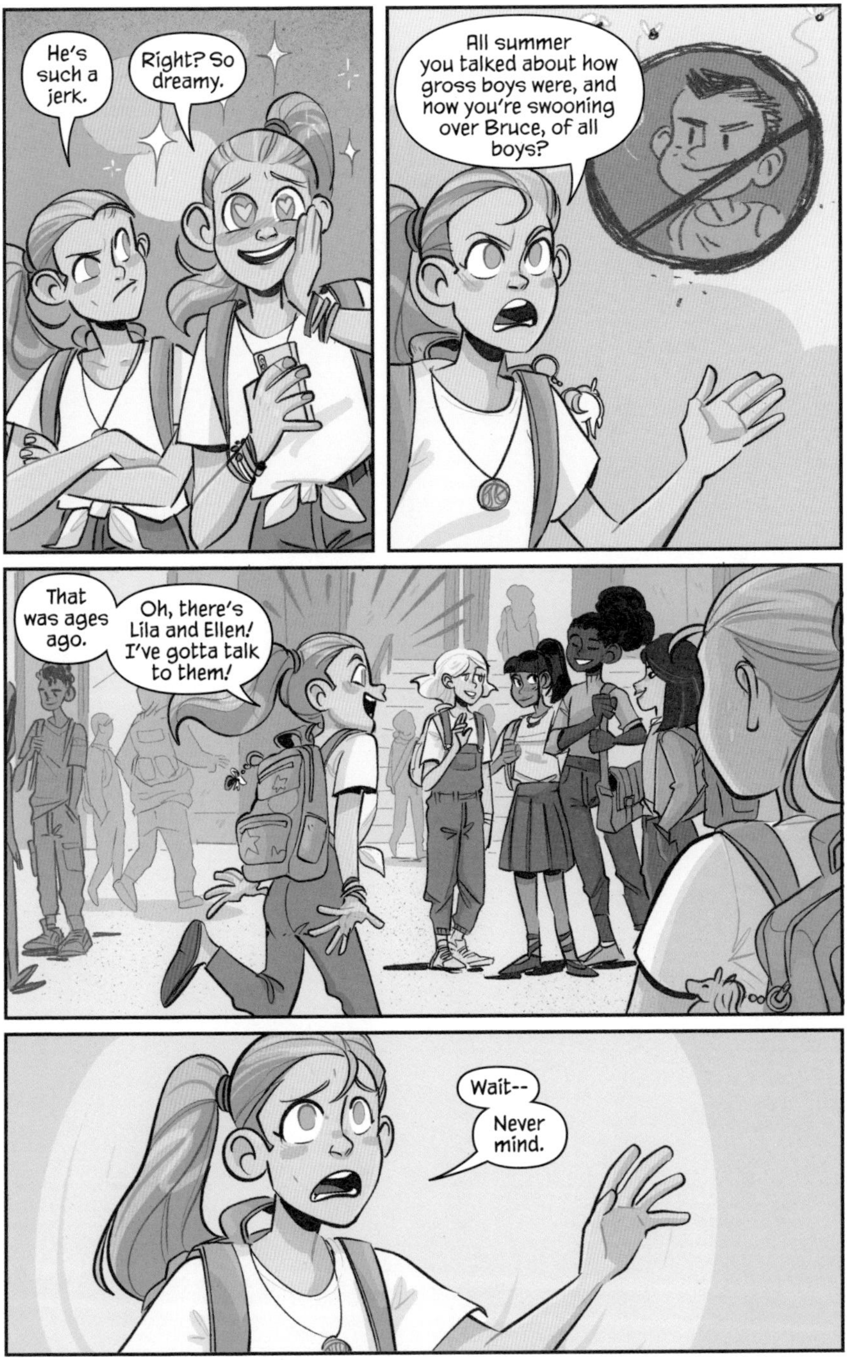
He's such a jerk.
Right? So dreamy.
All summer you talked about how gross boys were, and now you're swooning over Bruce, of all boys?
That was ages ago.
Oh, there's Lila and Ellen! I've gotta talk to them!
Wait--
Never mind.

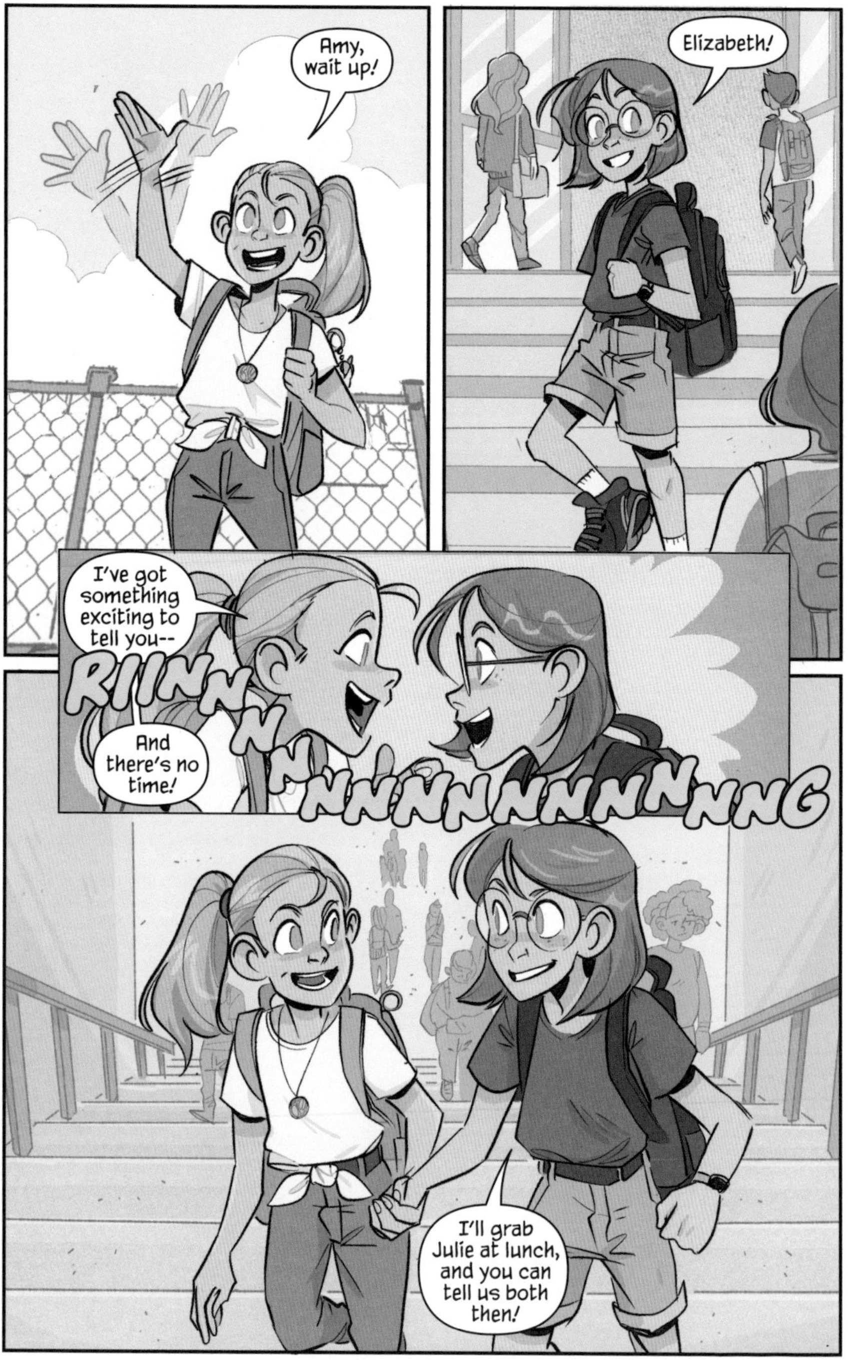

Amy, wait up!
Elizabeth!
I've got something exciting to tell you--
And there's no time!
RIINNNNNNNNNNNNNNNG
I'll grab Julie at lunch, and you can tell us both then!

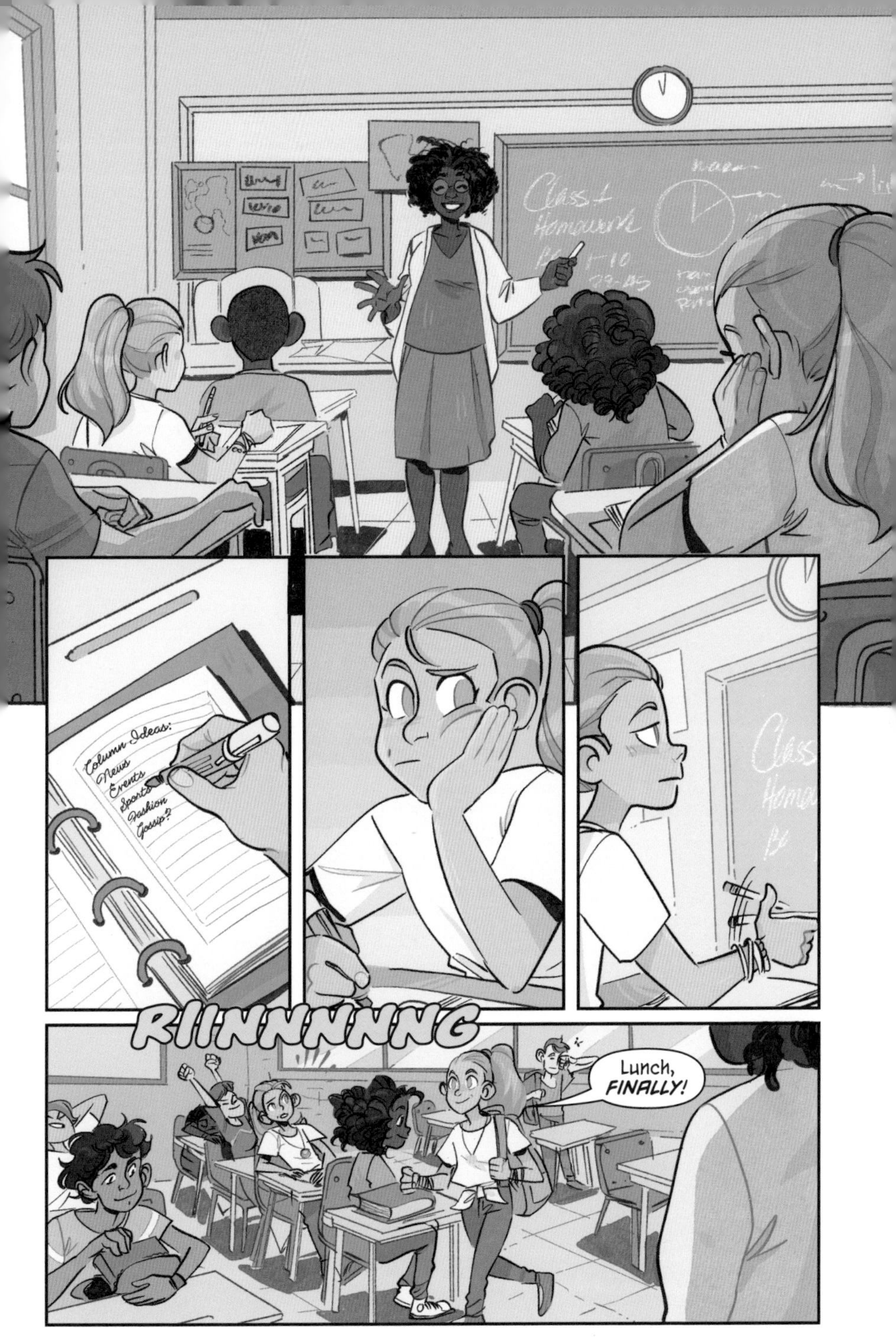
Column Ideas:
News
Events
Sports
Fashion
Gossip?
RIINNNNNG
Lunch, FINALLY!

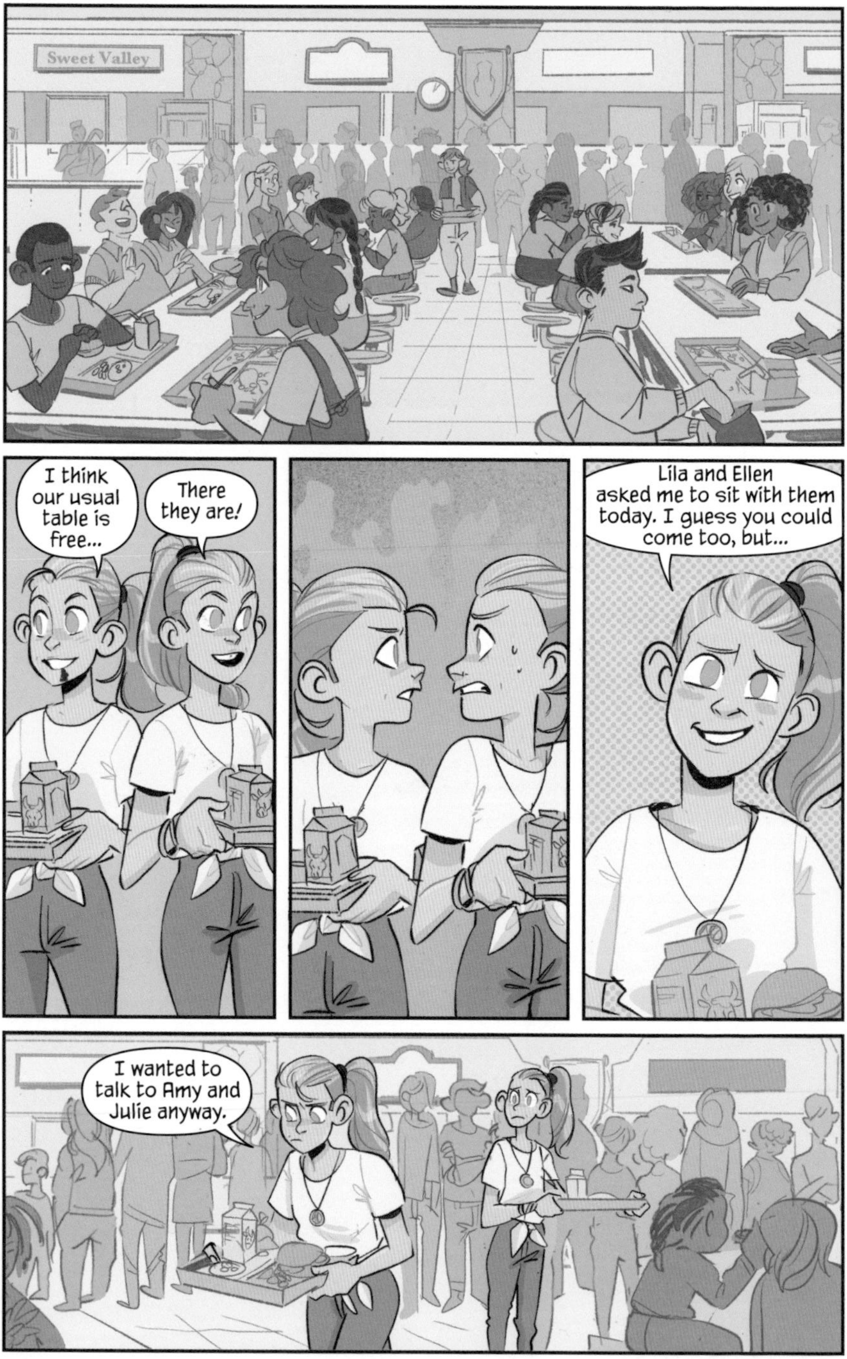
Sweet Valley
I think our usual table is free...
There they are!
Lila and Ellen asked me to sit with them today. I guess you could come too, but...
I wanted to talk to Amy and Julie anyway.

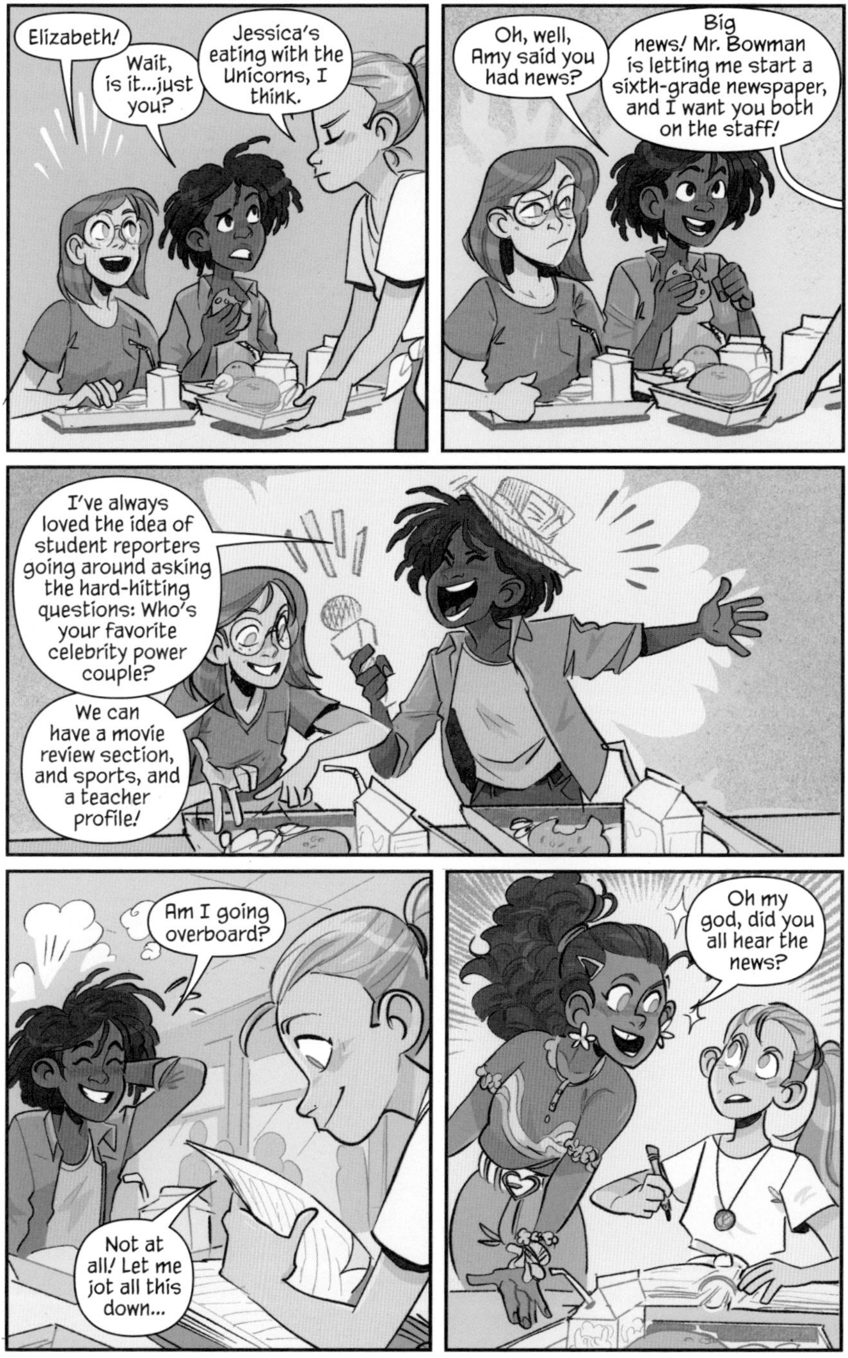
Elizabeth!
Wait, is it...just you?
Jessica's eating with the Unicorns, I think.
Oh, well, Amy said you had news?
Big news! Mr. Bowman is letting me start a sixth-grade newspaper, and I want you both on the staff!
I've always loved the idea of student reporters going around asking the hard-hitting questions: Who's your favorite celebrity power couple?
We can have a movie review section, and sports, and a teacher profile!
Am I going overboard?
Not at all! Let me jot all this down...
Oh my god, did you all hear the news?

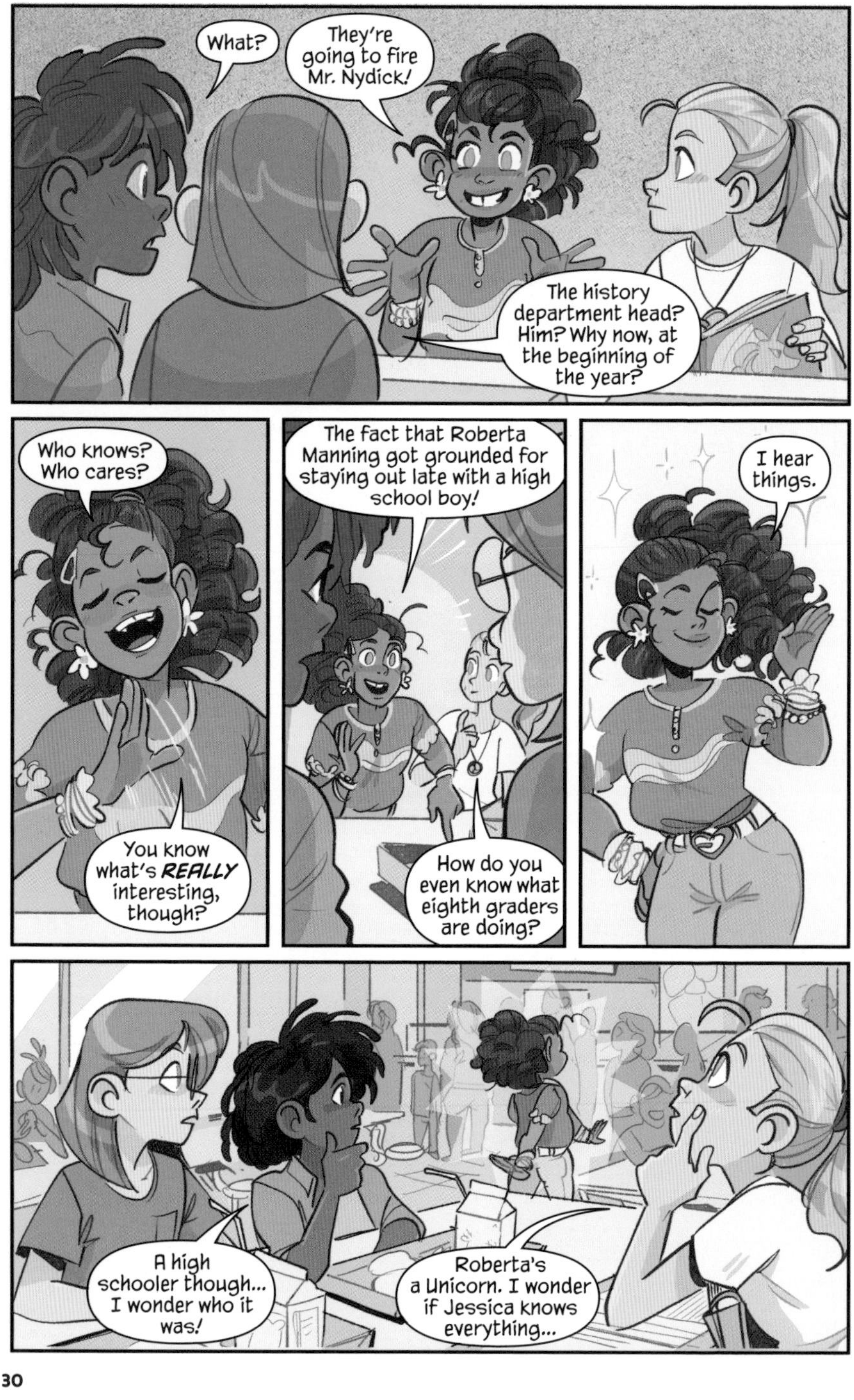
What?
They're going to fire Mr. Nydick!
The history department head? Him? Why now, at the beginning of the year?
Who knows? Who cares?
You know what's **REALLY** interesting, though?
The fact that Roberta Manning got grounded for staying out late with a high school boy!
How do you even know what eighth graders are doing?
I hear things.
A high schooler though... I wonder who it was!
Roberta's a Unicorn. I wonder if Jessica knows everything...

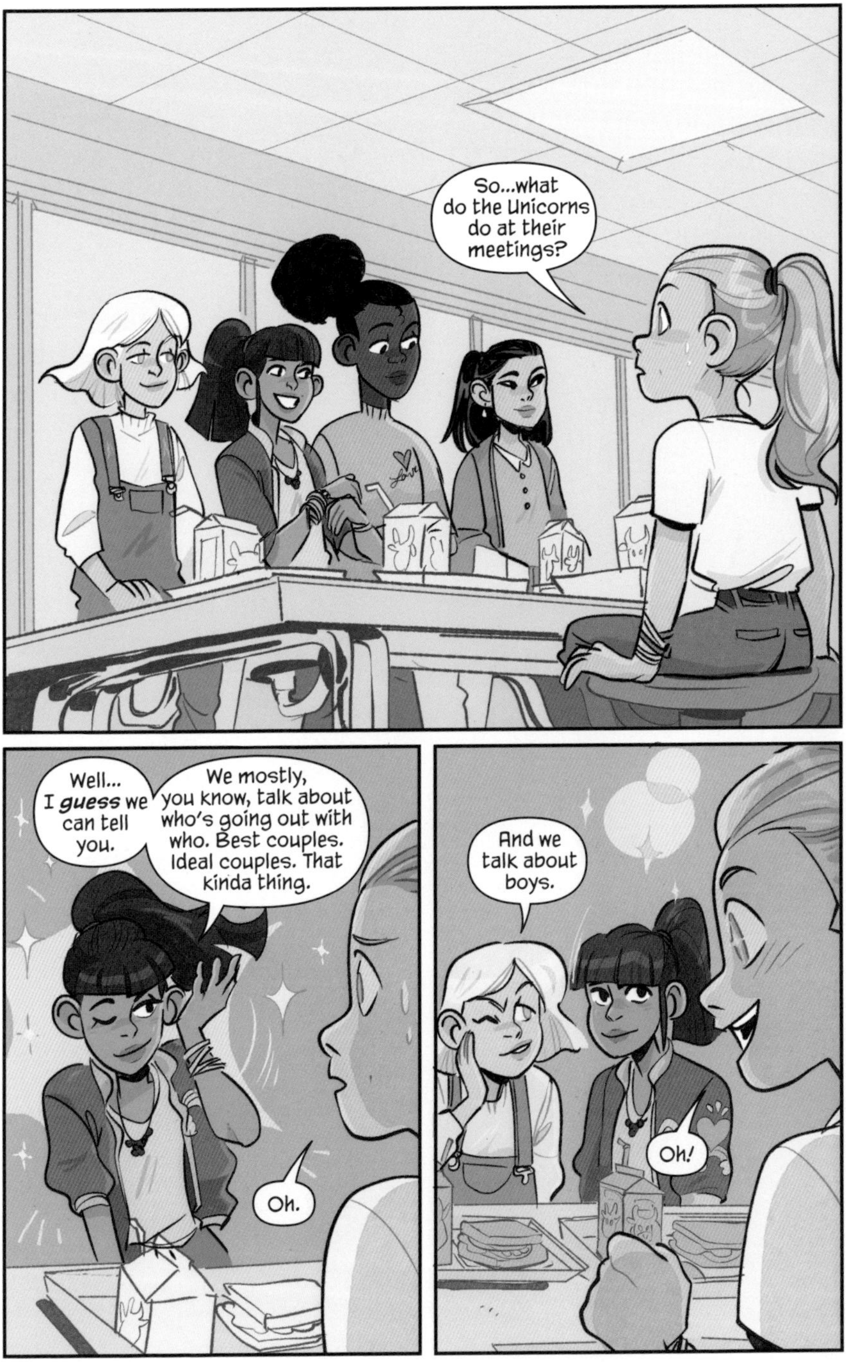
So...what do the Unicorns do at their meetings?
Well... I *guess* we can tell you.
We mostly, you know, talk about who's going out with who. Best couples. Ideal couples. That kinda thing.
Oh.
And we talk about boys.
Oh!

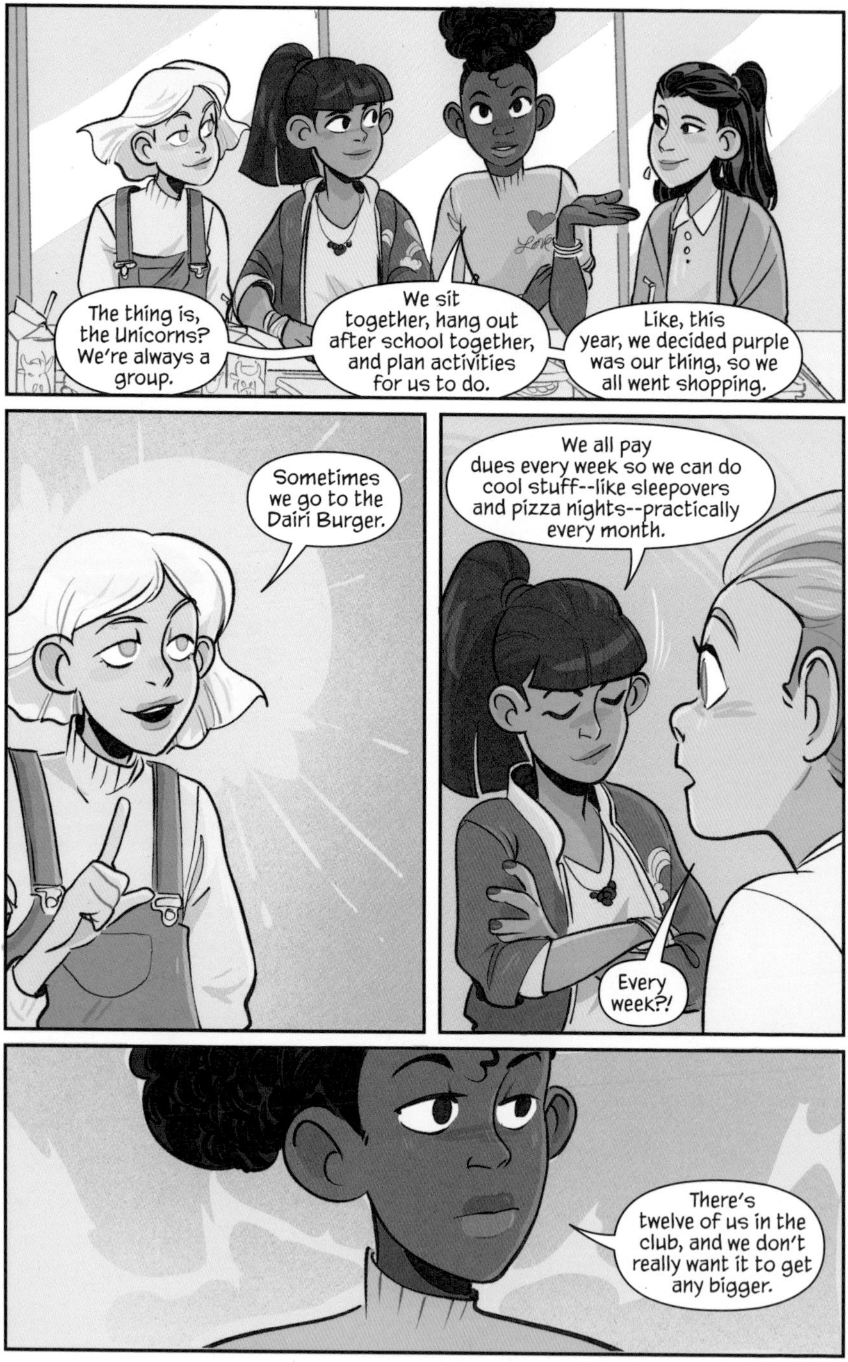
The thing is, the Unicorns? We're always a group.
We sit together, hang out after school together, and plan activities for us to do.
Like, this year, we decided purple was our thing, so we all went shopping.
Sometimes we go to the Dairi Burger.
We all pay dues every week so we can do cool stuff--like sleepovers and pizza nights--practically every month.
Every week?!
There's twelve of us in the club, and we don't really want it to get any bigger.

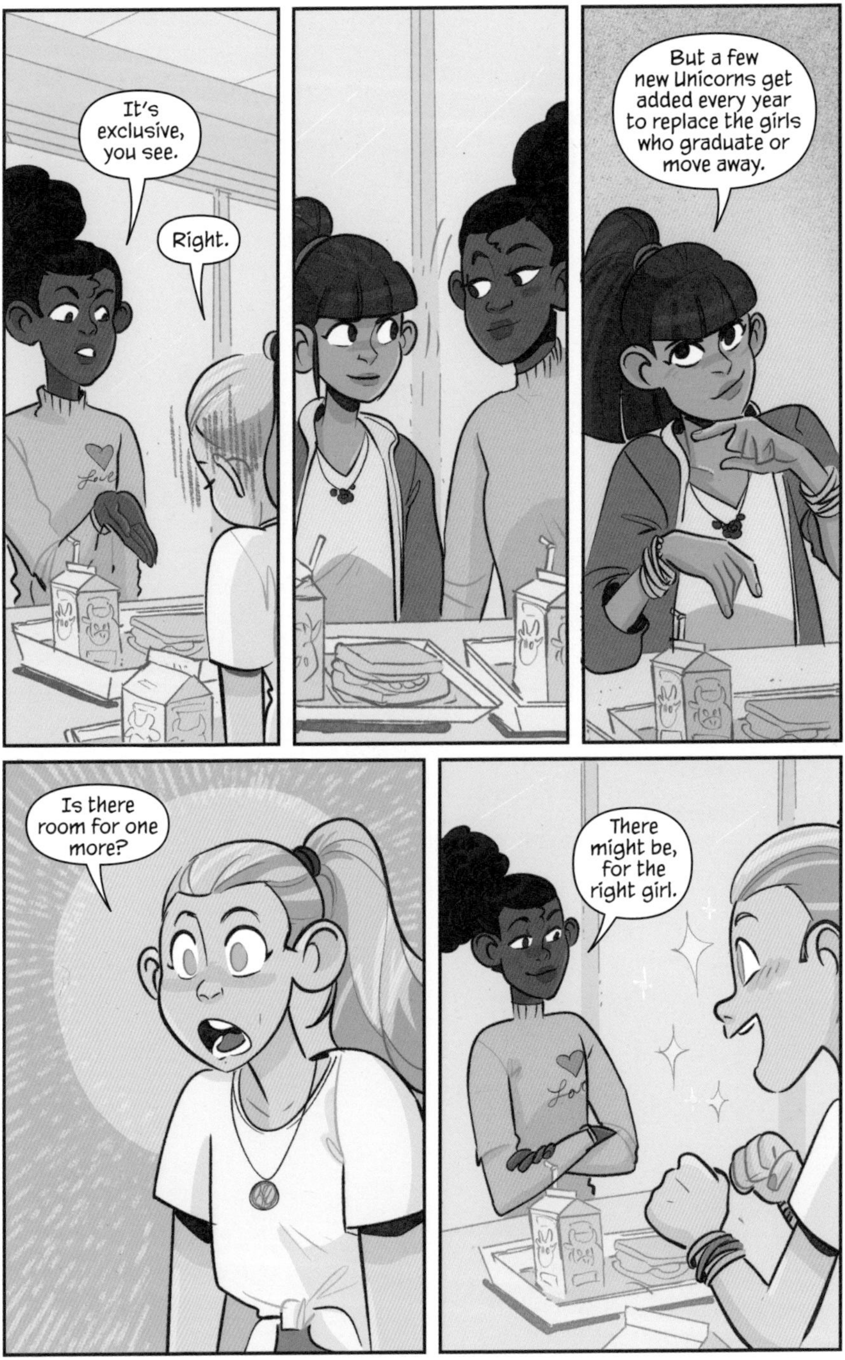
It's exclusive, you see.
Right.
But a few new Unicorns get added every year to replace the girls who graduate or move away.
Is there room for one more?
There might be, for the right girl.

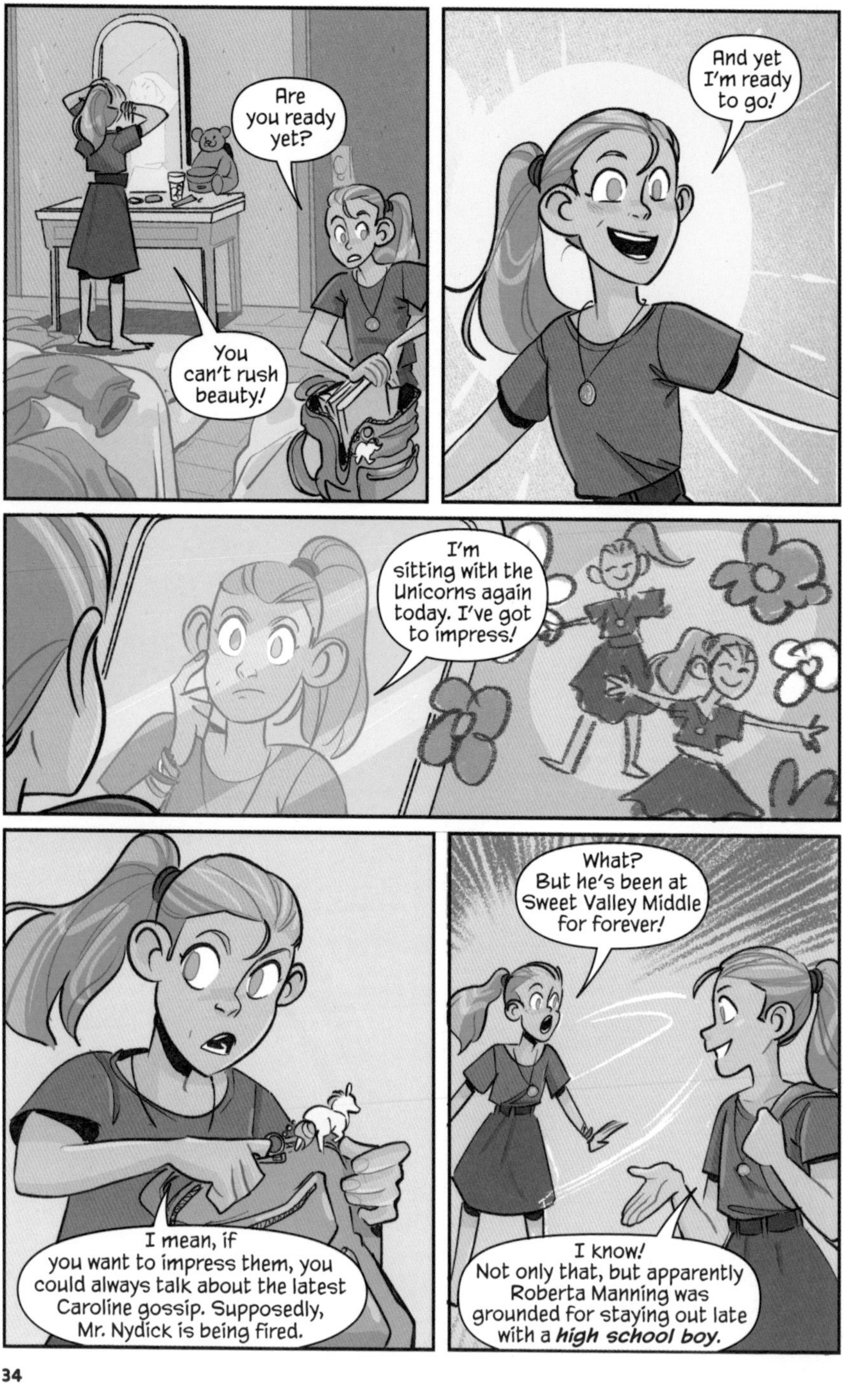
Are you ready yet?
You can't rush beauty!
And yet I'm ready to go!
I'm sitting with the Unicorns again today. I've got to impress!
I mean, if you want to impress them, you could always talk about the latest Caroline gossip. Supposedly, Mr. Nydick is being fired.
What? But he's been at Sweet Valley Middle for forever!
I know! Not only that, but apparently Roberta Manning was grounded for staying out late with a ***high school boy.***

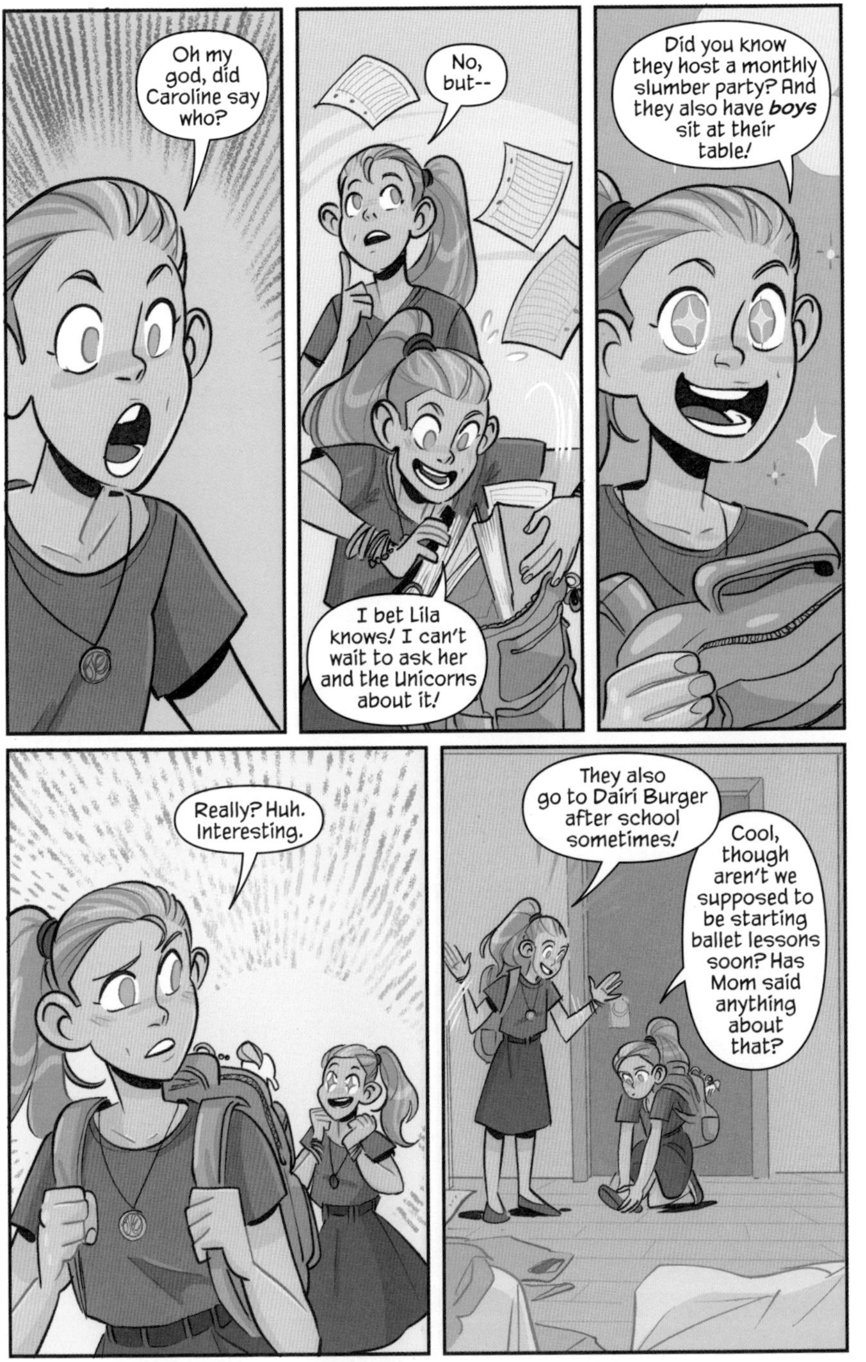

Oh my god, did Caroline say who?
No, but--
I bet Lila knows! I can't wait to ask her and the Unicorns about it!
Did you know they host a monthly slumber party? And they also have *boys* sit at their table!
Really? Huh. Interesting.
They also go to Dairi Burger after school sometimes!
Cool, though aren't we supposed to be starting ballet lessons soon? Has Mom said anything about that?

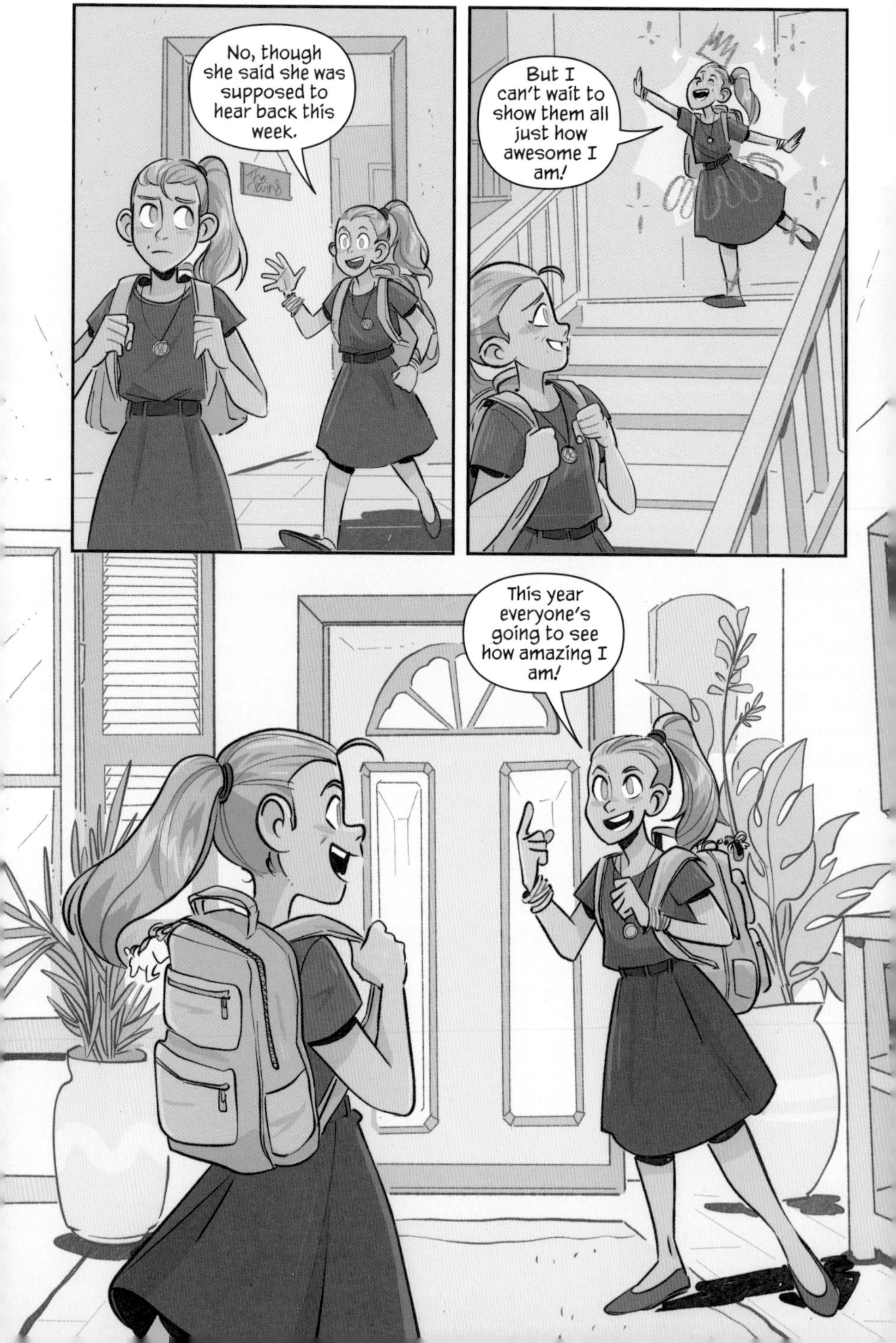
No, though she said she was supposed to hear back this week.
But I can't wait to show them all just how awesome I am!
This year everyone's going to see how amazing I am!

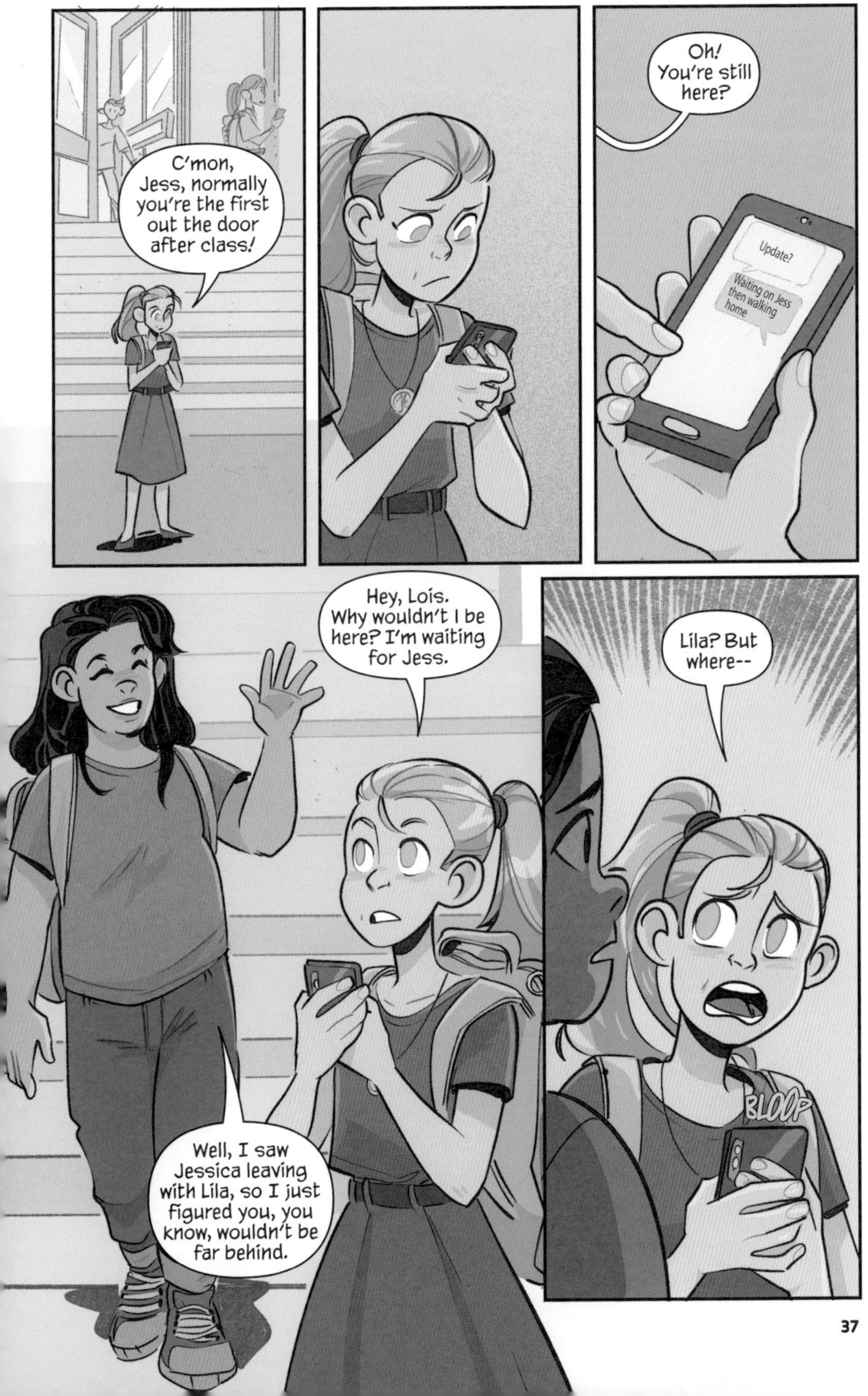

C'mon, Jess, normally you're the first out the door after class!
Oh! You're still here?
Update?
Waiting on Jess then walking home
Hey, Lois. Why wouldn't I be here? I'm waiting for Jess.
Well, I saw Jessica leaving with Lila, so I just figured you, you know, wouldn't be far behind.
Lila? But where--
BLOOP

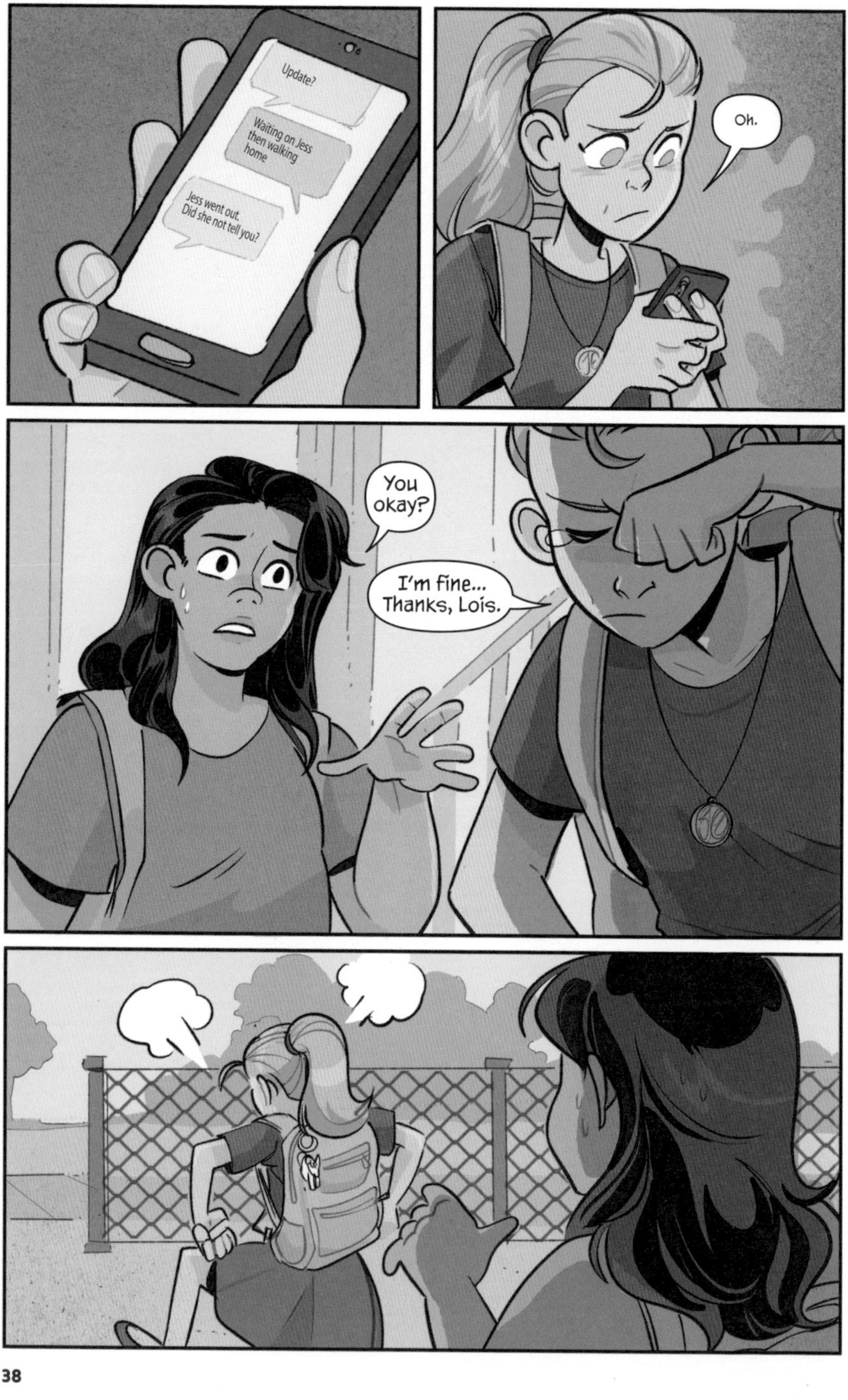
Update?
Waiting on Jess then walking home
Jess went out. Did she not tell you?
Oh.
You okay?
I'm fine... Thanks, Lois.

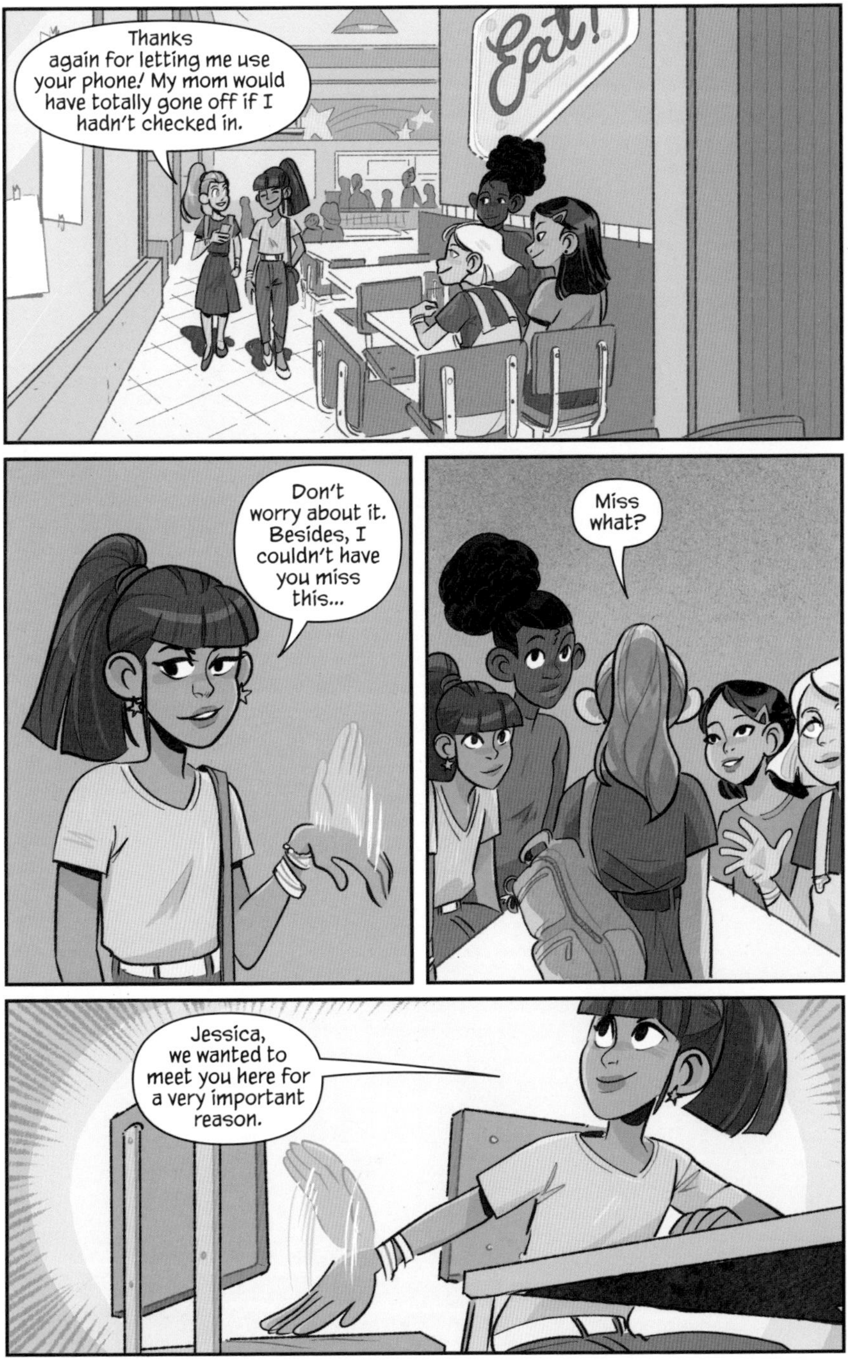

Thanks again for letting me use your phone! My mom would have totally gone off if I hadn't checked in.
Eat!
Don't worry about it. Besides, I couldn't have you miss this...
Miss what?
Jessica, we wanted to meet you here for a very important reason.

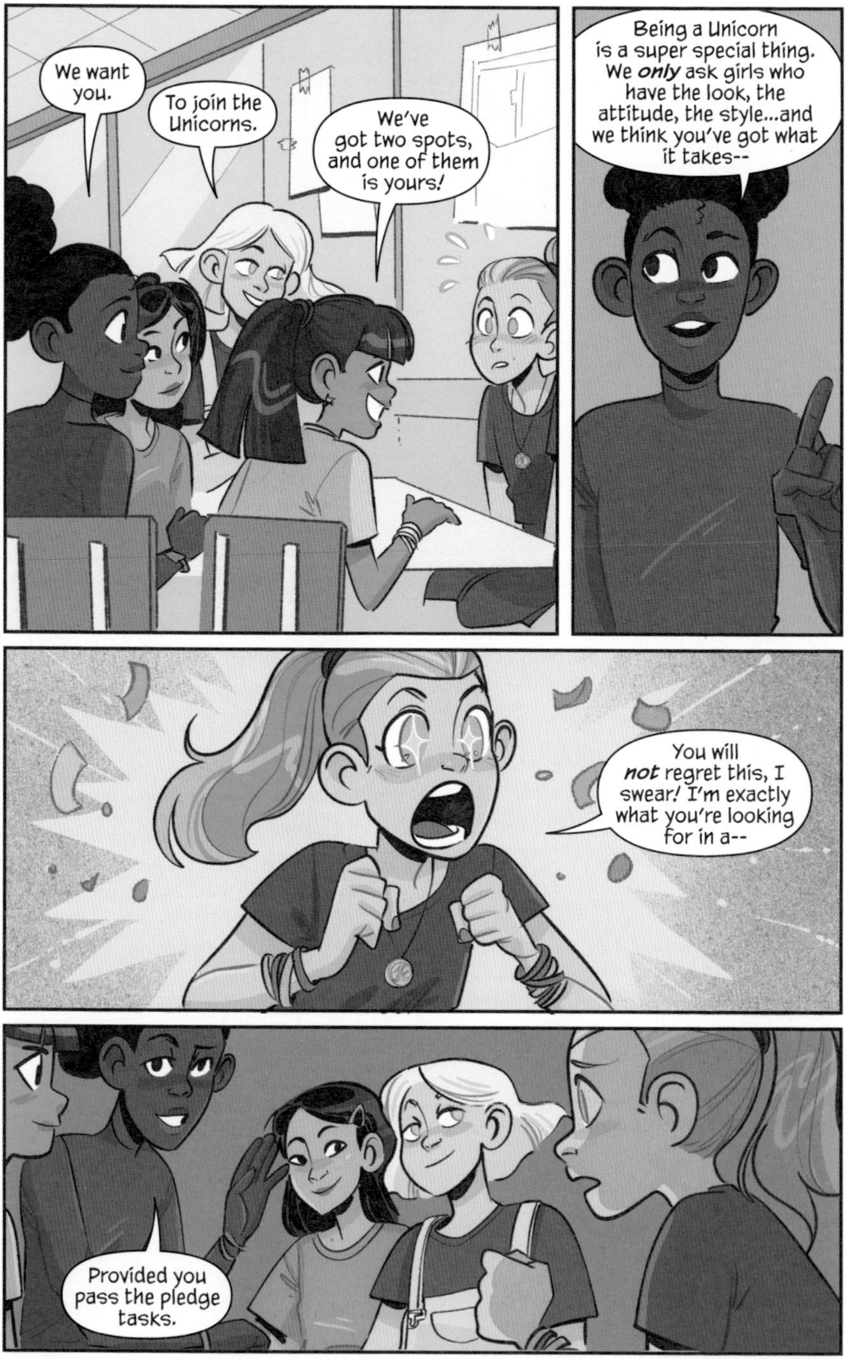
We want you.
To join the Unicorns.
We've got two spots, and one of them is yours!
Being a Unicorn is a super special thing. We *only* ask girls who have the look, the attitude, the style...and we think you've got what it takes--
You will **not** regret this, I swear! I'm exactly what you're looking for in a--
Provided you pass the pledge tasks.

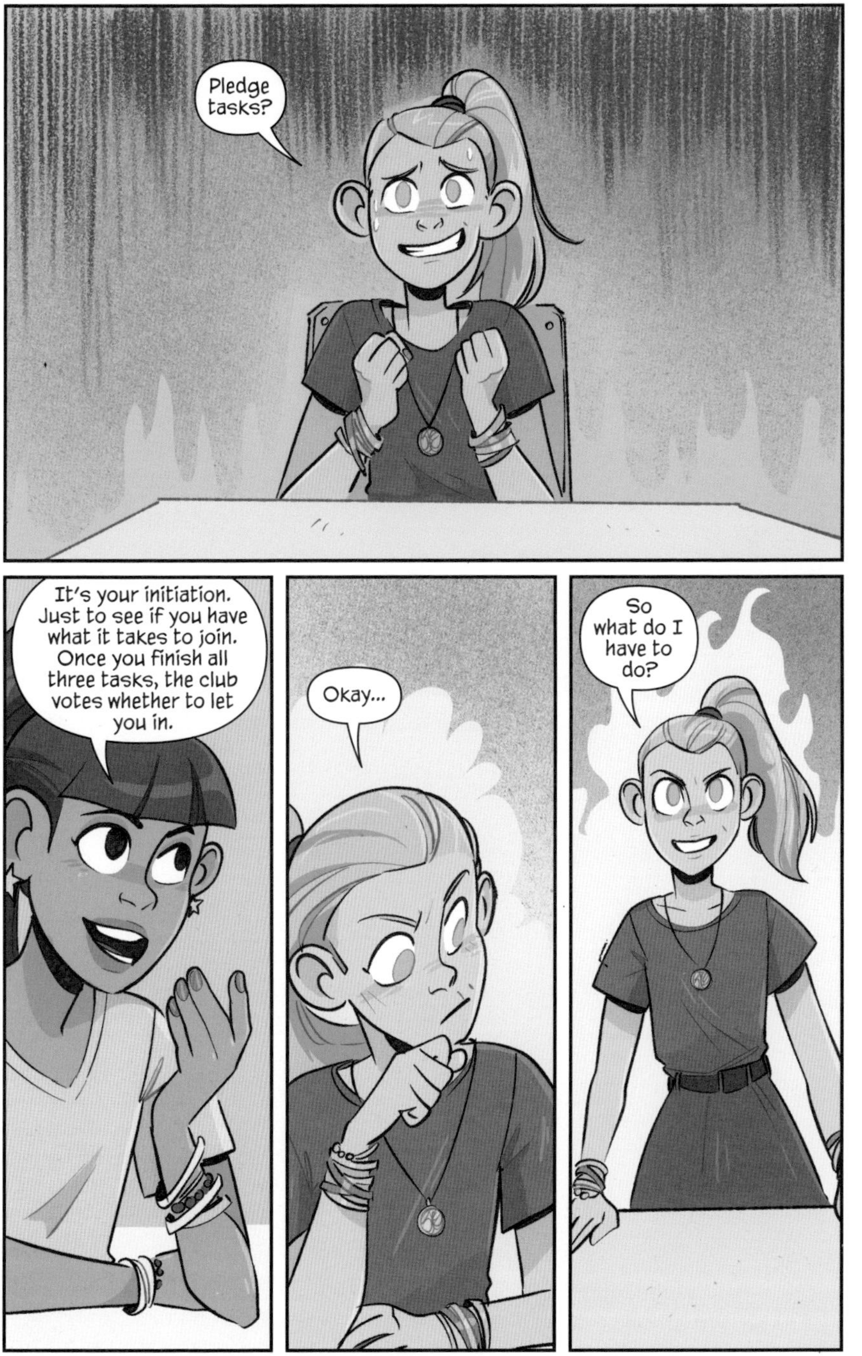

Pledge tasks?
It's your initiation. Just to see if you have what it takes to join. Once you finish all three tasks, the club votes whether to let you in.
Okay...
So what do I have to do?

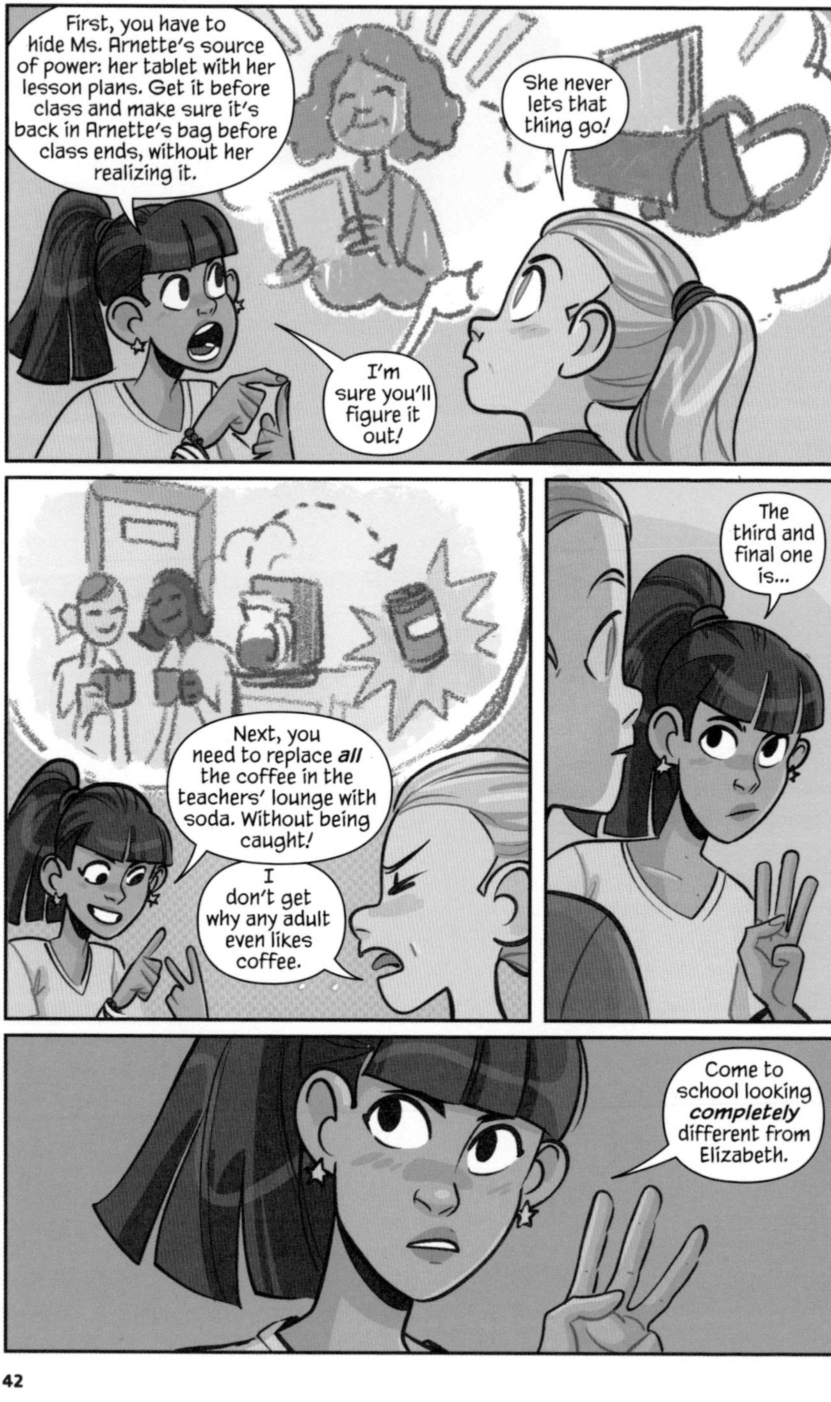
First, you have to hide Ms. Arnette's source of power: her tablet with her lesson plans. Get it before class and make sure it's back in Arnette's bag before class ends, without her realizing it.
She never lets that thing go!
I'm sure you'll figure it out!
Next, you need to replace *all* the coffee in the teachers' lounge with soda. Without being caught!
I don't get why any adult even likes coffee.
The third and final one is...
Come to school looking ***completely*** different from Elizabeth.

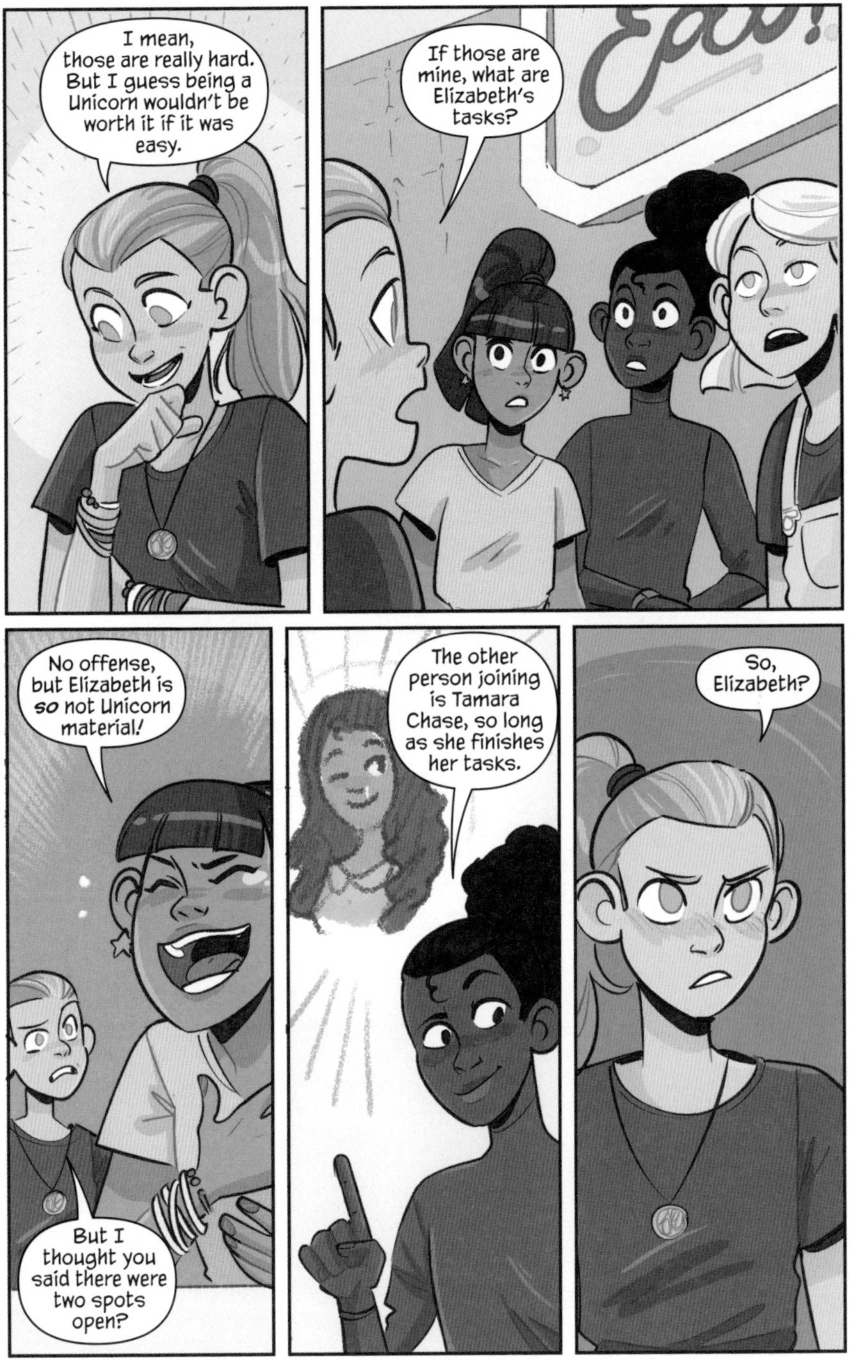
I mean, those are really hard. But I guess being a Unicorn wouldn't be worth it if it was easy.
If those are mine, what are Elizabeth's tasks?
No offense, but Elizabeth is *so* not Unicorn material!
But I thought you said there were two spots open?
The other person joining is Tamara Chase, so long as she finishes her tasks.
So, Elizabeth?

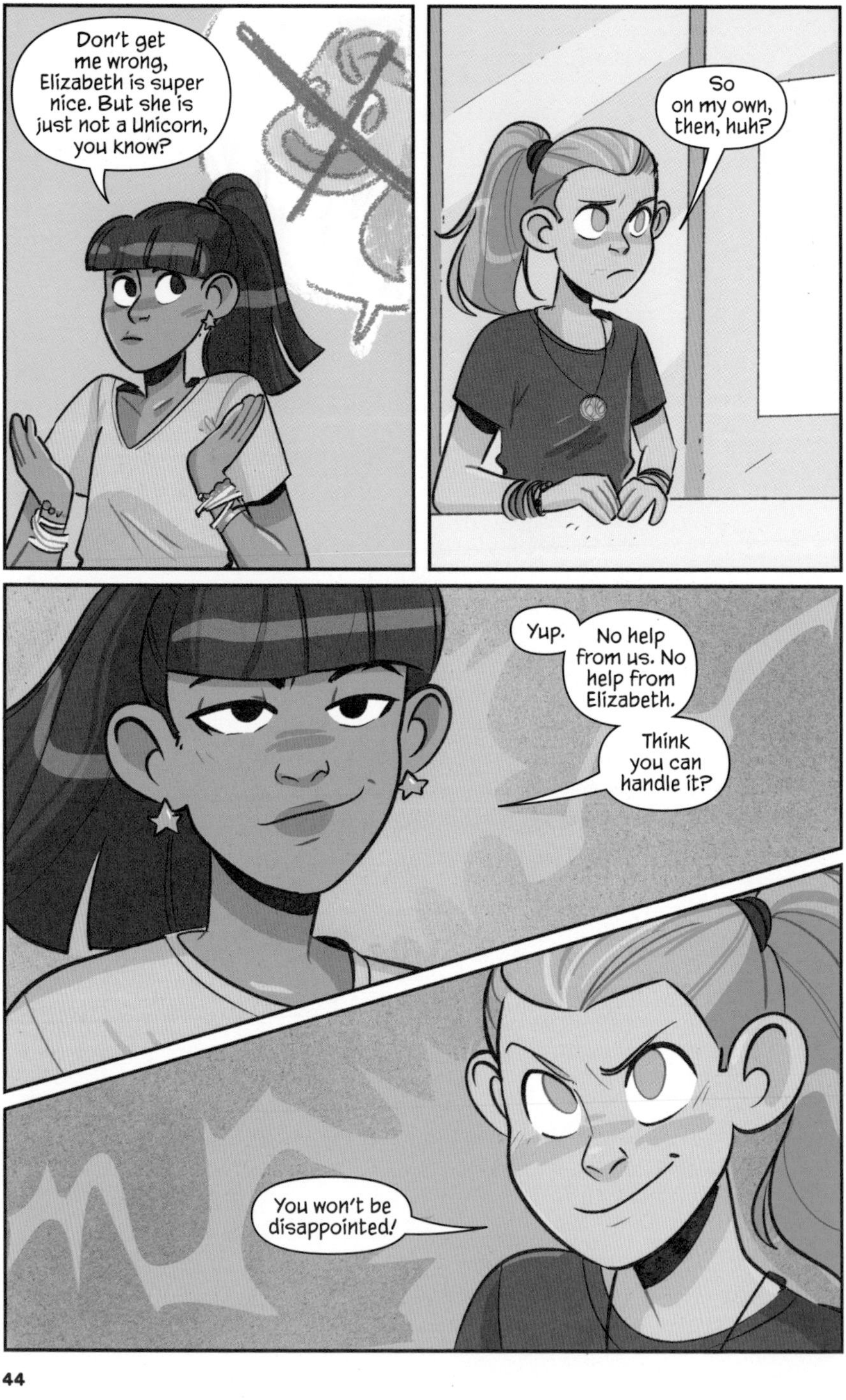
Don't get me wrong, Elizabeth is super nice. But she is just not a Unicorn, you know?
So on my own, then, huh?
Yup.
No help from us. No help from Elizabeth.
Think you can handle it?
You won't be disappointed!

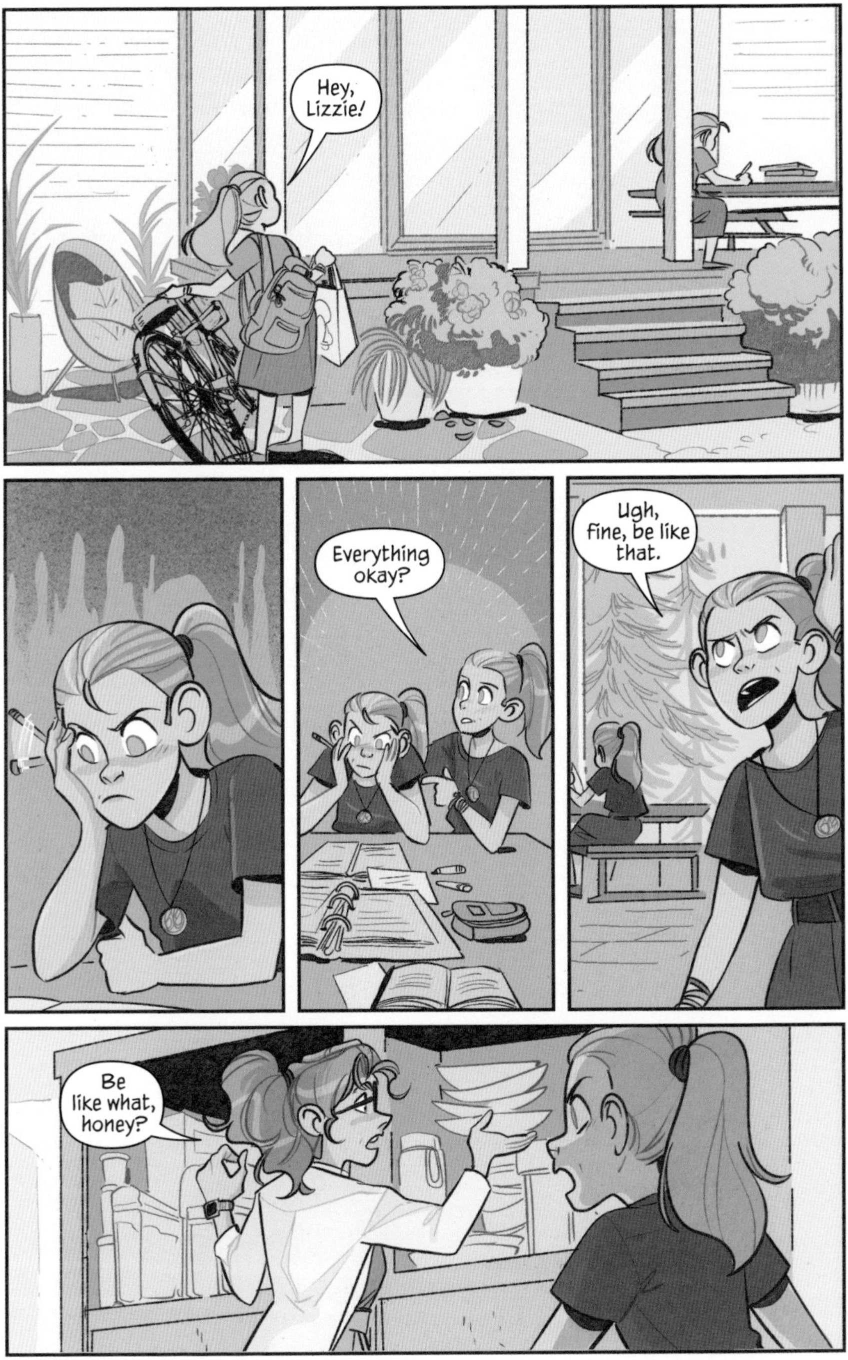
Hey, Lizzie!
Everything okay?
Ugh, fine, be like that.
Be like what, honey?

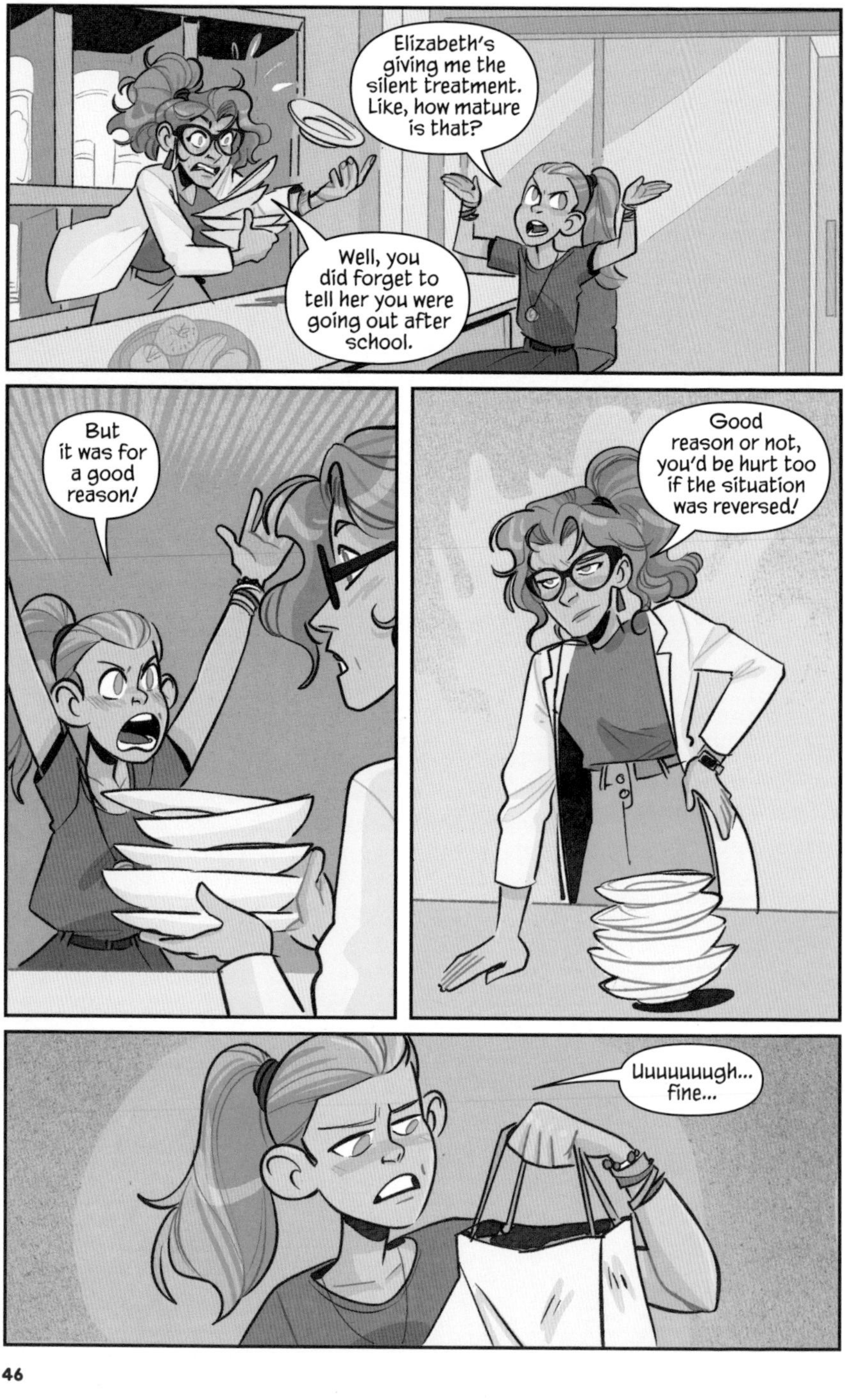
Elizabeth's giving me the silent treatment. Like, how mature is that?
Well, you did forget to tell her you were going out after school.
But it was for a good reason!
Good reason or not, you'd be hurt too if the situation was reversed!
Uuuuuuugh... fine...

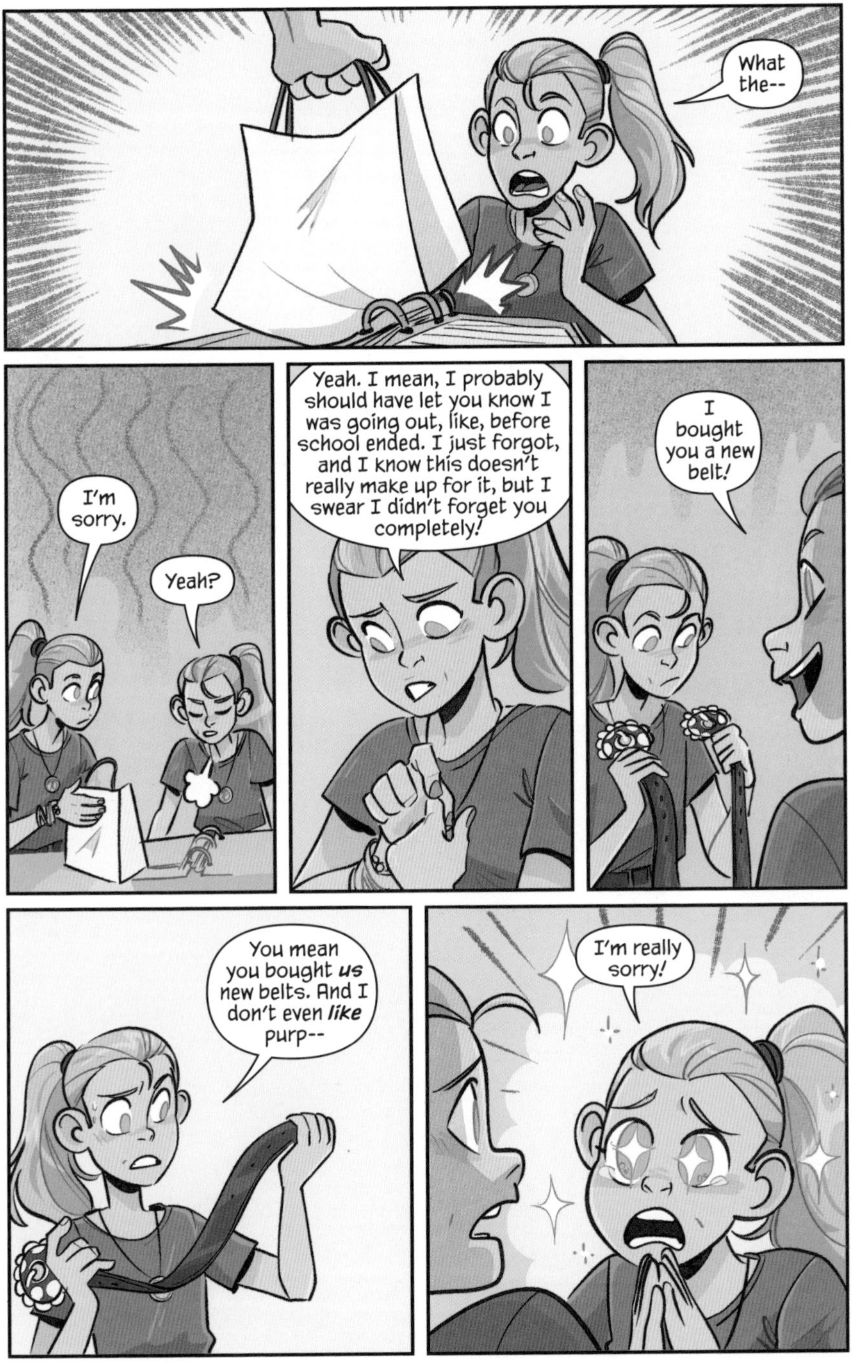
What the--
I'm sorry.
Yeah?
Yeah. I mean, I probably should have let you know I was going out, like, before school ended. I just forgot, and I know this doesn't really make up for it, but I swear I didn't forget you completely!
I bought you a new belt!
You mean you bought **us** new belts. And I don't even ***like*** purp--
I'm really sorry!

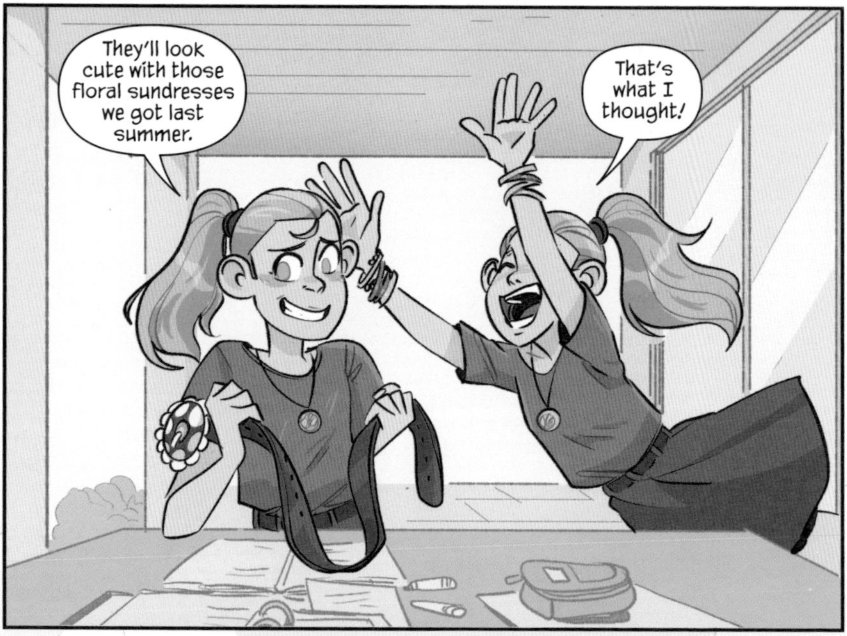
They'll look cute with those floral sundresses we got last summer.
That's what I thought!

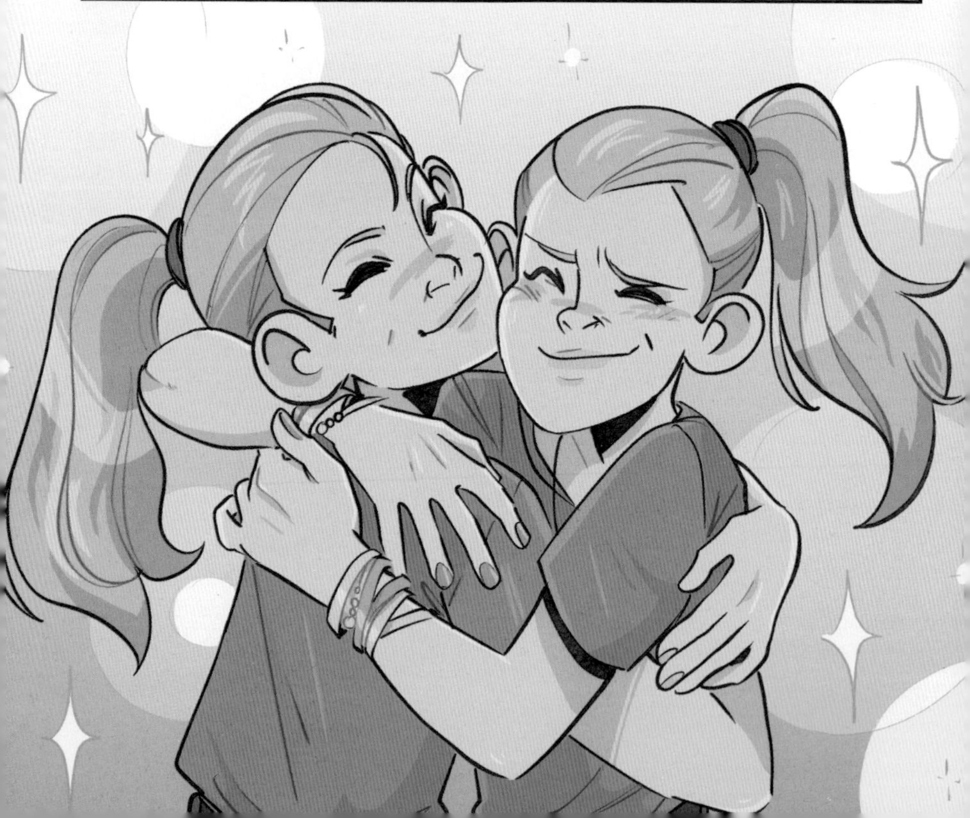

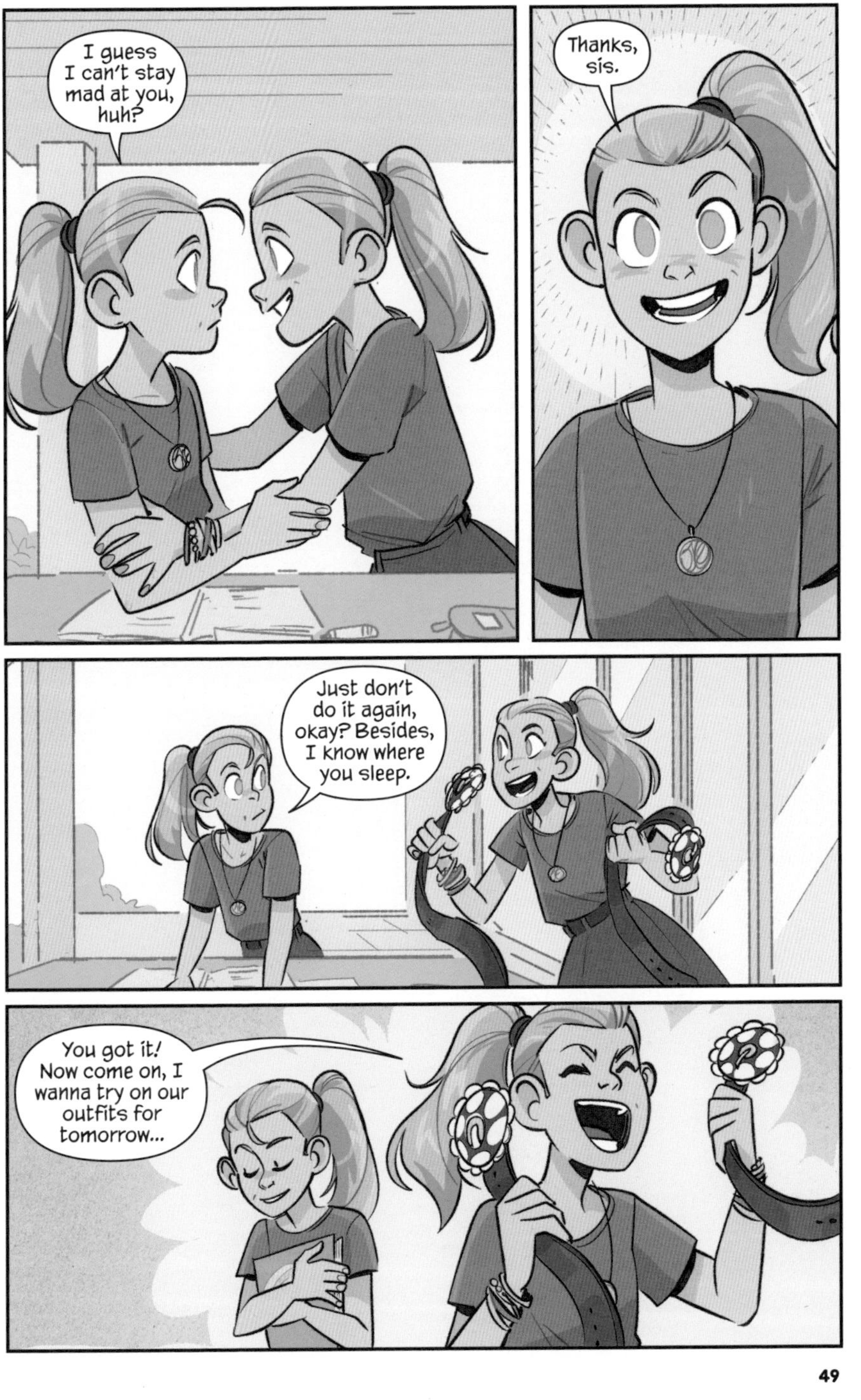
I guess I can't stay mad at you, huh?
Thanks, sis.
Just don't do it again, okay? Besides, I know where you sleep.
You got it! Now come on, I wanna try on our outfits for tomorrow...

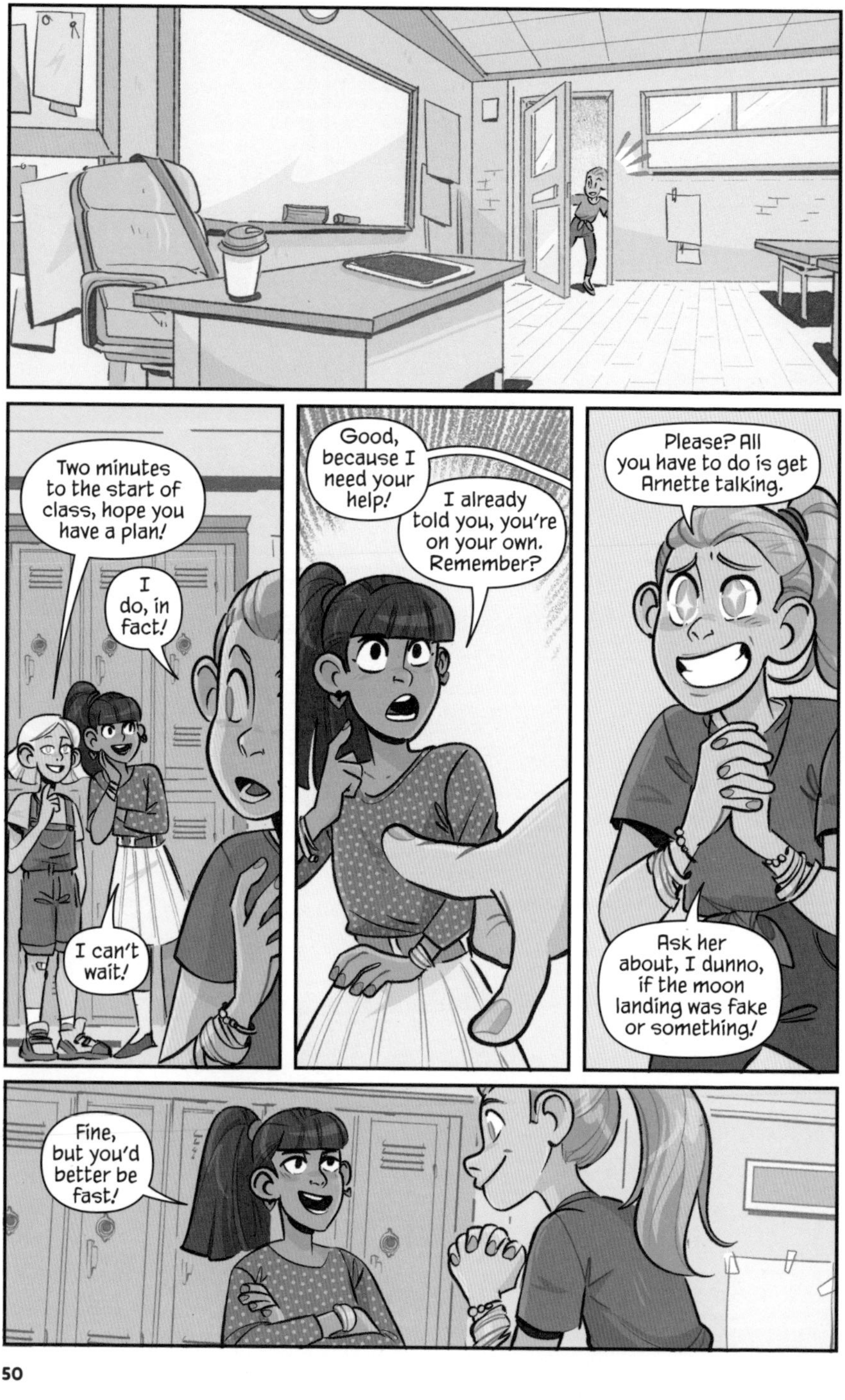
Two minutes to the start of class, hope you have a plan!
I do, in fact!
I can't wait!
Good, because I need your help!
I already told you, you're on your own. Remember?
Please? All you have to do is get Arnette talking.
Ask her about, I dunno, if the moon landing was fake or something!
Fine, but you'd better be fast!

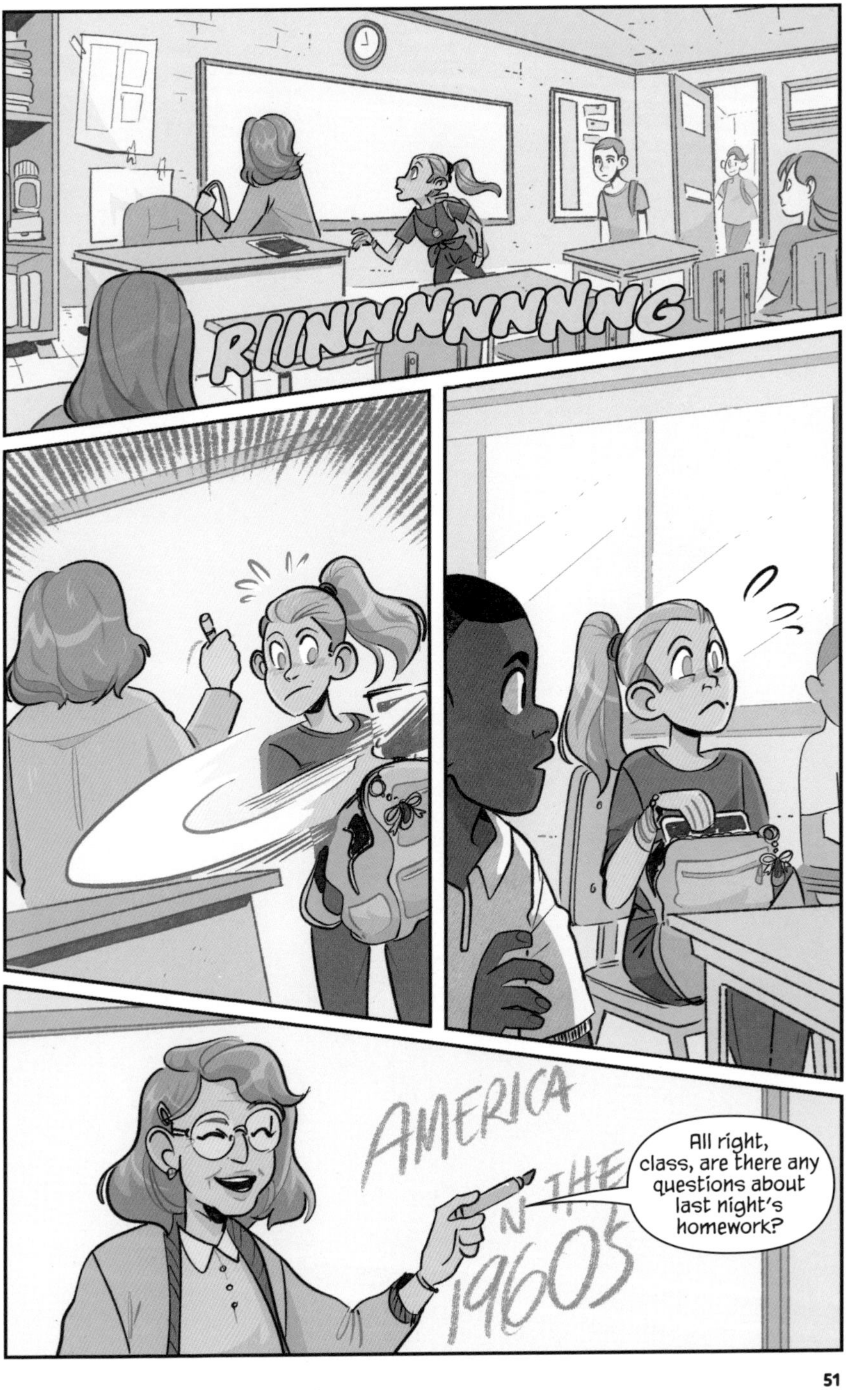
RIINNNNNNNG
AMERICA IN THE 1960S
All right, class, are there any questions about last night's homework?

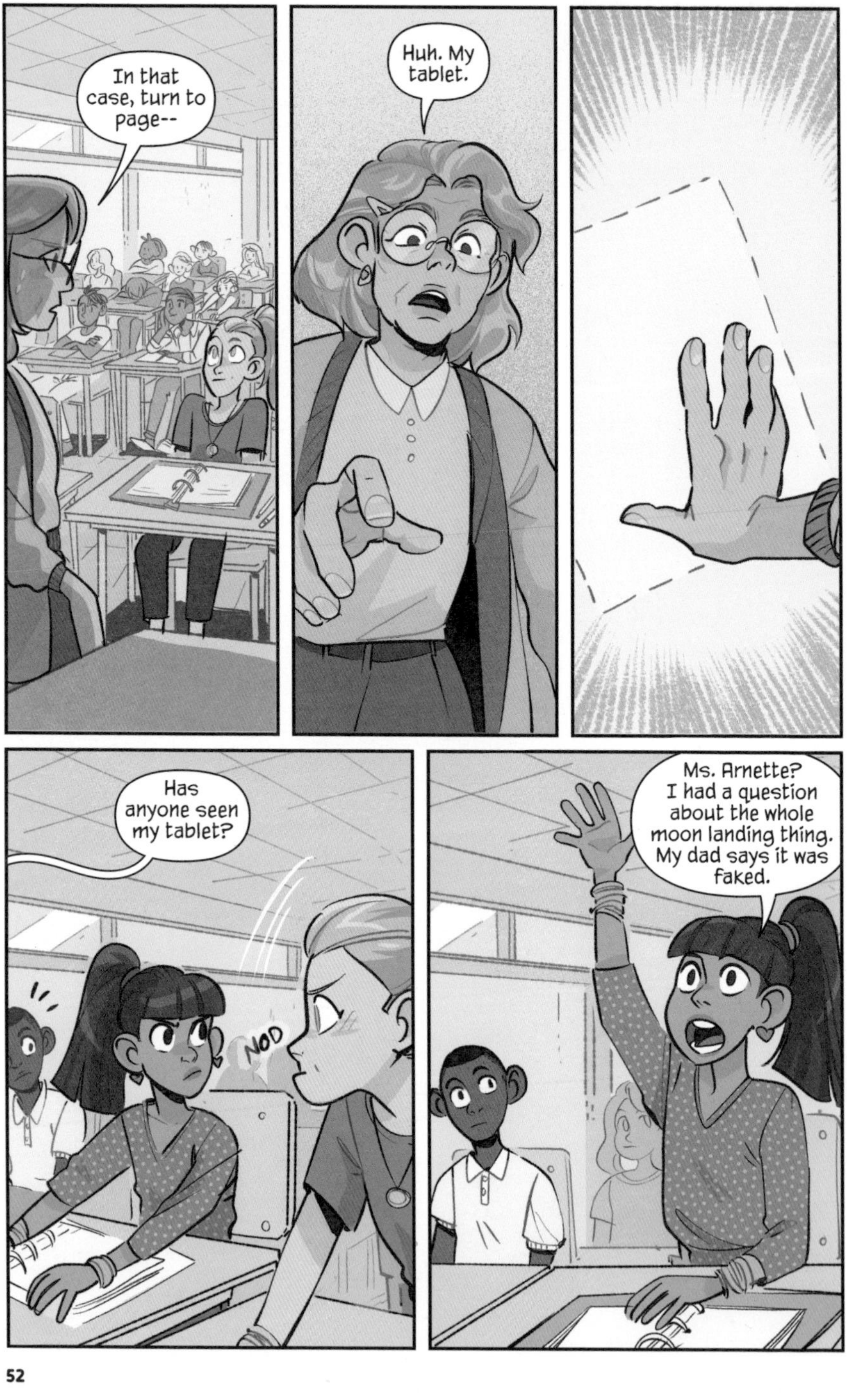
In that case, turn to page--
Huh. My tablet.
Has anyone seen my tablet?
NOD
Ms. Arnette? I had a question about the whole moon landing thing. My dad says it was faked.

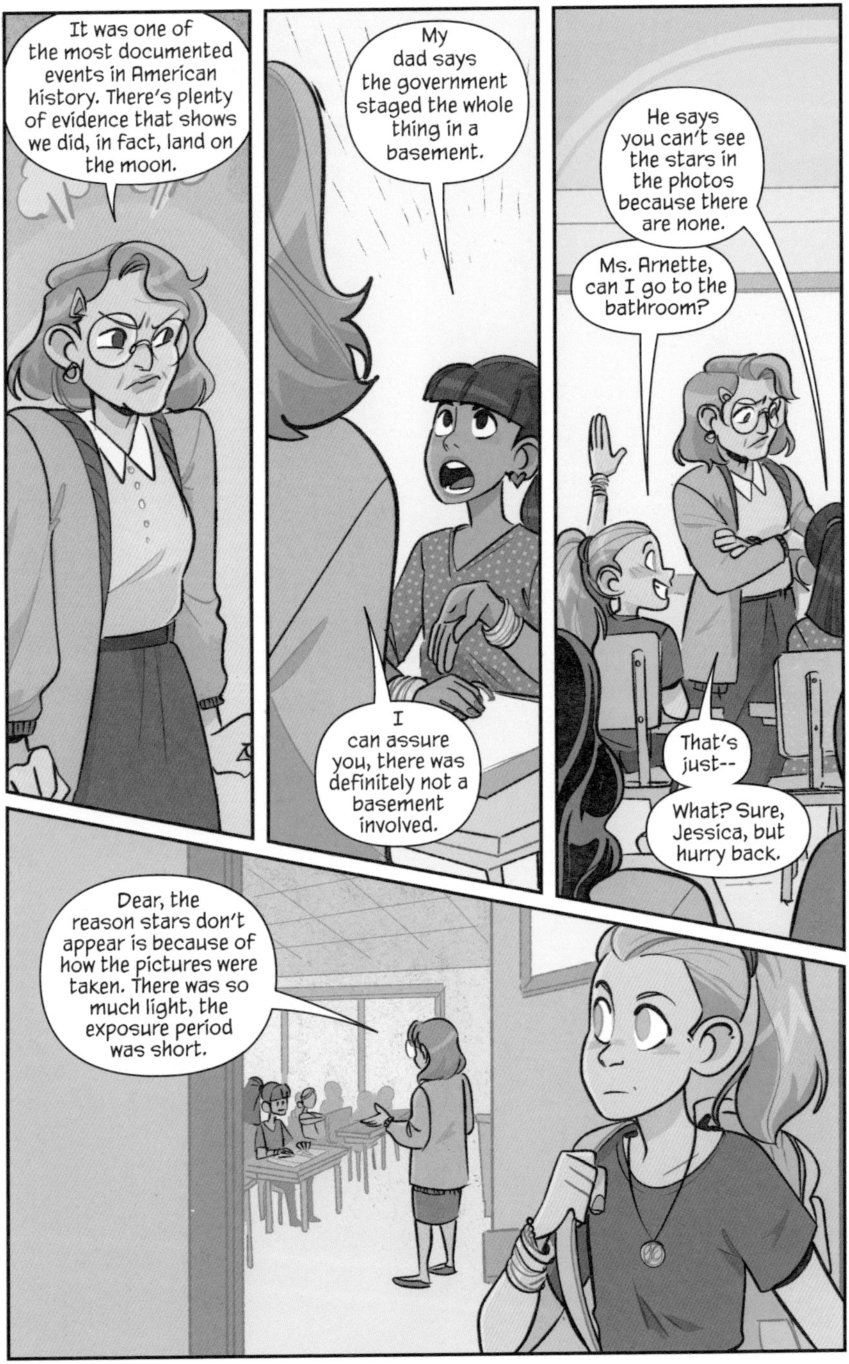
It was one of the most documented events in American history. There's plenty of evidence that shows we did, in fact, land on the moon.
My dad says the government staged the whole thing in a basement.
I can assure you, there was definitely not a basement involved.
He says you can't see the stars in the photos because there are none.
Ms. Arnette, can I go to the bathroom?
That's just--
What? Sure, Jessica, but hurry back.
Dear, the reason stars don't appear is because of how the pictures were taken. There was so much light, the exposure period was short.

"Yes, I understand it all *sounds* very convincing, but that's why we need to be critical in our thinking. And why examining sources is so important...

"We can't believe everything we're told."

Now that we've settled that--

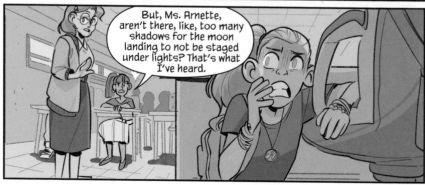

But, Ms. Arnette, aren't there, like, too many shadows for the moon landing to not be staged under lights? That's what I've heard.

That argument assumes that the sun is the only source of illumination.

"There were other sources of illumination, however."

"Like what?"

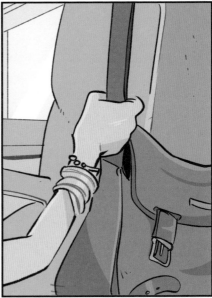

"Well, the lunar ground for one."

"Like, rocks?"

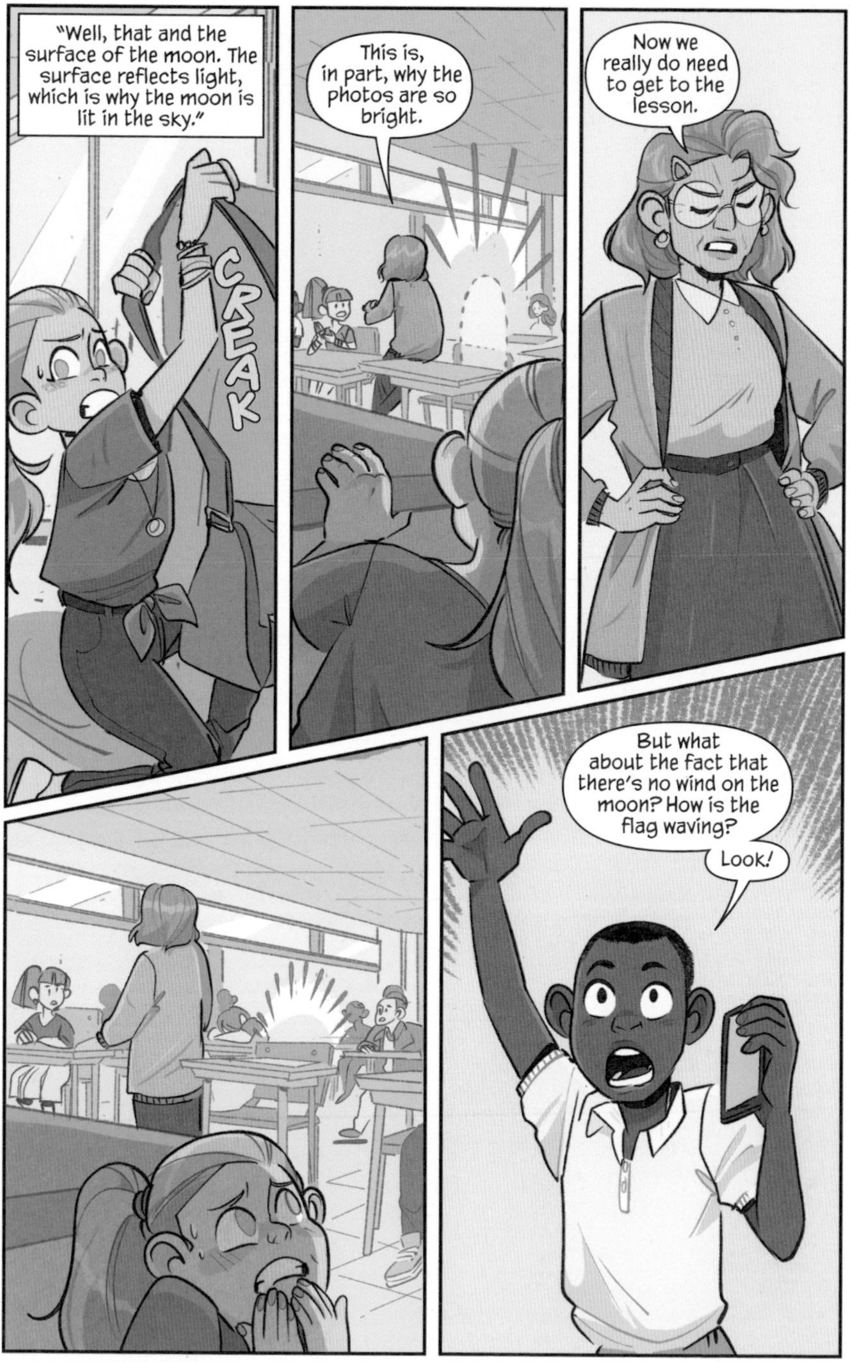
"Well, that and the surface of the moon. The surface reflects light, which is why the moon is lit in the sky."
CREAK
This is, in part, why the photos are so bright.
Now we really do need to get to the lesson.
But what about the fact that there's no wind on the moon? How is the flag waving?
Look!

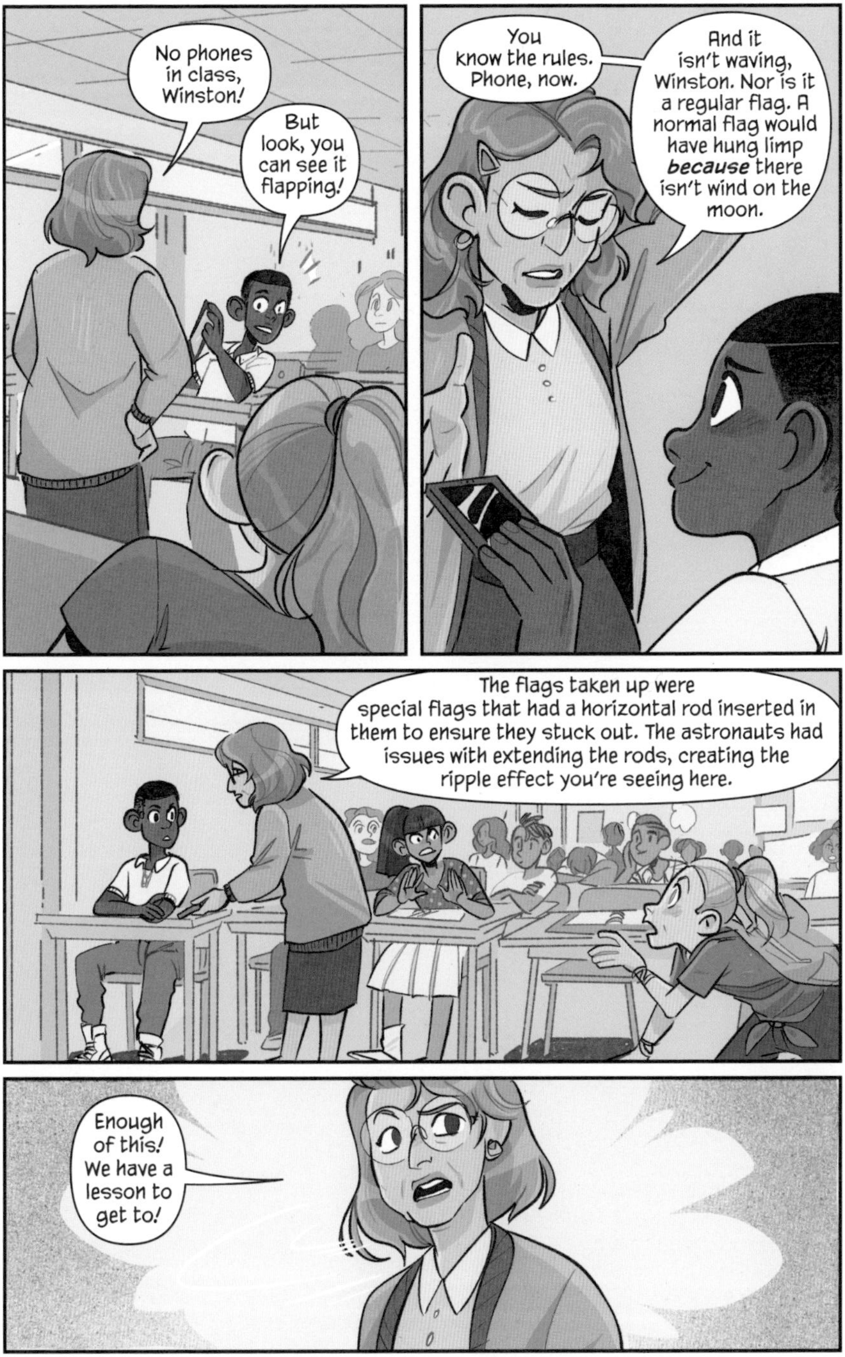
No phones in class, Winston!
But look, you can see it flapping!
You know the rules. Phone, now.
And it isn't waving, Winston. Nor is it a regular flag. A normal flag would have hung limp *because* there isn't wind on the moon.
The flags taken up were special flags that had a horizontal rod inserted in them to ensure they stuck out. The astronauts had issues with extending the rods, creating the ripple effect you're seeing here.
Enough of this! We have a lesson to get to!

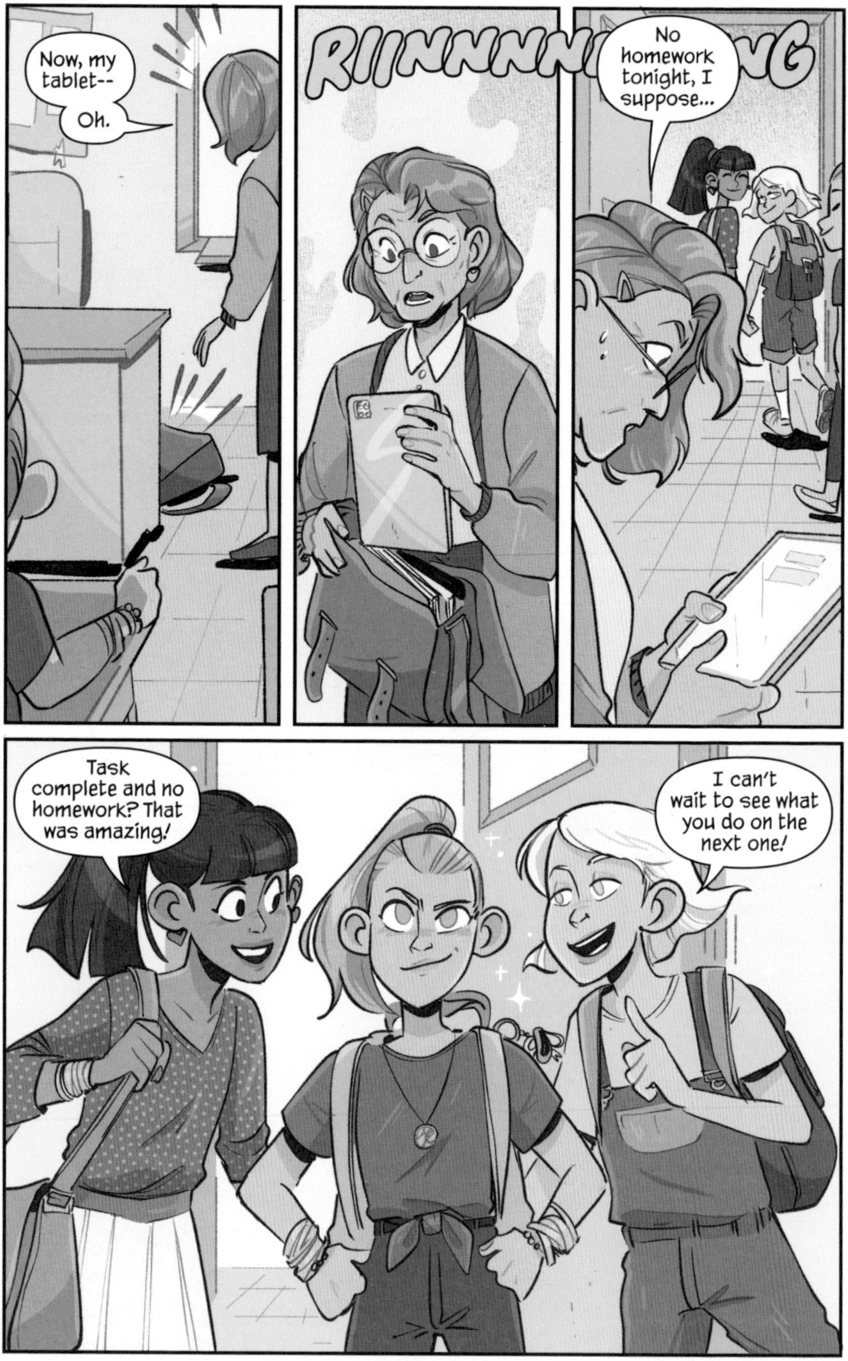
Now, my tablet--
Oh.
RIINNNNNNNNNG
No homework tonight, I suppose...
Task complete and no homework? That was amazing!
I can't wait to see what you do on the next one!

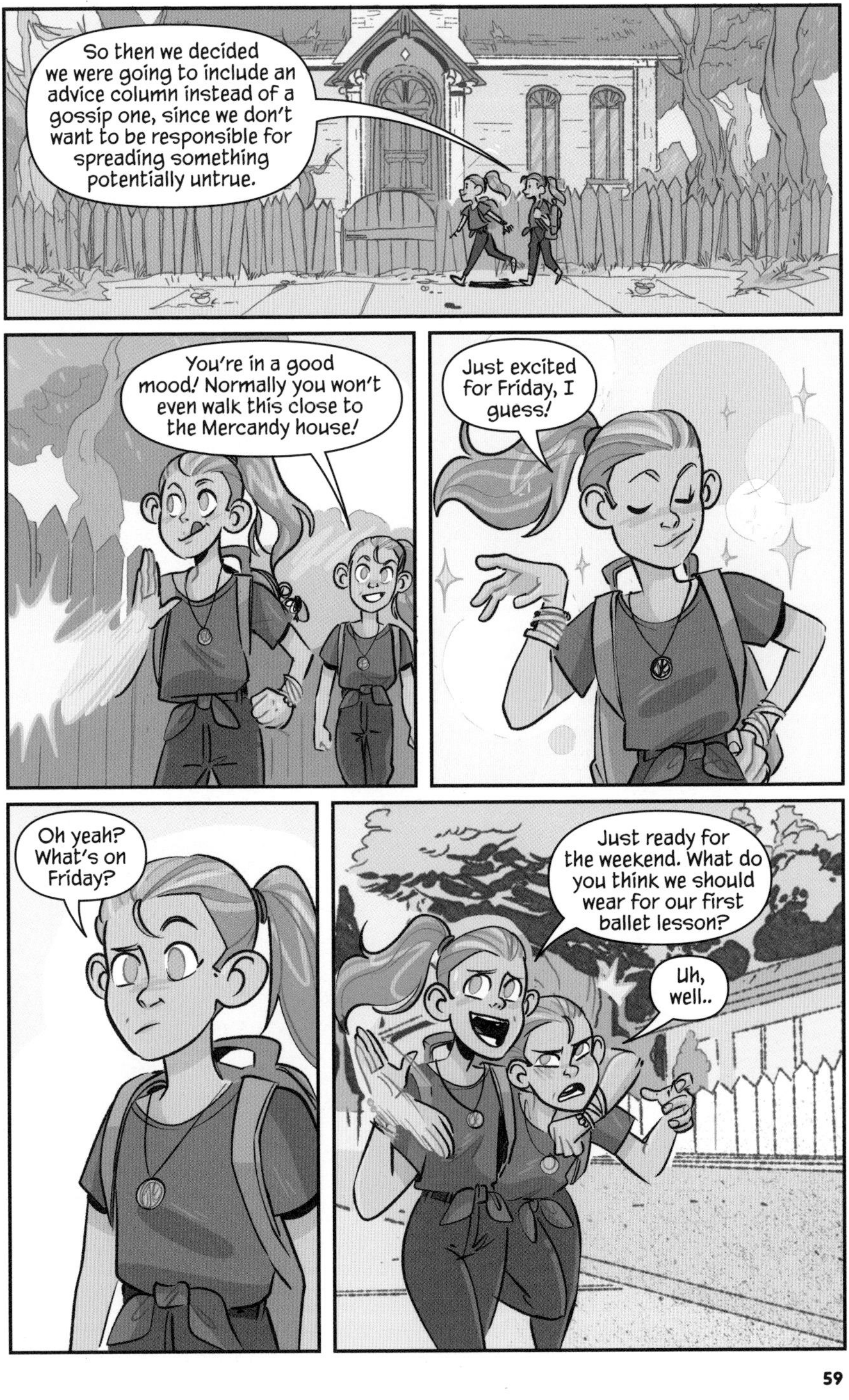
So then we decided we were going to include an advice column instead of a gossip one, since we don't want to be responsible for spreading something potentially untrue.
You're in a good mood! Normally you won't even walk this close to the Mercandy house!
Just excited for Friday, I guess!
Oh yeah? What's on Friday?
Just ready for the weekend. What do you think we should wear for our first ballet lesson?
Uh, well..

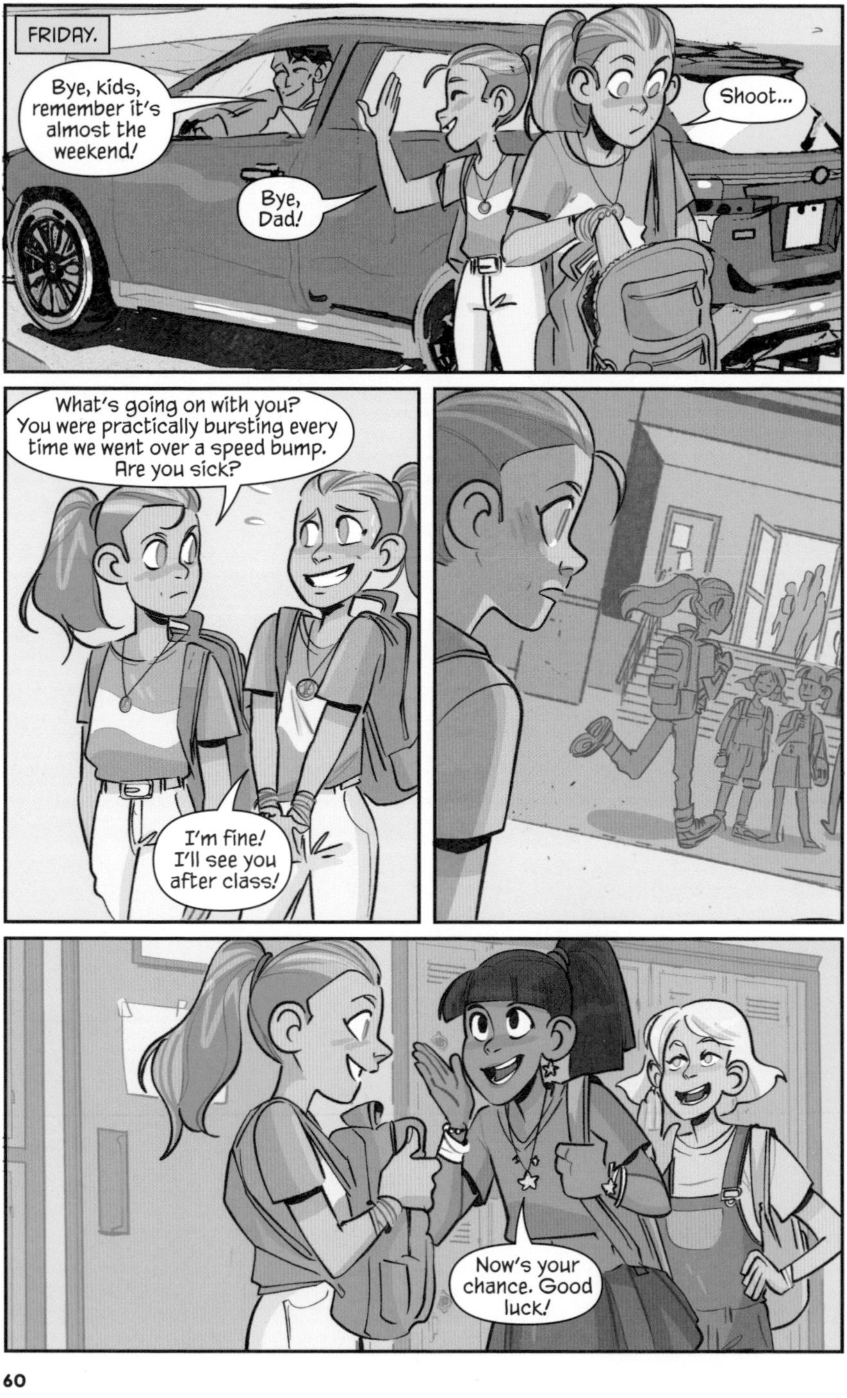
FRIDAY.
Bye, kids, remember it's almost the weekend!
Bye, Dad!
Shoot...
What's going on with you? You were practically bursting every time we went over a speed bump. Are you sick?
I'm fine! I'll see you after class!
Now's your chance. Good luck!

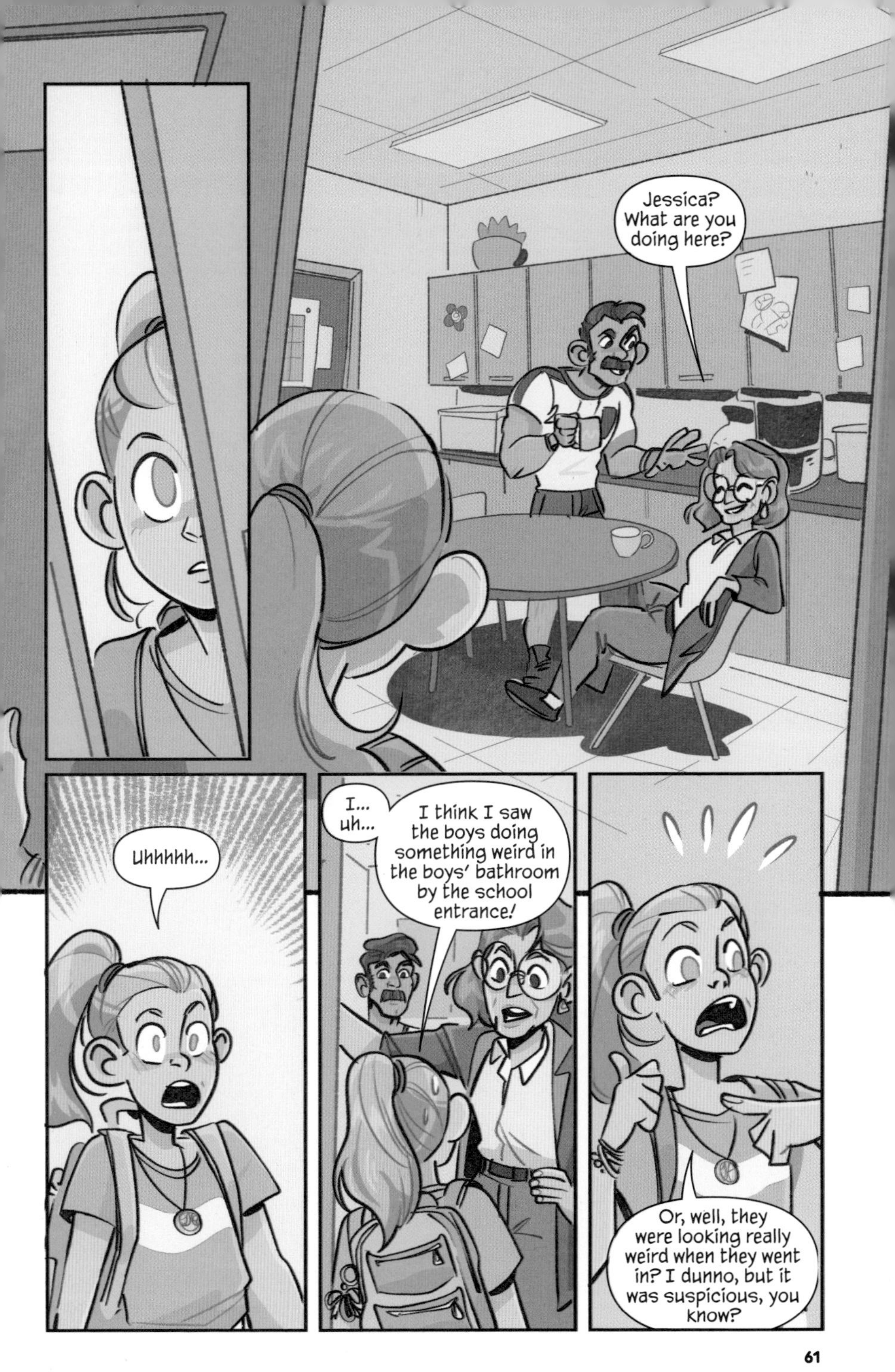
Jessica? What are you doing here?
Uhhhhh...
I... uh...
I think I saw the boys doing something weird in the boys' bathroom by the school entrance!
Or, well, they were looking really weird when they went in? I dunno, but it was suspicious, you know?

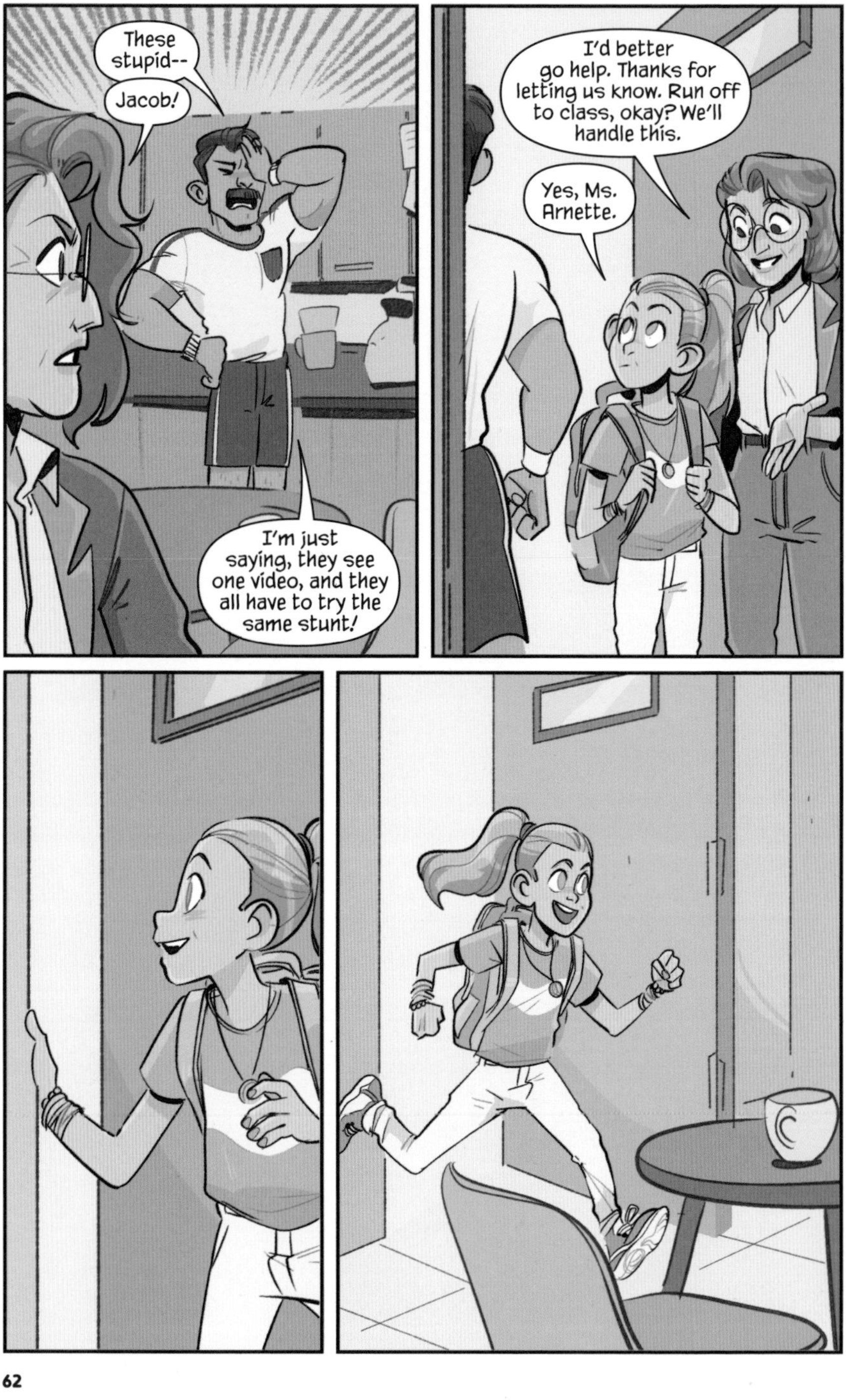
These stupid--
Jacob!
I'm just saying, they see one video, and they all have to try the same stunt!
I'd better go help. Thanks for letting us know. Run off to class, okay? We'll handle this.
Yes, Ms. Arnette.

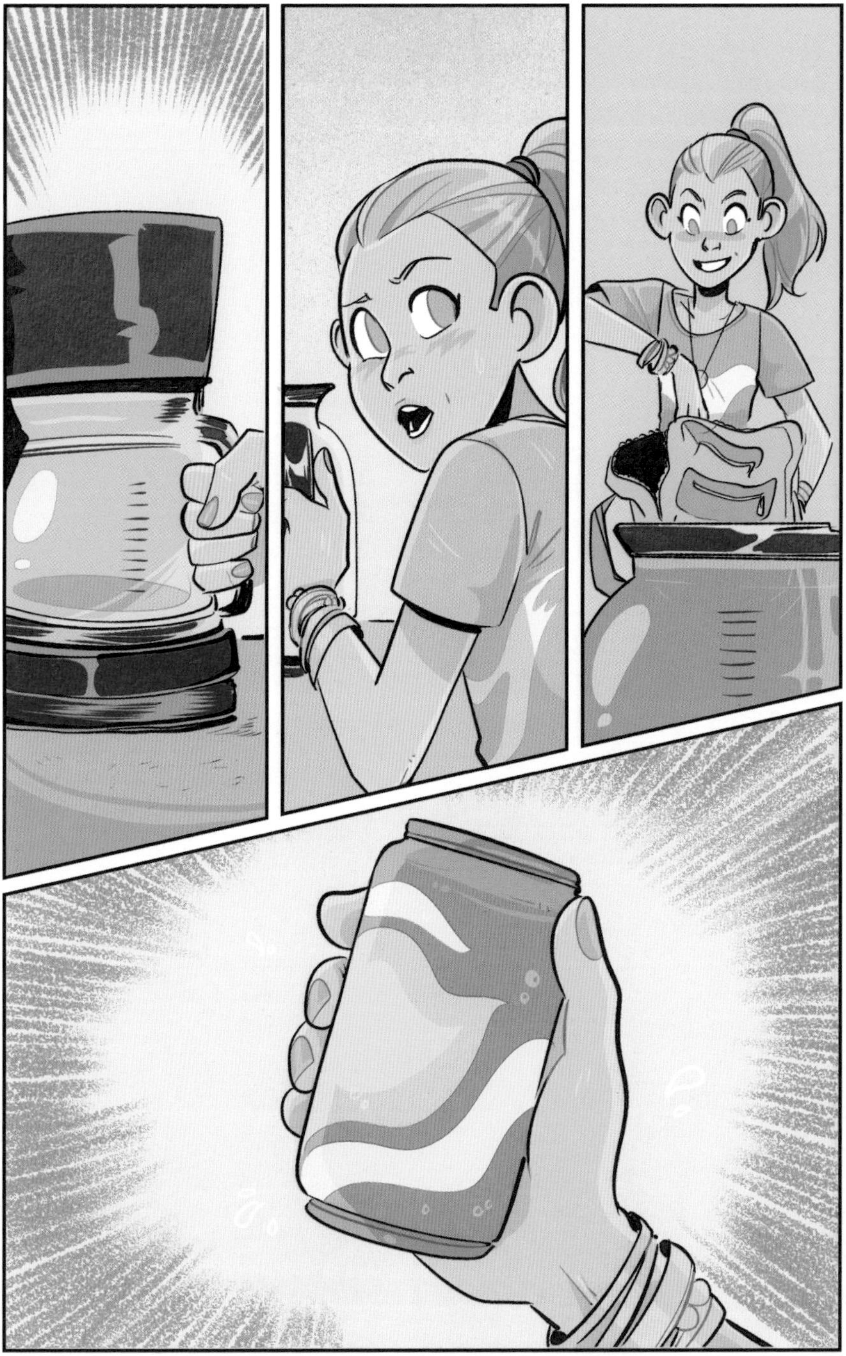

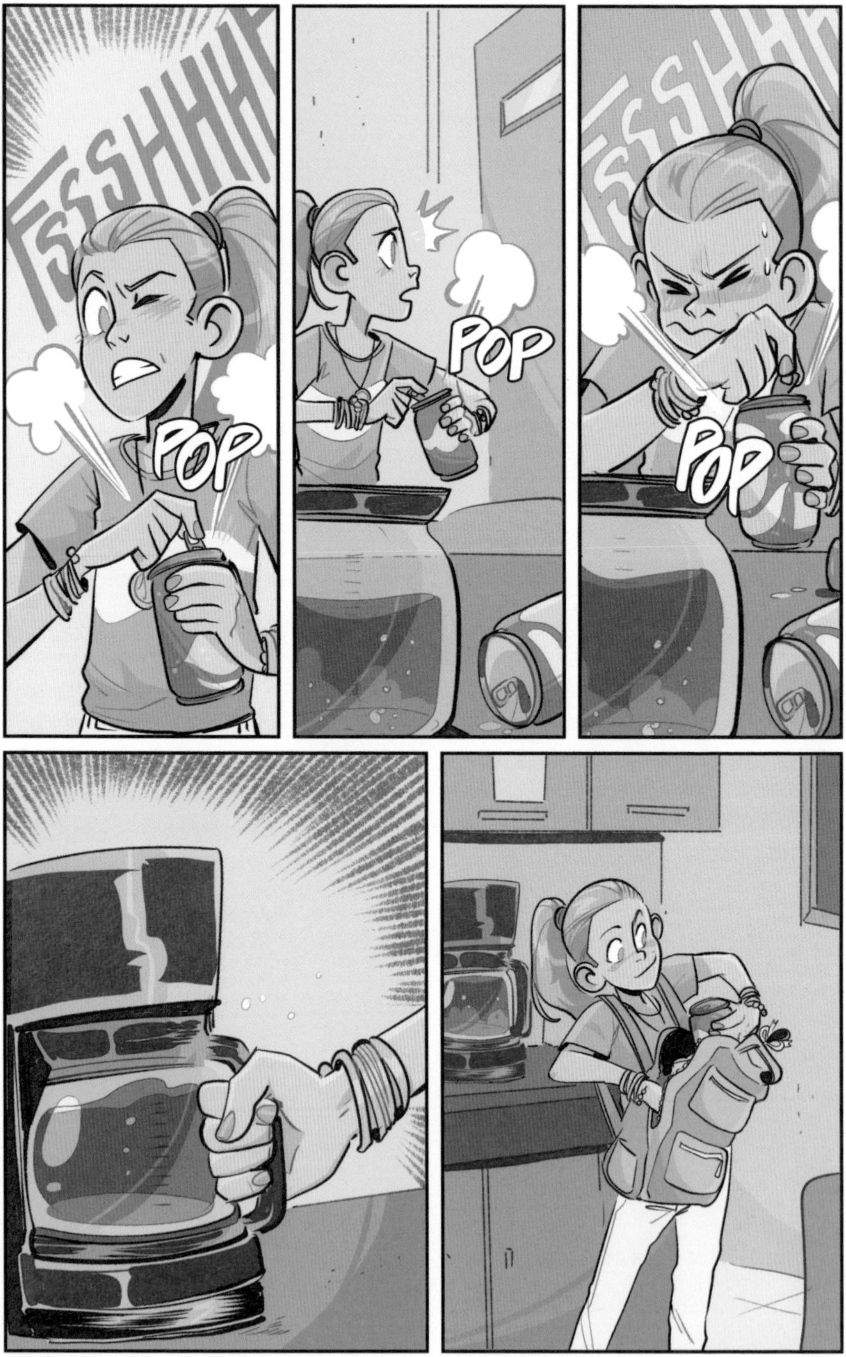
FSSSHHH
POP
POP
FSSSHHH
POP

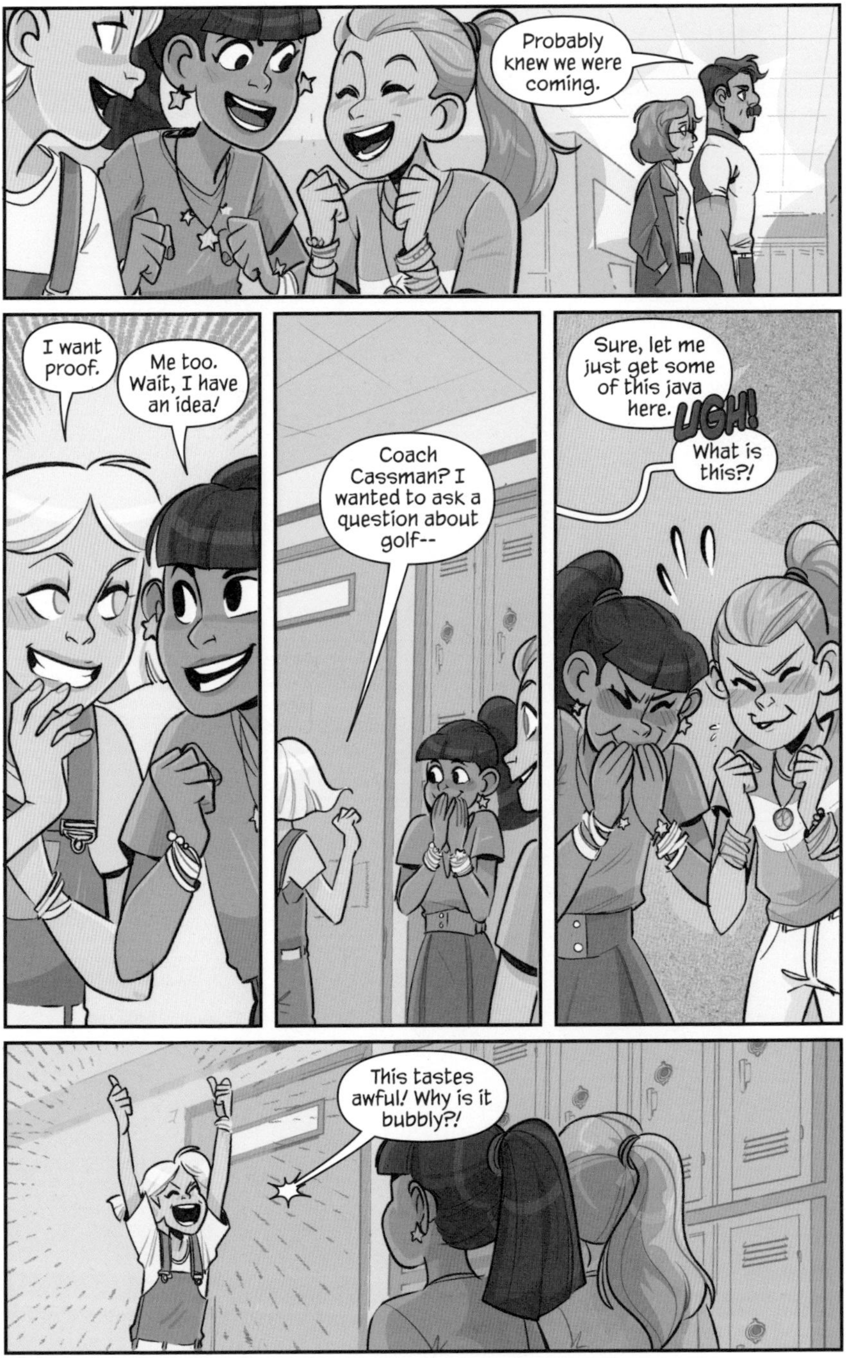
Probably knew we were coming.
I want proof.
Me too. Wait, I have an idea!
Coach Cassman? I wanted to ask a question about golf--
Sure, let me just get some of this java here.
UGH!
What is this?!
This tastes awful! Why is it bubbly?!

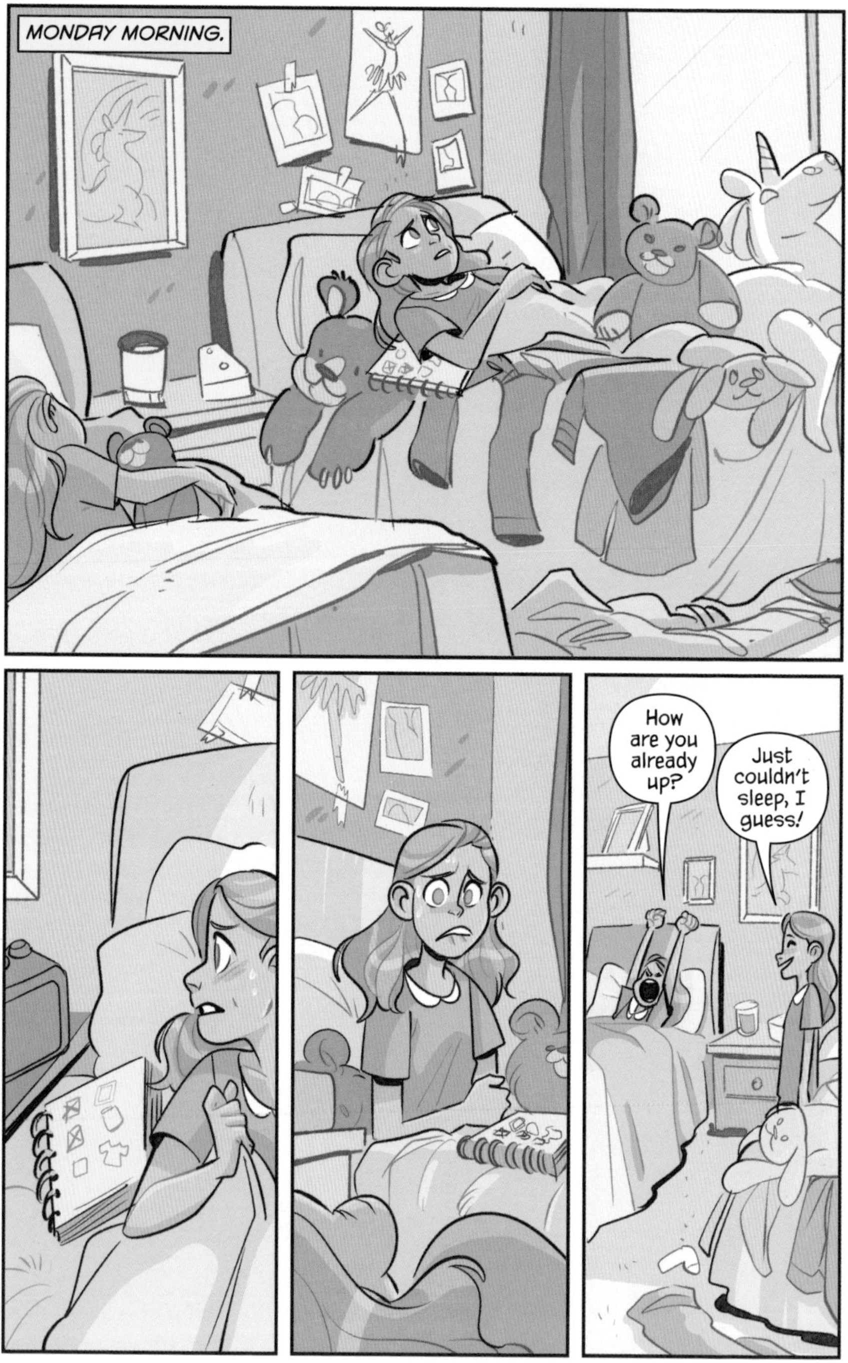
MONDAY MORNING.
How are you already up?
Just couldn't sleep, I guess!

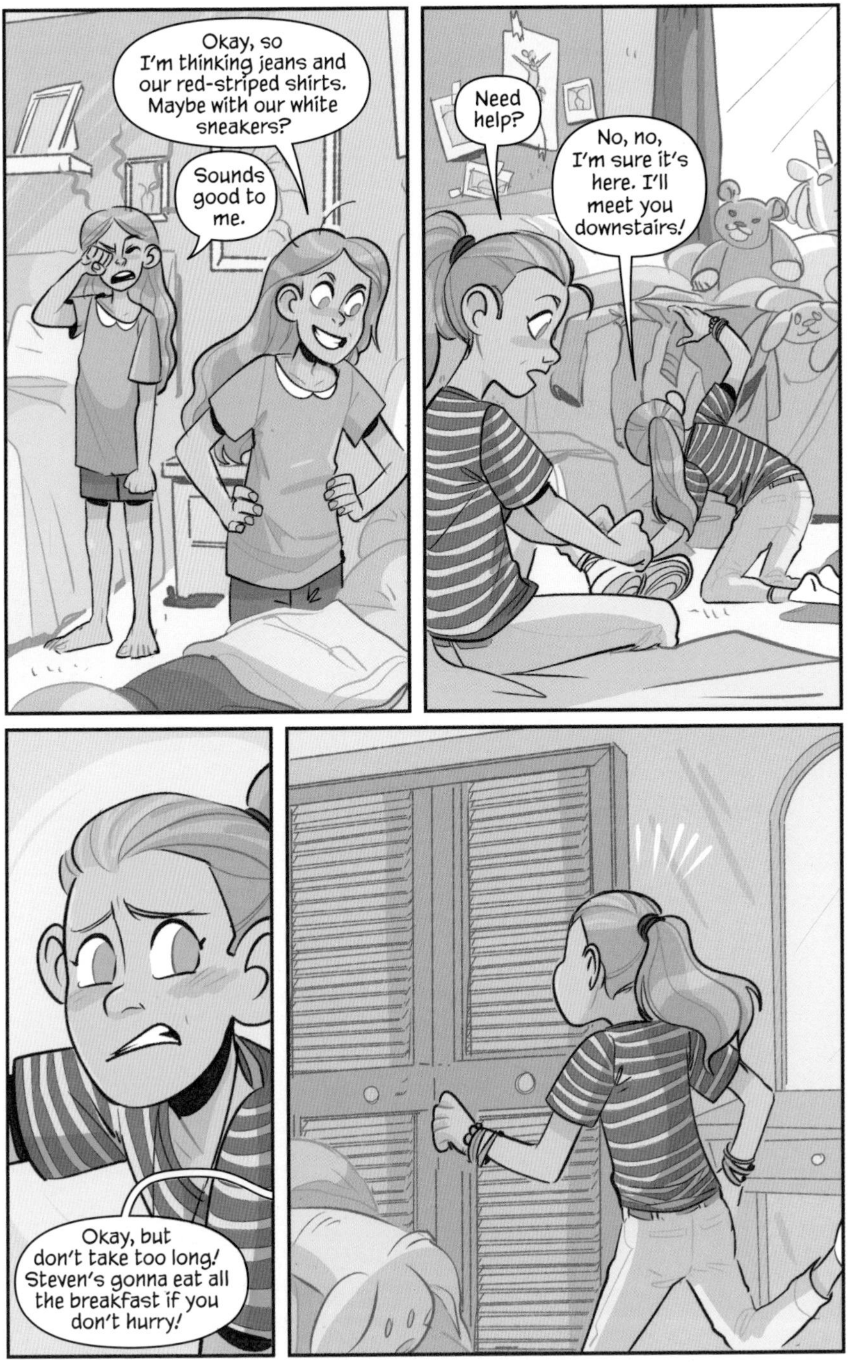
Okay, so I'm thinking jeans and our red-striped shirts. Maybe with our white sneakers?
Sounds good to me.
Need help?
No, no, I'm sure it's here. I'll meet you downstairs!
Okay, but don't take too long! Steven's gonna eat all the breakfast if you don't hurry!

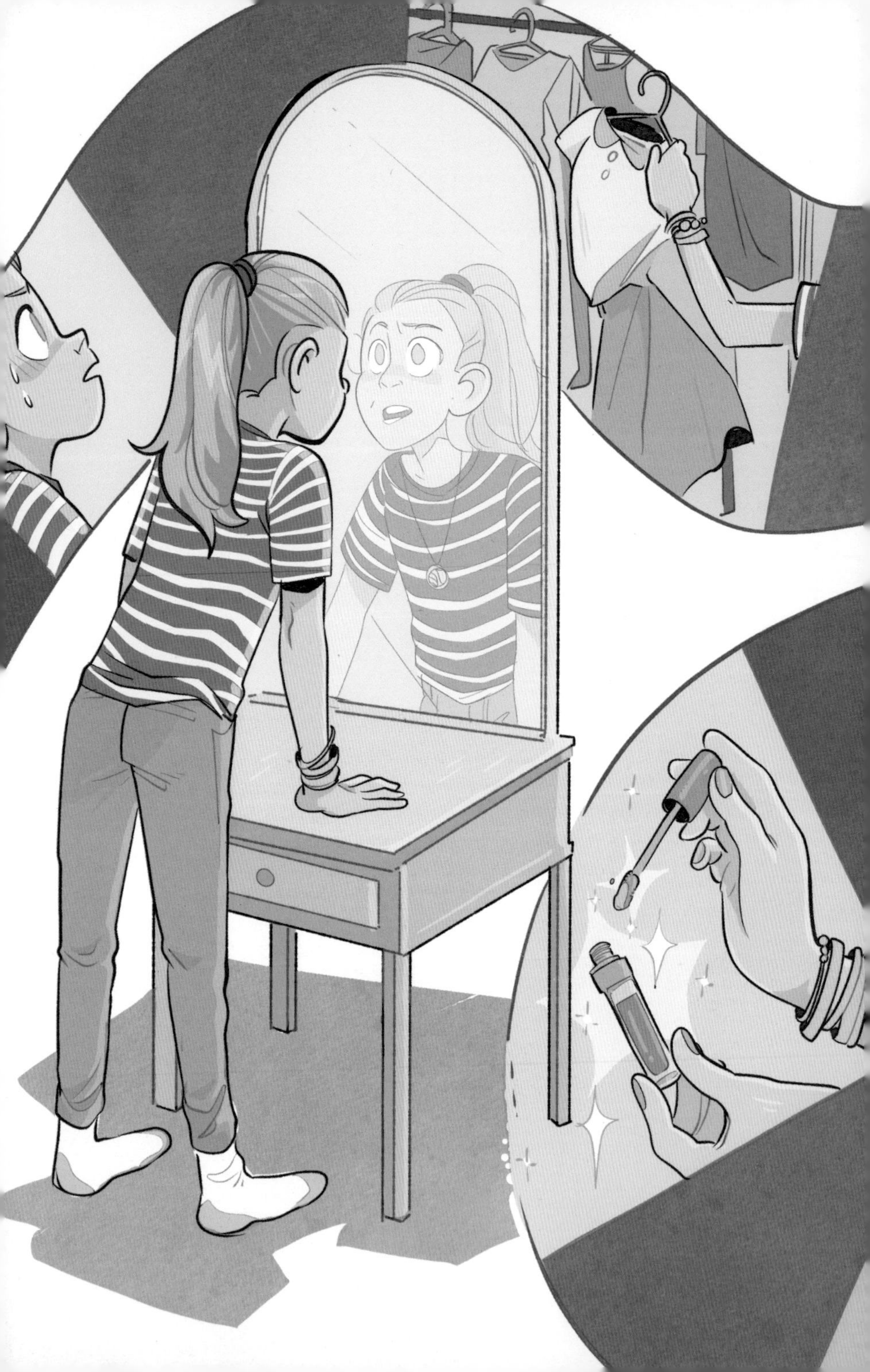

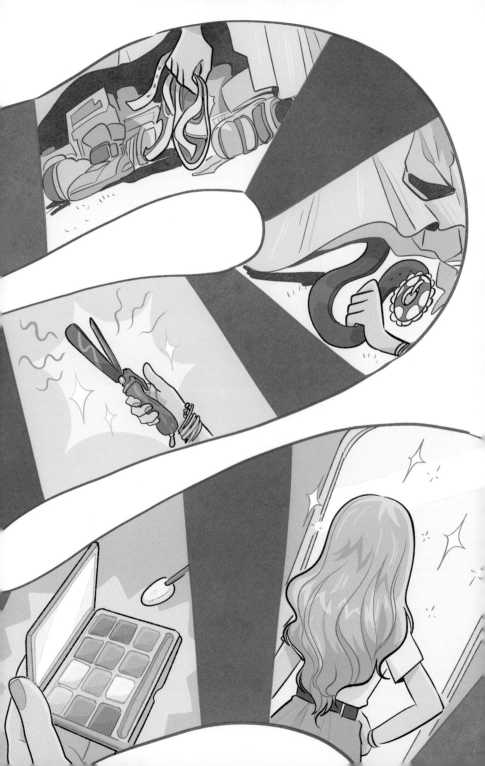

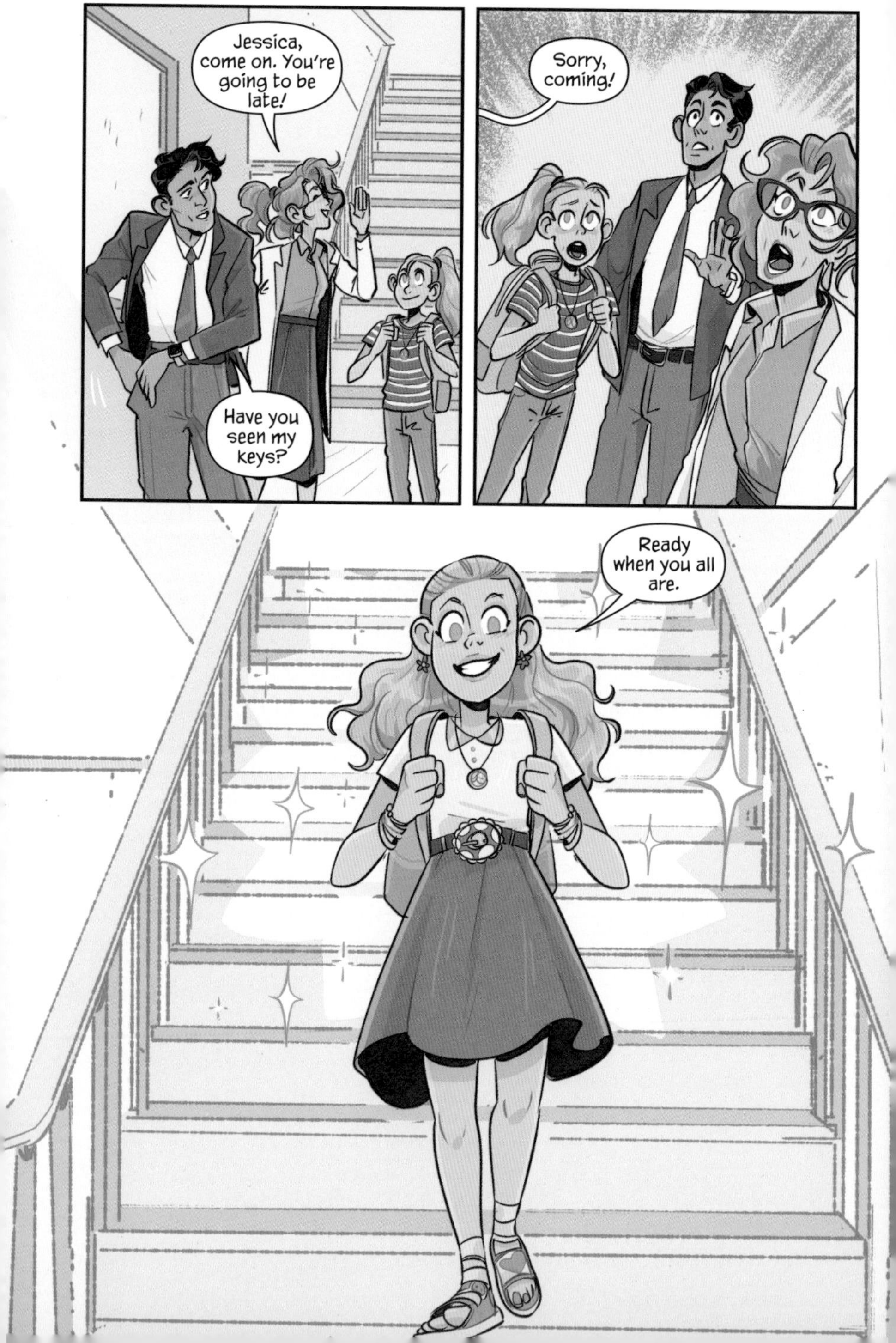
Jessica, come on. You're going to be late!
Have you seen my keys?
Sorry, coming!
Ready when you all are.

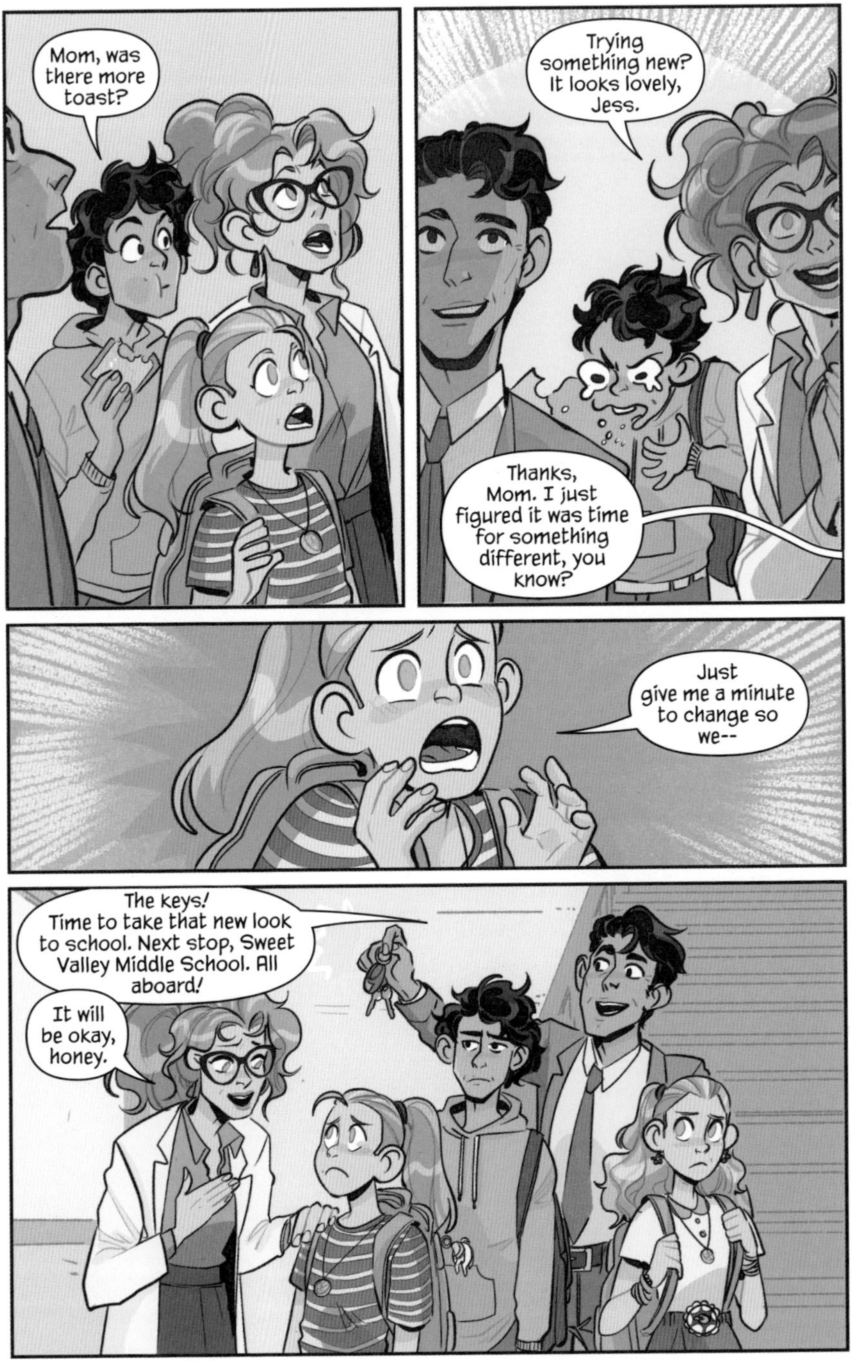

Mom, was there more toast?
Trying something new? It looks lovely, Jess.
Thanks, Mom. I just figured it was time for something different, you know?
Just give me a minute to change so we--
The keys! Time to take that new look to school. Next stop, Sweet Valley Middle School. All aboard!
It will be okay, honey.

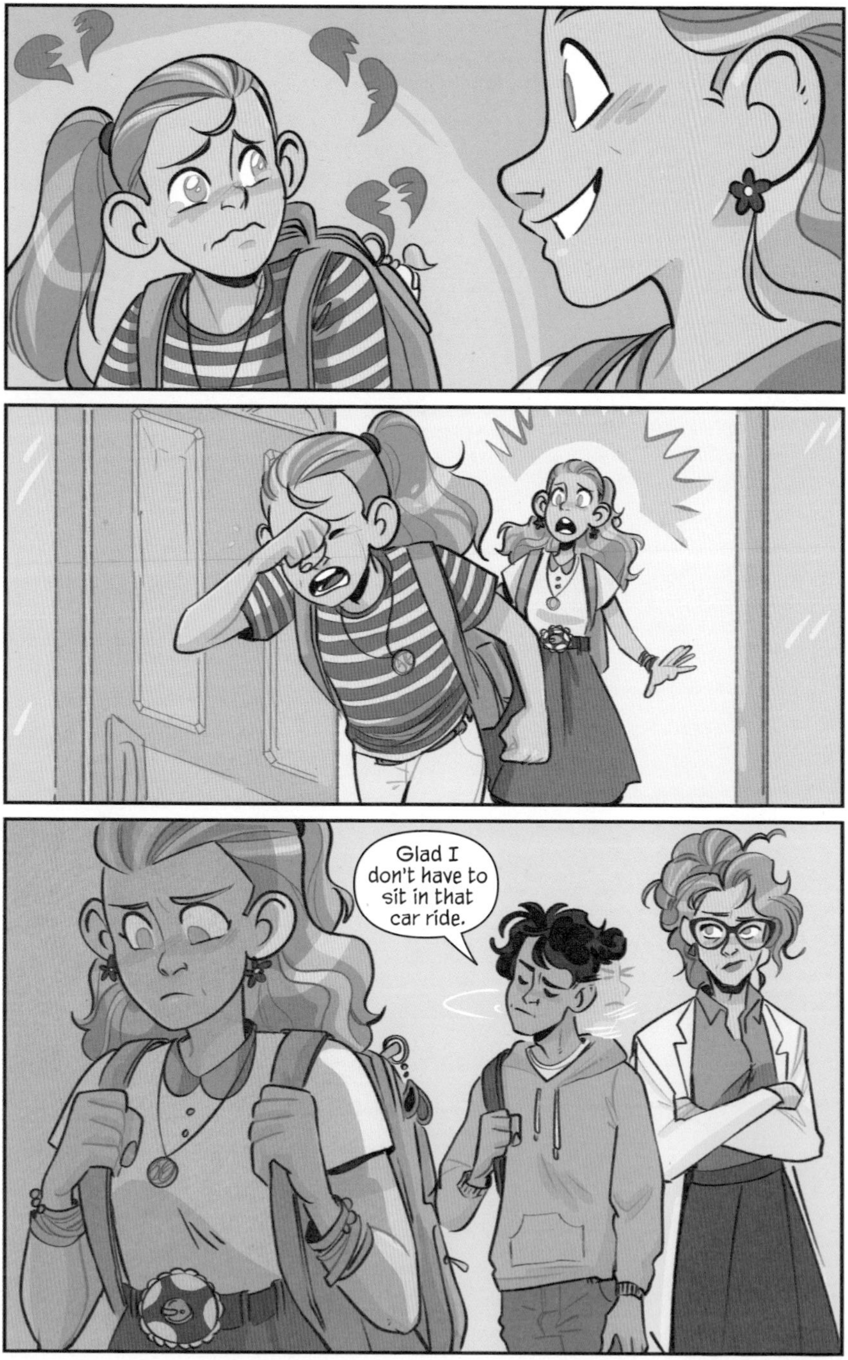
Glad I don't have to sit in that car ride.

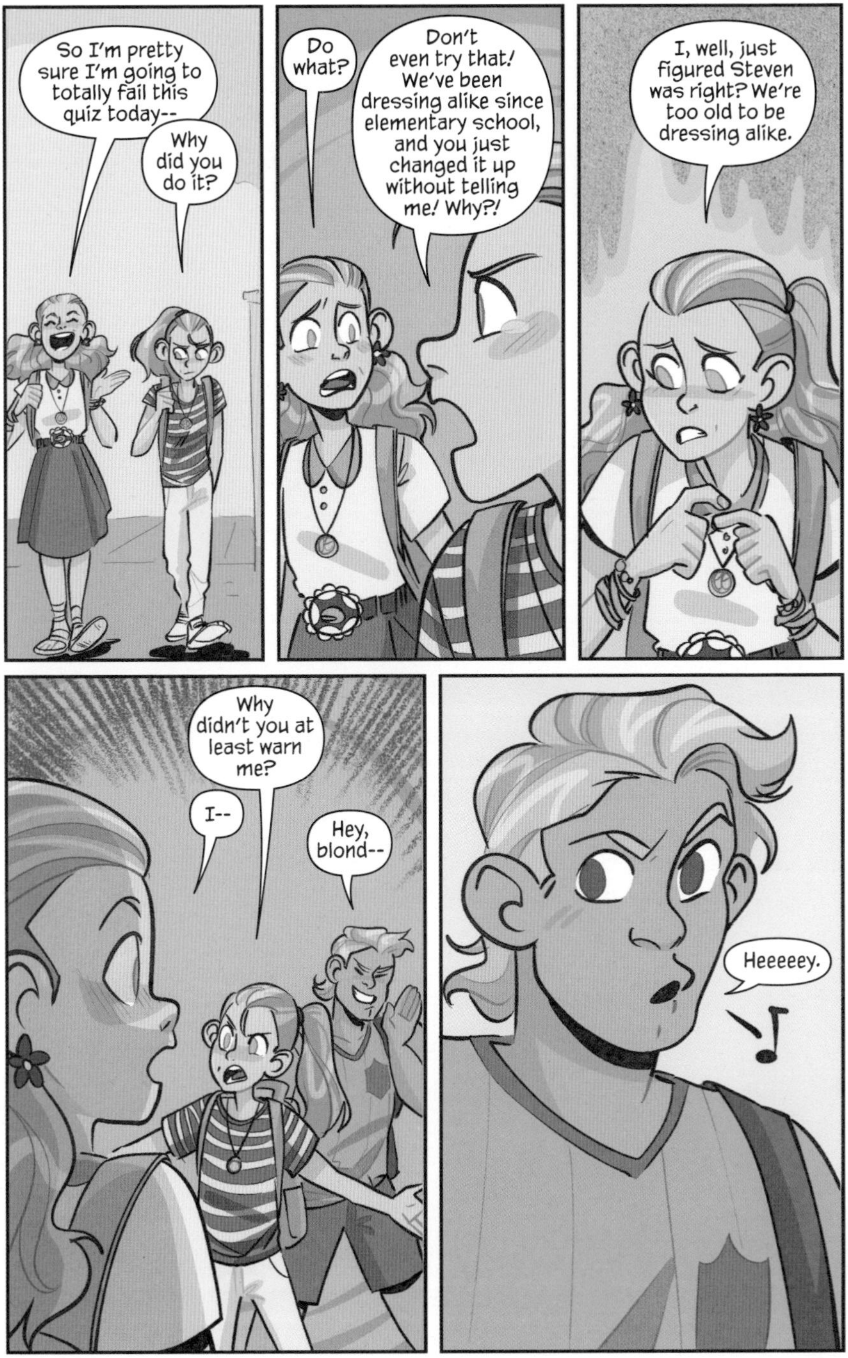
So I'm pretty sure I'm going to totally fail this quiz today--
Why did you do it?
Do what?
Don't even try that! We've been dressing alike since elementary school, and you just changed it up without telling me! Why?!
I, well, just figured Steven was right? We're too old to be dressing alike.
Why didn't you at least warn me?
I--
Hey, blond--
Heeeeey.

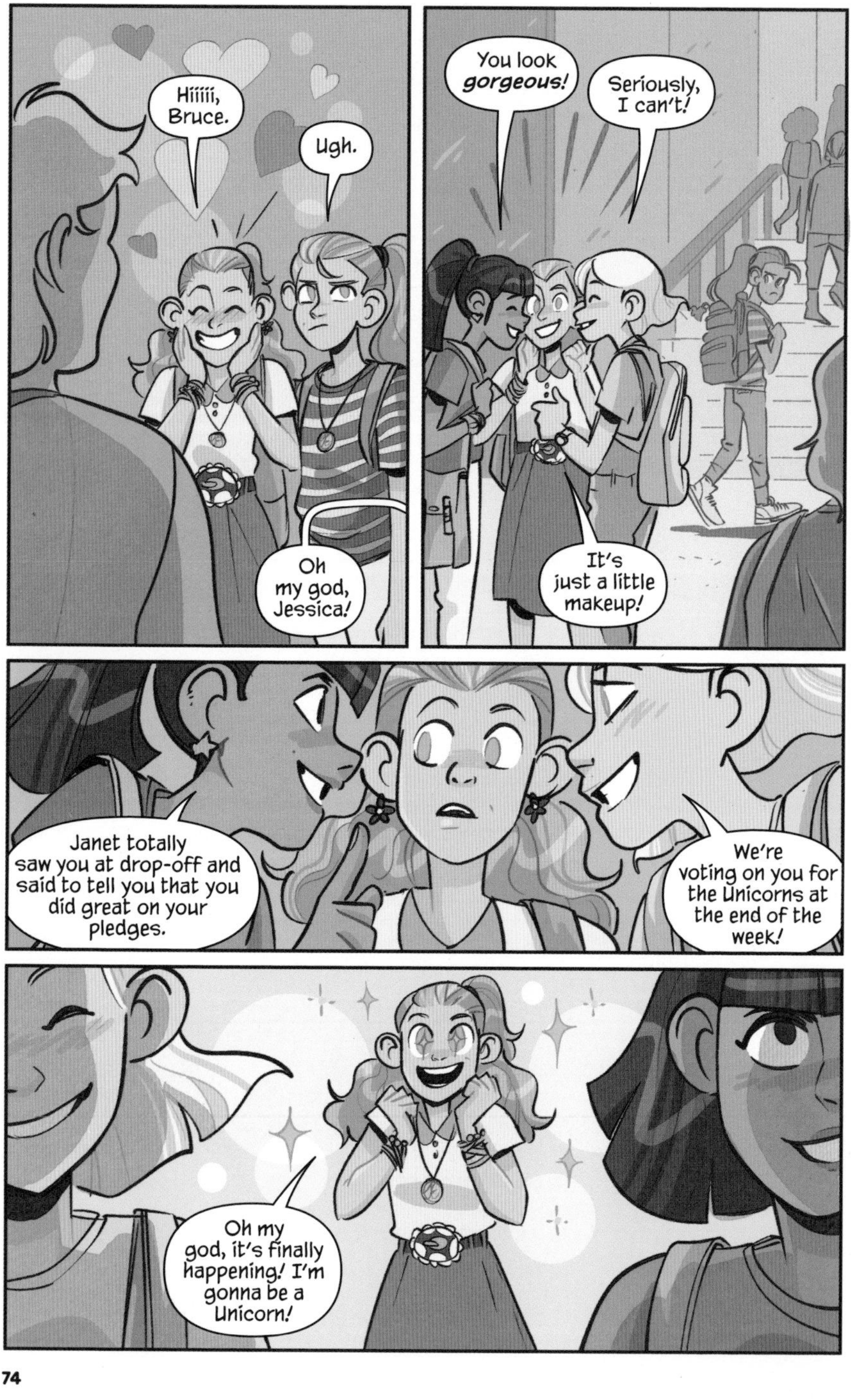
Hiiiii, Bruce.
Ugh.
Oh my god, Jessica!
You look *gorgeous!*
Seriously, I can't!
It's just a little makeup!
Janet totally saw you at drop-off and said to tell you that you did great on your pledges.
We're voting on you for the Unicorns at the end of the week!
Oh my god, it's finally happening! I'm gonna be a Unicorn!

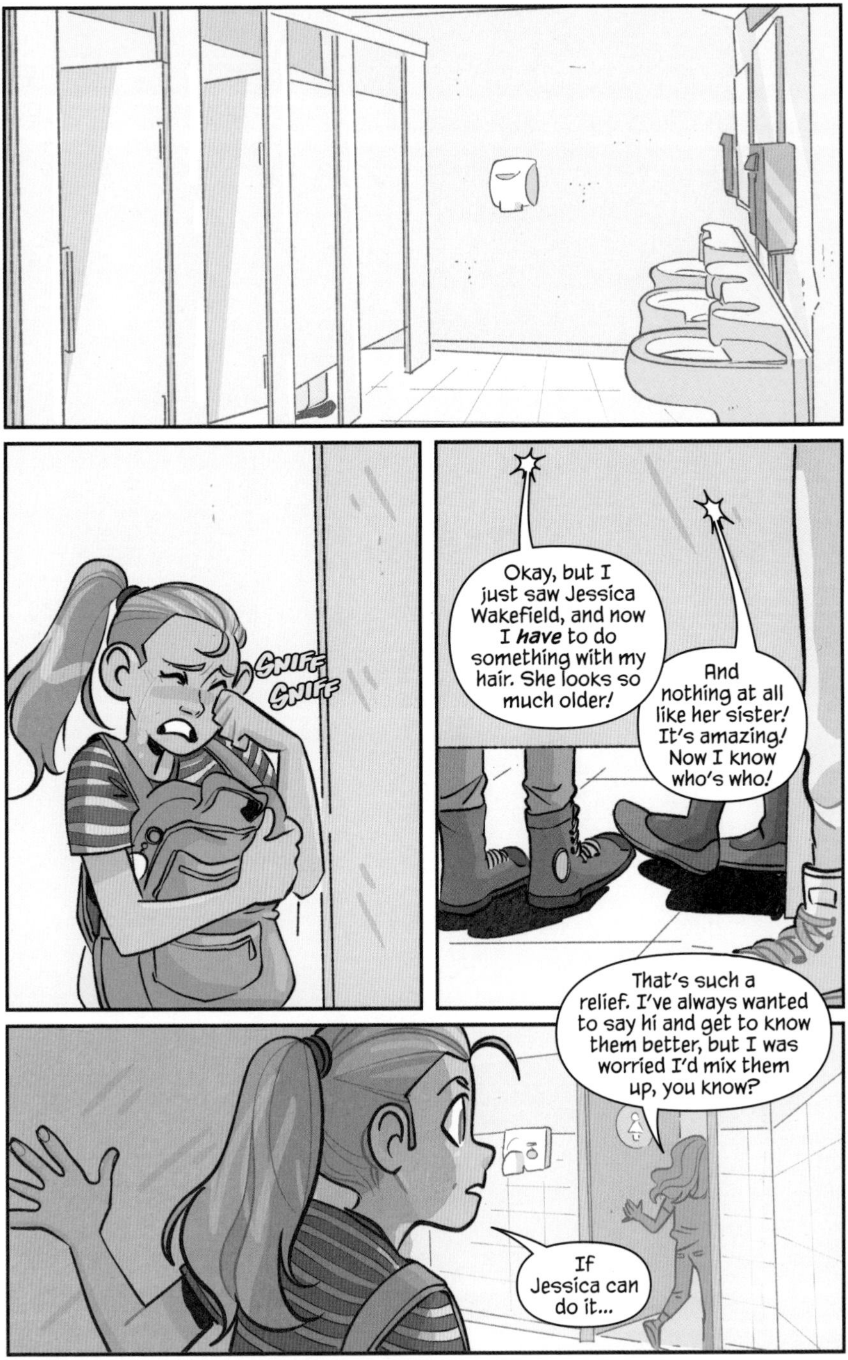
SNIFF SNIFF
Okay, but I just saw Jessica Wakefield, and now I *have* to do something with my hair. She looks so much older!
And nothing at all like her sister! It's amazing! Now I know who's who!
That's such a relief. I've always wanted to say hi and get to know them better, but I was worried I'd mix them up, you know?
If Jessica can do it...

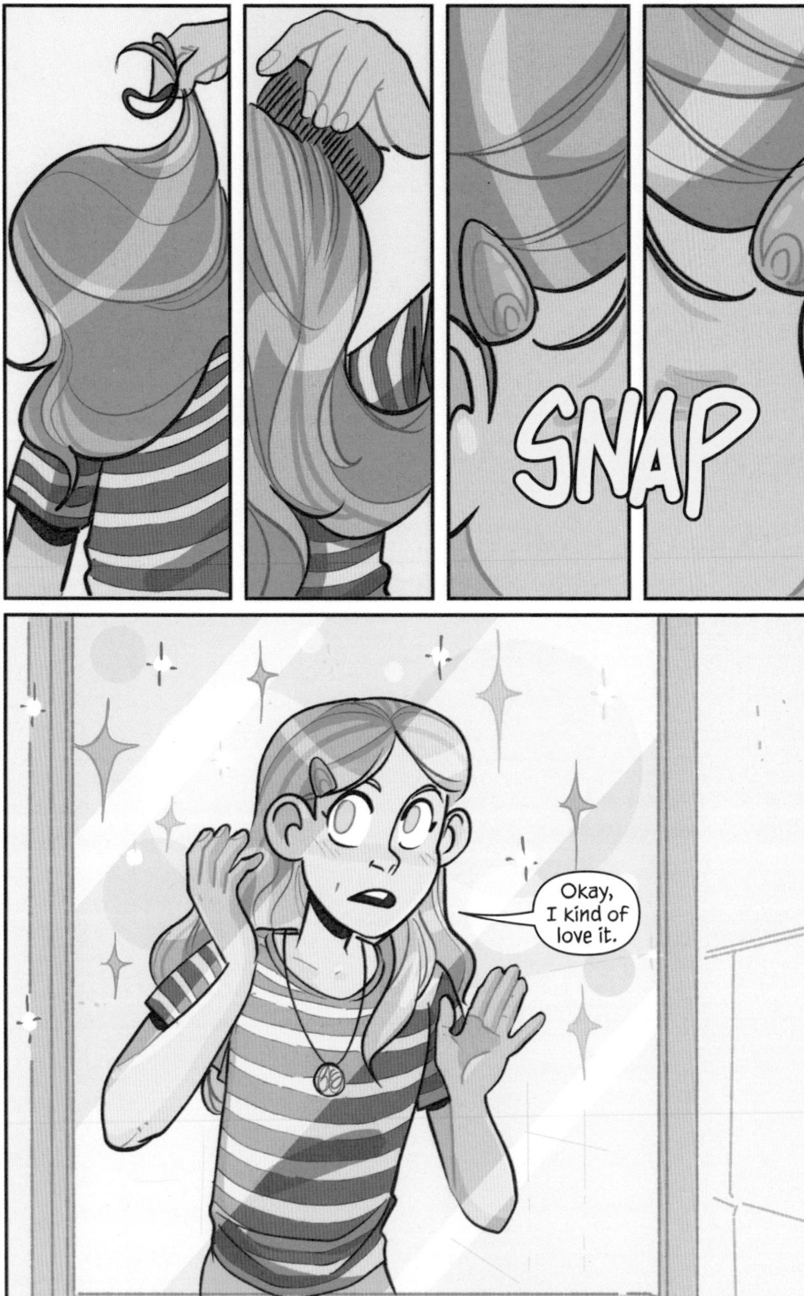
SNAP
Okay, I kind of love it.

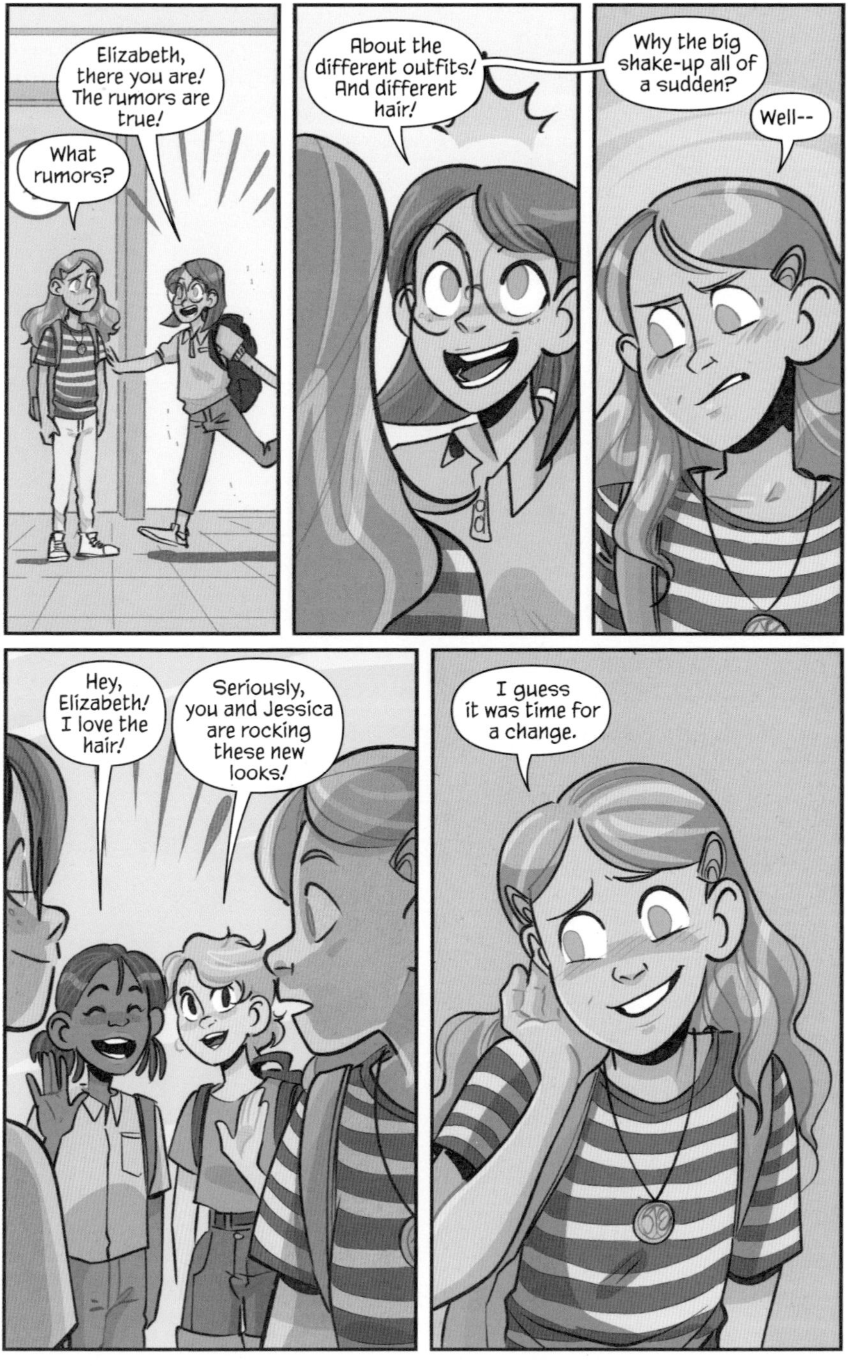
Elizabeth, there you are! The rumors are true!
What rumors?
About the different outfits! And different hair!
Why the big shake-up all of a sudden?
Well--
Hey, Elizabeth! I love the hair!
Seriously, you and Jessica are rocking these new looks!
I guess it was time for a change.

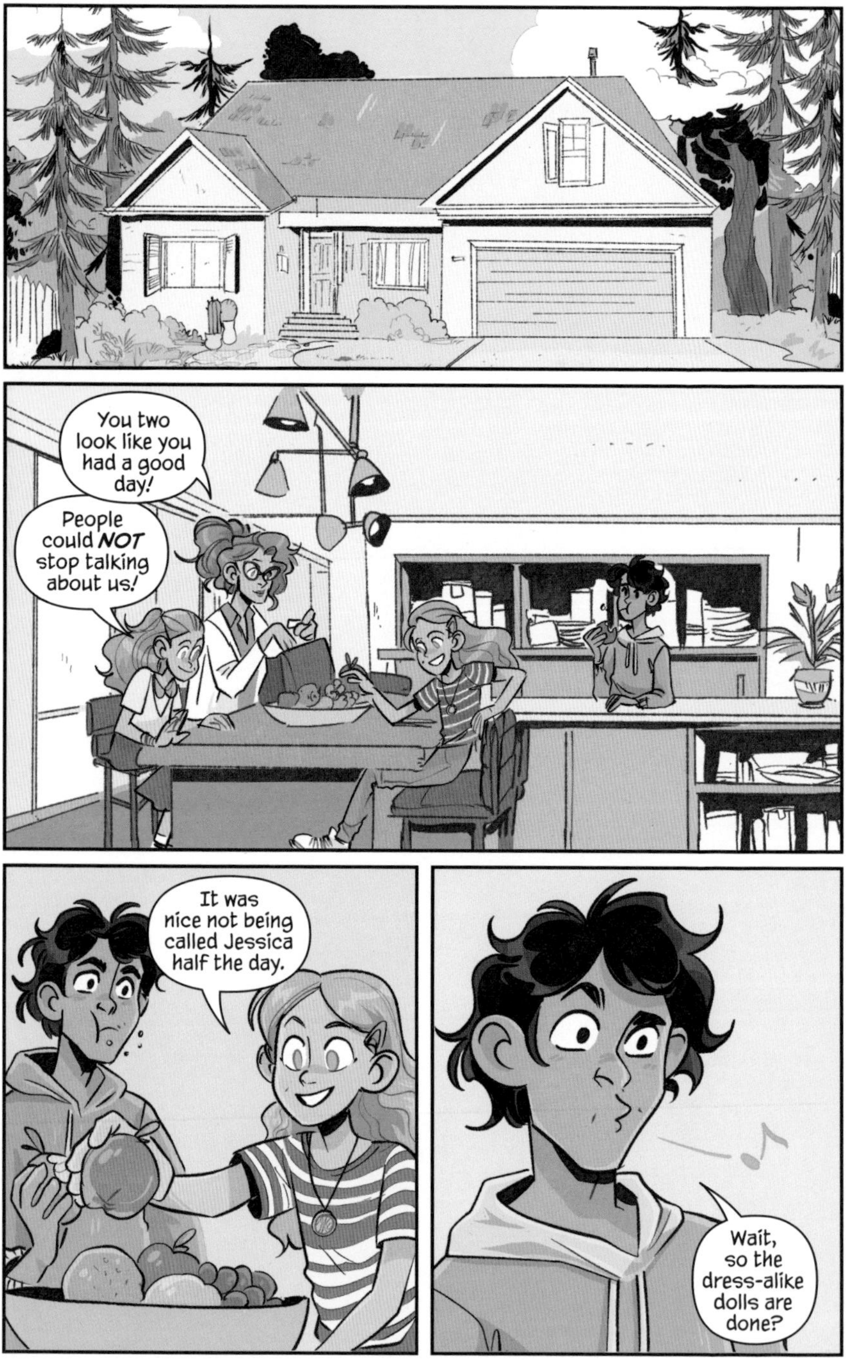

You two look like you had a good day!
People could ***NOT*** stop talking about us!
It was nice not being called Jessica half the day.
Wait, so the dress-alike dolls are done?

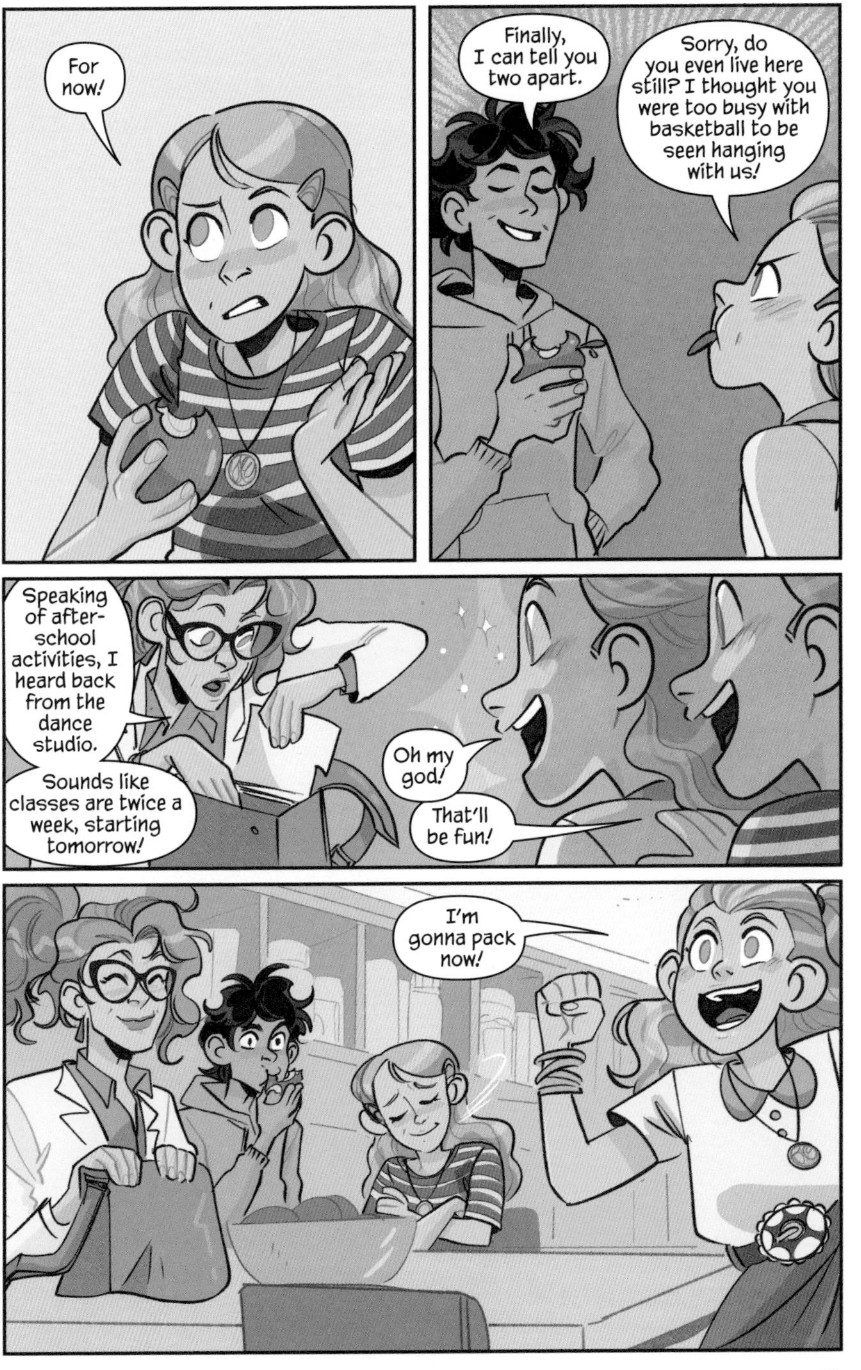
For now!
Finally, I can tell you two apart.
Sorry, do you even live here still? I thought you were too busy with basketball to be seen hanging with us!
Speaking of after-school activities, I heard back from the dance studio.
Sounds like classes are twice a week, starting tomorrow!
Oh my god!
That'll be fun!
I'm gonna pack now!

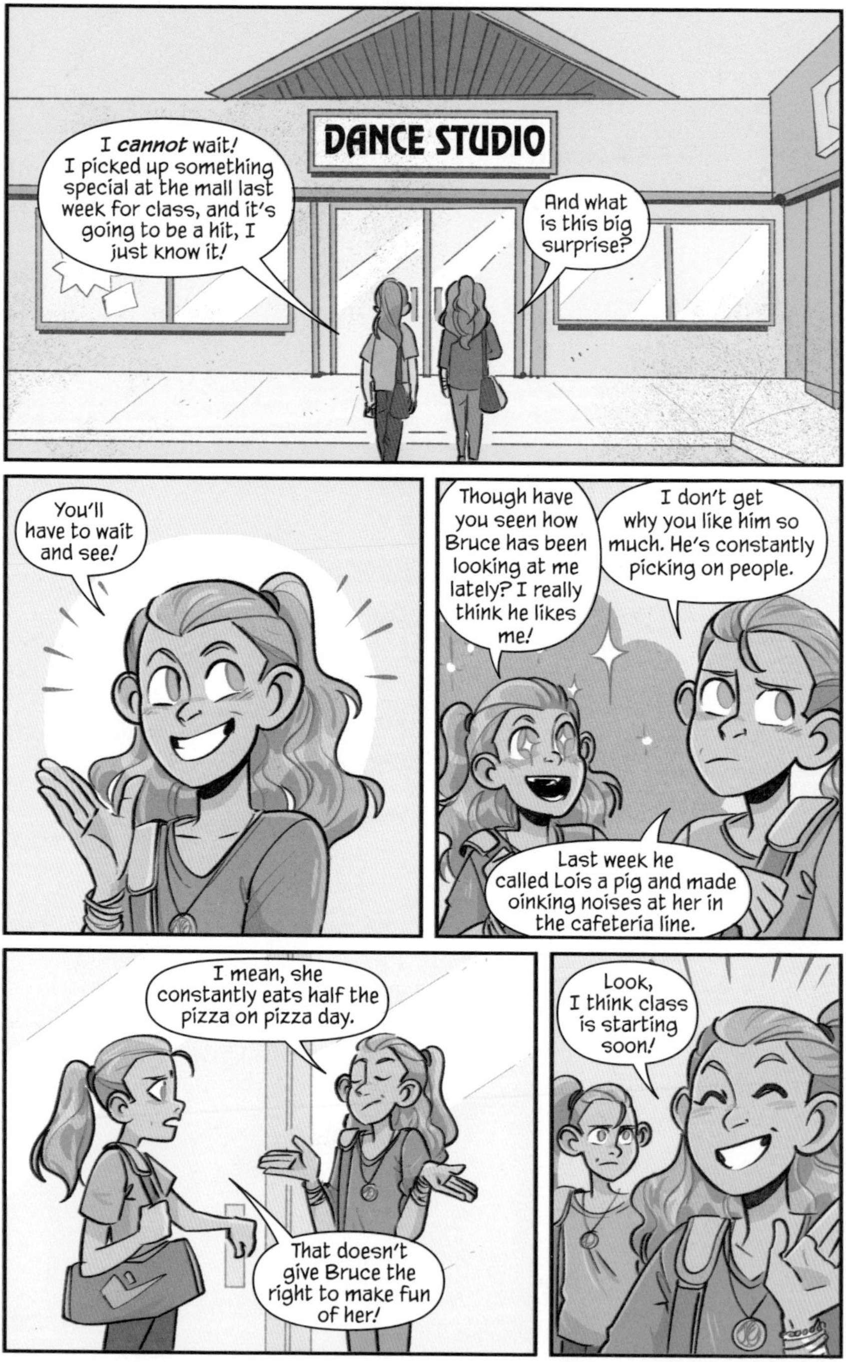
DANCE STUDIO
I *cannot* wait! I picked up something special at the mall last week for class, and it's going to be a hit, I just know it!
And what is this big surprise?
You'll have to wait and see!
Though have you seen how Bruce has been looking at me lately? I really think he likes me!
I don't get why you like him so much. He's constantly picking on people.
Last week he called Lois a pig and made oinking noises at her in the cafeteria line.
I mean, she constantly eats half the pizza on pizza day.
That doesn't give Bruce the right to make fun of her!
Look, I think class is starting soon!

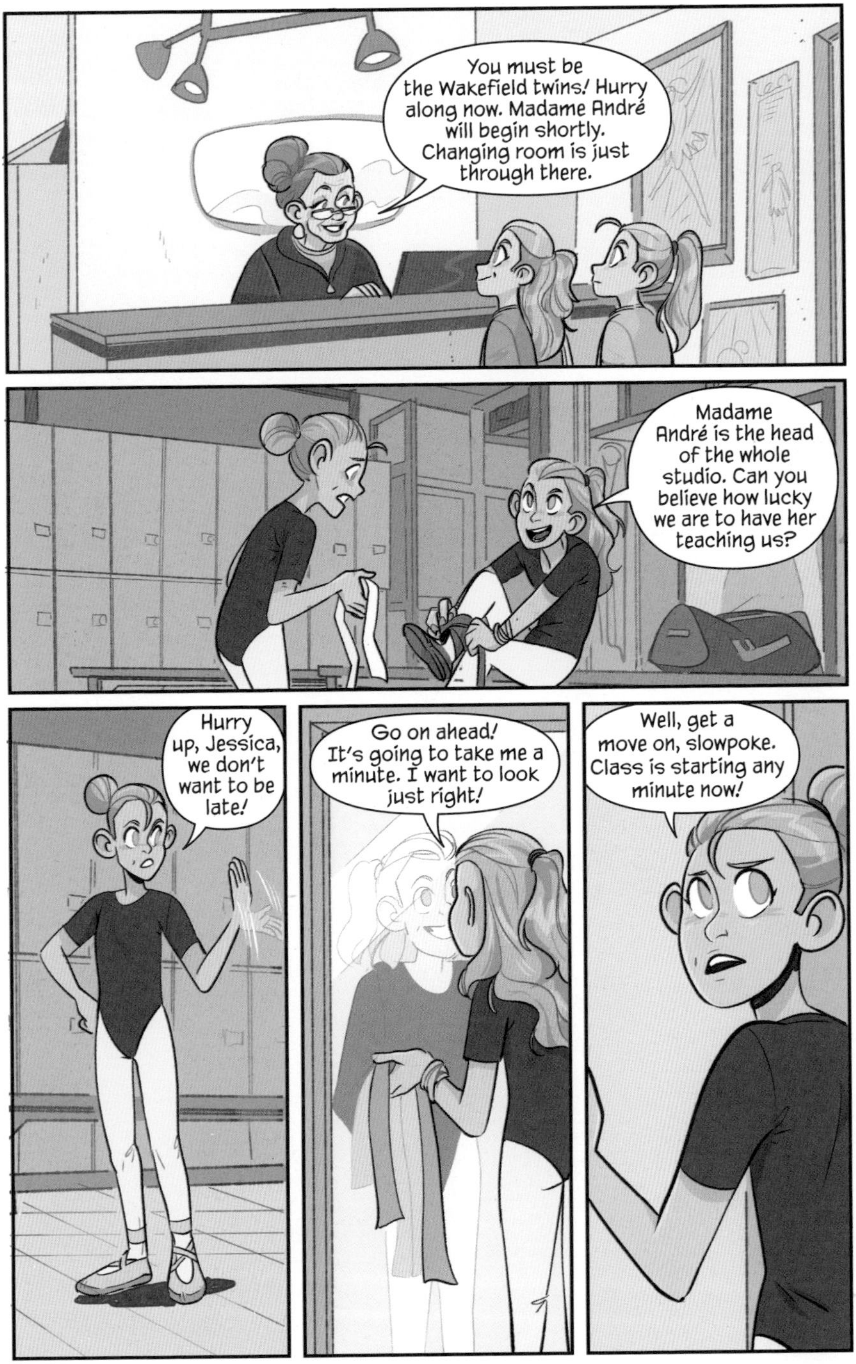

You must be the Wakefield twins! Hurry along now. Madame André will begin shortly. Changing room is just through there.
Madame André is the head of the whole studio. Can you believe how lucky we are to have her teaching us?
Hurry up, Jessica, we don't want to be late!
Go on ahead! It's going to take me a minute. I want to look just right!
Well, get a move on, slowpoke. Class is starting any minute now!

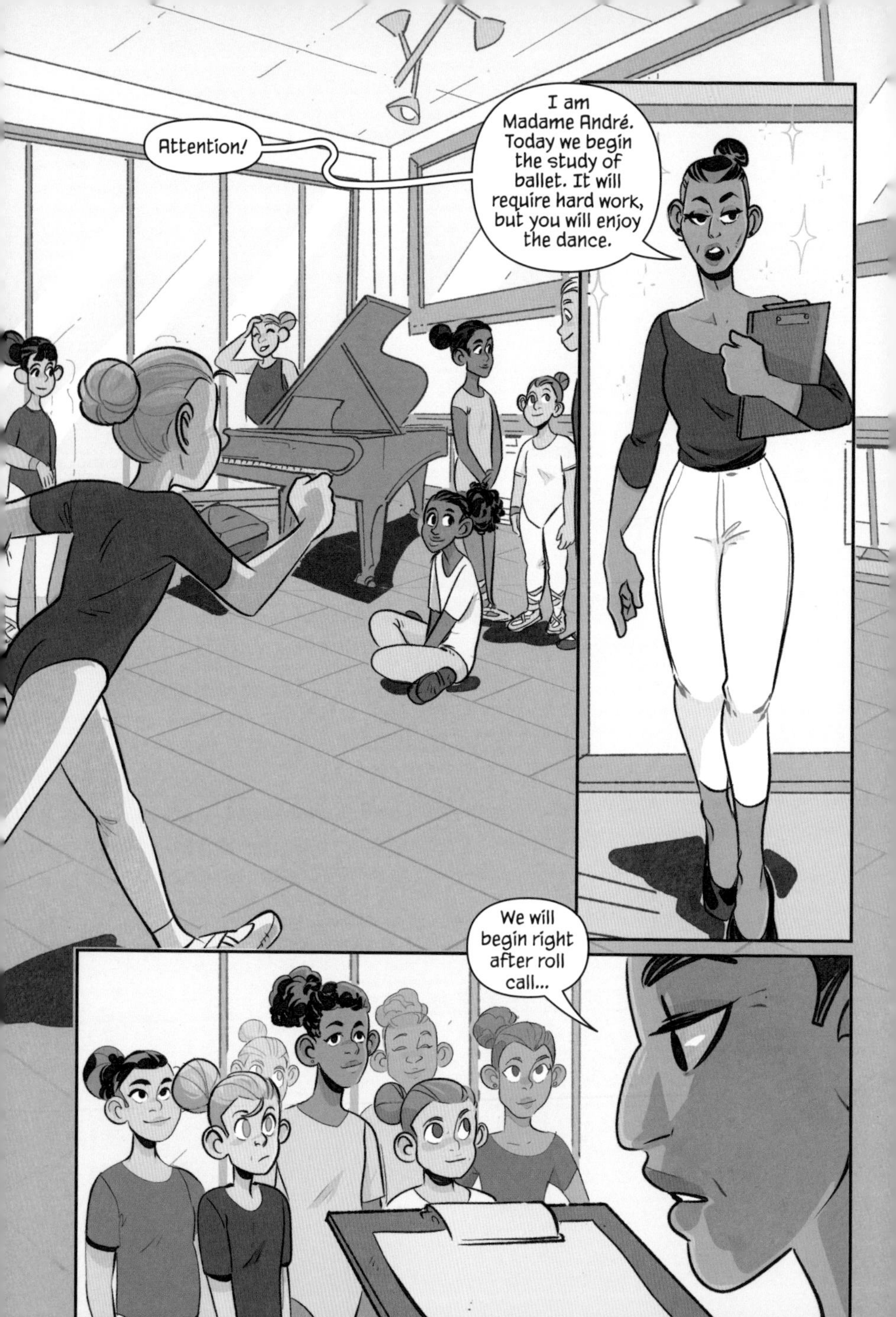
Attention!
I am Madame André. Today we begin the study of ballet. It will require hard work, but you will enjoy the dance.
We will begin right after roll call...

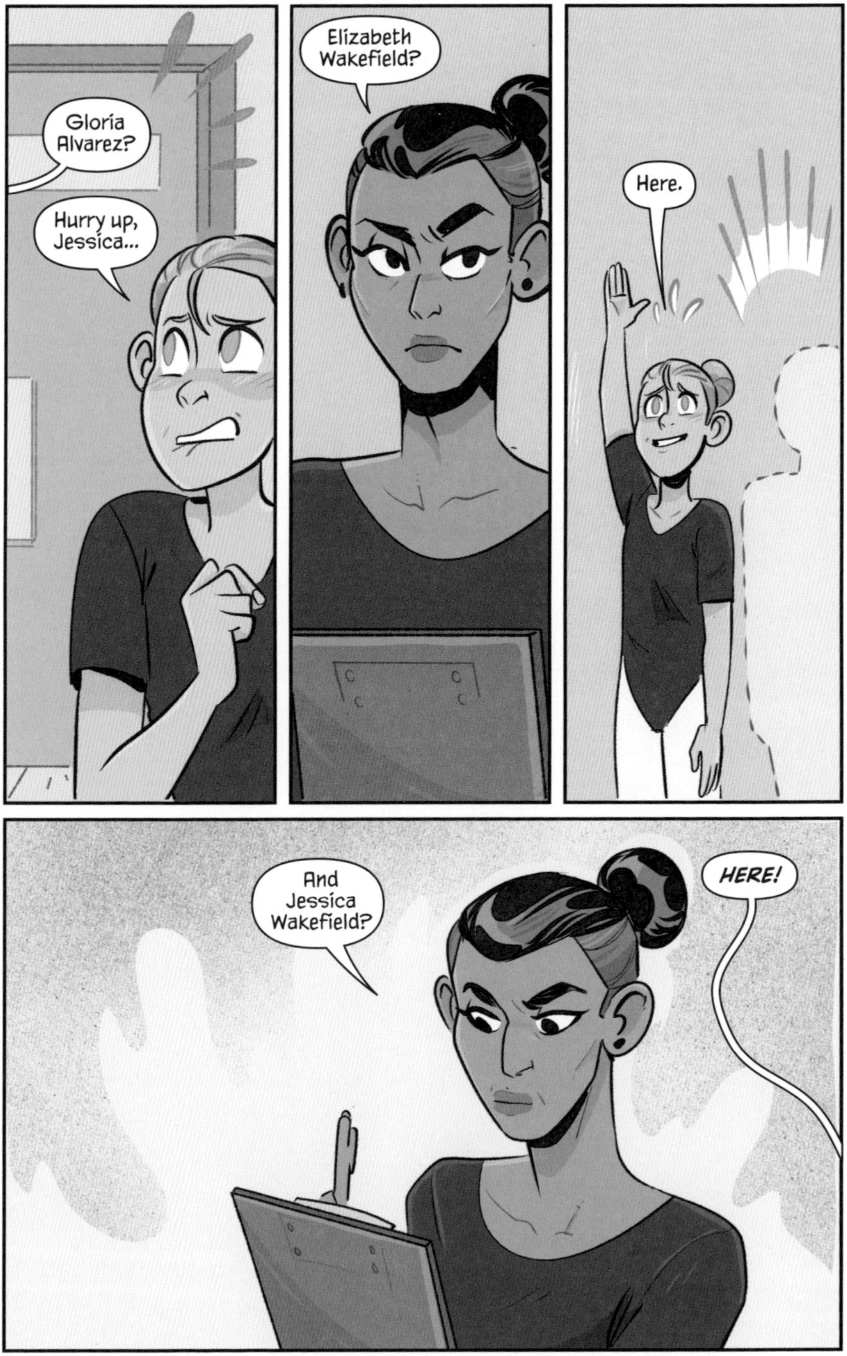
Gloria Alvarez?
Hurry up, Jessica...
Elizabeth Wakefield?
Here.
And Jessica Wakefield?
HERE!

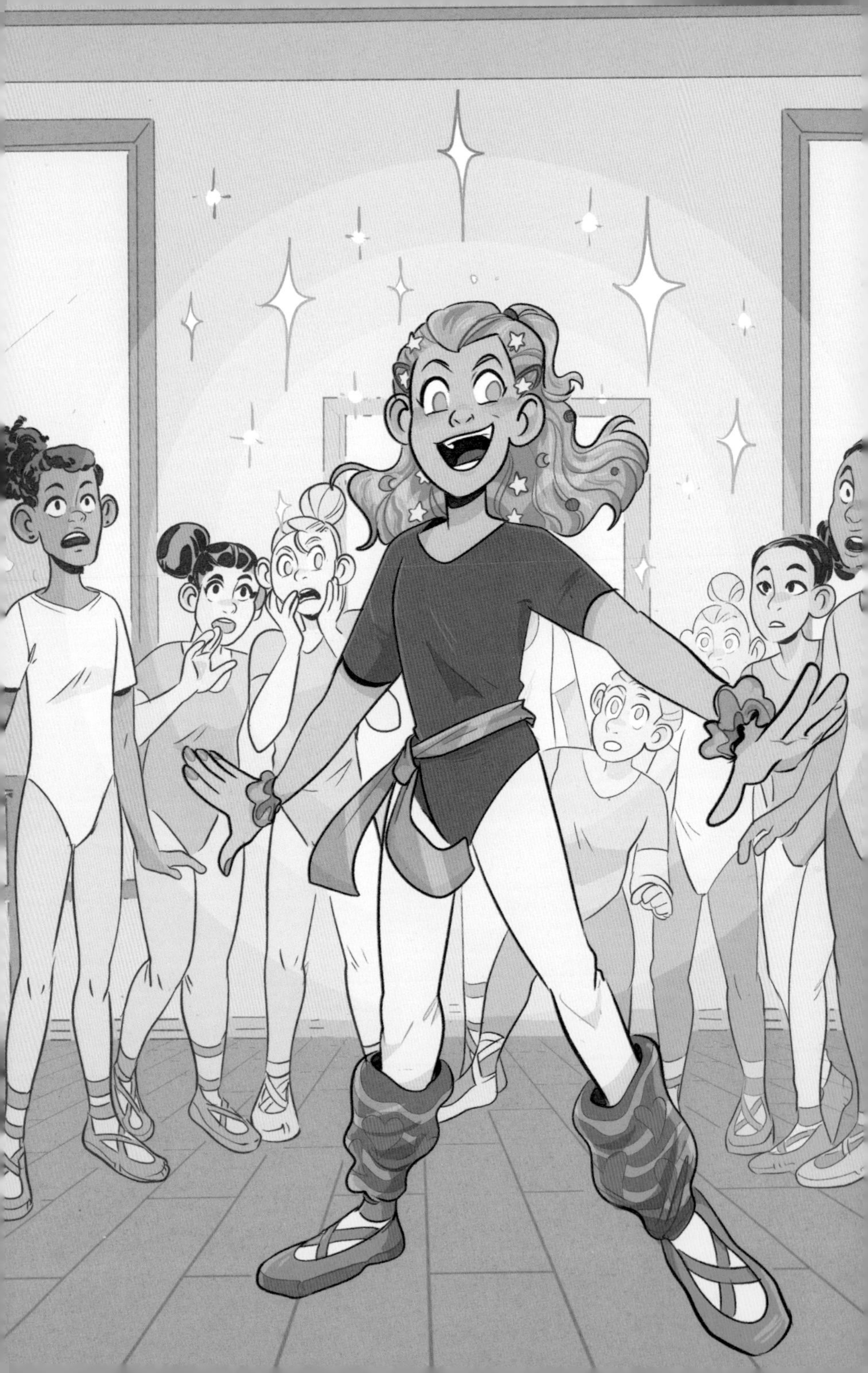

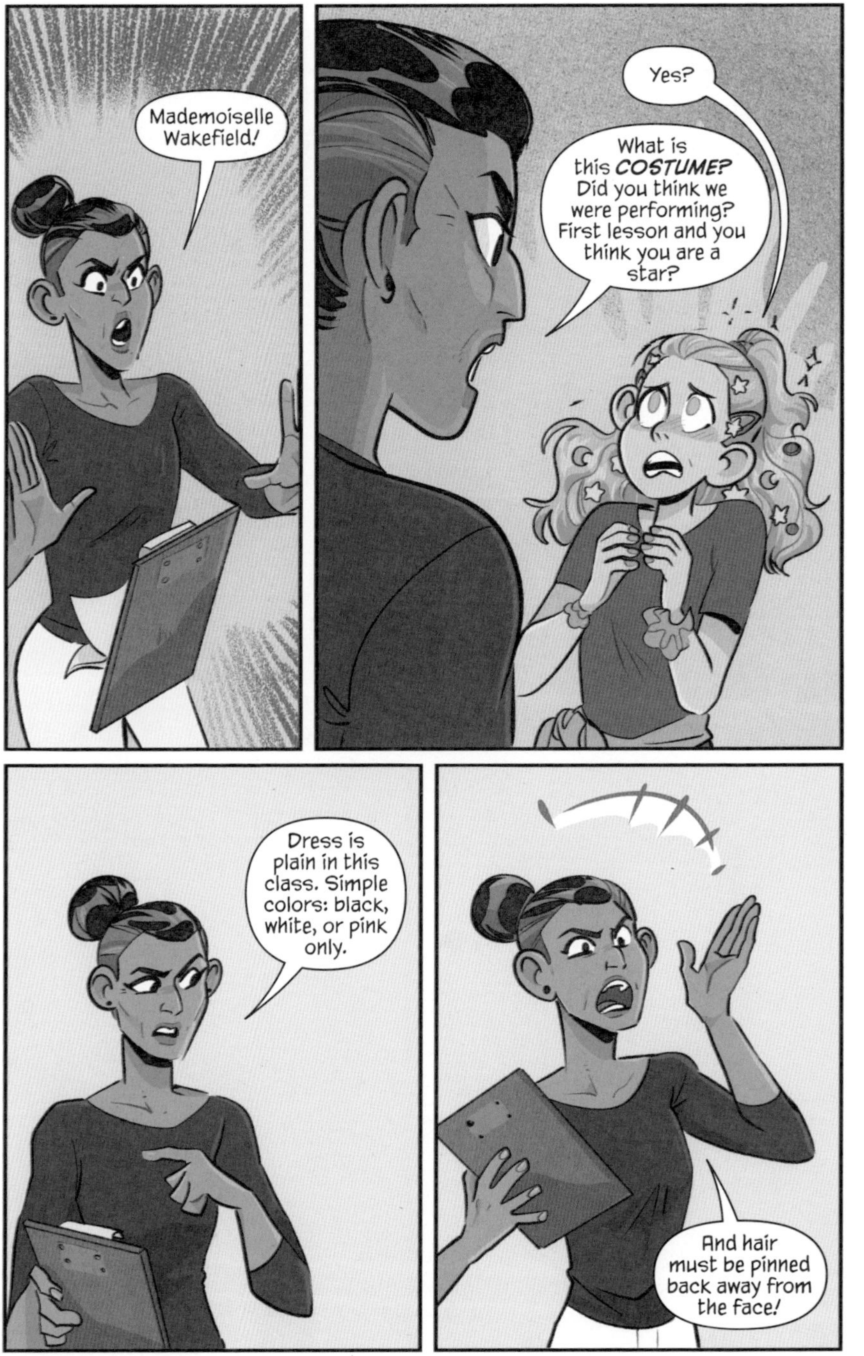
Mademoiselle Wakefield!
Yes?
What is this COSTUME? Did you think we were performing? First lesson and you think you are a star?
Dress is plain in this class. Simple colors: black, white, or pink only.
And hair must be pinned back away from the face!

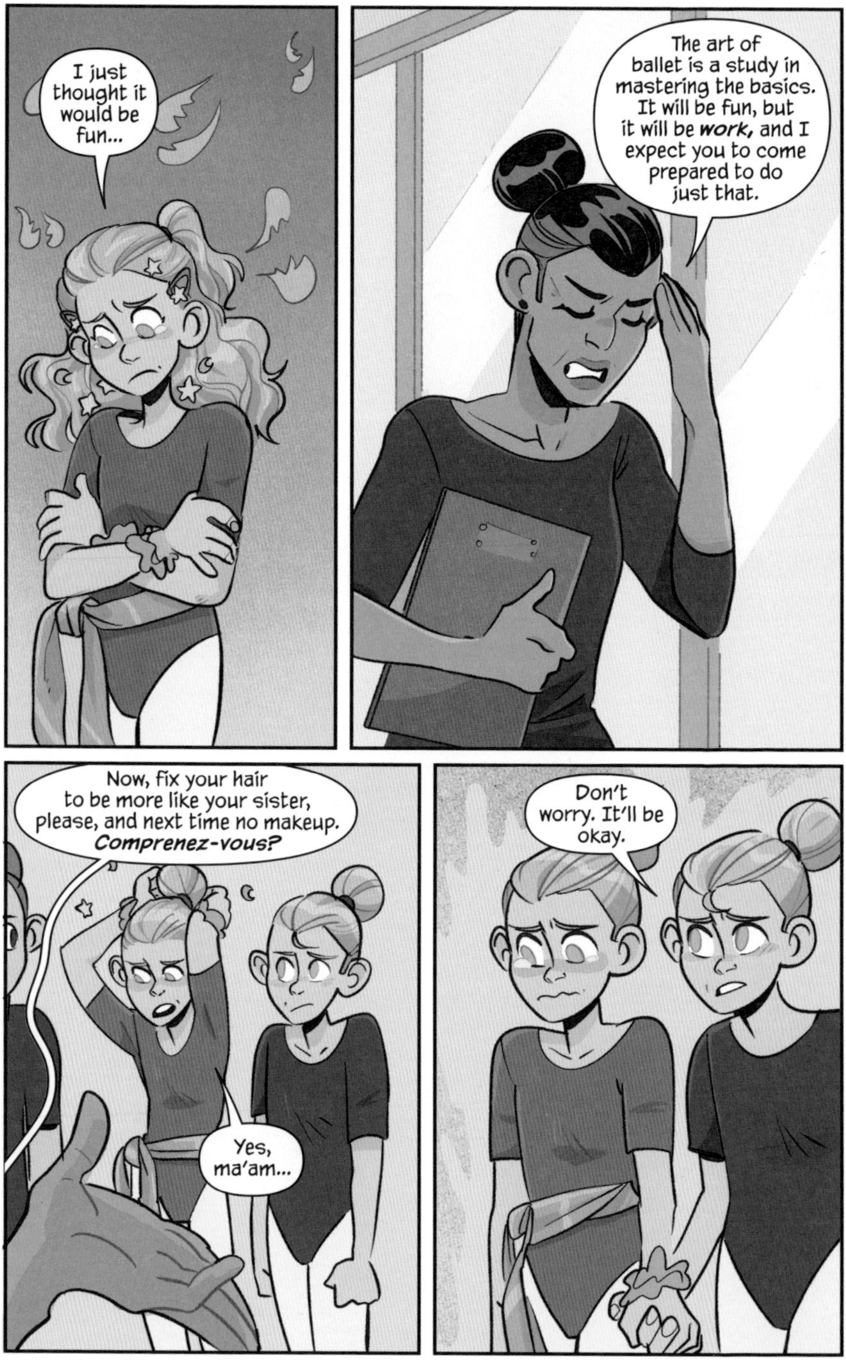
I just thought it would be fun...
The art of ballet is a study in mastering the basics. It will be fun, but it will be *work,* and I expect you to come prepared to do just that.
Now, fix your hair to be more like your sister, please, and next time no makeup. *Comprenez-vous?*
Yes, ma'am...
Don't worry. It'll be okay.

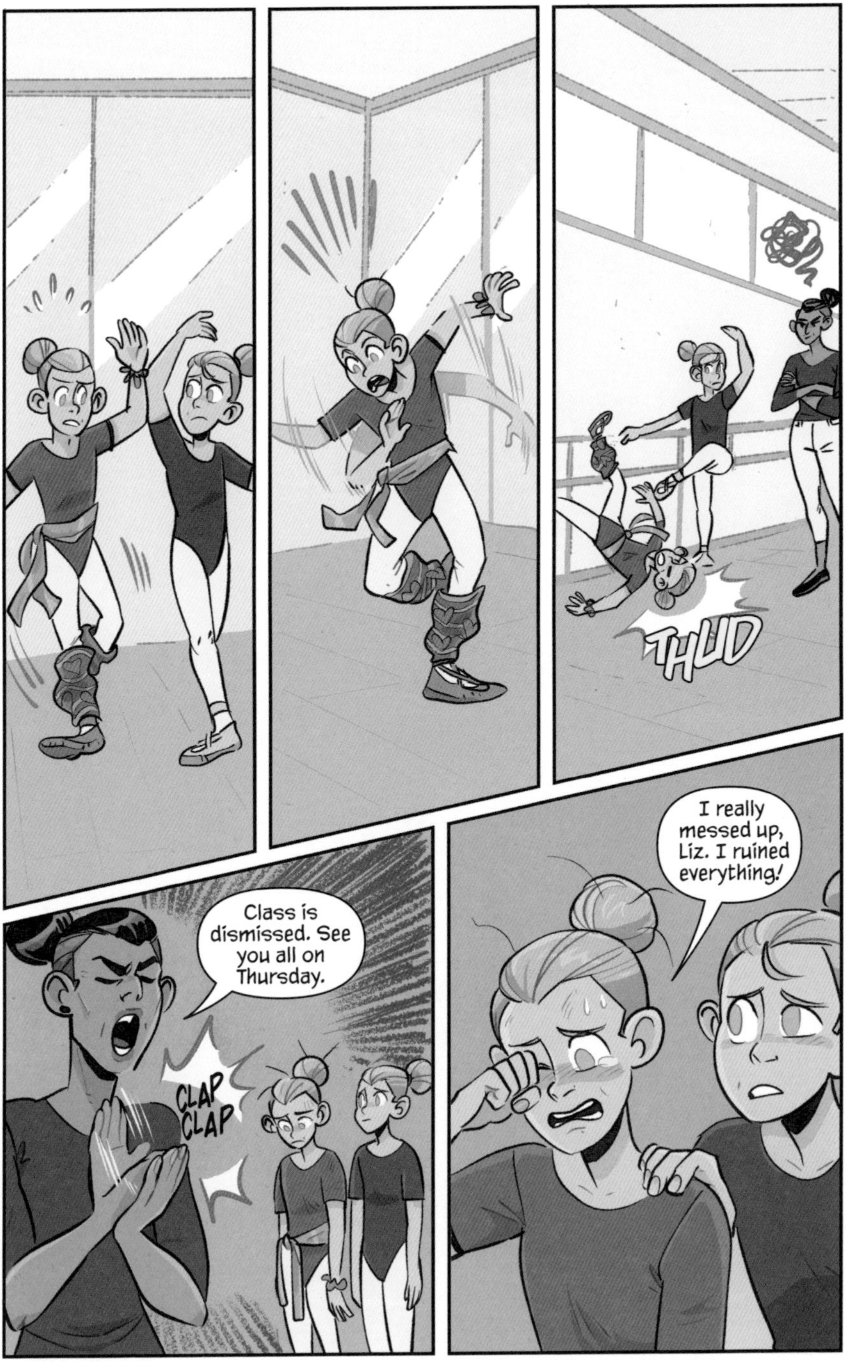
THUD
Class is dismissed. See you all on Thursday.
CLAP CLAP
I really messed up, Liz. I ruined everything!

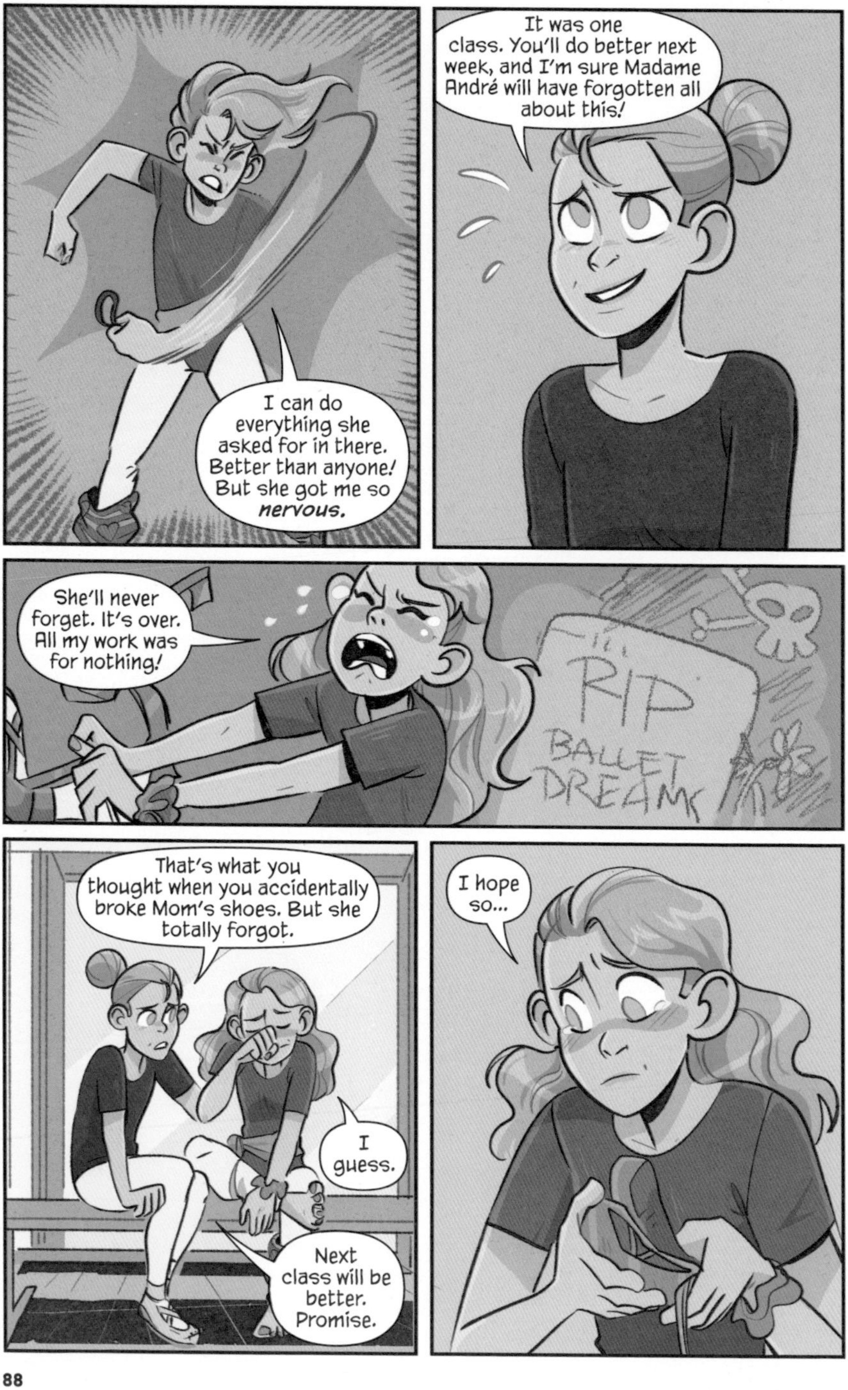
I can do everything she asked for in there. Better than anyone! But she got me so *nervous.*
It was one class. You'll do better next week, and I'm sure Madame André will have forgotten all about this!
She'll never forget. It's over. All my work was for nothing!
RIP BALLET DREAM
That's what you thought when you accidentally broke Mom's shoes. But she totally forgot.
I guess.
Next class will be better. Promise.
I hope so...

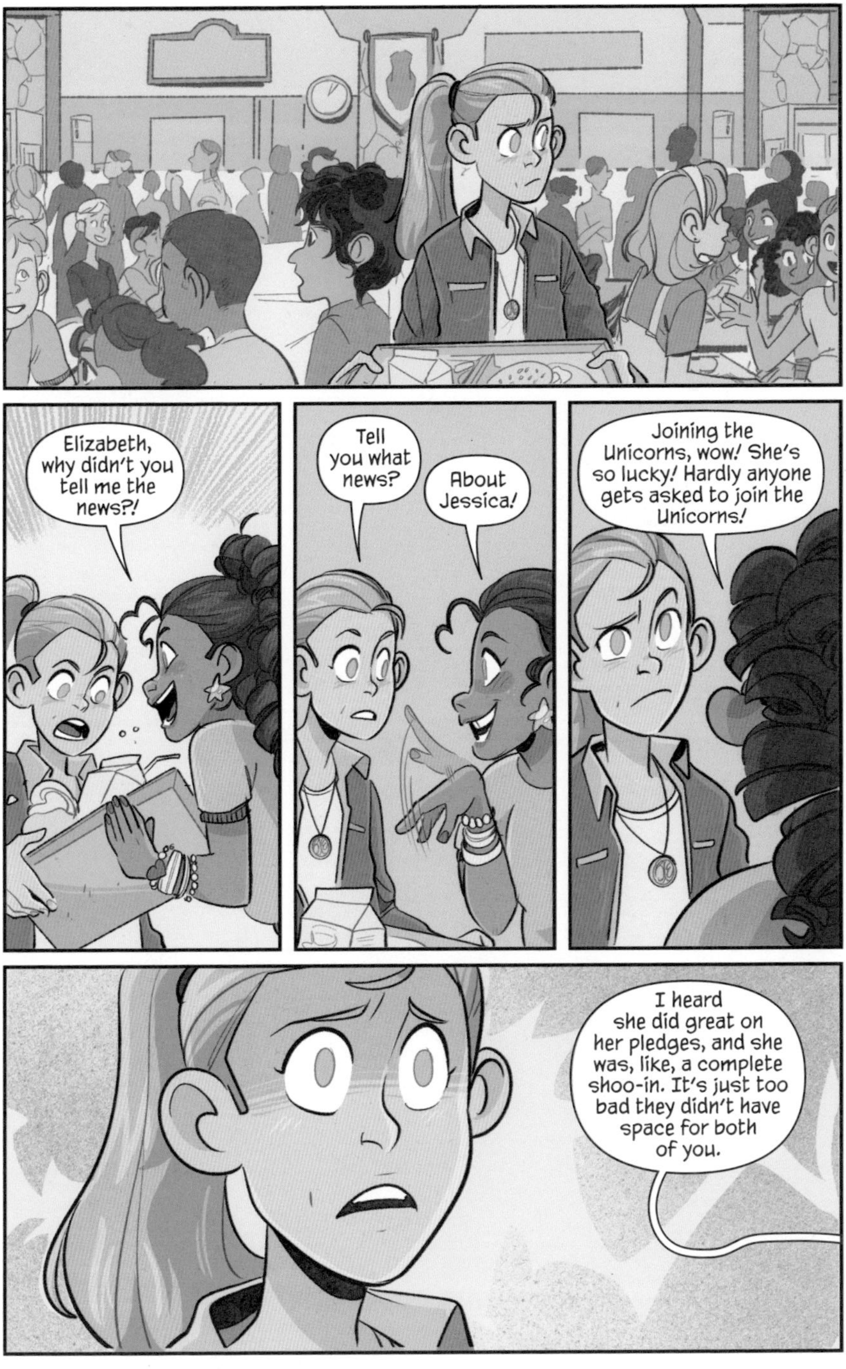
Elizabeth, why didn't you tell me the news?!
Tell you what news?
About Jessica!
Joining the Unicorns, wow! She's so lucky! Hardly anyone gets asked to join the Unicorns!
I heard she did great on her pledges, and she was, like, a complete shoo-in. It's just too bad they didn't have space for both of you.

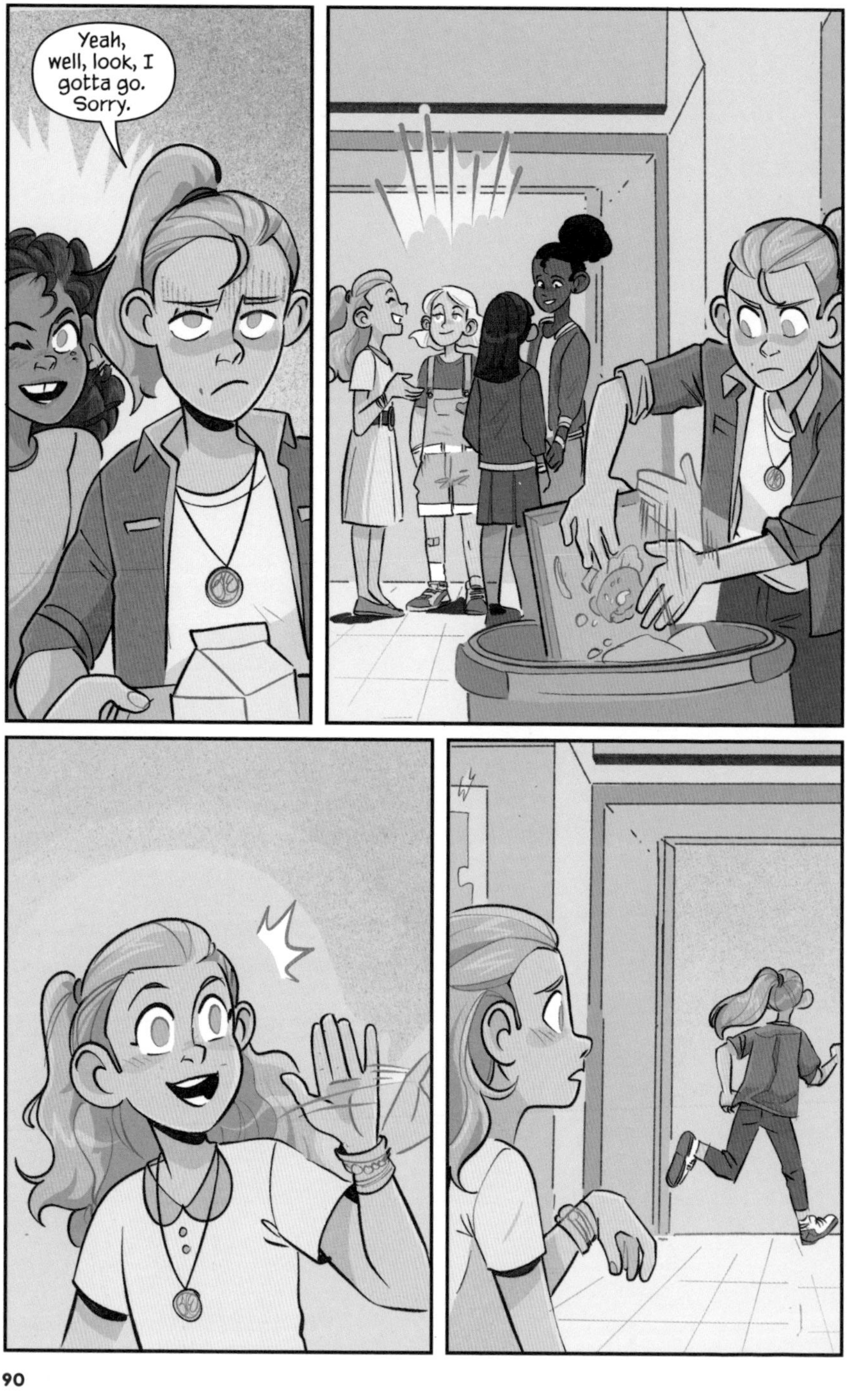
Yeah, well, look, I gotta go. Sorry.

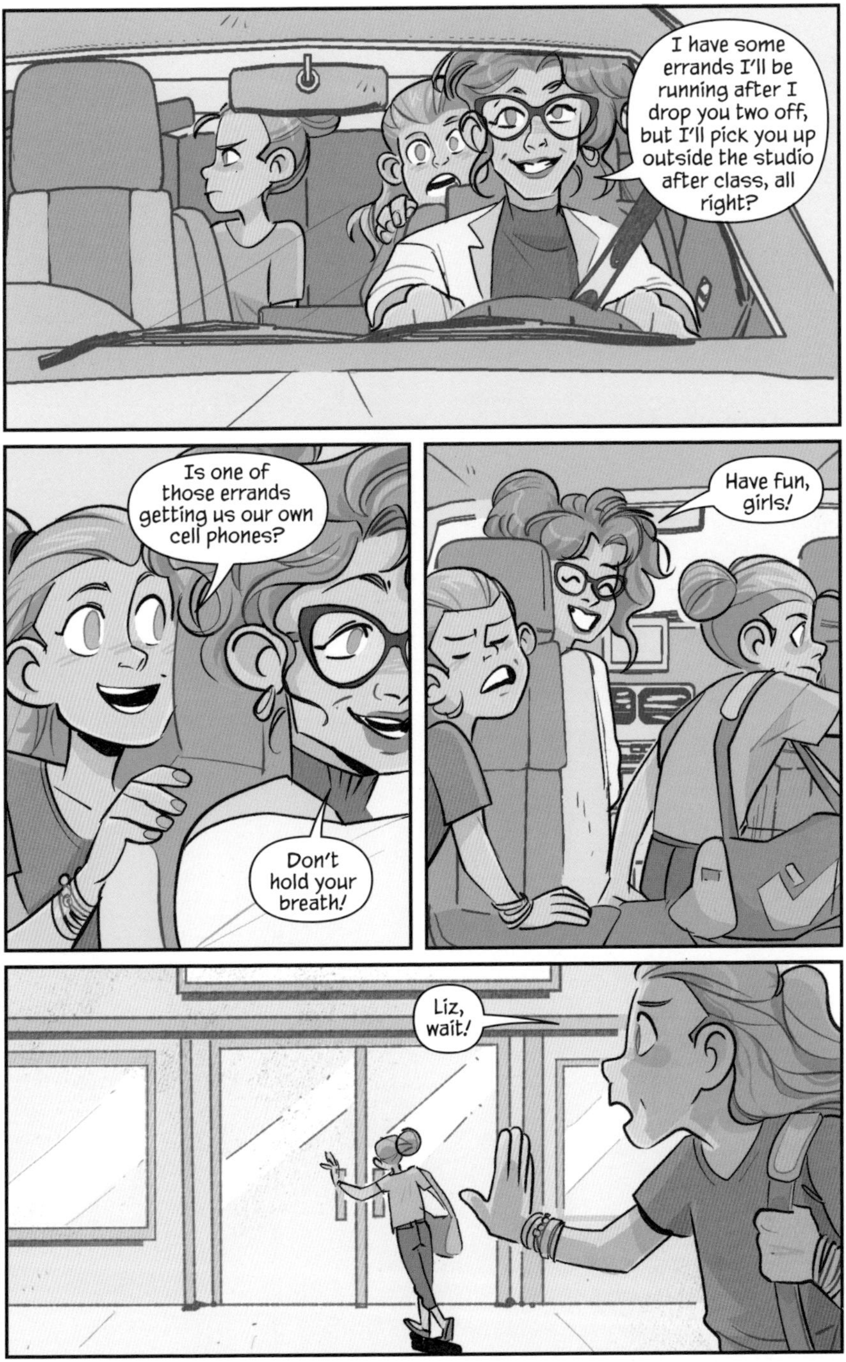

I have some errands I'll be running after I drop you two off, but I'll pick you up outside the studio after class, all right?
Is one of those errands getting us our own cell phones?
Don't hold your breath!
Have fun, girls!
Liz, wait!

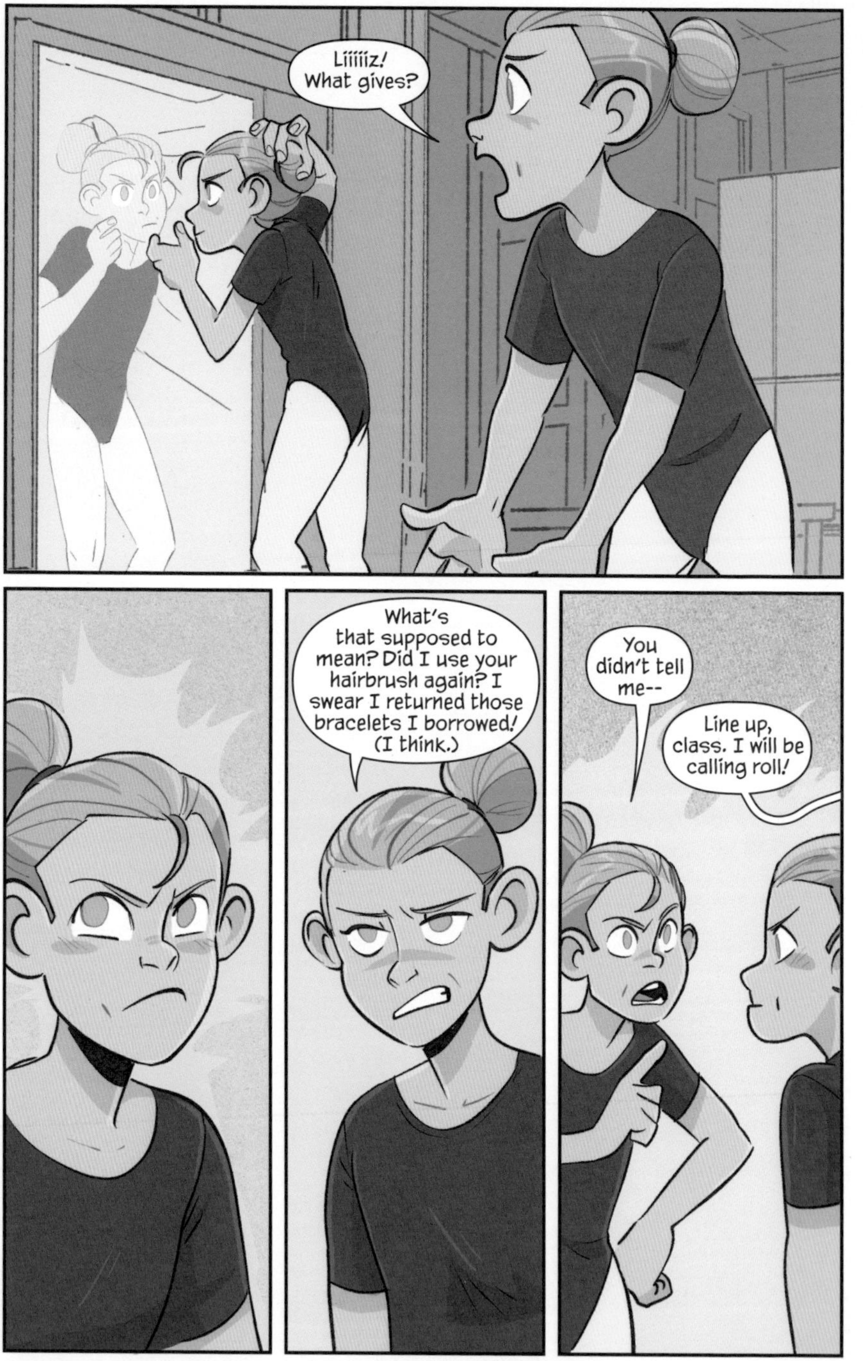
Liiiiiz! What gives?
What's that supposed to mean? Did I use your hairbrush again? I swear I returned those bracelets I borrowed! (I think.)
You didn't tell me--
Line up, class. I will be calling roll!

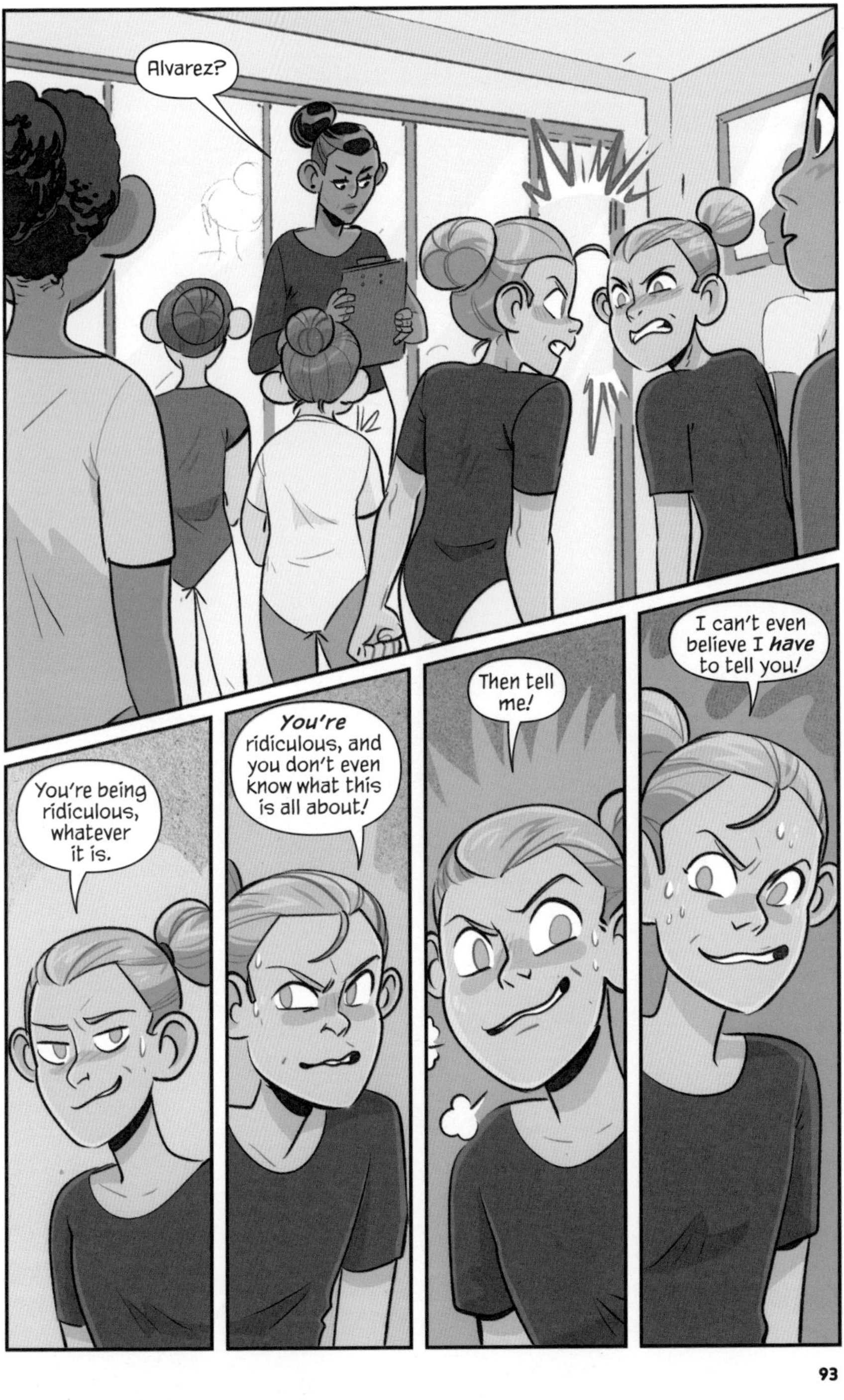
Alvarez?
You're being ridiculous, whatever it is.
You're ridiculous, and you don't even know what this is all about!
Then tell me!
I can't even believe I ***have*** to tell you!

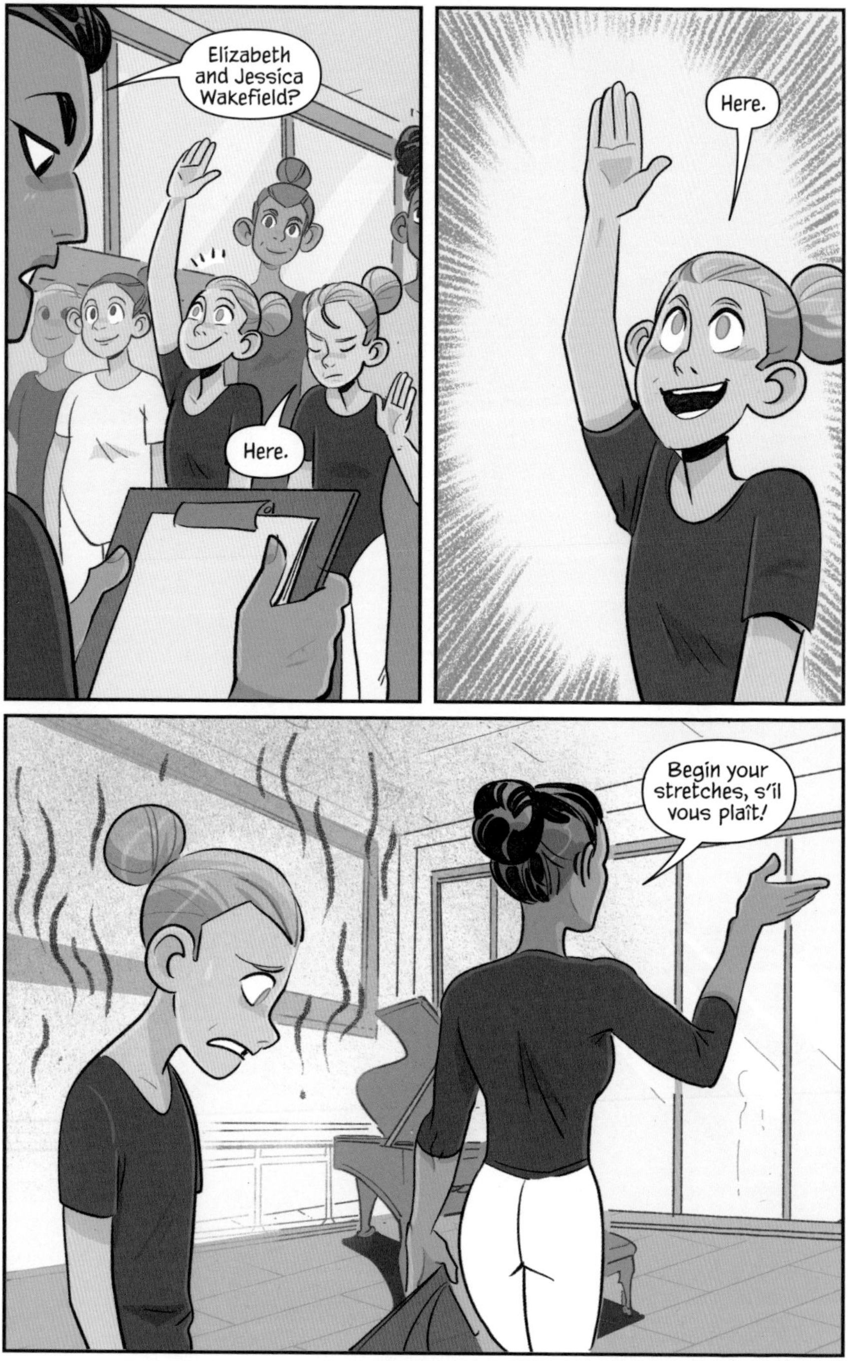
Elizabeth and Jessica Wakefield?
Here.
Here.
Begin your stretches, s'il vous plaît!

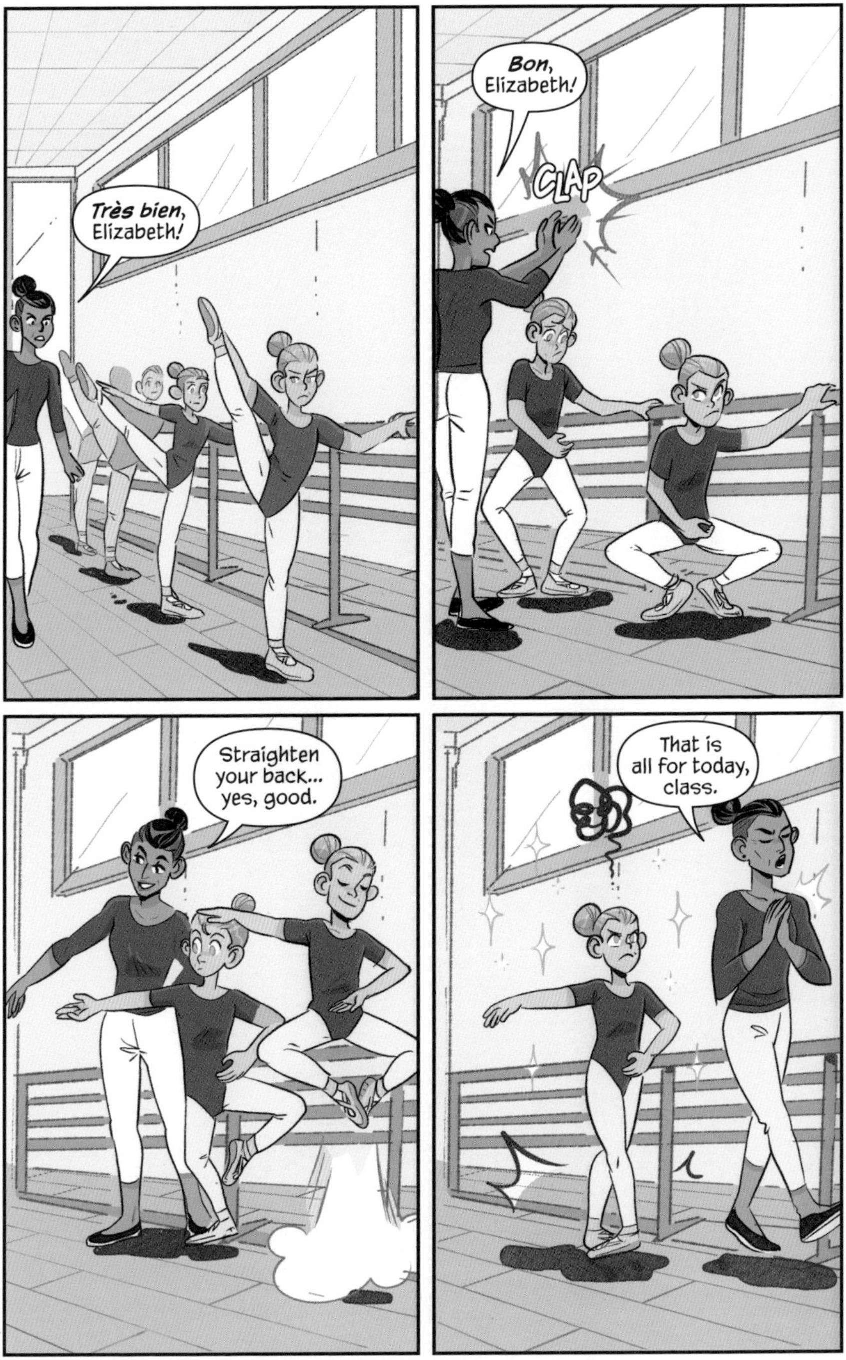
Très bien, Elizabeth!
Bon, Elizabeth!
CLAP
Straighten your back... yes, good.
That is all for today, class.

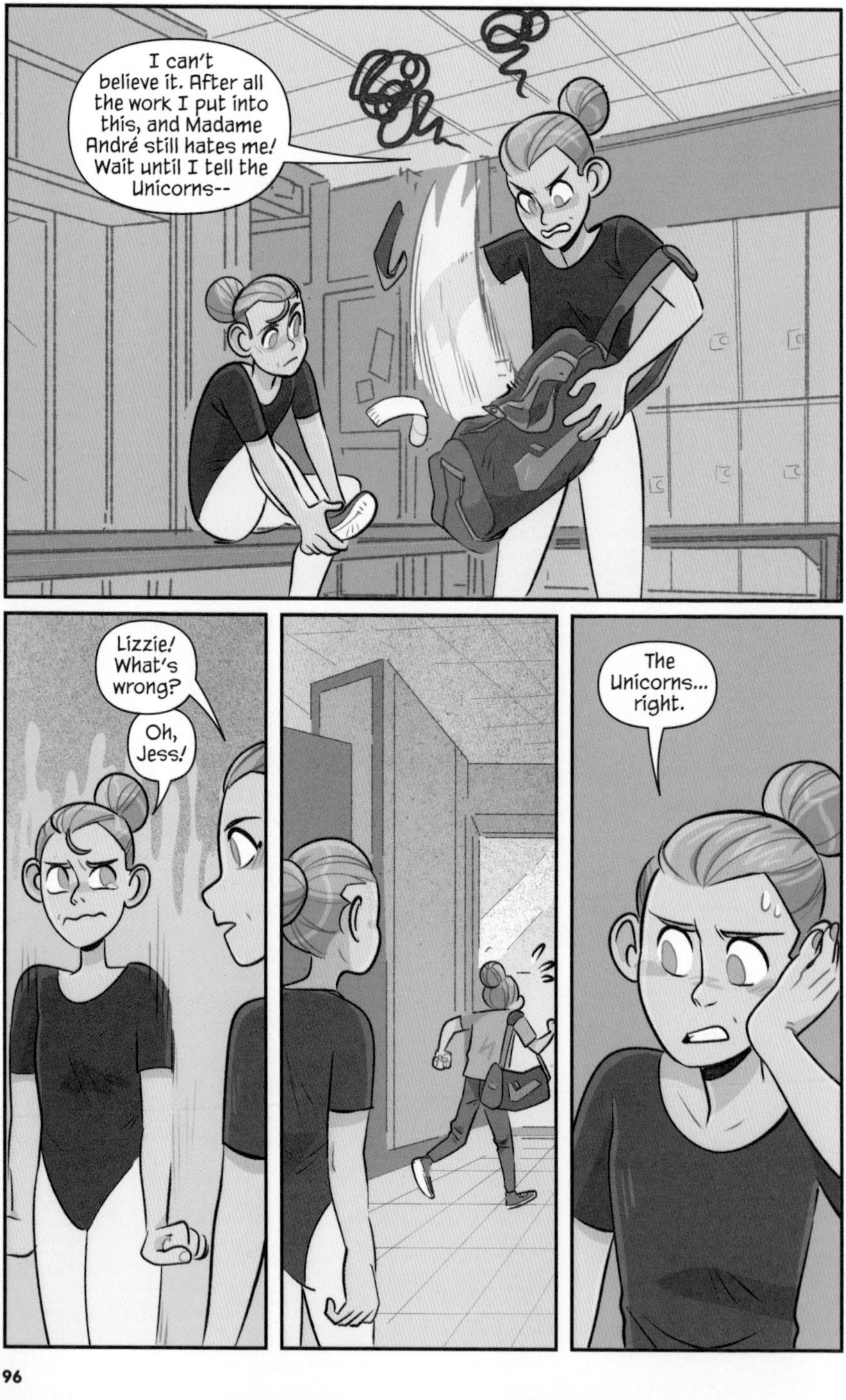
I can't believe it. After all the work I put into this, and Madame André still hates me! Wait until I tell the Unicorns--
Lizzie! What's wrong?
Oh, Jess!
The Unicorns... right.

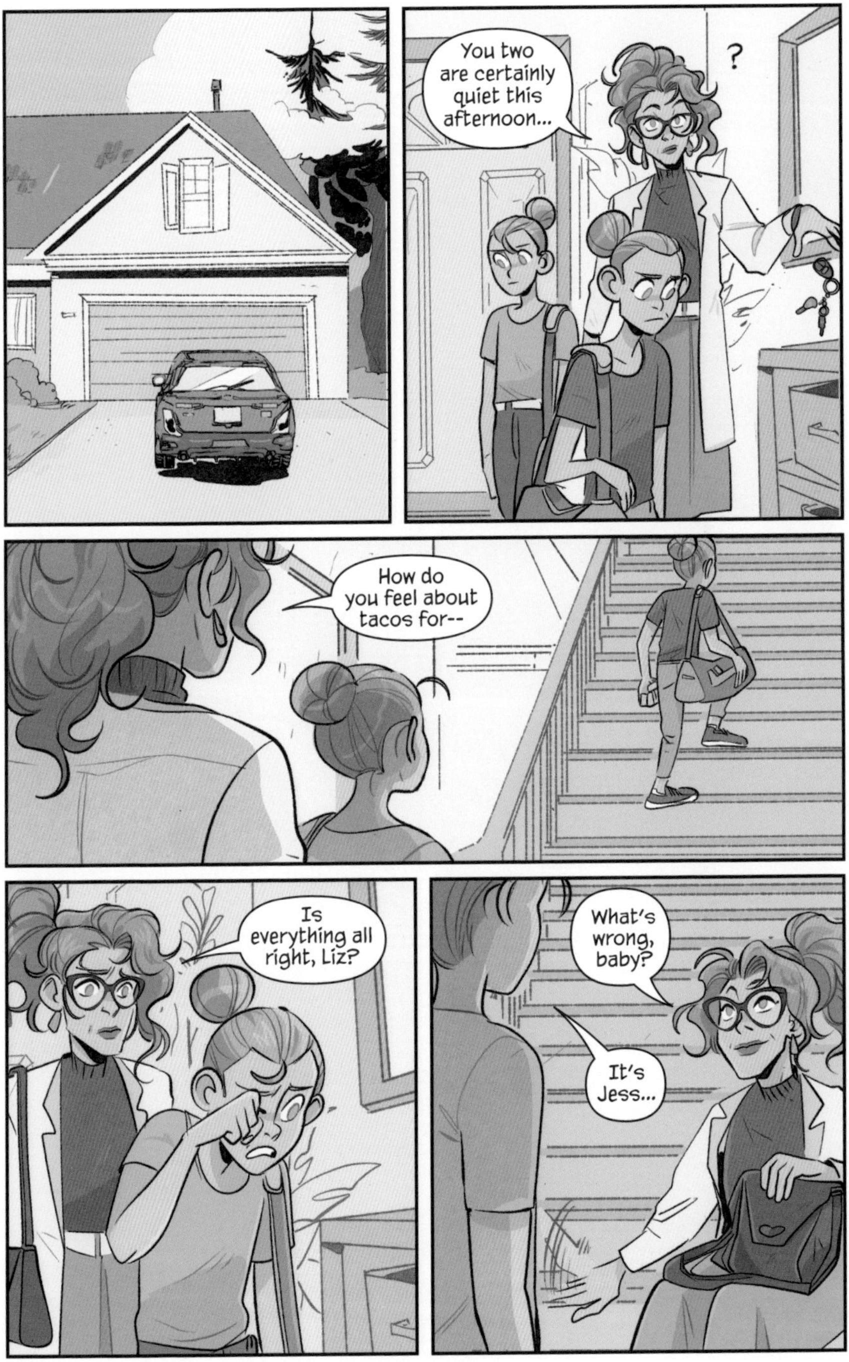
You two are certainly quiet this afternoon...
?
How do you feel about tacos for--
Is everything all right, Liz?
What's wrong, baby?
It's Jess...

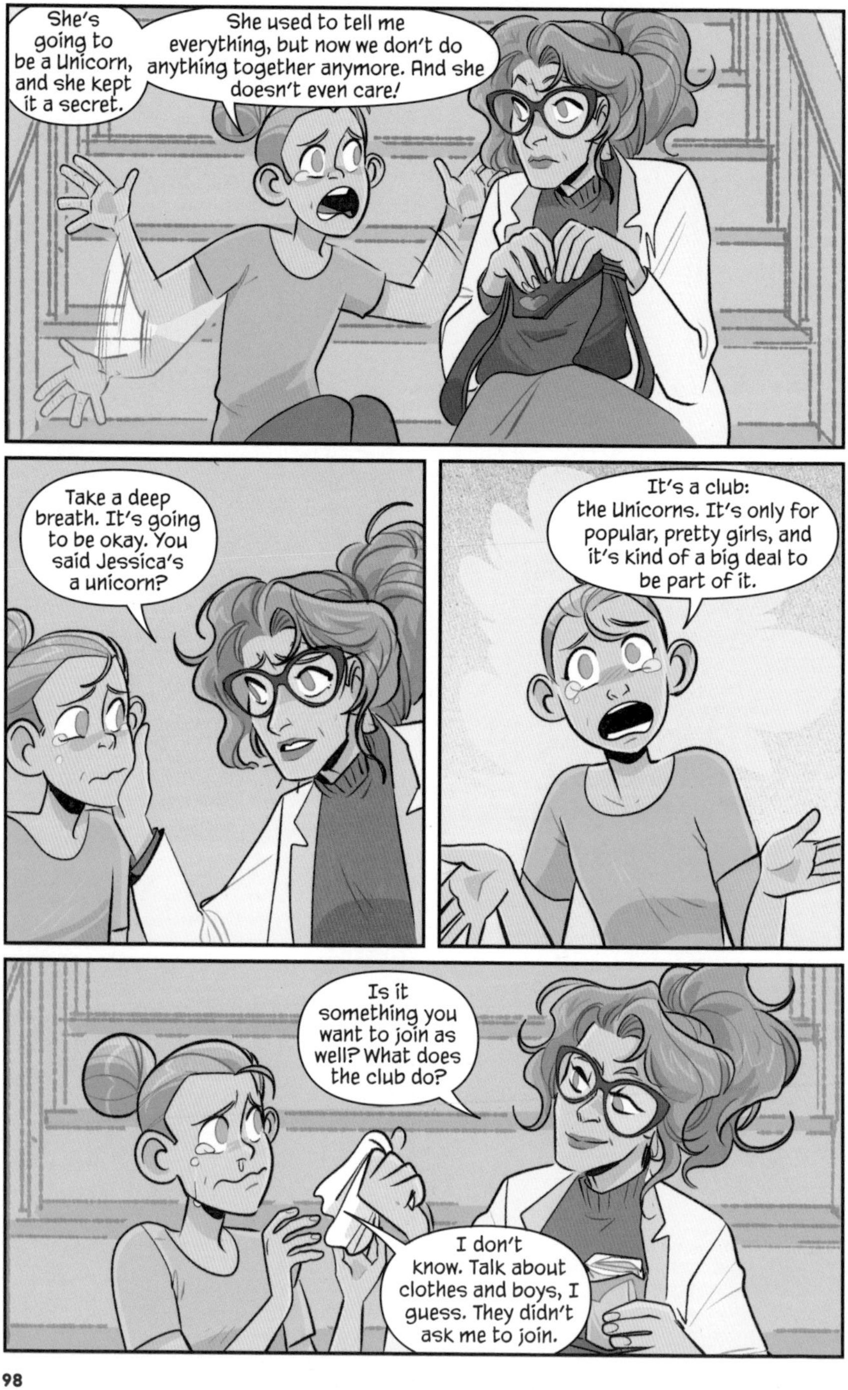
She's going to be a Unicorn, and she kept it a secret.
She used to tell me everything, but now we don't do anything together anymore. And she doesn't even care!
Take a deep breath. It's going to be okay. You said Jessica's a unicorn?
It's a club: the Unicorns. It's only for popular, pretty girls, and it's kind of a big deal to be part of it.
Is it something you want to join as well? What does the club do?
I don't know. Talk about clothes and boys, I guess. They didn't ask me to join.

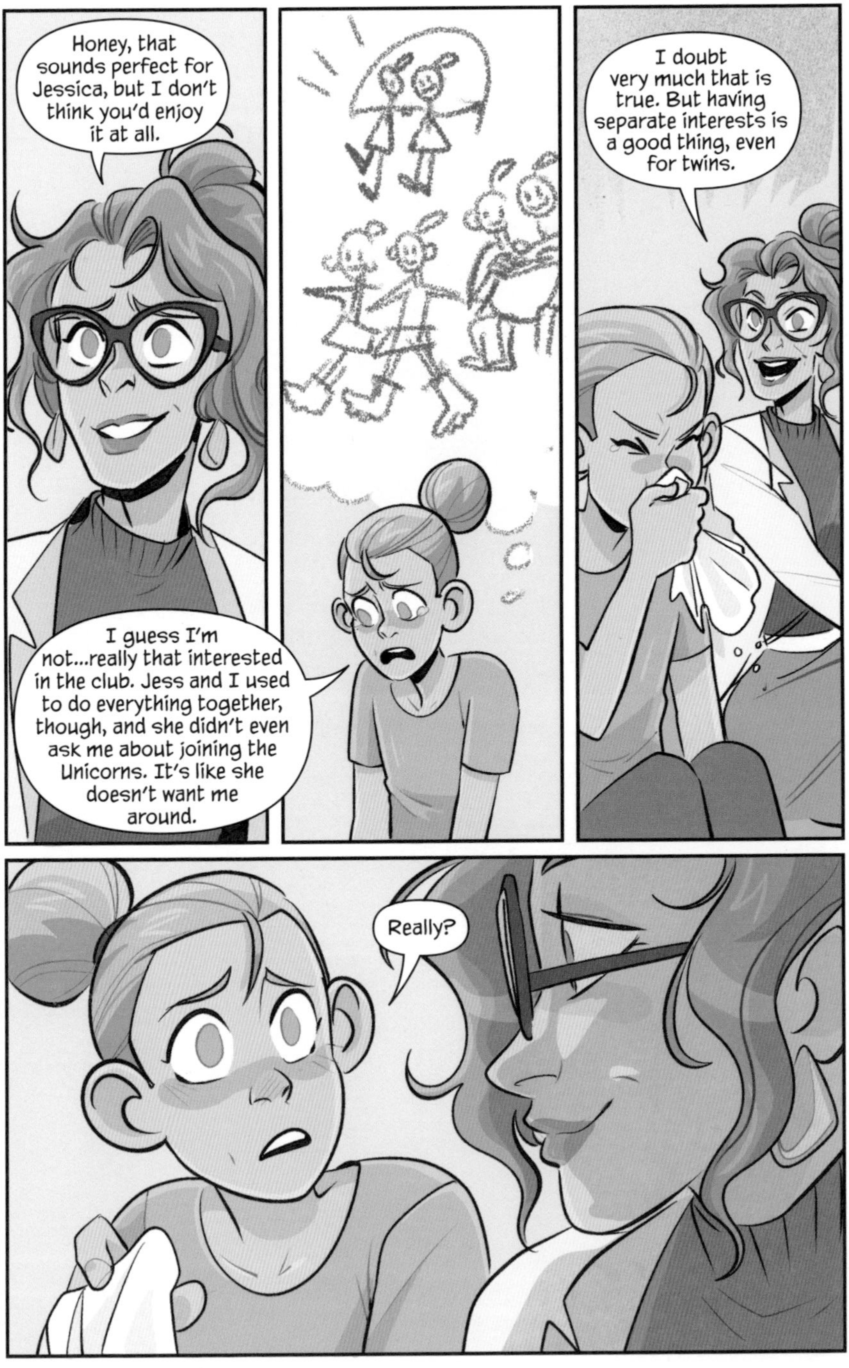
Honey, that sounds perfect for Jessica, but I don't think you'd enjoy it at all.
I guess I'm not...really that interested in the club. Jess and I used to do everything together, though, and she didn't even ask me about joining the Unicorns. It's like she doesn't want me around.
I doubt very much that is true. But having separate interests is a good thing, even for twins.
Really?

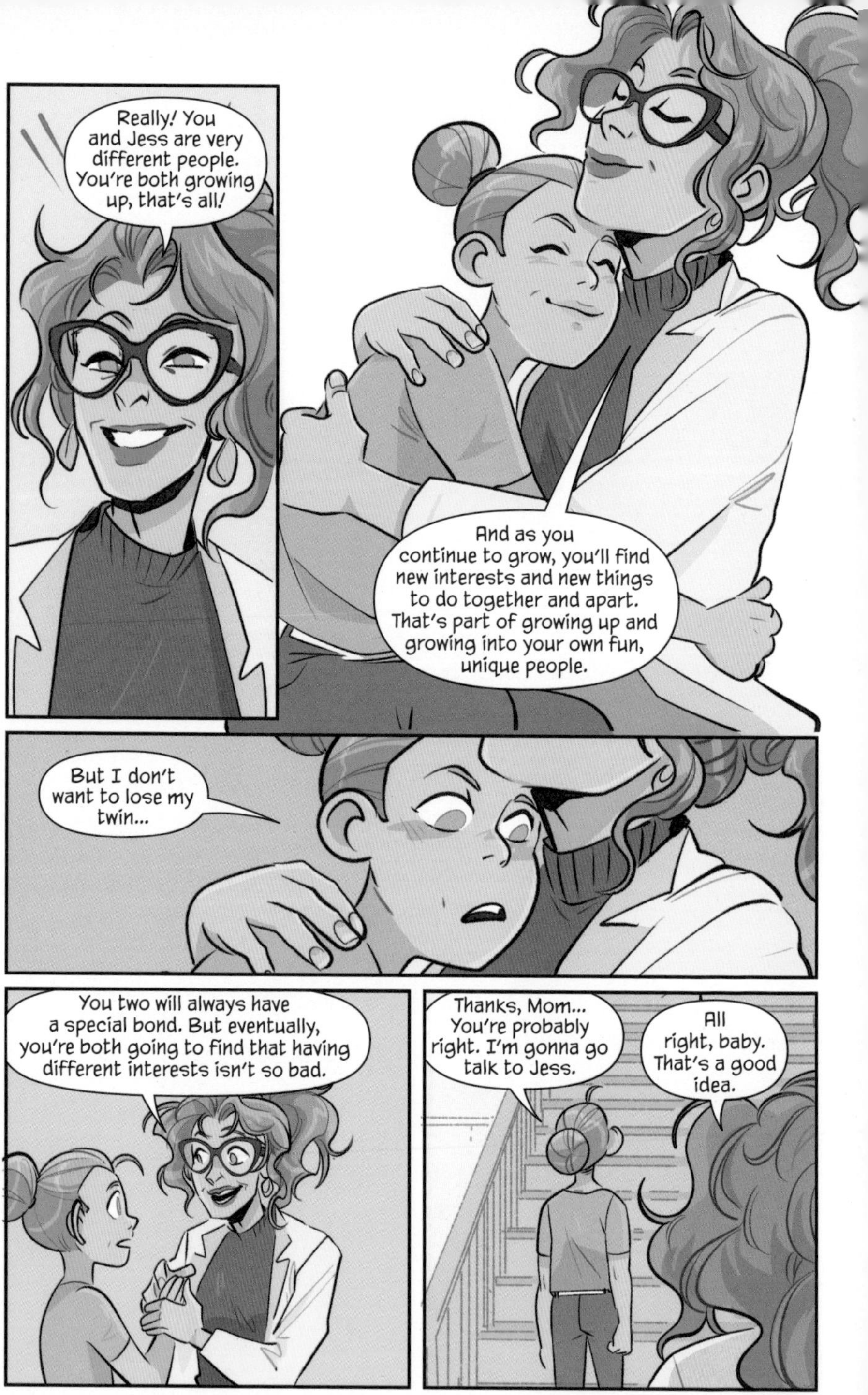
Really! You and Jess are very different people. You're both growing up, that's all!
And as you continue to grow, you'll find new interests and new things to do together and apart. That's part of growing up and growing into your own fun, unique people.
But I don't want to lose my twin...
You two will always have a special bond. But eventually, you're both going to find that having different interests isn't so bad.
Thanks, Mom... You're probably right. I'm gonna go talk to Jess.
All right, baby. That's a good idea.

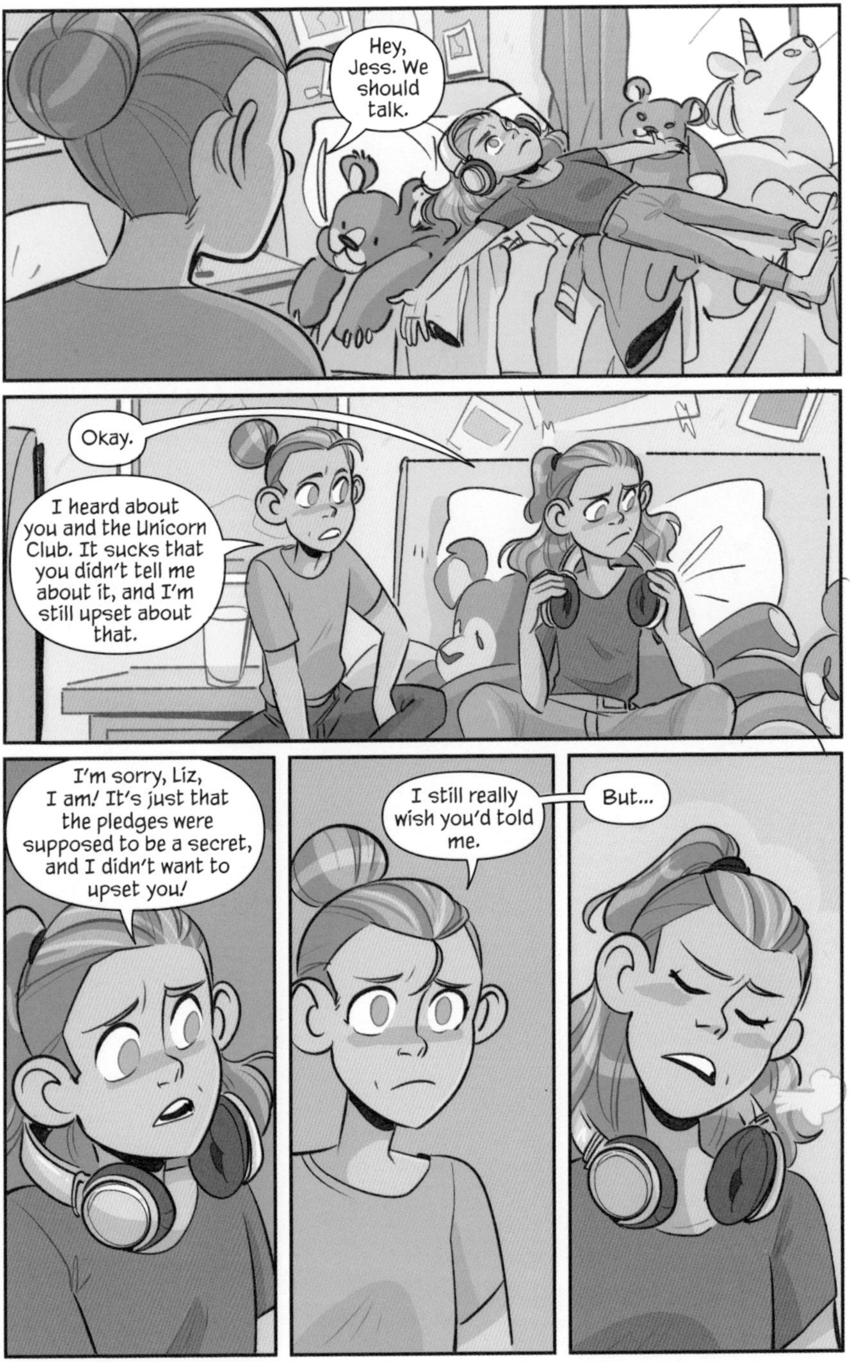
Hey, Jess. We should talk.
Okay.
I heard about you and the Unicorn Club. It sucks that you didn't tell me about it, and I'm still upset about that.
I'm sorry, Liz, I am! It's just that the pledges were supposed to be a secret, and I didn't want to upset you!
I still really wish you'd told me.
But...

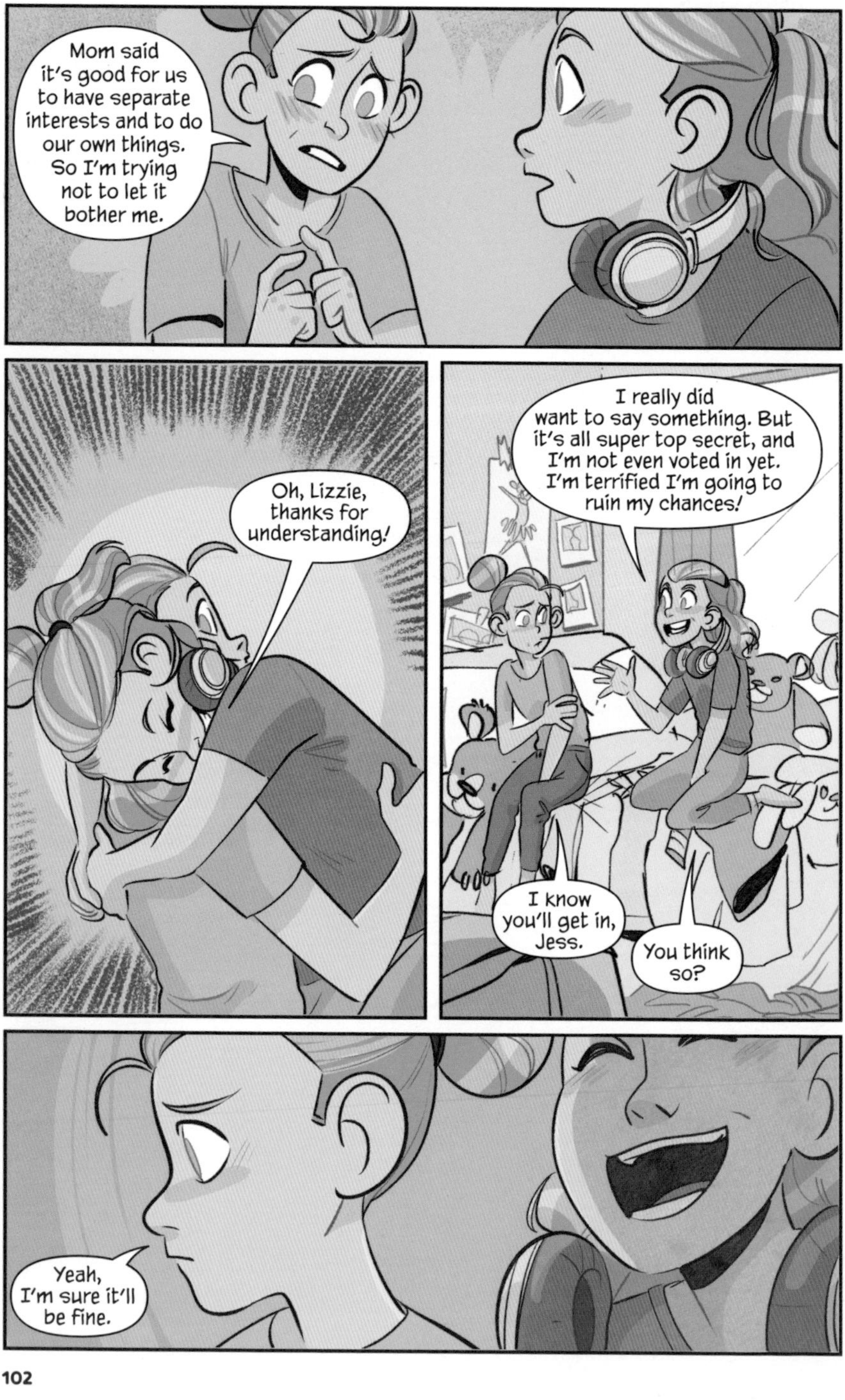
Mom said it's good for us to have separate interests and to do our own things. So I'm trying not to let it bother me.
Oh, Lizzie, thanks for understanding!
I really did want to say something. But it's all super top secret, and I'm not even voted in yet. I'm terrified I'm going to ruin my chances!
I know you'll get in, Jess.
You think so?
Yeah, I'm sure it'll be fine.

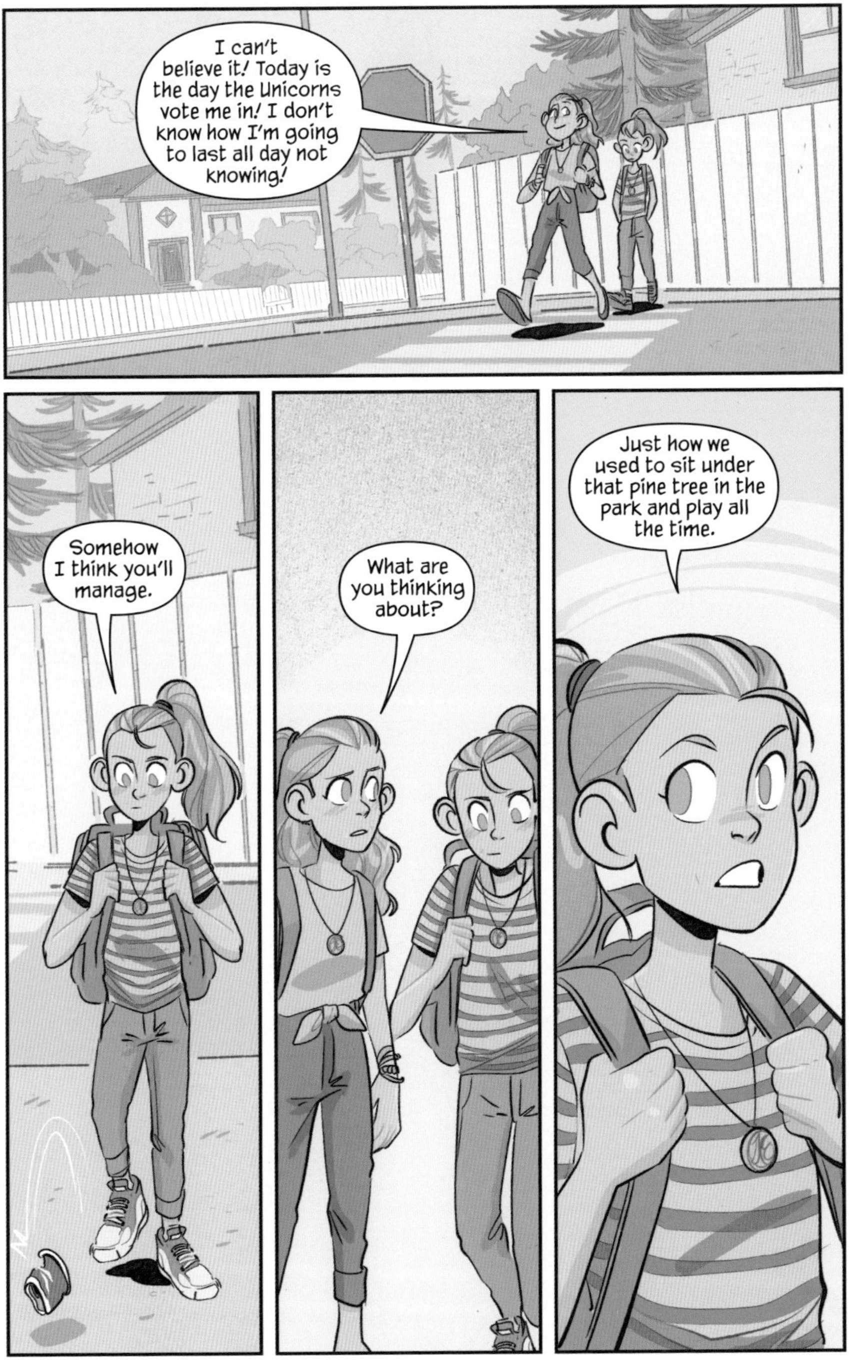
I can't believe it! Today is the day the Unicorns vote me in! I don't know how I'm going to last all day not knowing!
Somehow I think you'll manage.
What are you thinking about?
Just how we used to sit under that pine tree in the park and play all the time.

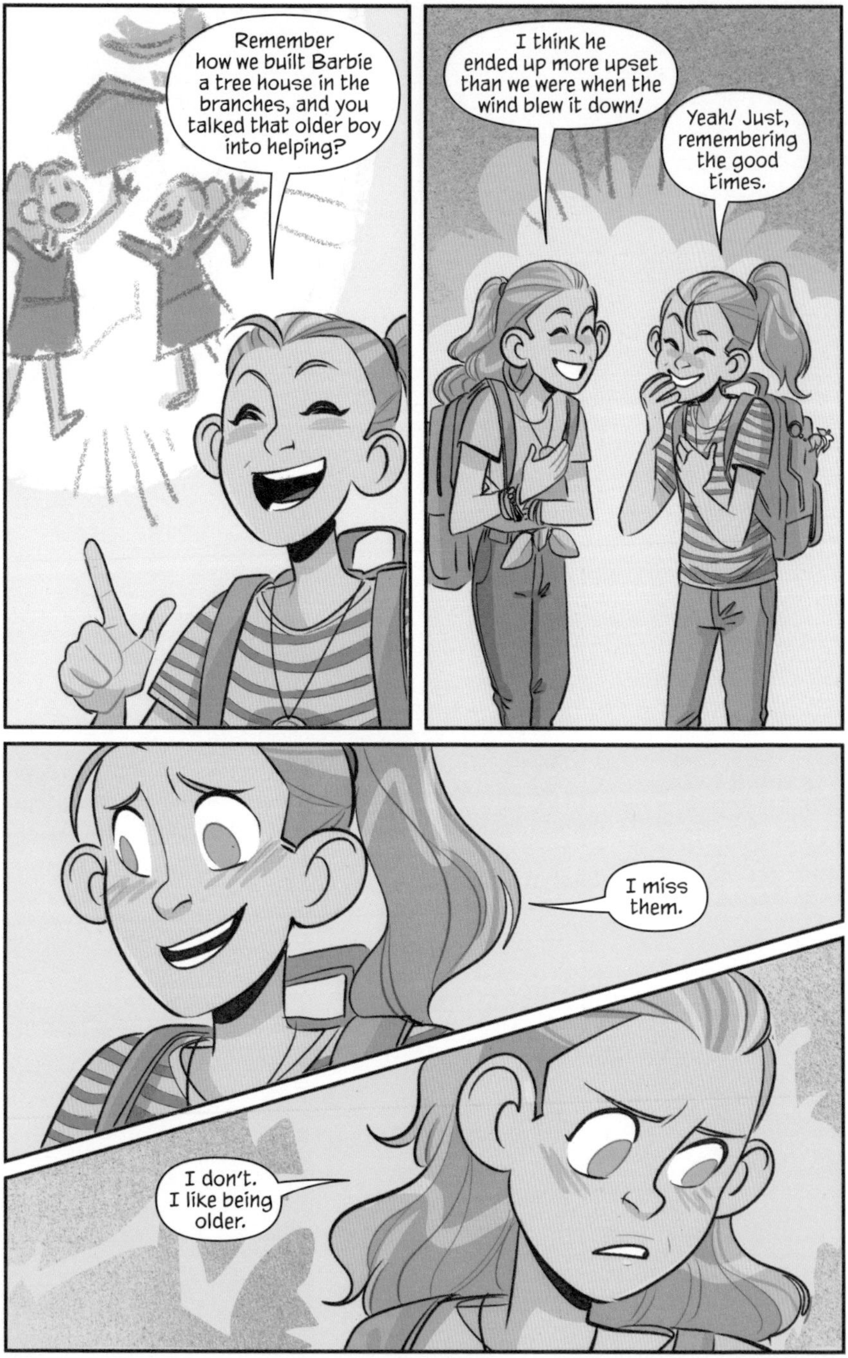
Remember how we built Barbie a tree house in the branches, and you talked that older boy into helping?
I think he ended up more upset than we were when the wind blew it down!
Yeah! Just, remembering the good times.
I miss them.
I don't. I like being older.

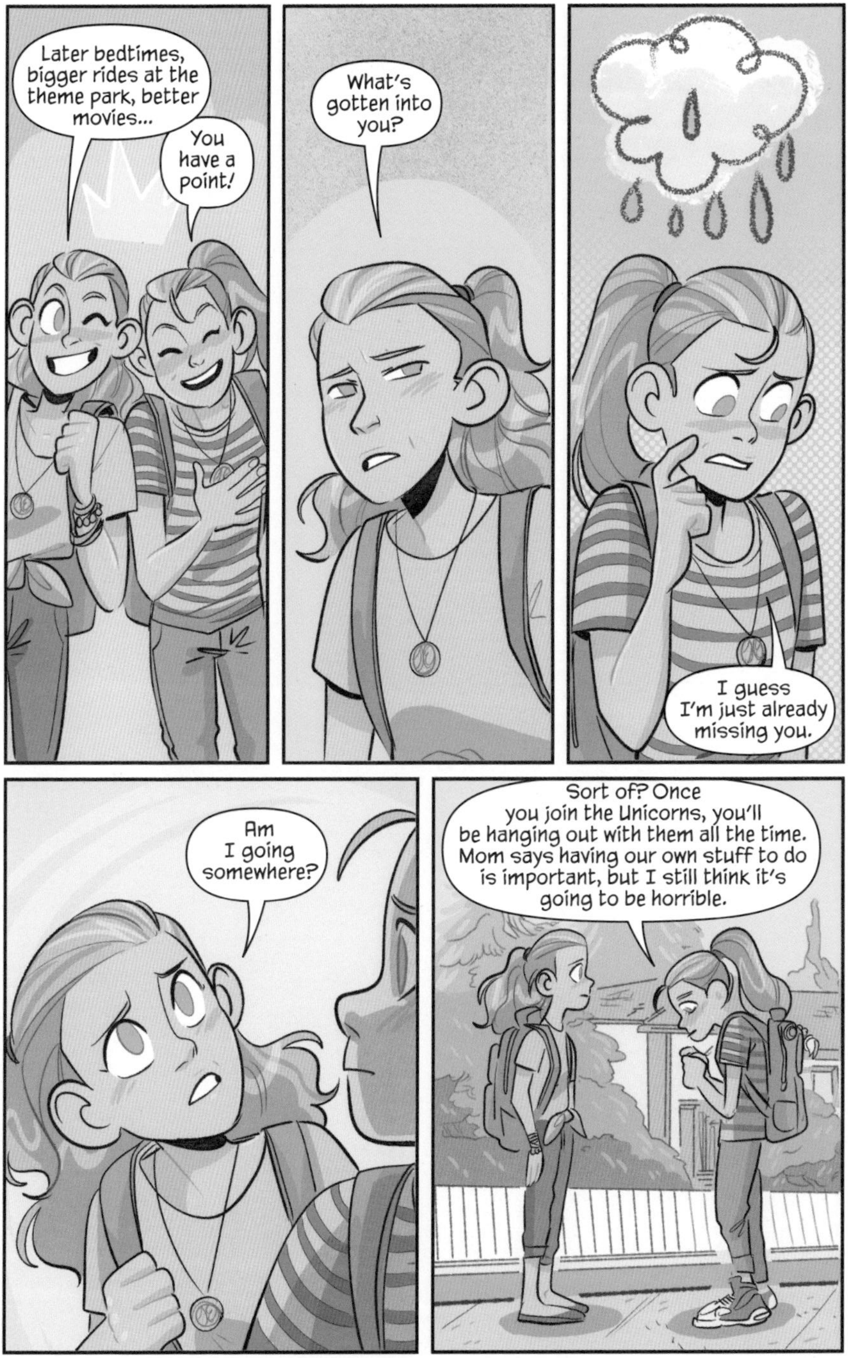
Later bedtimes, bigger rides at the theme park, better movies...
You have a point!
What's gotten into you?
I guess I'm just already missing you.
Am I going somewhere?
Sort of? Once you join the Unicorns, you'll be hanging out with them all the time. Mom says having our own stuff to do is important, but I still think it's going to be horrible.

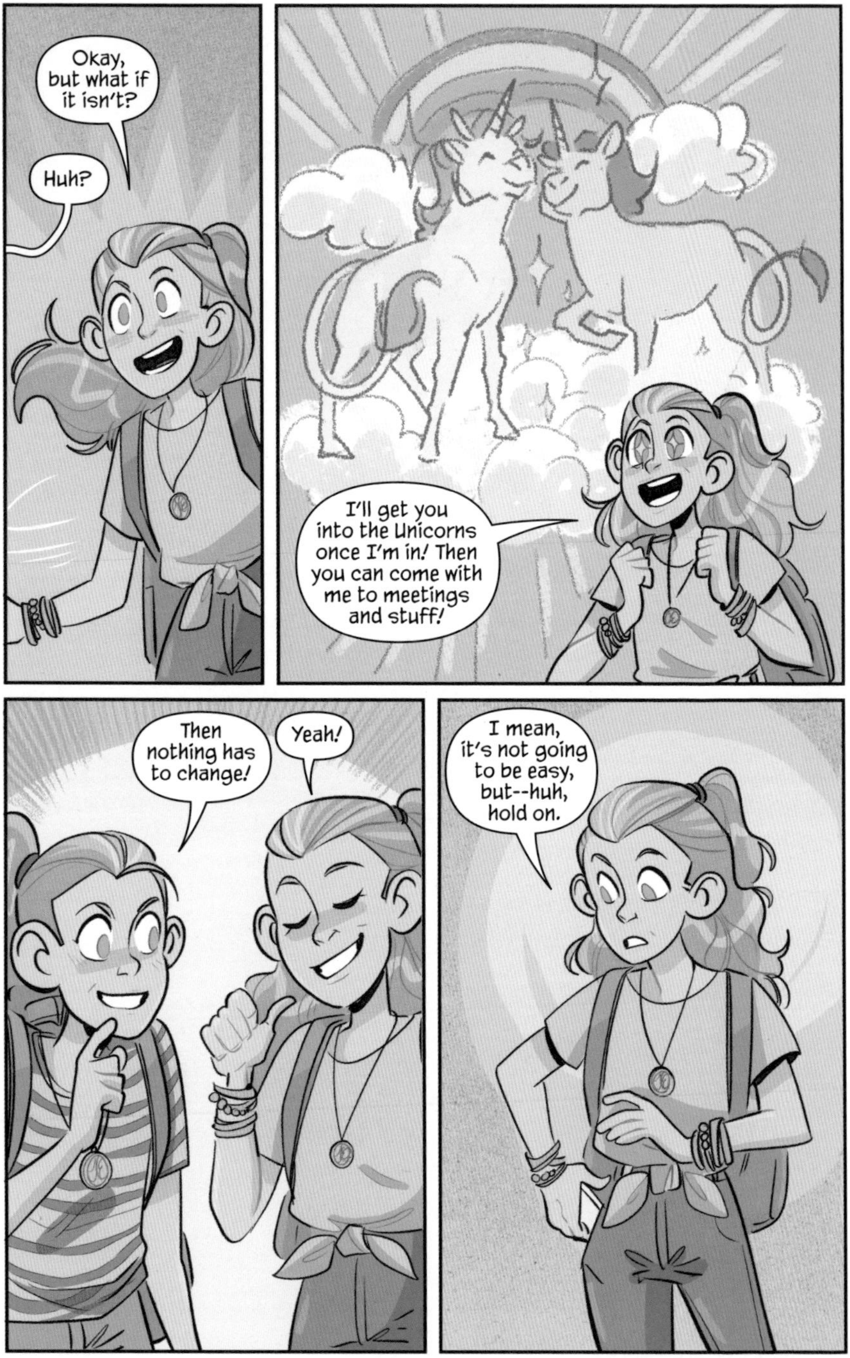
Okay, but what if it isn't?
Huh?
I'll get you into the Unicorns once I'm in! Then you can come with me to meetings and stuff!
Then nothing has to change!
Yeah!
I mean, it's not going to be easy, but--huh, hold on.

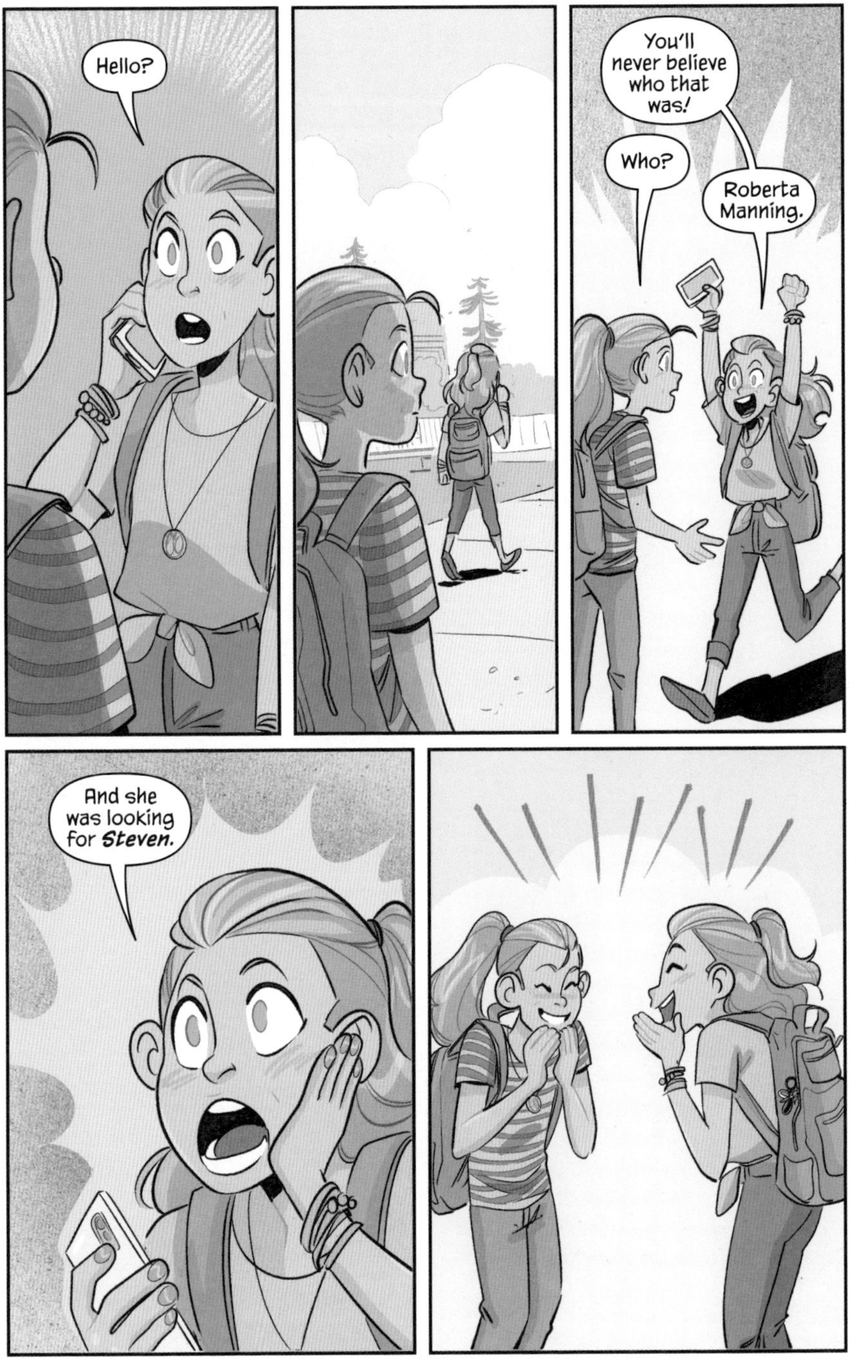
Hello?
You'll never believe who that was!
Who?
Roberta Manning.
And she was looking for *Steven.*

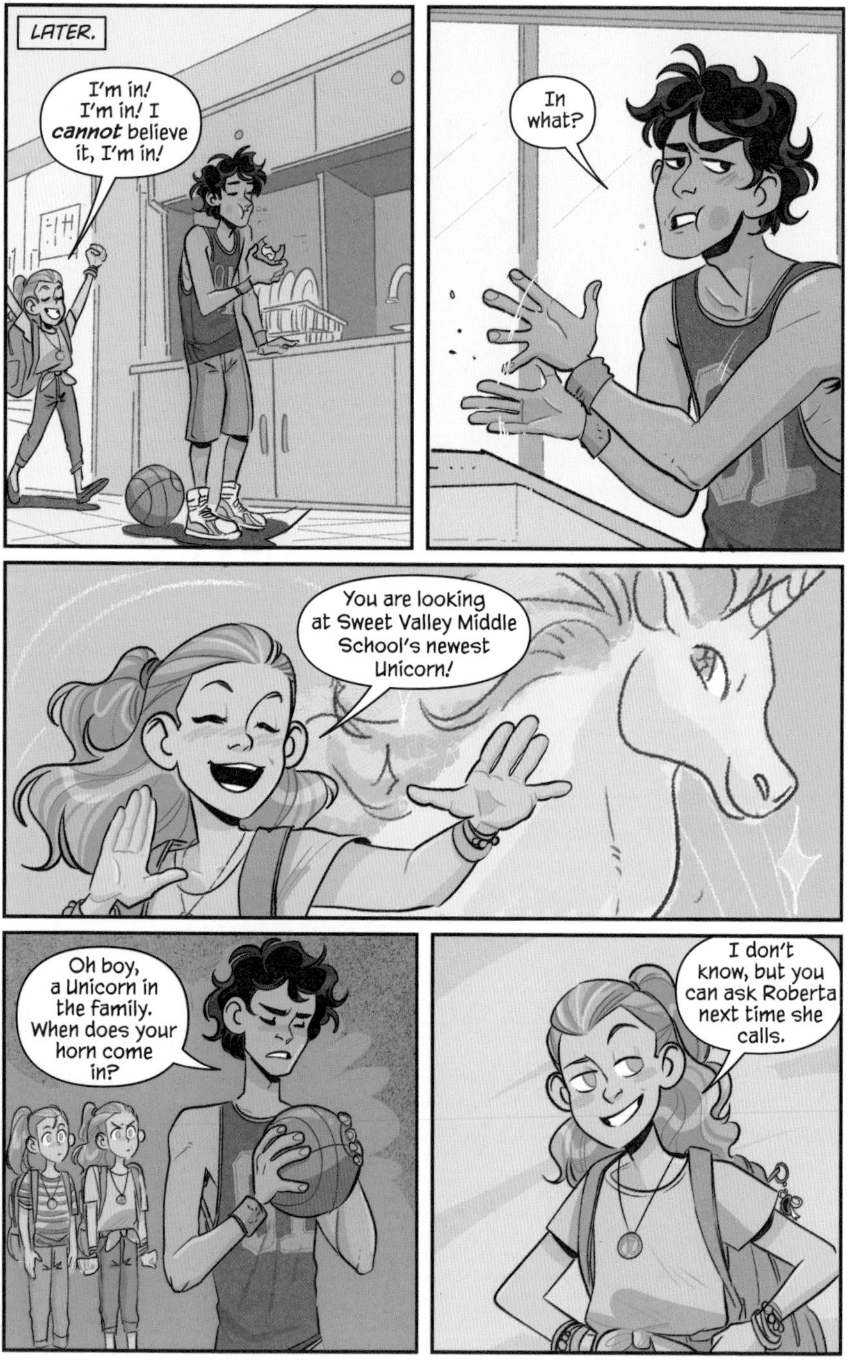
LATER.
I'm in! I'm in! I *cannot* believe it, I'm in!
In what?
You are looking at Sweet Valley Middle School's newest Unicorn!
Oh boy, a Unicorn in the family. When does your horn come in?
I don't know, but you can ask Roberta next time she calls.

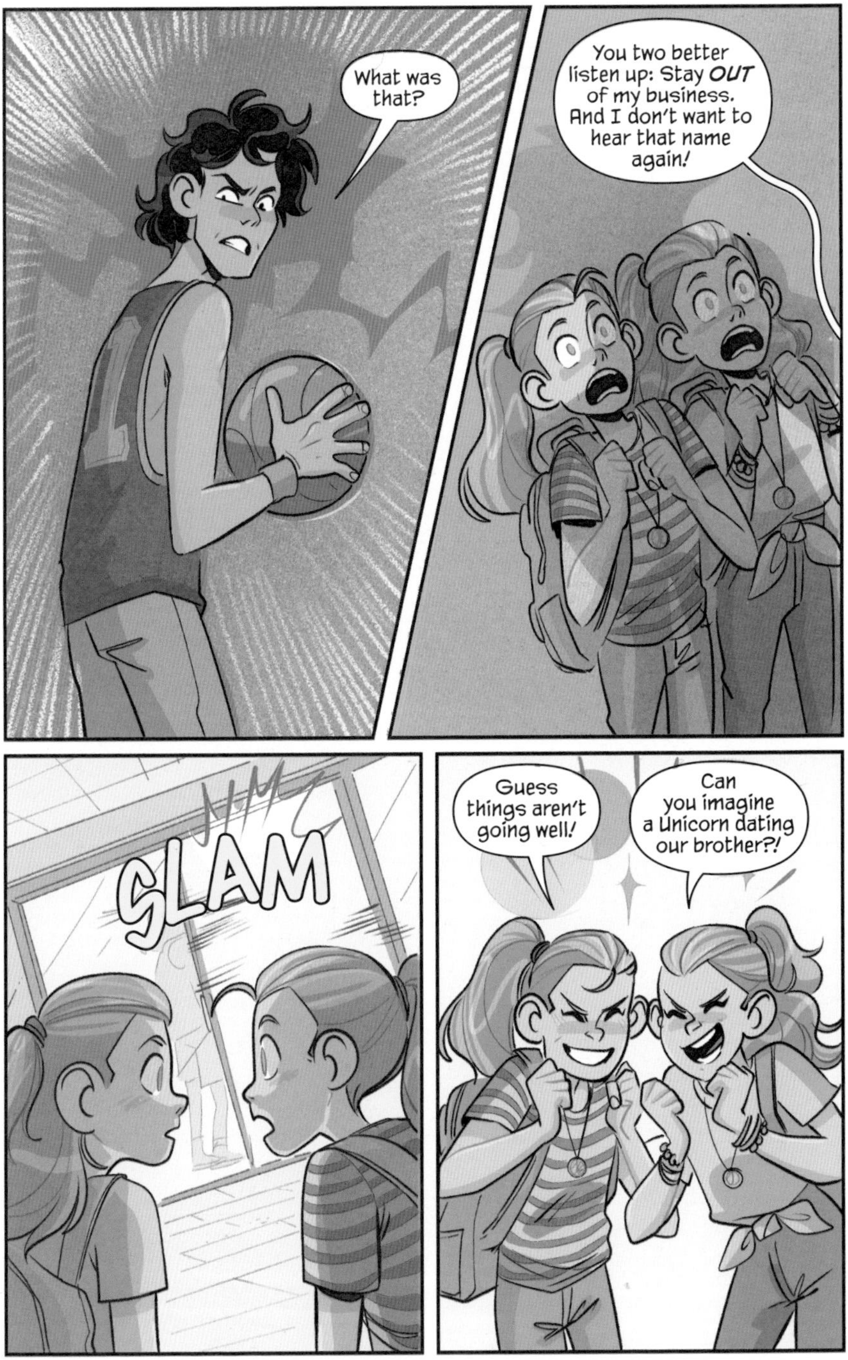
What was that?
You two better listen up: Stay OUT of my business. And I don't want to hear that name again!
SLAM
Guess things aren't going well!
Can you imagine a Unicorn dating our brother?!

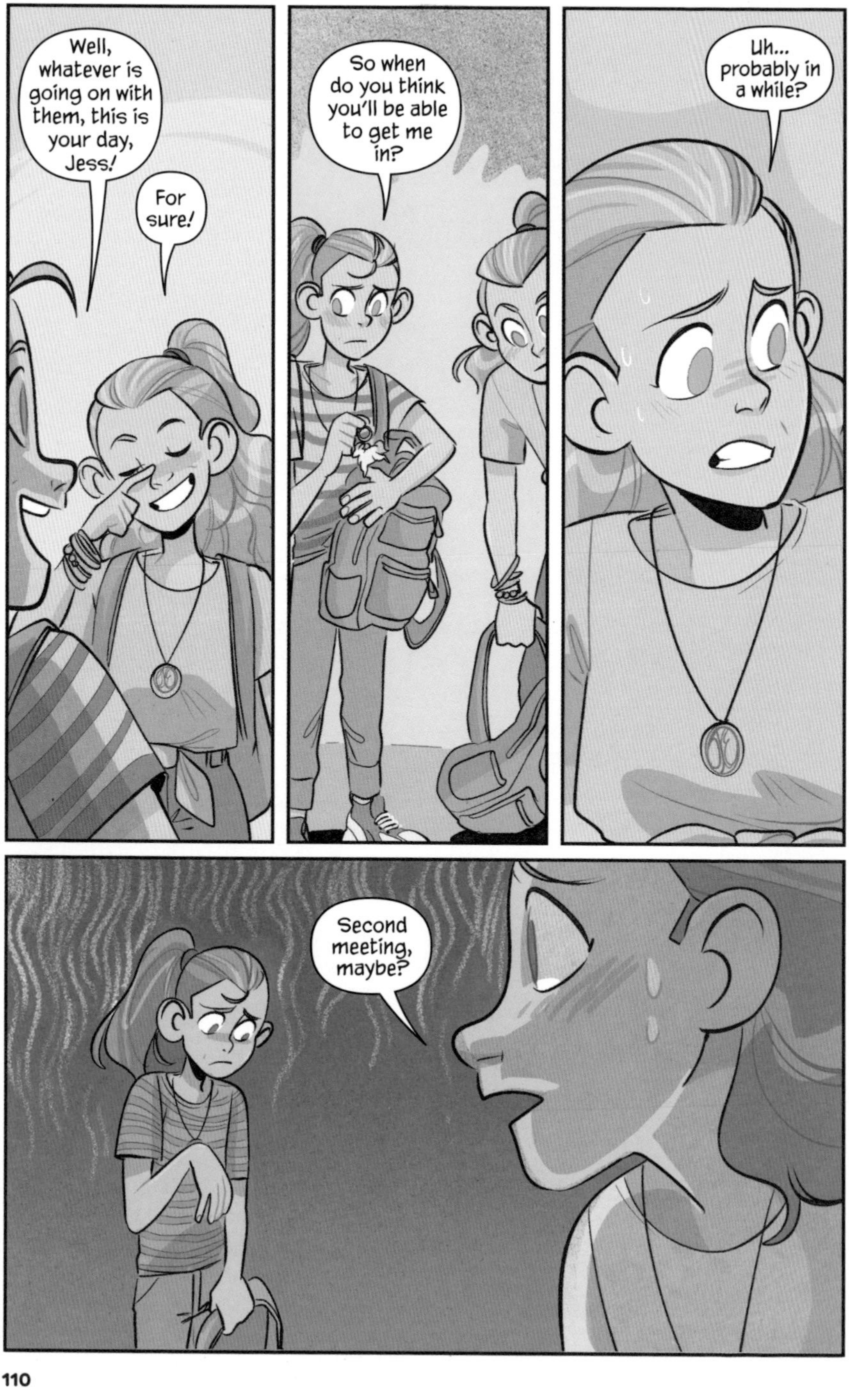
Well, whatever is going on with them, this is your day, Jess!
For sure!
So when do you think you'll be able to get me in?
Uh... probably in a while?
Second meeting, maybe?

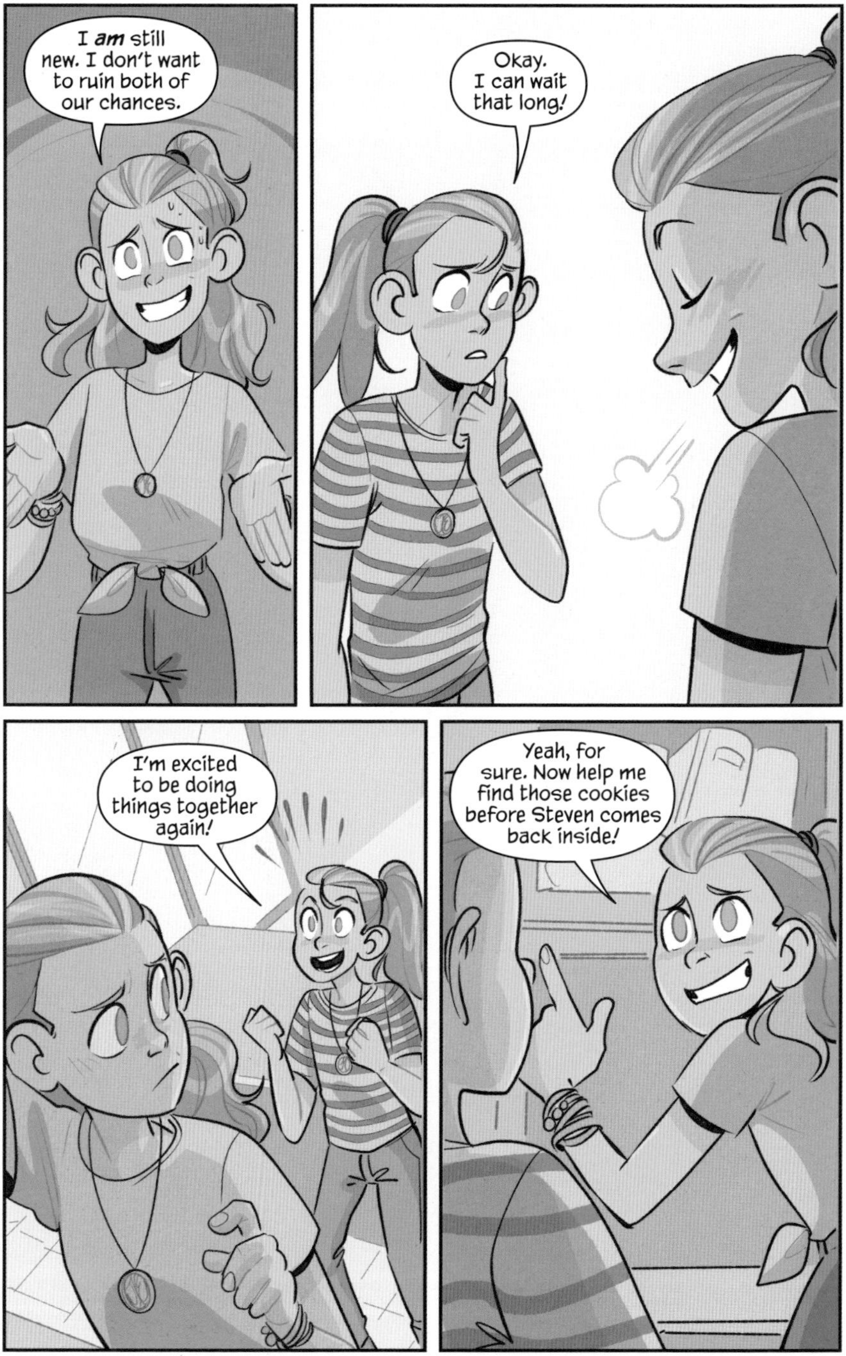
I *am* still new. I don't want to ruin both of our chances.
Okay. I can wait that long!
I'm excited to be doing things together again!
Yeah, for sure. Now help me find those cookies before Steven comes back inside!

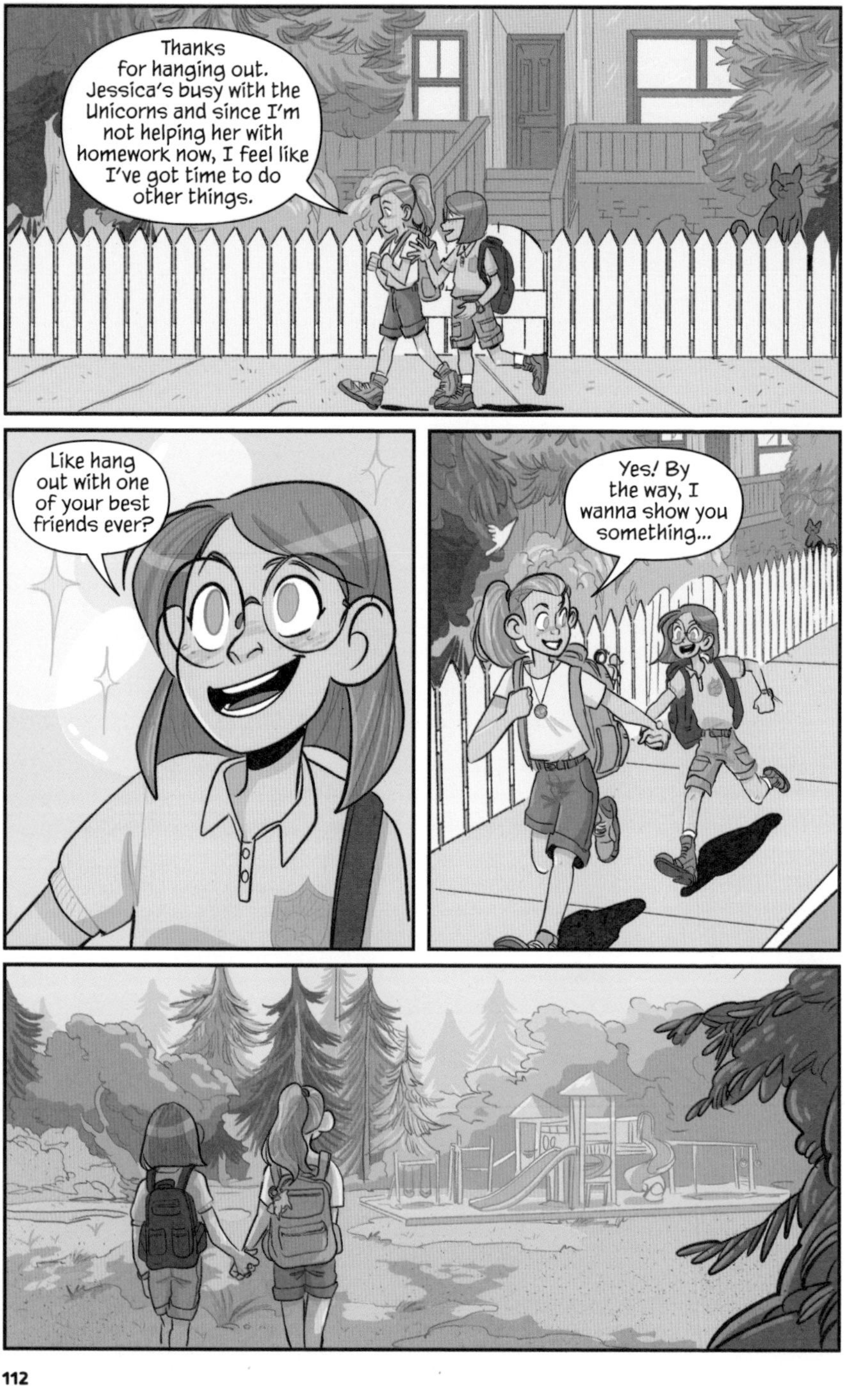
Thanks for hanging out. Jessica's busy with the Unicorns and since I'm not helping her with homework now, I feel like I've got time to do other things.
Like hang out with one of your best friends ever?
Yes! By the way, I wanna show you something...

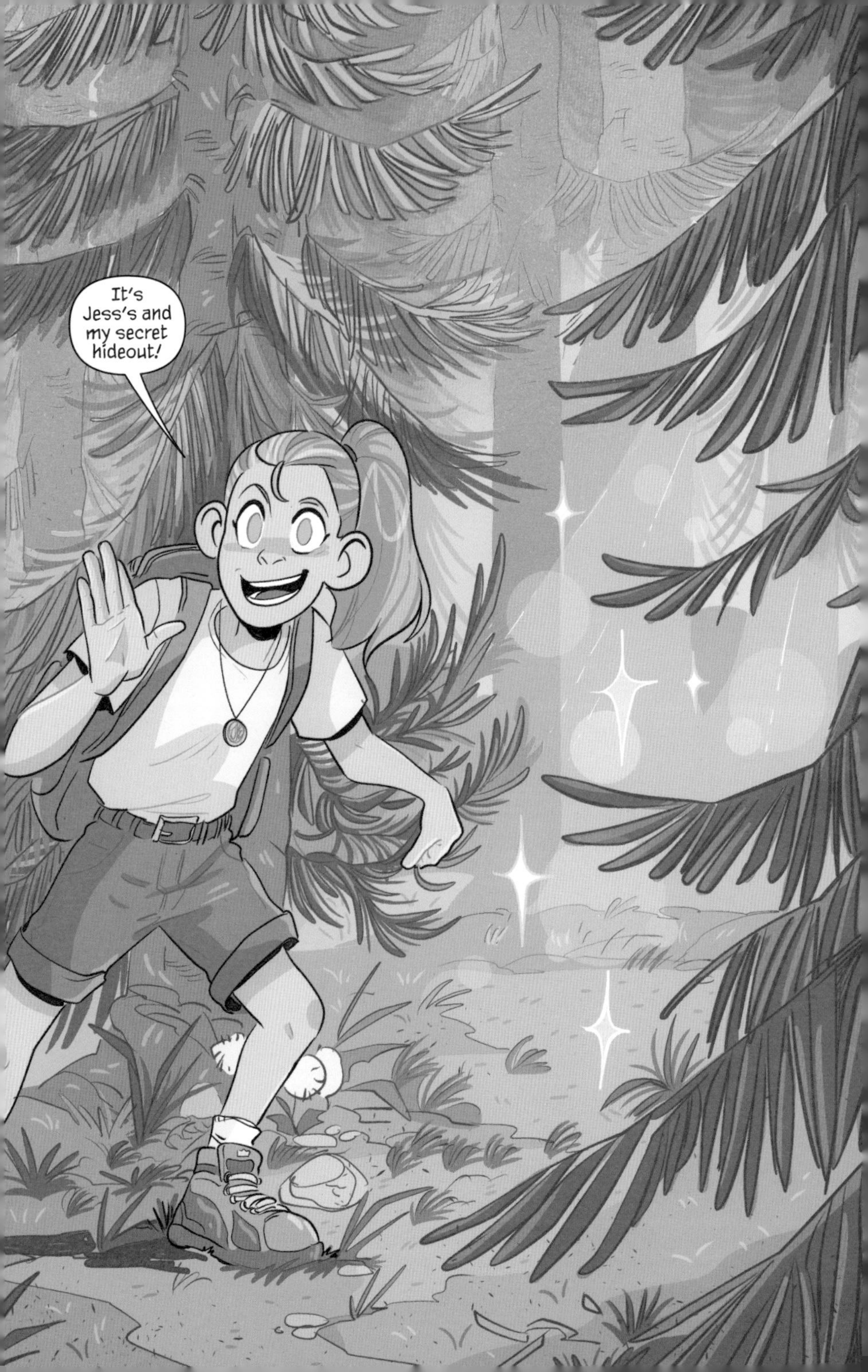
It's Jess's and my secret hideout!

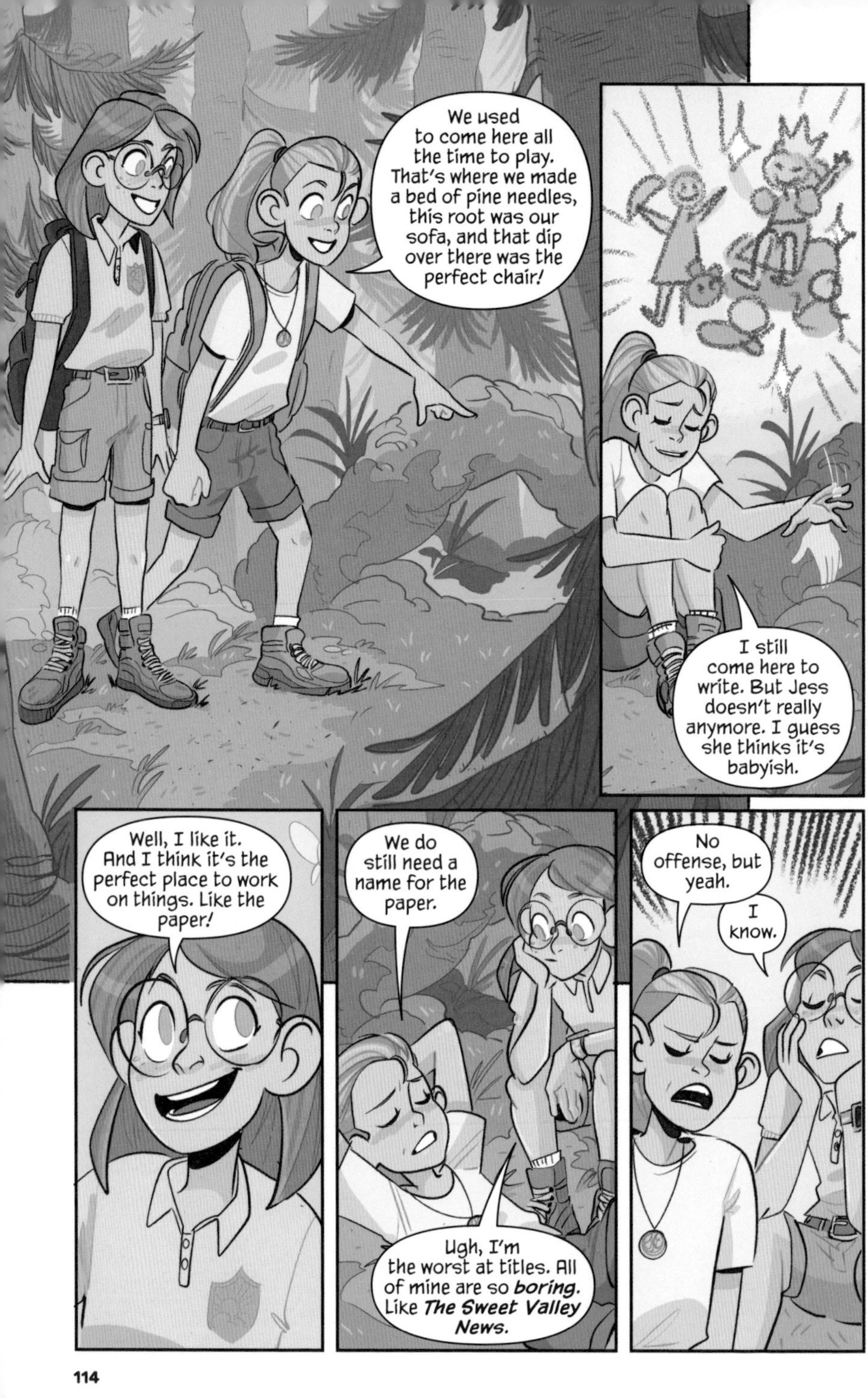
We used to come here all the time to play. That's where we made a bed of pine needles, this root was our sofa, and that dip over there was the perfect chair!
I still come here to write. But Jess doesn't really anymore. I guess she thinks it's babyish.
Well, I like it. And I think it's the perfect place to work on things. Like the paper!
We do still need a name for the paper.
Ugh, I'm the worst at titles. All of mine are so *boring*. Like ***The Sweet Valley News***.
No offense, but yeah.
I know.

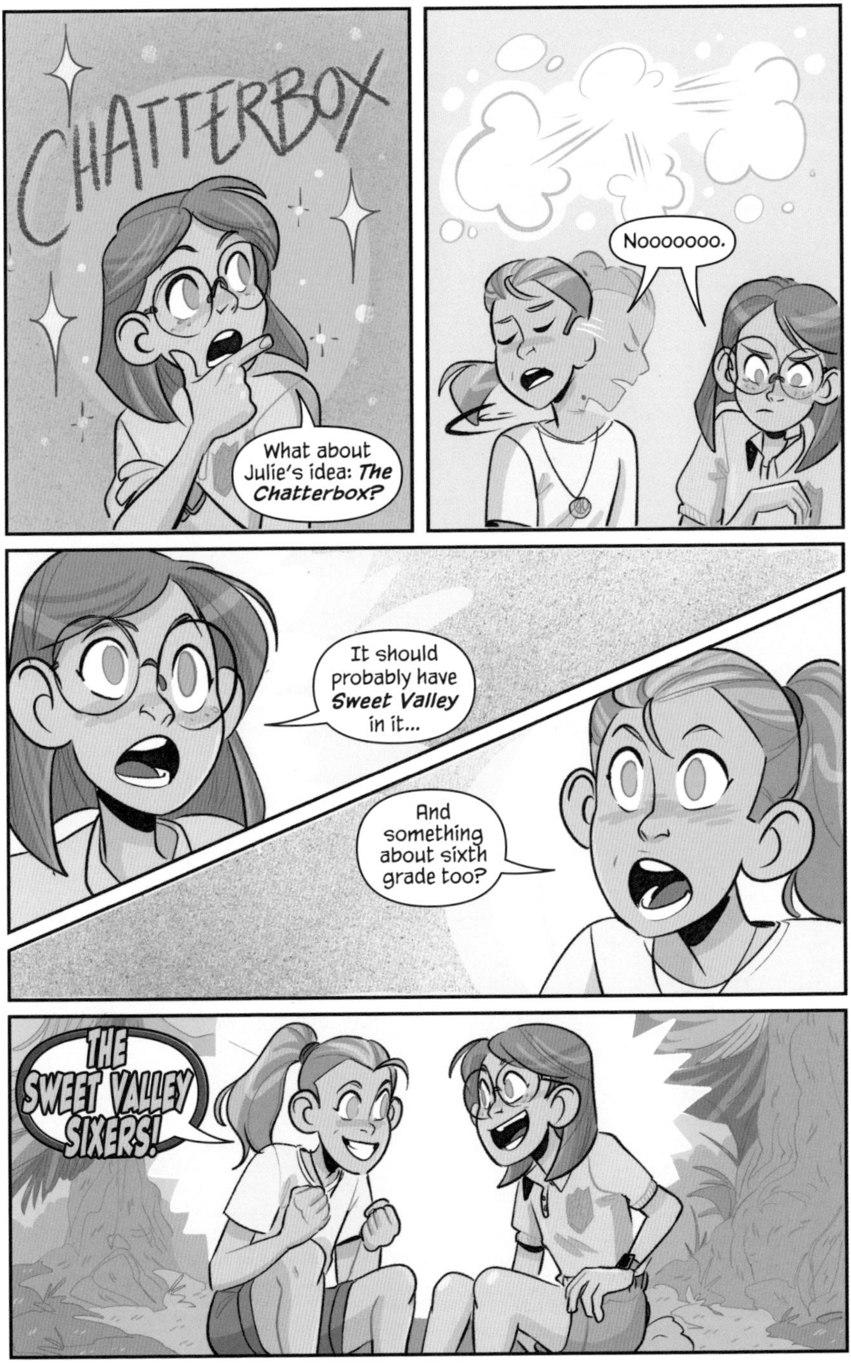
CHATTERBOX
What about Julie's idea: *The Chatterbox?*
Noooooo.
It should probably have ***Sweet Valley*** in it...
And something about sixth grade too?
THE SWEET VALLEY SIXERS!

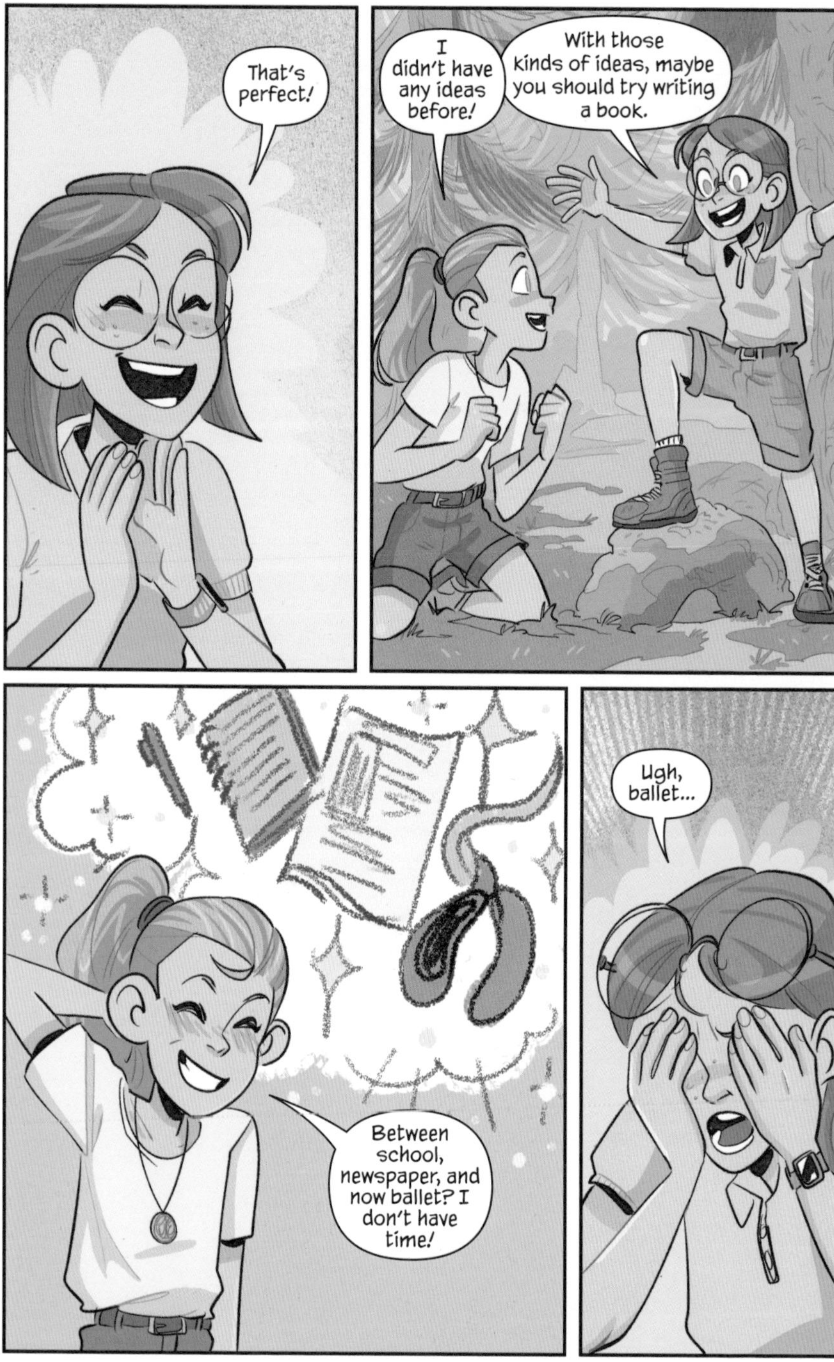
That's perfect!
I didn't have any ideas before!
With those kinds of ideas, maybe you should try writing a book.
Between school, newspaper, and now ballet? I don't have time!
Ugh, ballet...

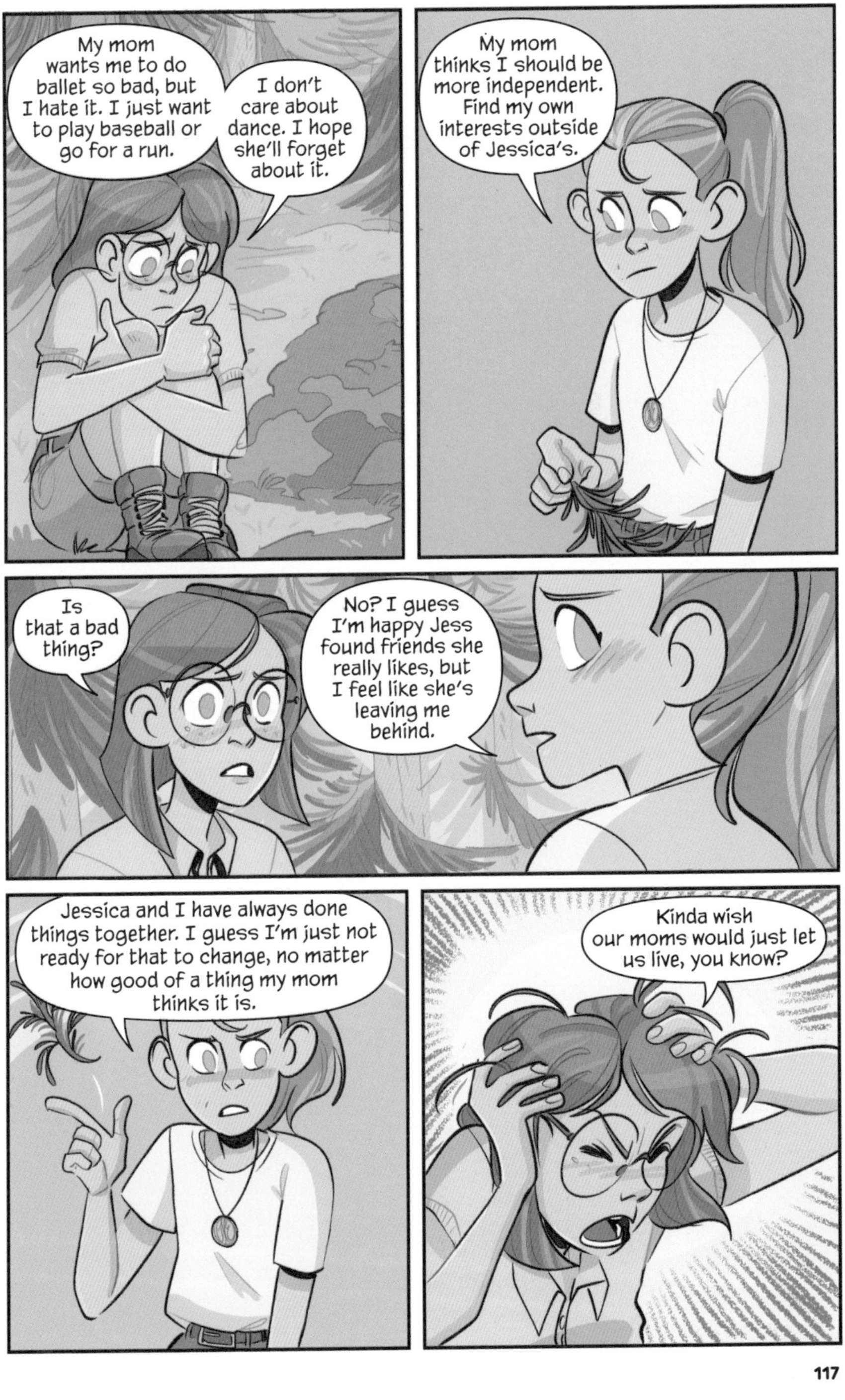
My mom wants me to do ballet so bad, but I hate it. I just want to play baseball or go for a run.
I don't care about dance. I hope she'll forget about it.
My mom thinks I should be more independent. Find my own interests outside of Jessica's.
Is that a bad thing?
No? I guess I'm happy Jess found friends she really likes, but I feel like she's leaving me behind.
Jessica and I have always done things together. I guess I'm just not ready for that to change, no matter how good of a thing my mom thinks it is.
Kinda wish our moms would just let us live, you know?

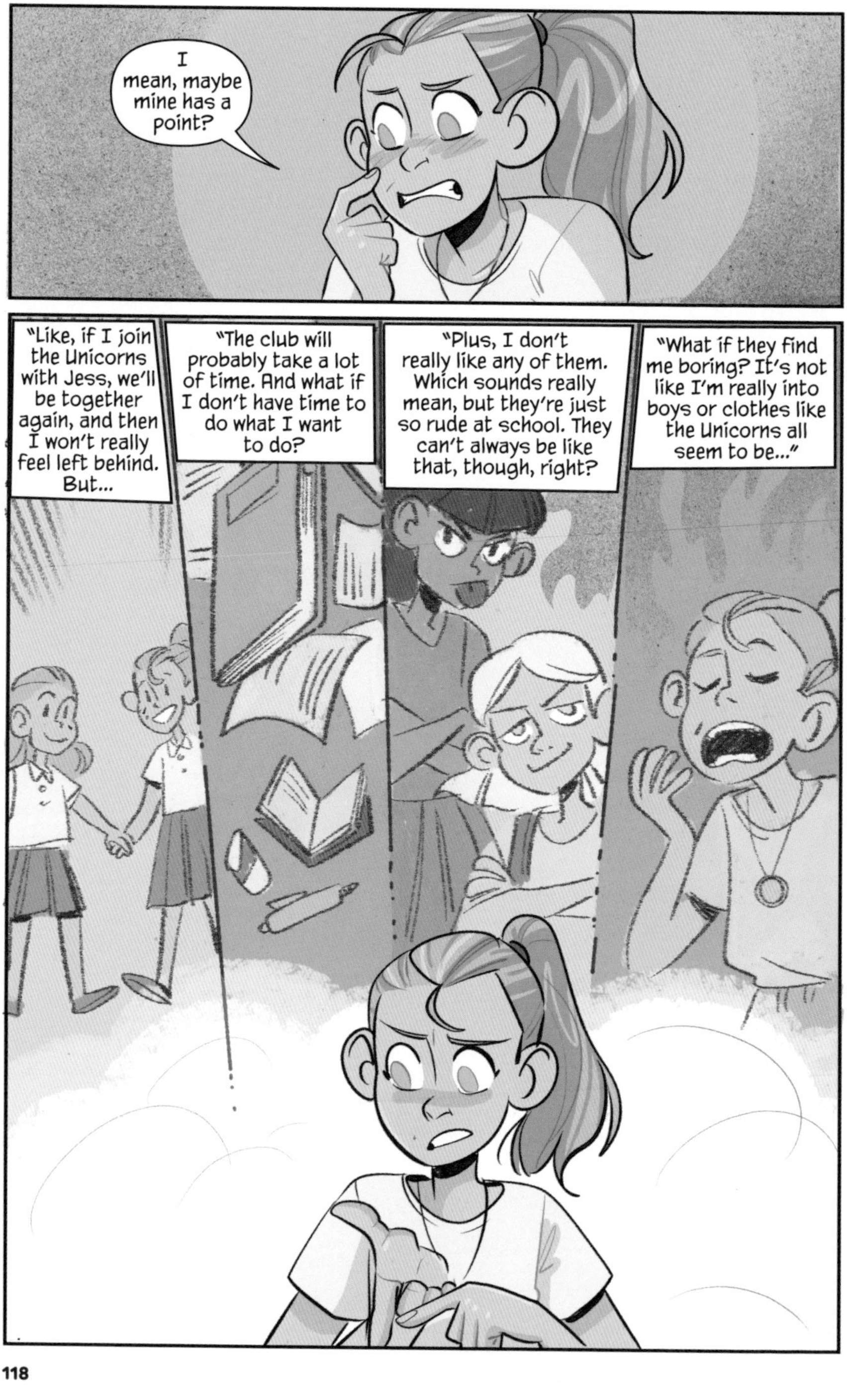
I mean, maybe mine has a point?
"Like, if I join the Unicorns with Jess, we'll be together again, and then I won't really feel left behind. But...
"The club will probably take a lot of time. And what if I don't have time to do what I want to do?
"Plus, I don't really like any of them. Which sounds really mean, but they're just so rude at school. They can't always be like that, though, right?
"What if they find me boring? It's not like I'm really into boys or clothes like the Unicorns all seem to be..."

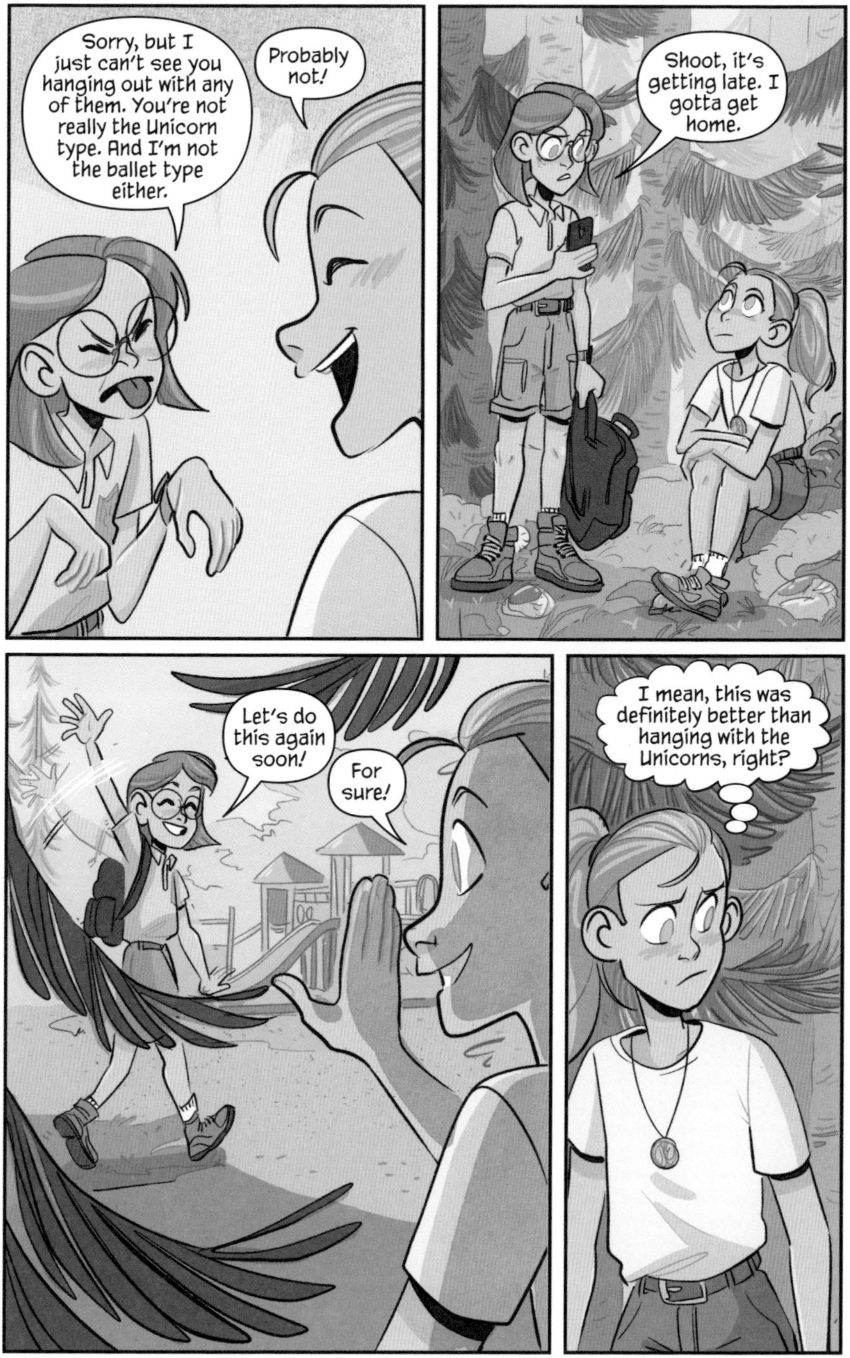
Sorry, but I just can't see you hanging out with any of them. You're not really the Unicorn type. And I'm not the ballet type either.
Probably not!
Shoot, it's getting late. I gotta get home.
Let's do this again soon!
For sure!
I mean, this was definitely better than hanging with the Unicorns, right?

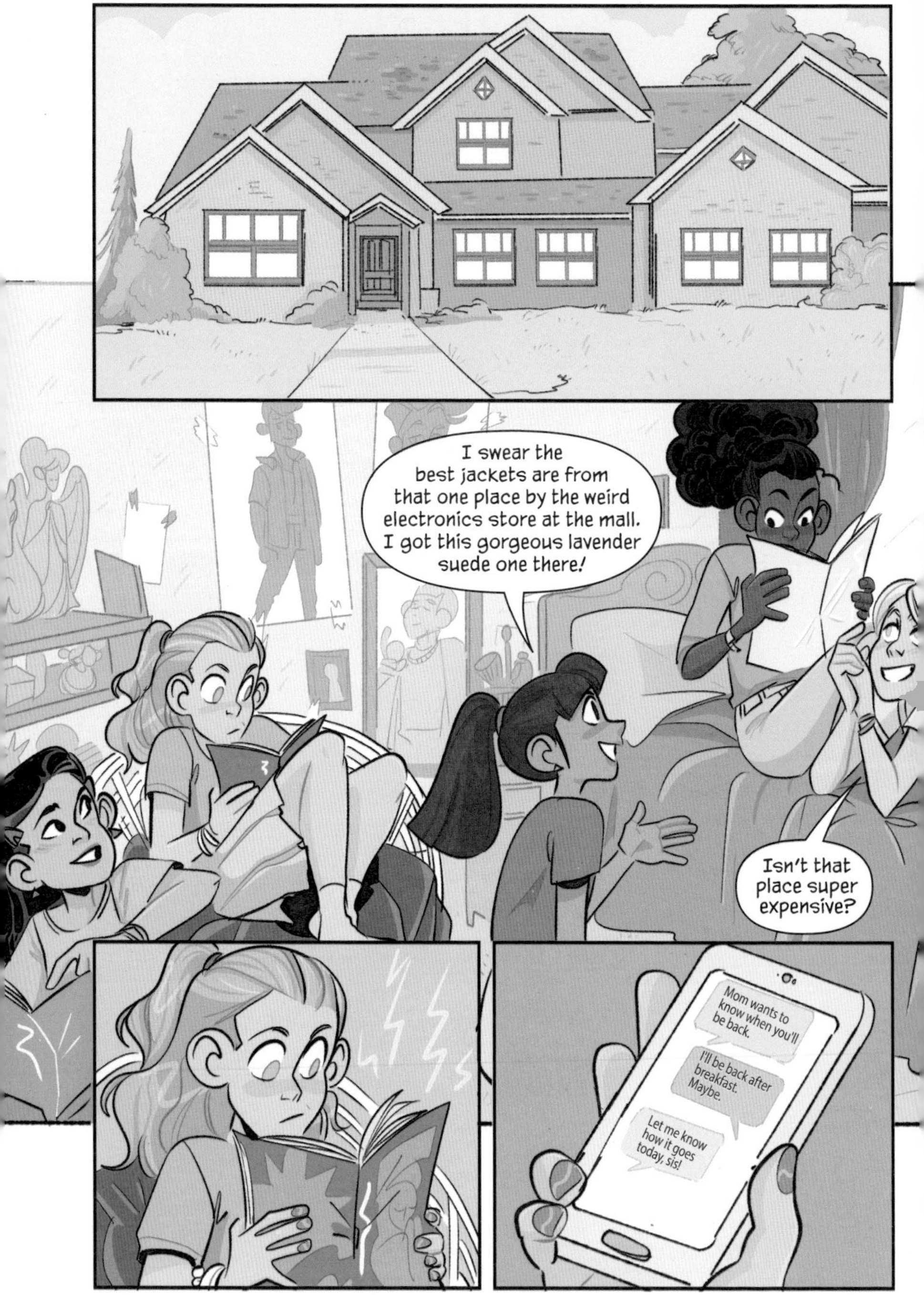
I swear the best jackets are from that one place by the weird electronics store at the mall. I got this gorgeous lavender suede one there!
Isn't that place super expensive?
Mom wants to know when you'll be back.
I'll be back after breakfast. Maybe.
Let me know how it goes today, sis!

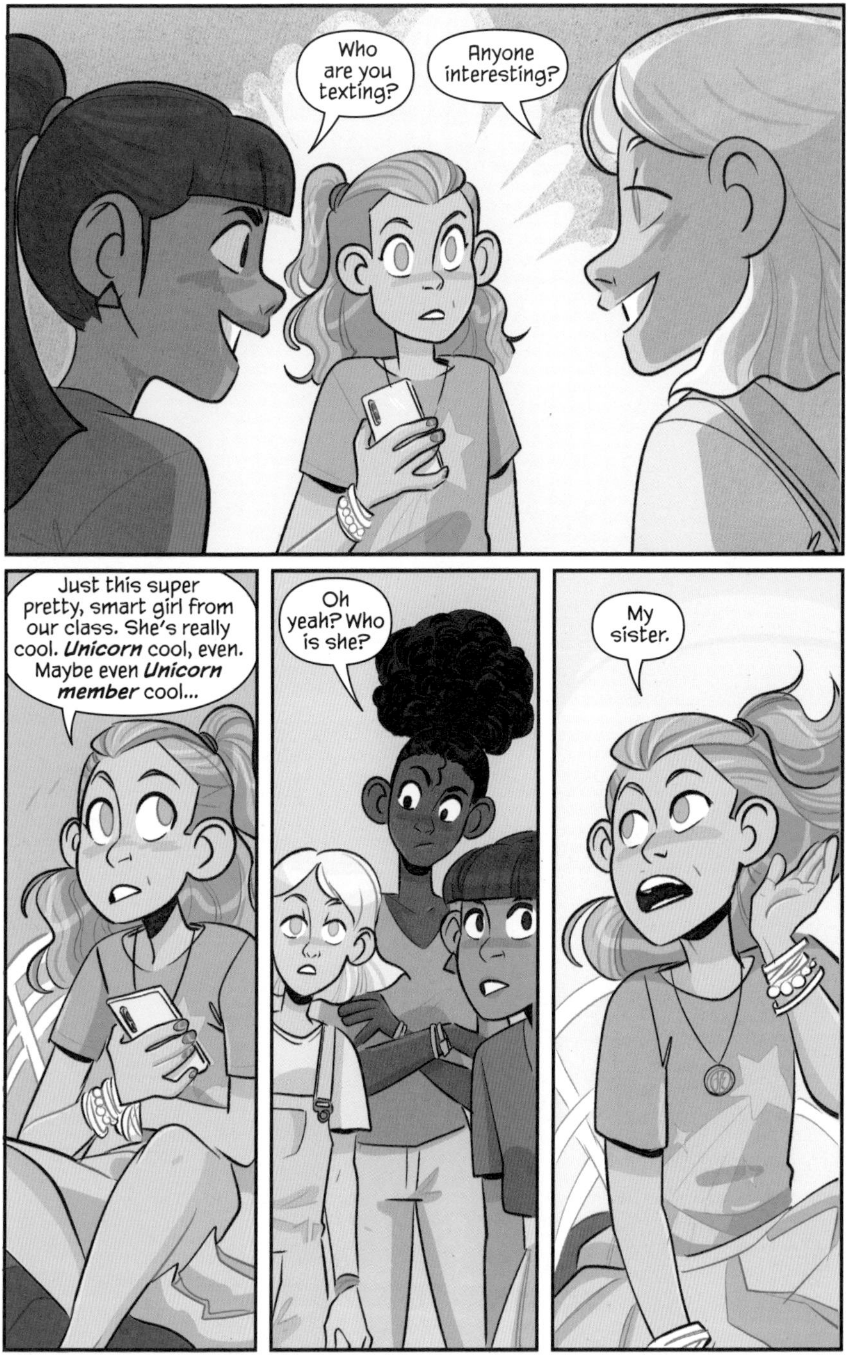
Who are you texting?
Anyone interesting?
Just this super pretty, smart girl from our class. She's really cool. *Unicorn* cool, even. Maybe even *Unicorn member* cool...
Oh yeah? Who is she?
My sister.

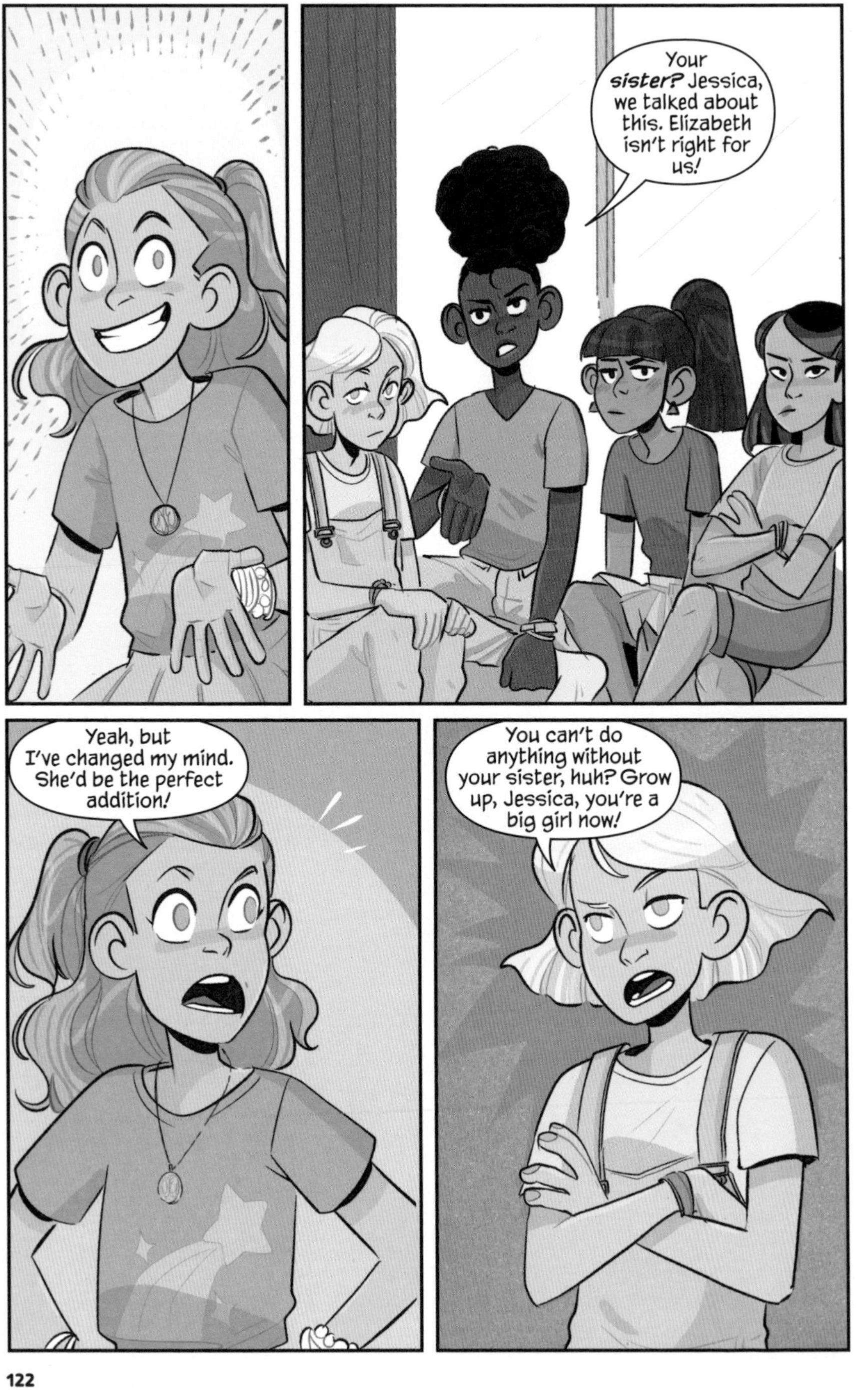
Your *sister?* Jessica, we talked about this. Elizabeth isn't right for us!
Yeah, but I've changed my mind. She'd be the perfect addition!
You can't do anything without your sister, huh? Grow up, Jessica, you're a big girl now!

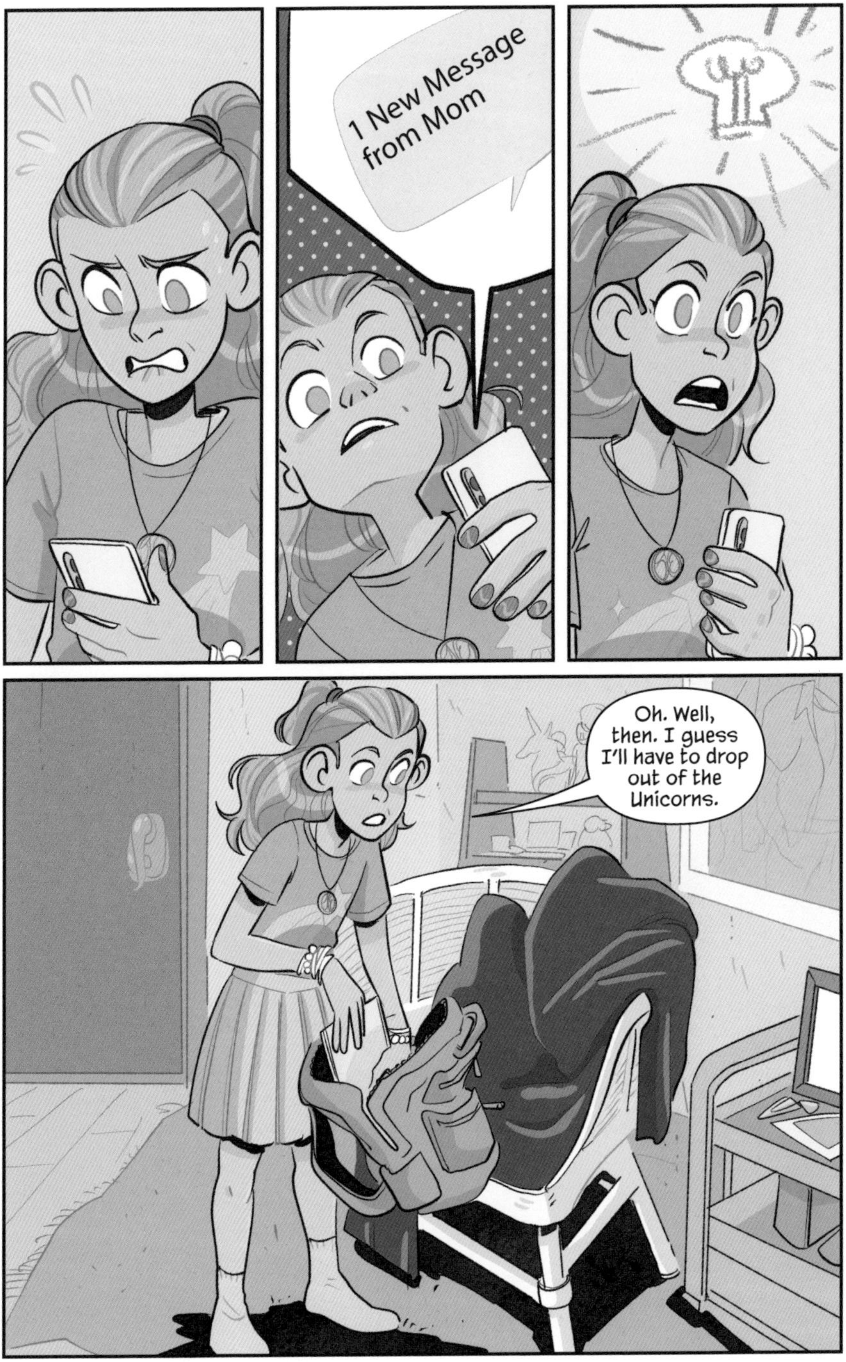
1 New Message from Mom
Oh. Well, then. I guess I'll have to drop out of the Unicorns.

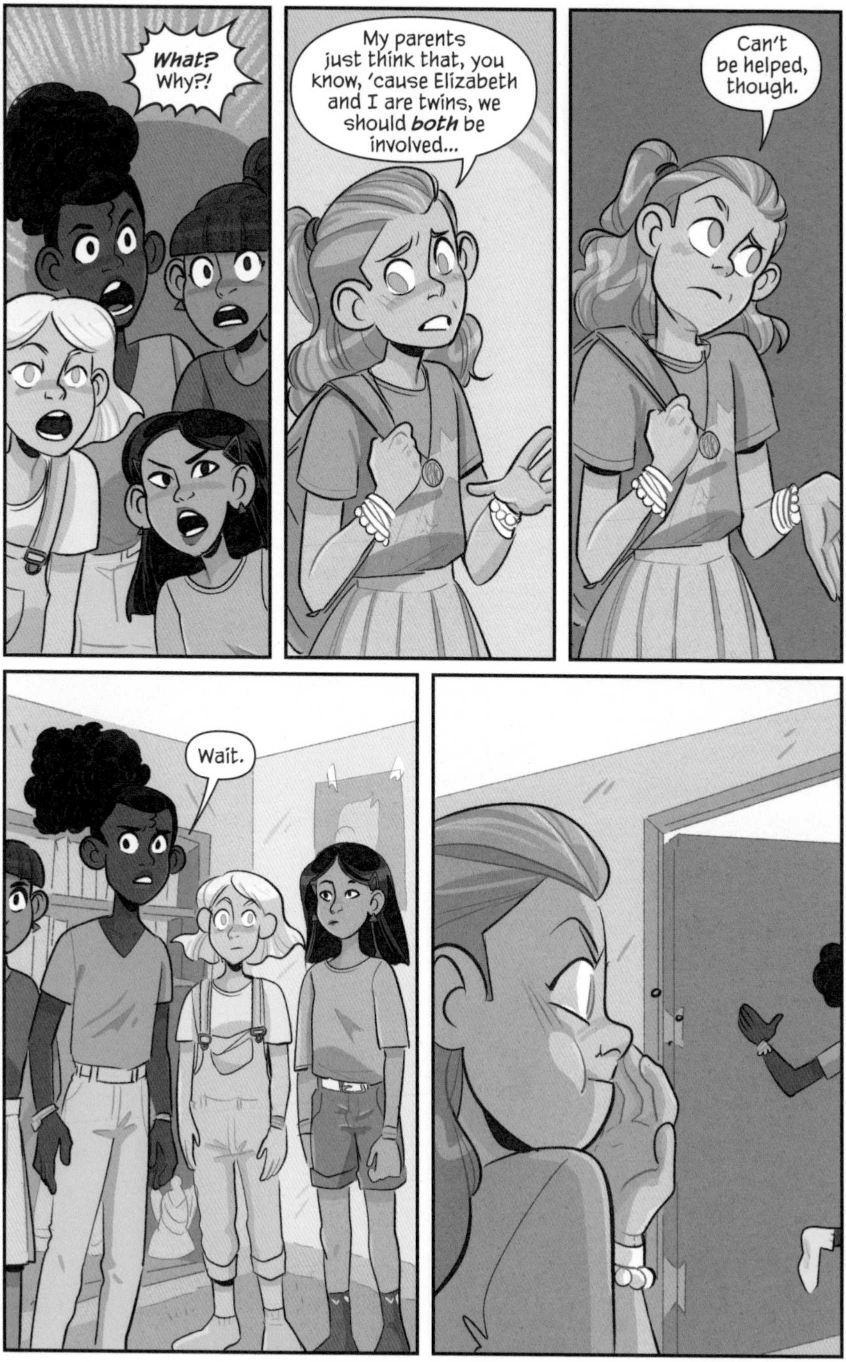
What? Why?!
My parents just think that, you know, 'cause Elizabeth and I are twins, we should both be involved...
Can't be helped, though.
Wait.

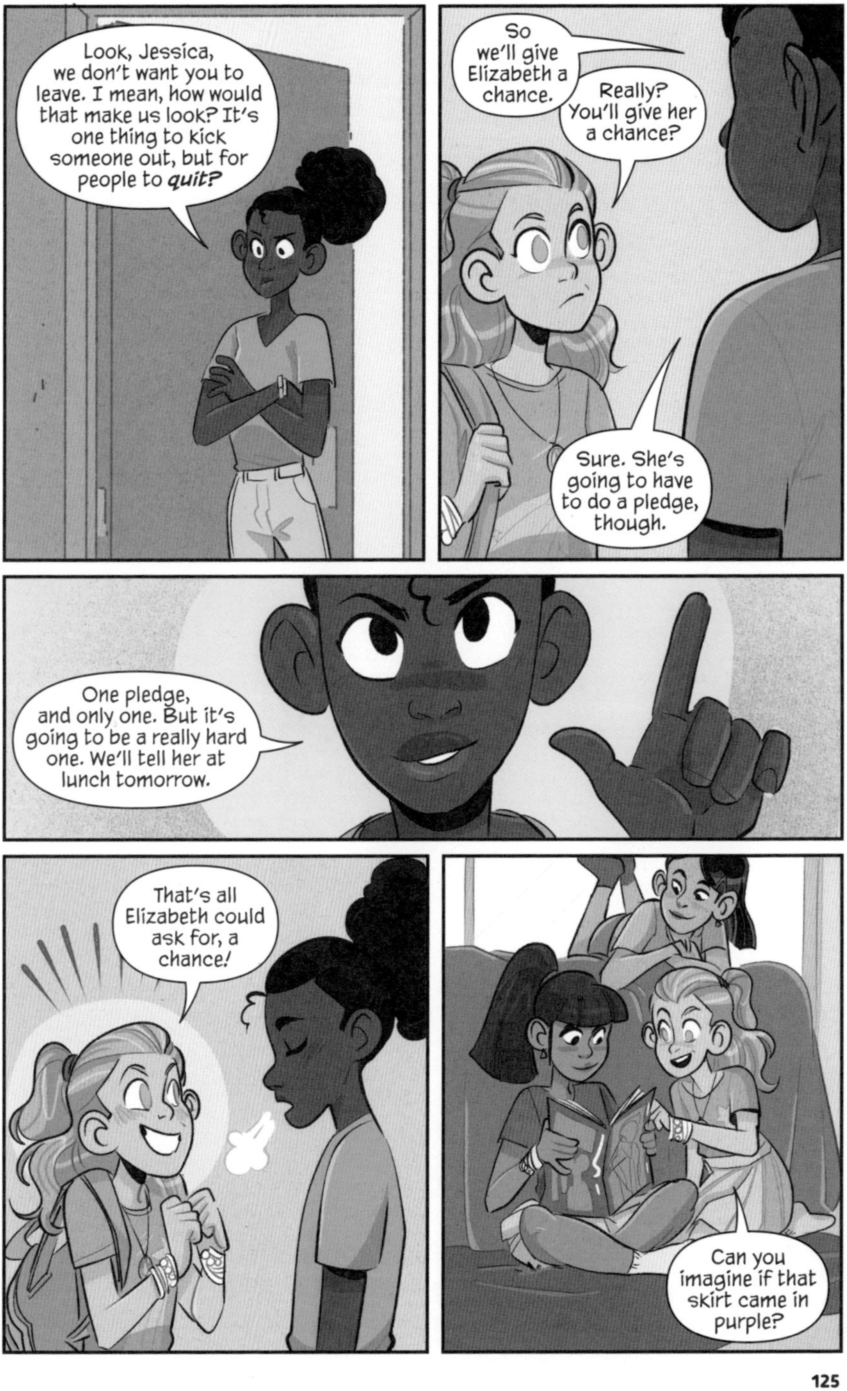
Look, Jessica, we don't want you to leave. I mean, how would that make us look? It's one thing to kick someone out, but for people to *quit?*
So we'll give Elizabeth a chance.
Really? You'll give her a chance?
Sure. She's going to have to do a pledge, though.
One pledge, and only one. But it's going to be a really hard one. We'll tell her at lunch tomorrow.
That's all Elizabeth could ask for, a chance!
Can you imagine if that skirt came in purple?

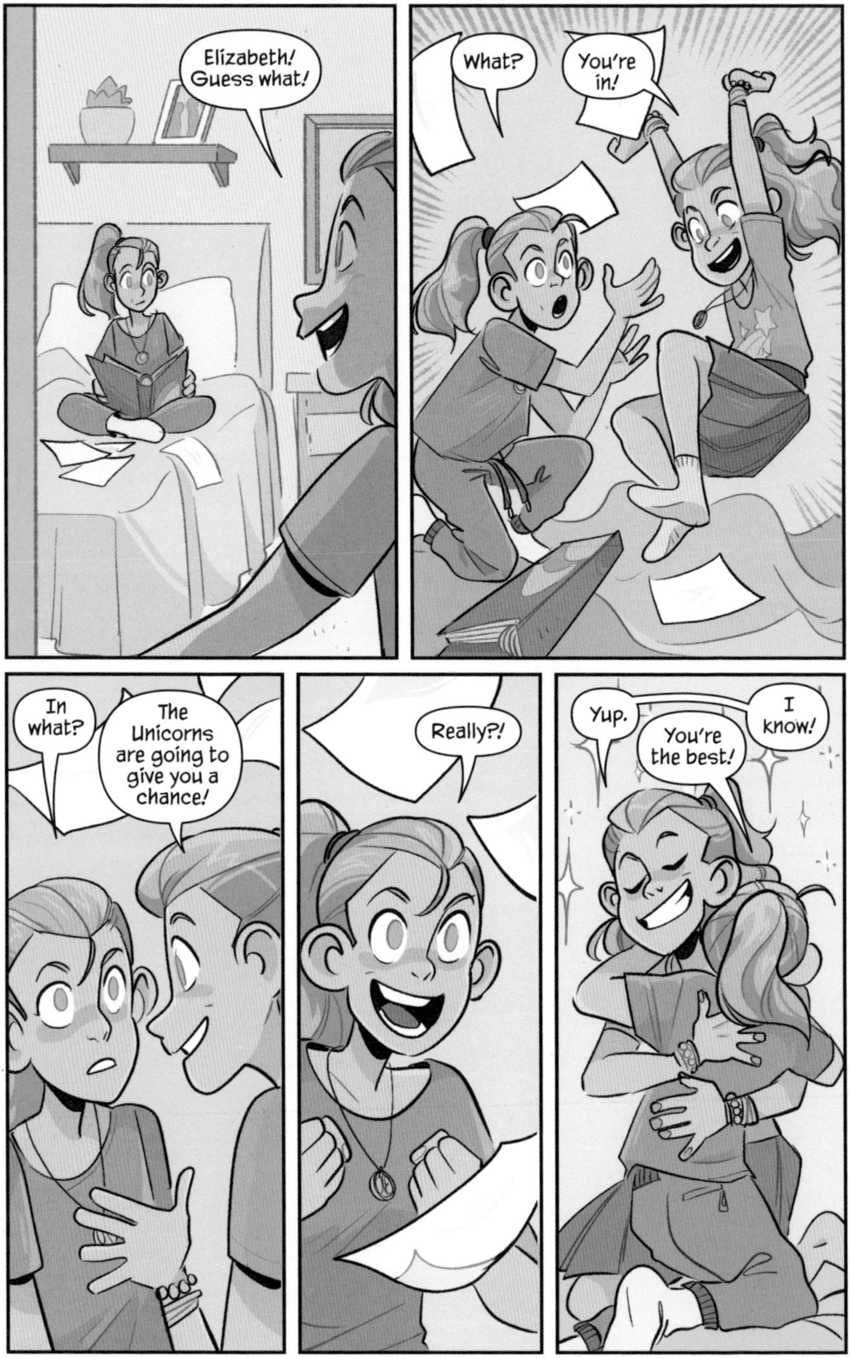

Elizabeth! Guess what!
What?
You're in!
In what?
The Unicorns are going to give you a chance!
Really?!
Yup.
You're the best!
I know!

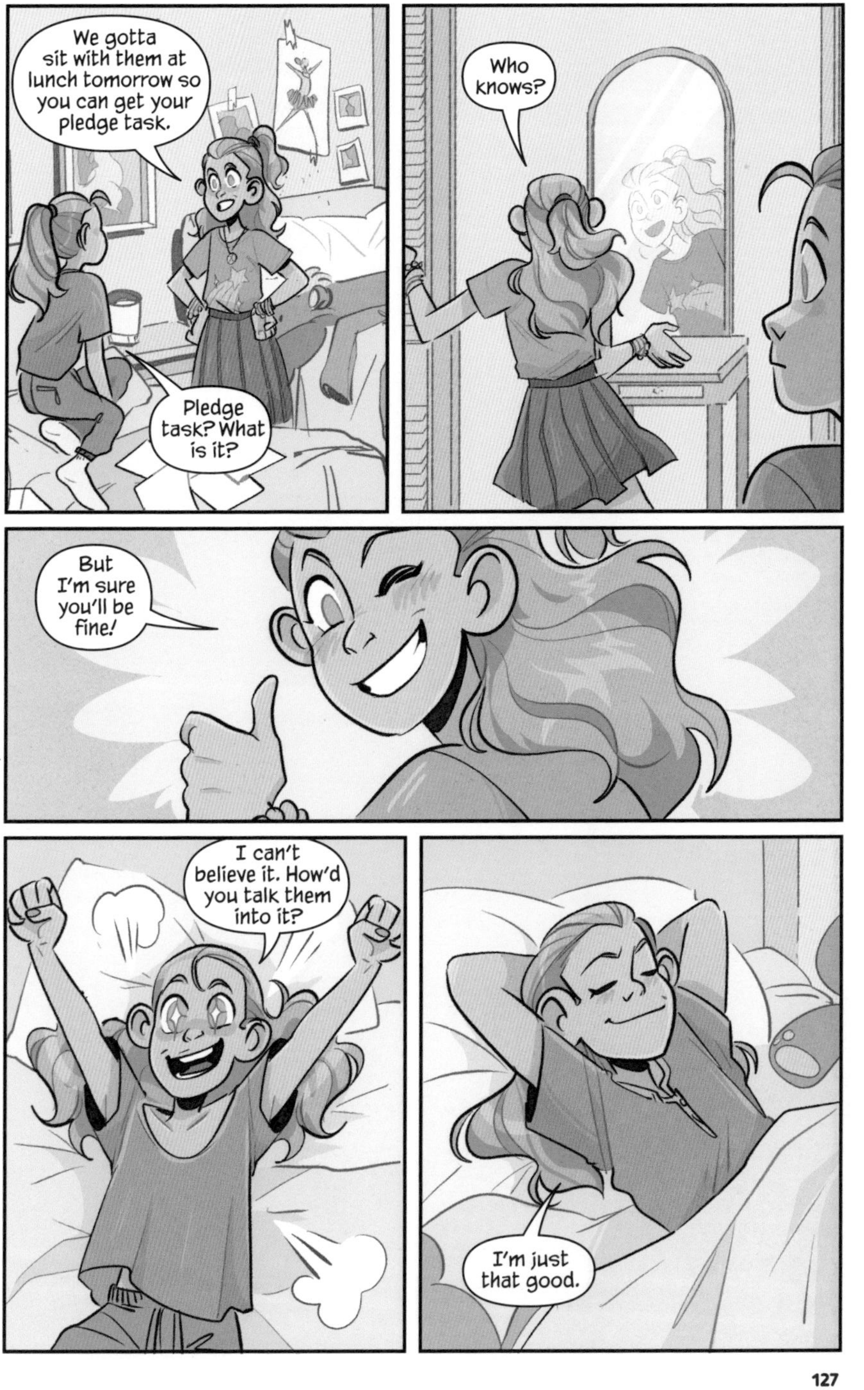
We gotta sit with them at lunch tomorrow so you can get your pledge task.
Pledge task? What is it?
Who knows?
But I'm sure you'll be fine!
I can't believe it. How'd you talk them into it?
I'm just that good.

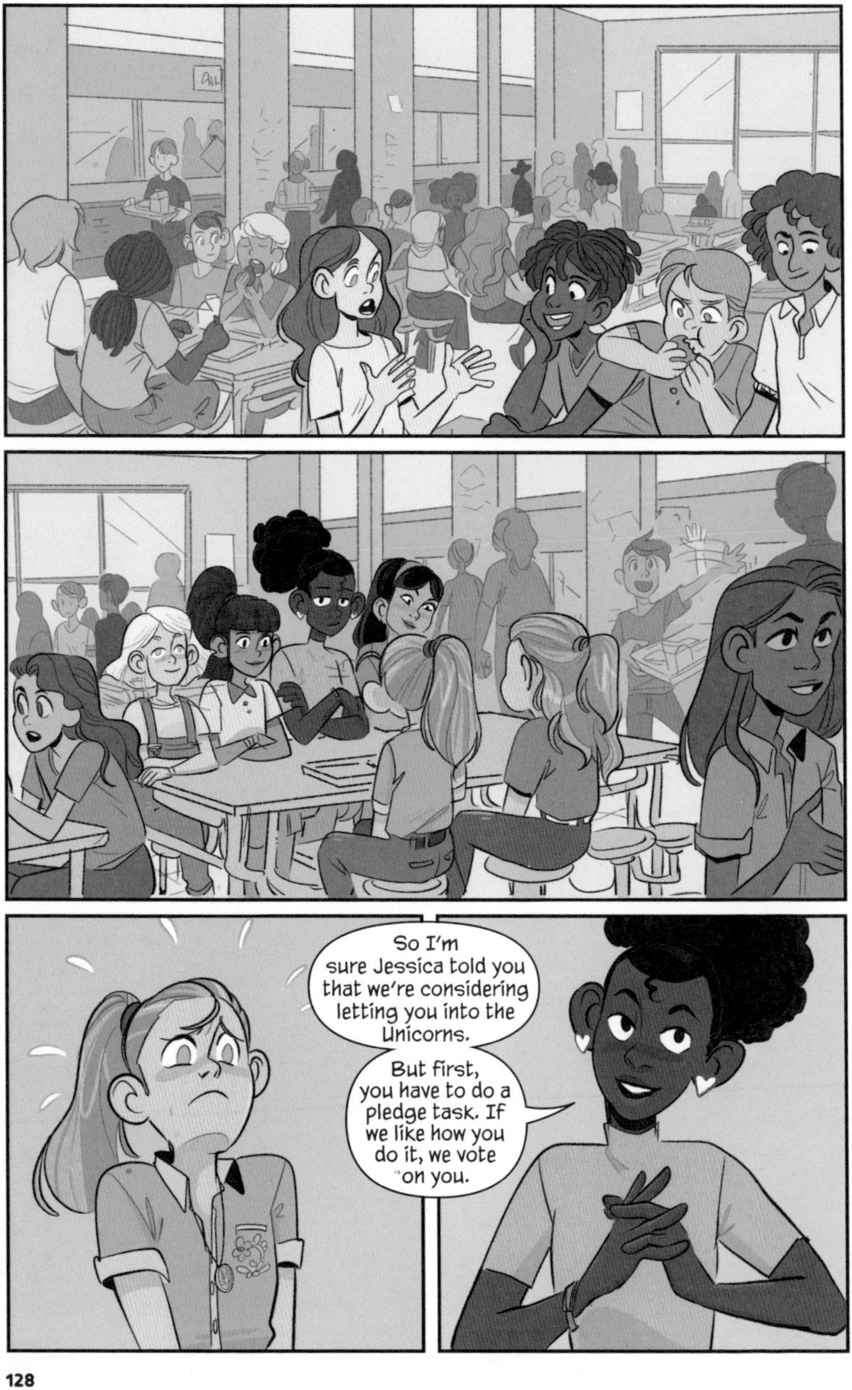
So I'm sure Jessica told you that we're considering letting you into the Unicorns.
But first, you have to do a pledge task. If we like how you do it, we vote on you.

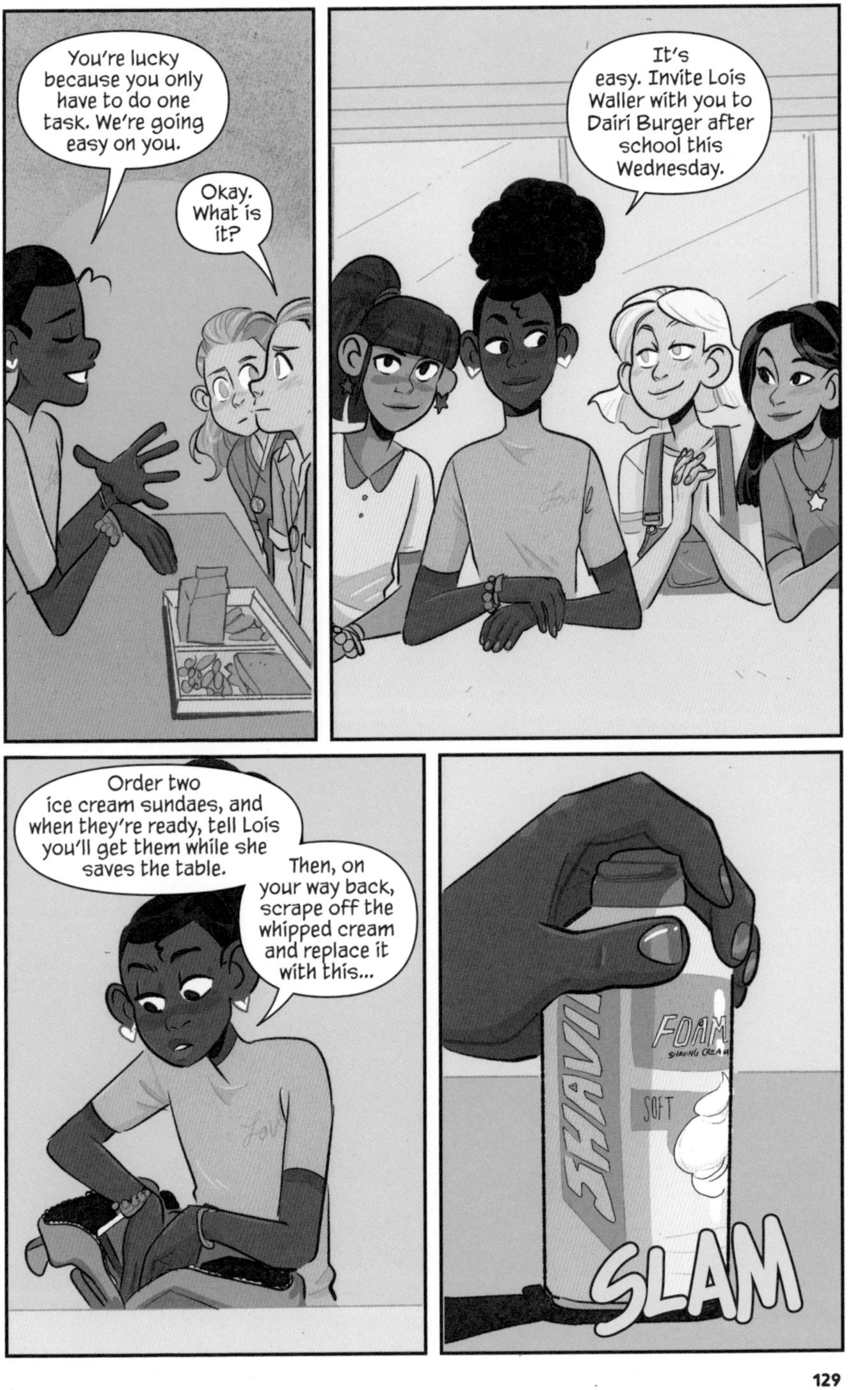
You're lucky because you only have to do one task. We're going easy on you.
Okay. What is it?
It's easy. Invite Lois Waller with you to Dairi Burger after school this Wednesday.
Order two ice cream sundaes, and when they're ready, tell Lois you'll get them while she saves the table.
Then, on your way back, scrape off the whipped cream and replace it with this...
FOAM
SHAVING CREAM
SOFT
SLAM

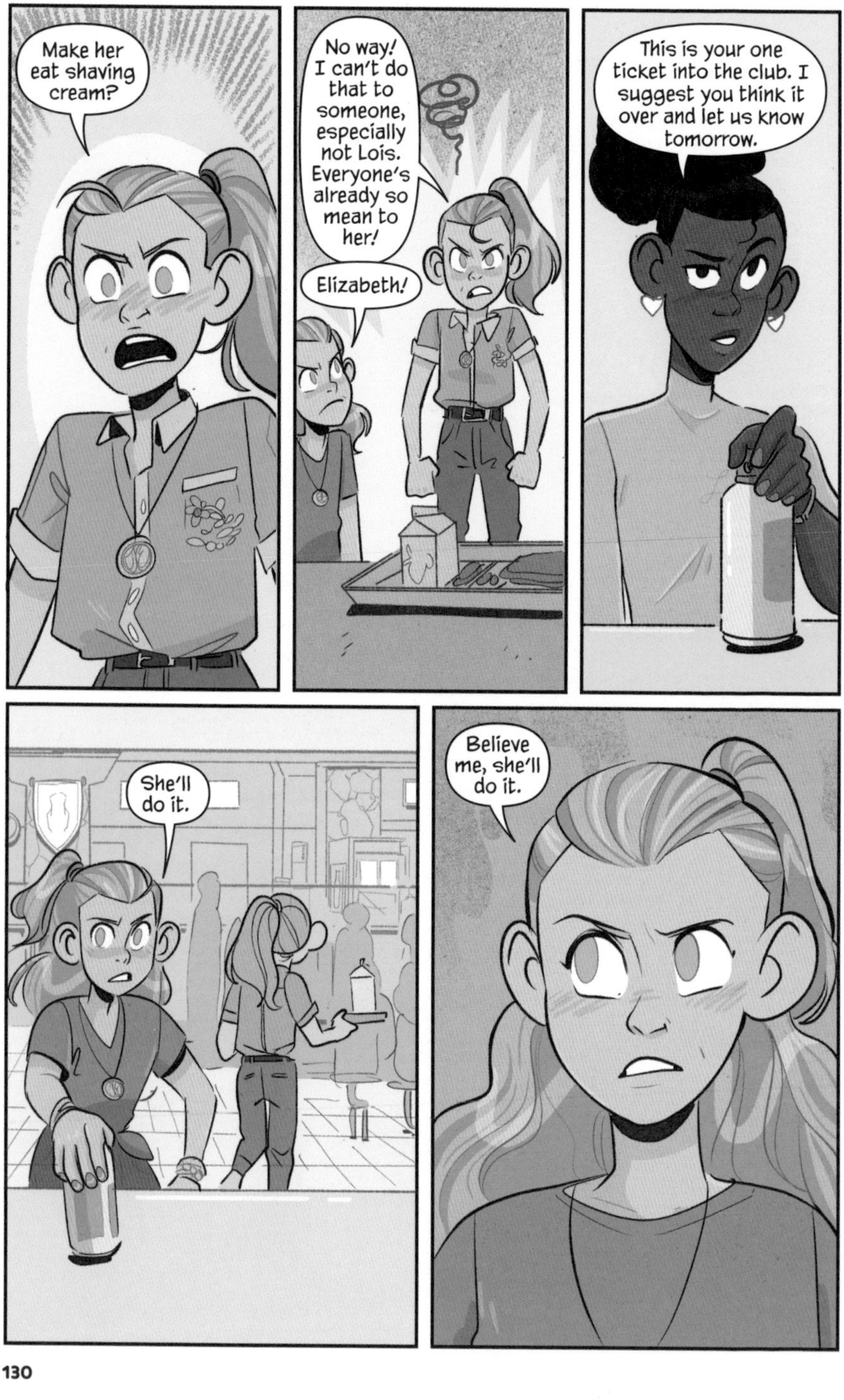
Make her eat shaving cream?
No way! I can't do that to someone, especially not Lois. Everyone's already so mean to her!
Elizabeth!
This is your one ticket into the club. I suggest you think it over and let us know tomorrow.
She'll do it.
Believe me, she'll do it.

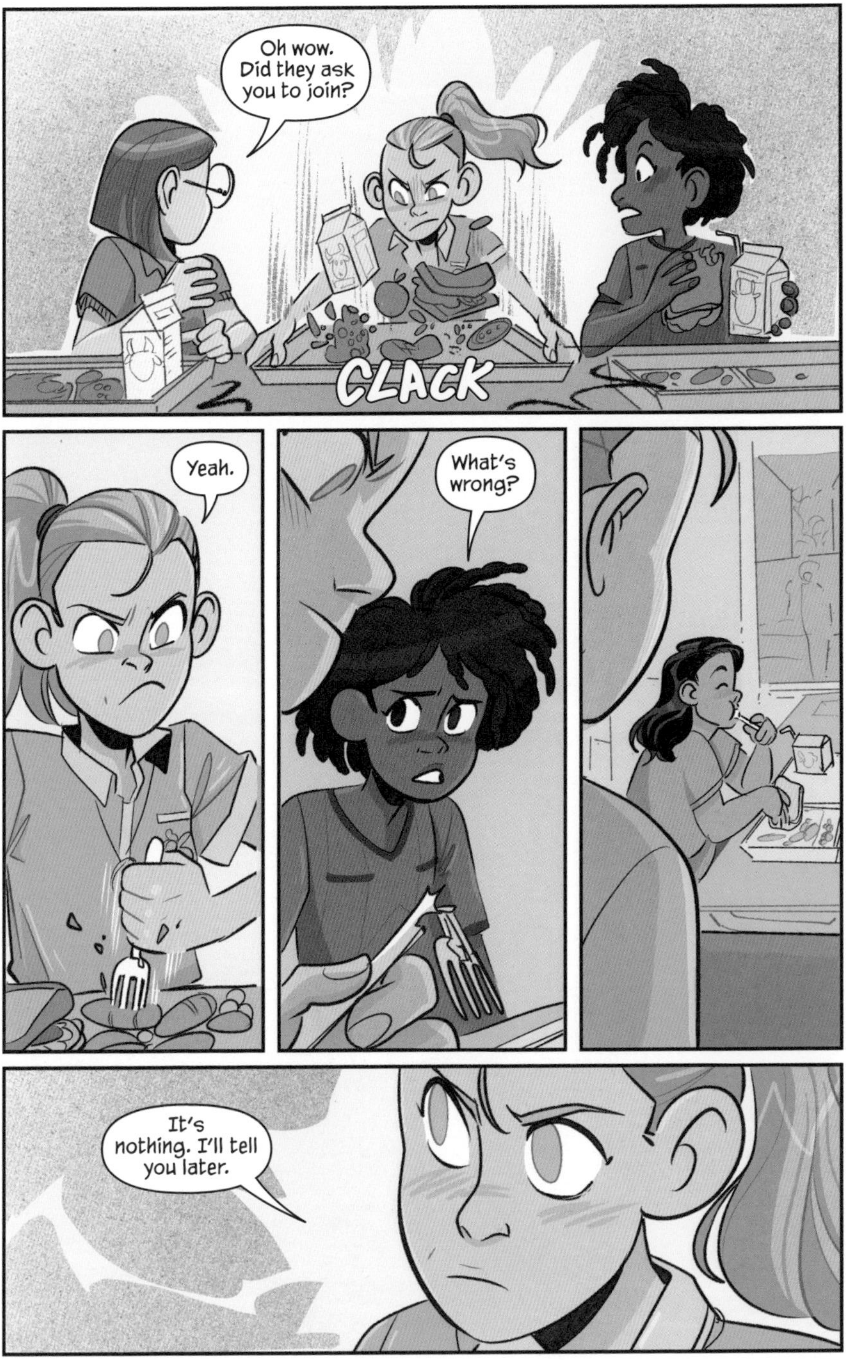
Oh wow. Did they ask you to join?
CLACK
Yeah.
What's wrong?
It's nothing. I'll tell you later.

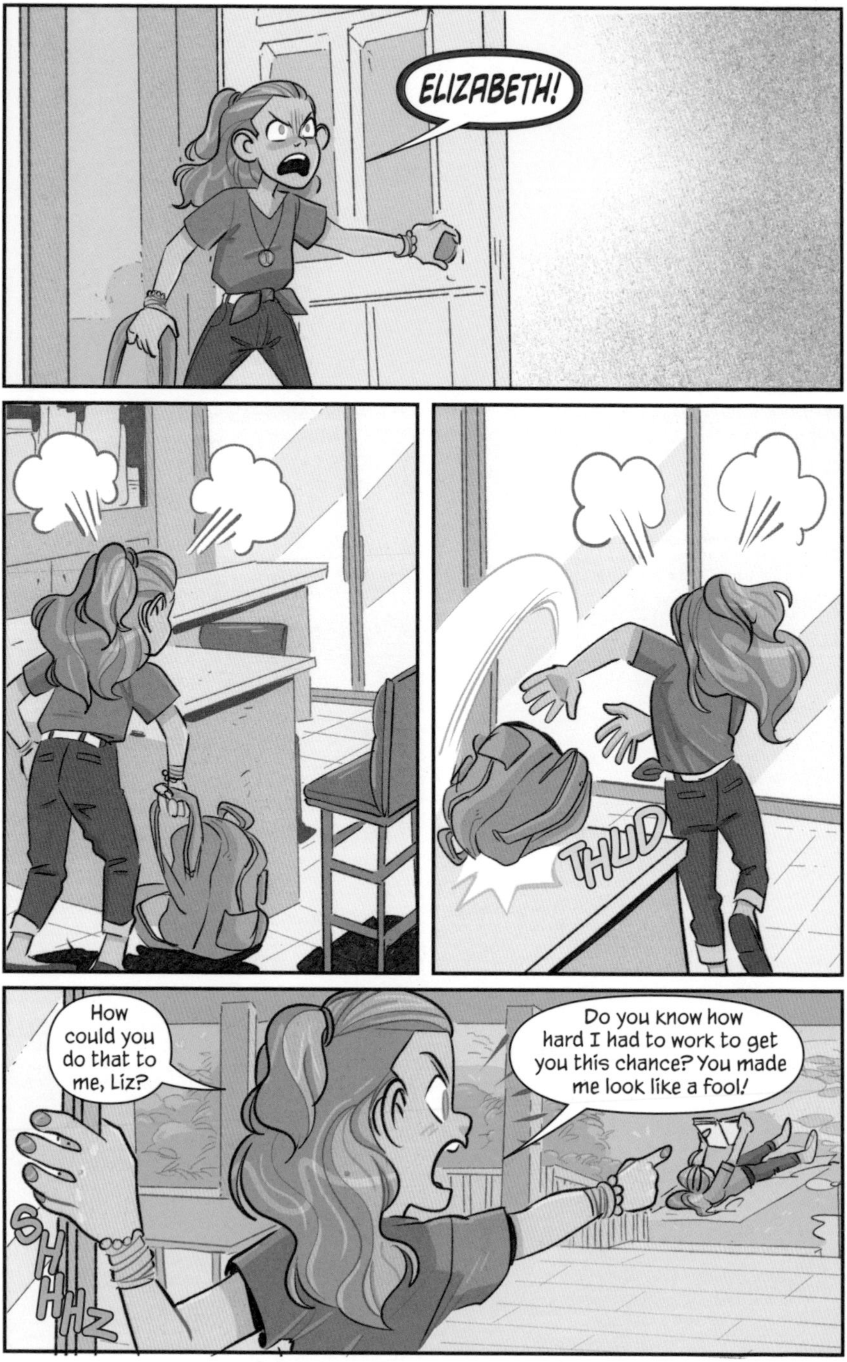
ELIZABETH!
THUD
How could you do that to me, Liz?
Do you know how hard I had to work to get you this chance? You made me look like a fool!
SHHHZ

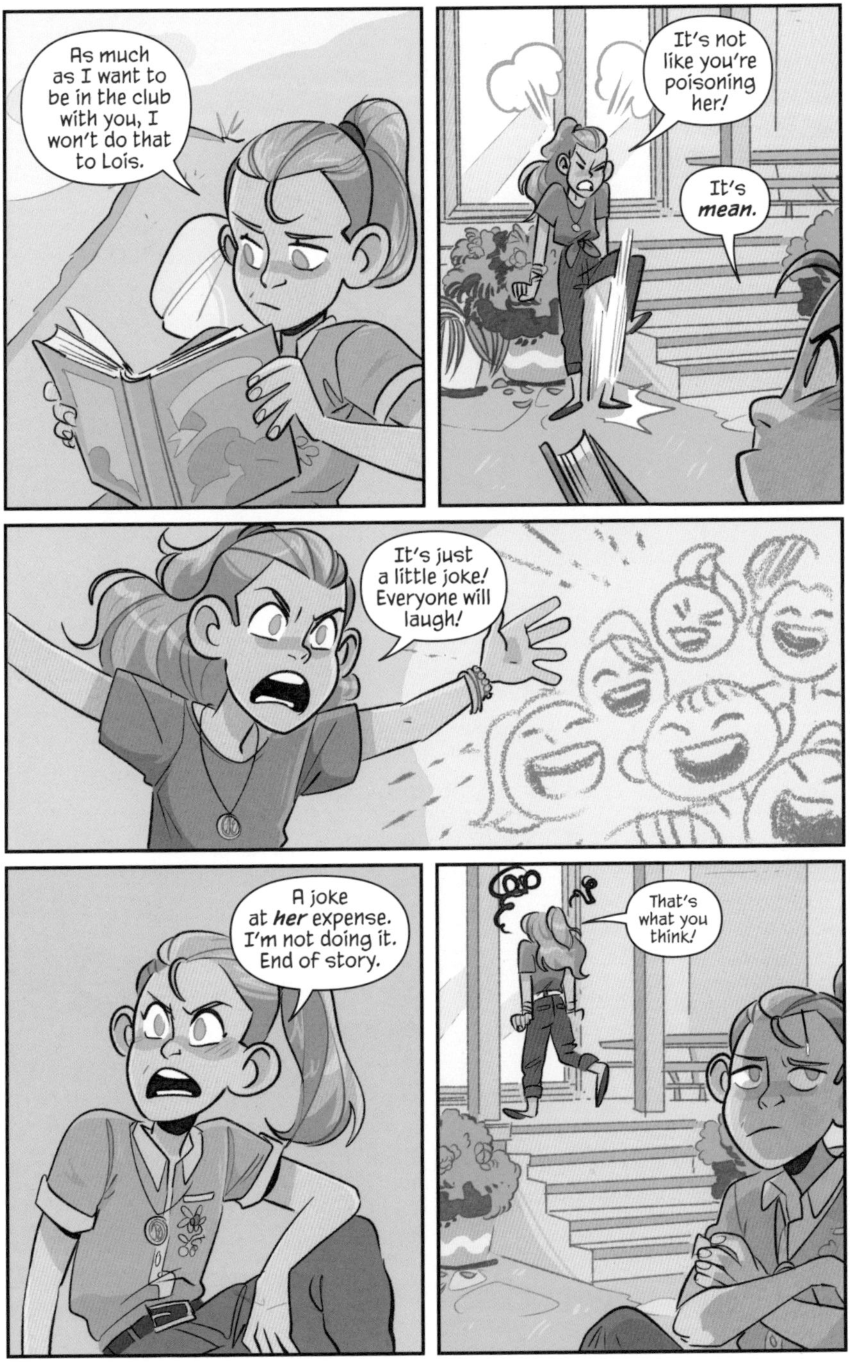
As much as I want to be in the club with you, I won't do that to Lois.
It's not like you're poisoning her!
It's *mean.*
It's just a little joke! Everyone will laugh!
A joke at *her* expense. I'm not doing it. End of story.
That's what you think!

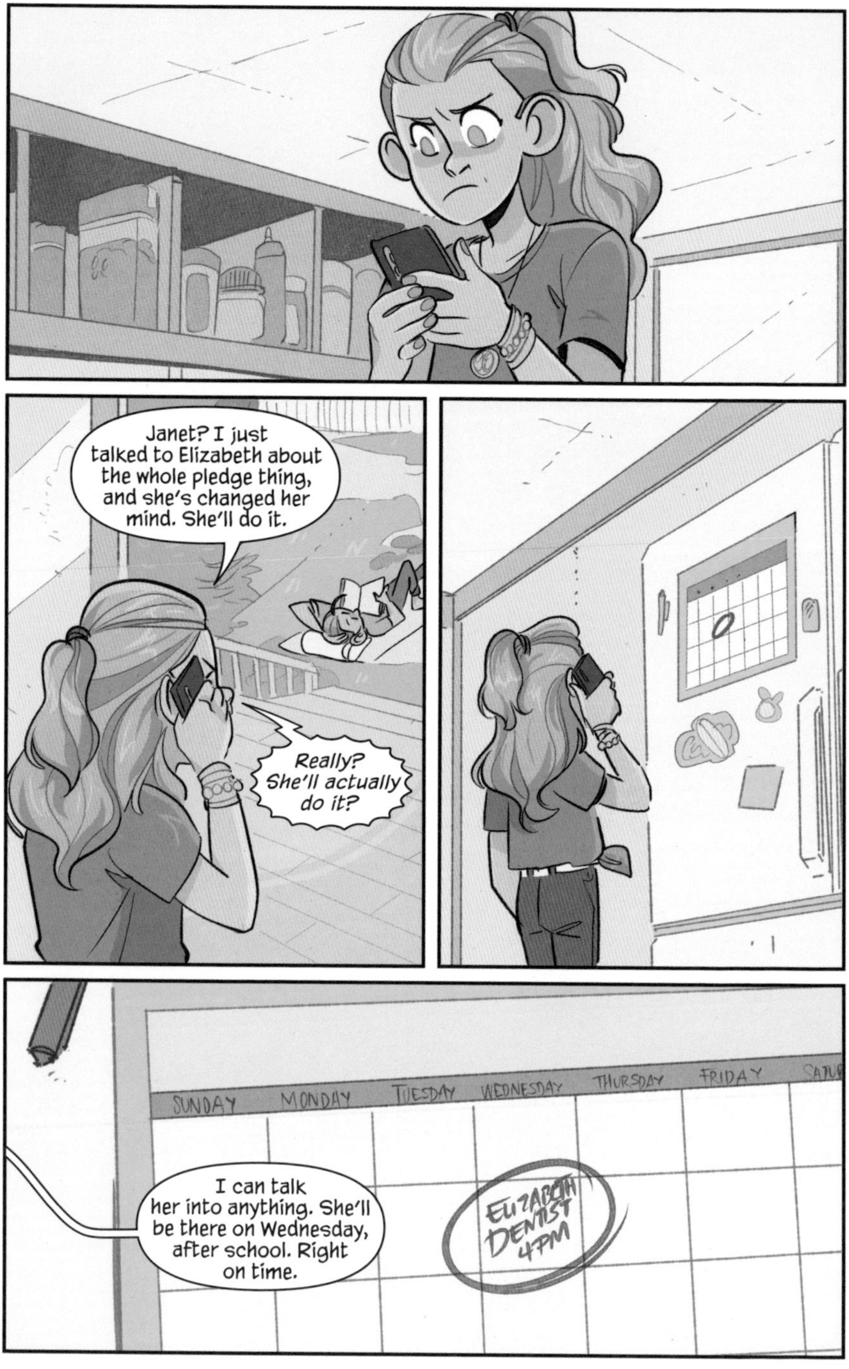
Janet? I just talked to Elizabeth about the whole pledge thing, and she's changed her mind. She'll do it.
Really? She'll actually do it?
SUNDAY MONDAY TUESDAY WEDNESDAY THURSDAY FRIDAY
ELIZABETH DENTIST 4PM
I can talk her into anything. She'll be there on Wednesday, after school. Right on time.

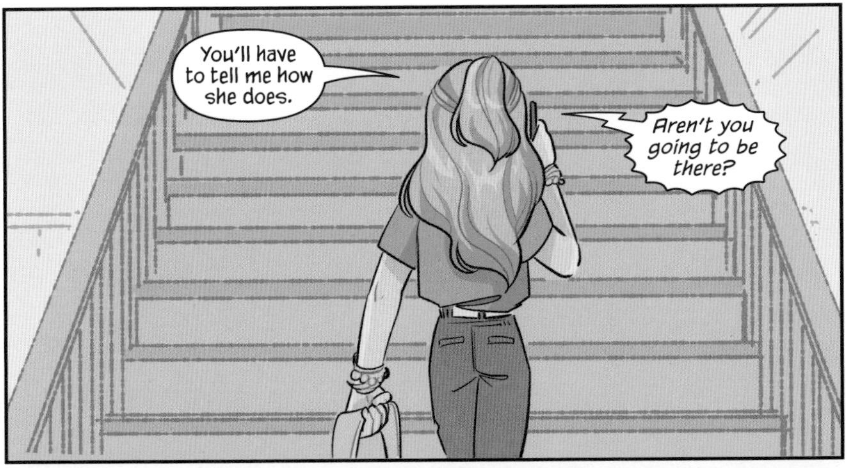
You'll have to tell me how she does.
Aren't you going to be there?

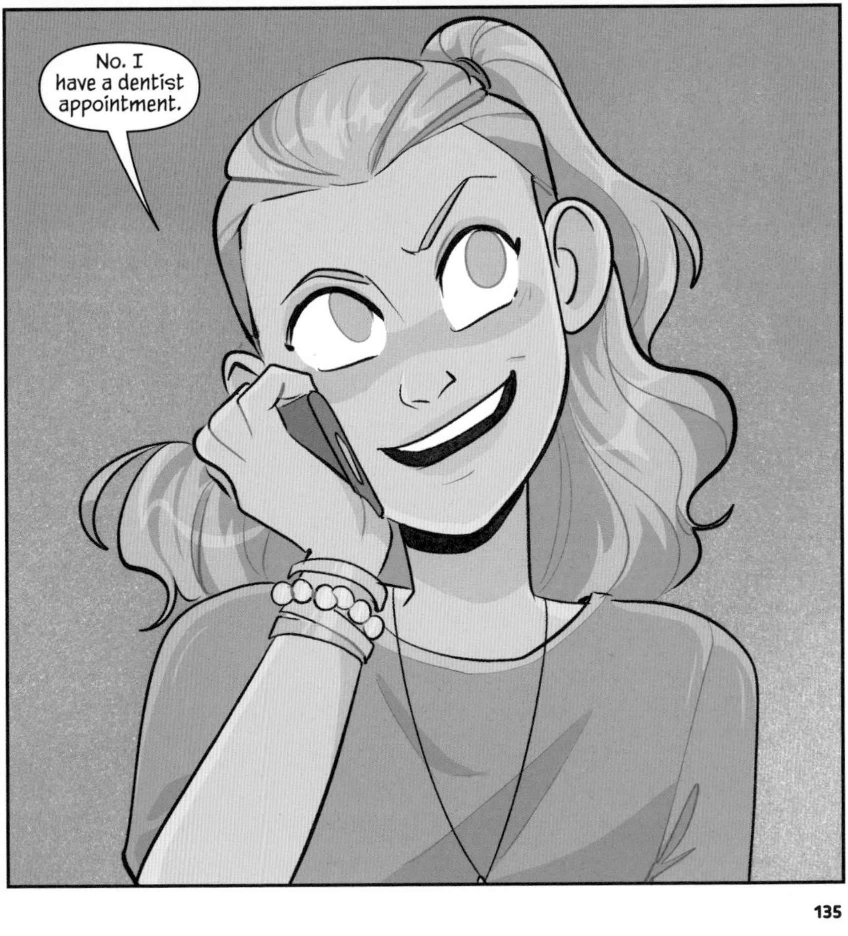
No. I have a dentist appointment.

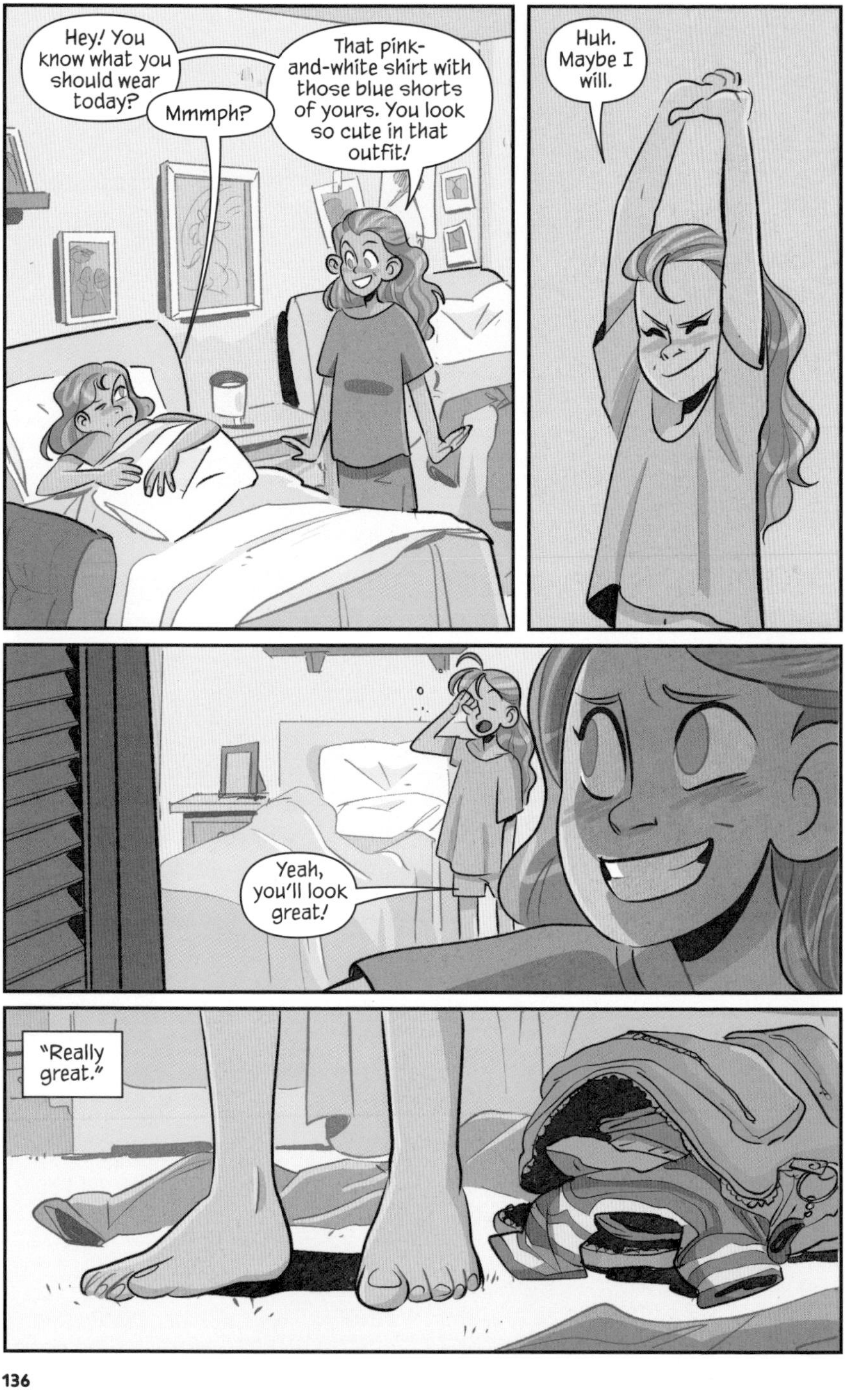
Hey! You know what you should wear today?
Mmmph?
That pink-and-white shirt with those blue shorts of yours. You look so cute in that outfit!
Huh. Maybe I will.
Yeah, you'll look great!
"Really great."

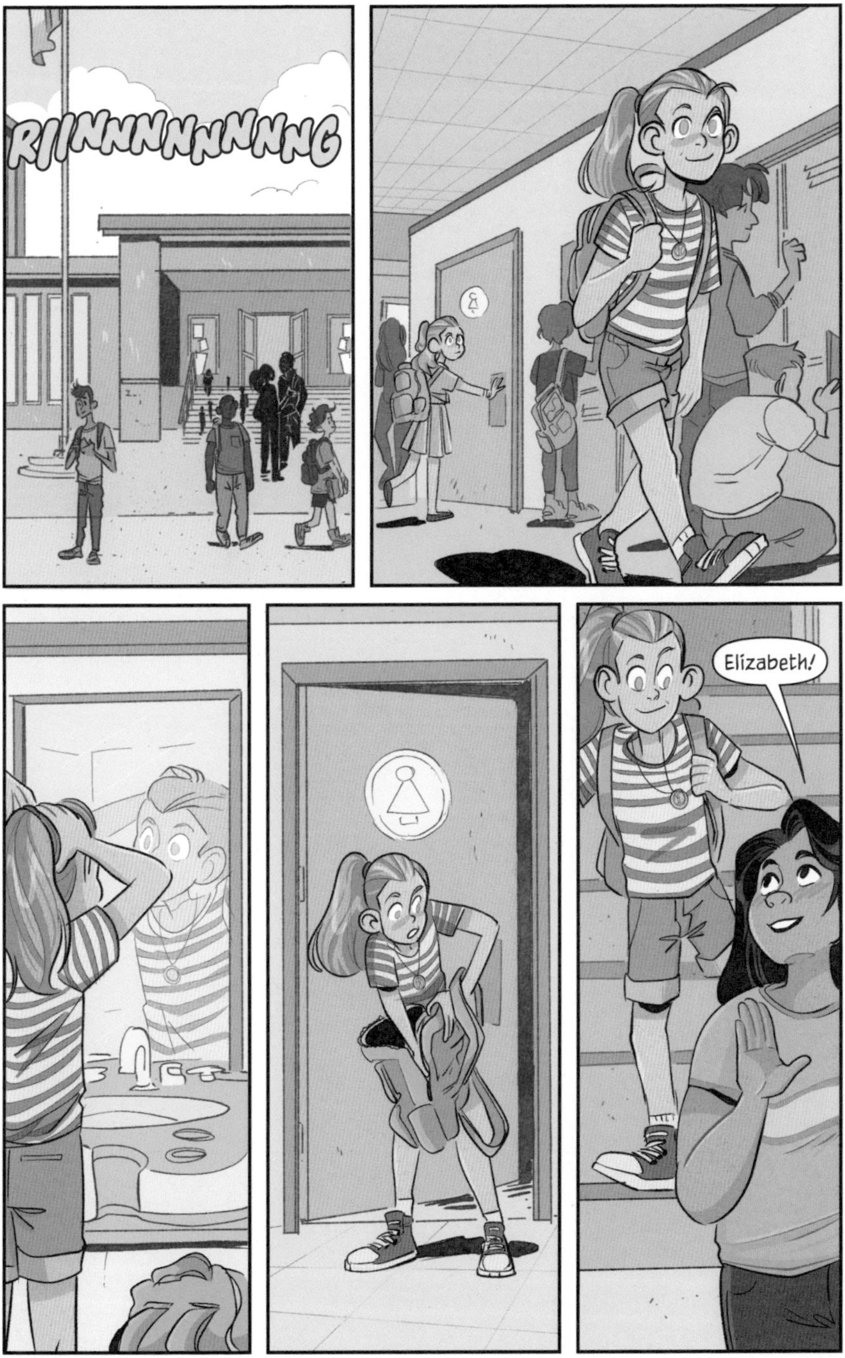
RIINNNNNNNNNG
Elizabeth!

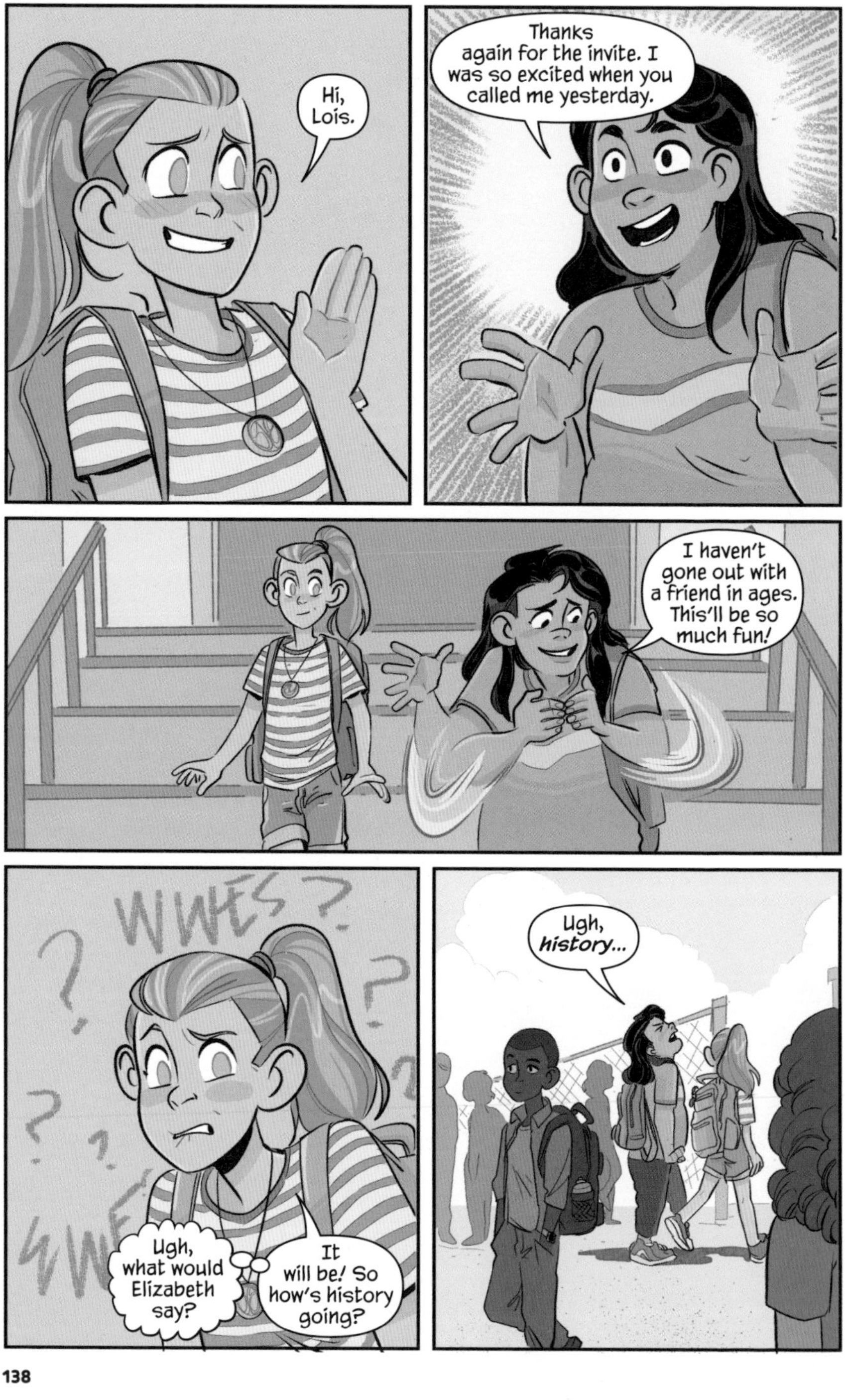
Hi, Lois.
Thanks again for the invite. I was so excited when you called me yesterday.
I haven't gone out with a friend in ages. This'll be so much fun!
WWES?
Ugh, what would Elizabeth say?
It will be! So how's history going?
Ugh, *history*...

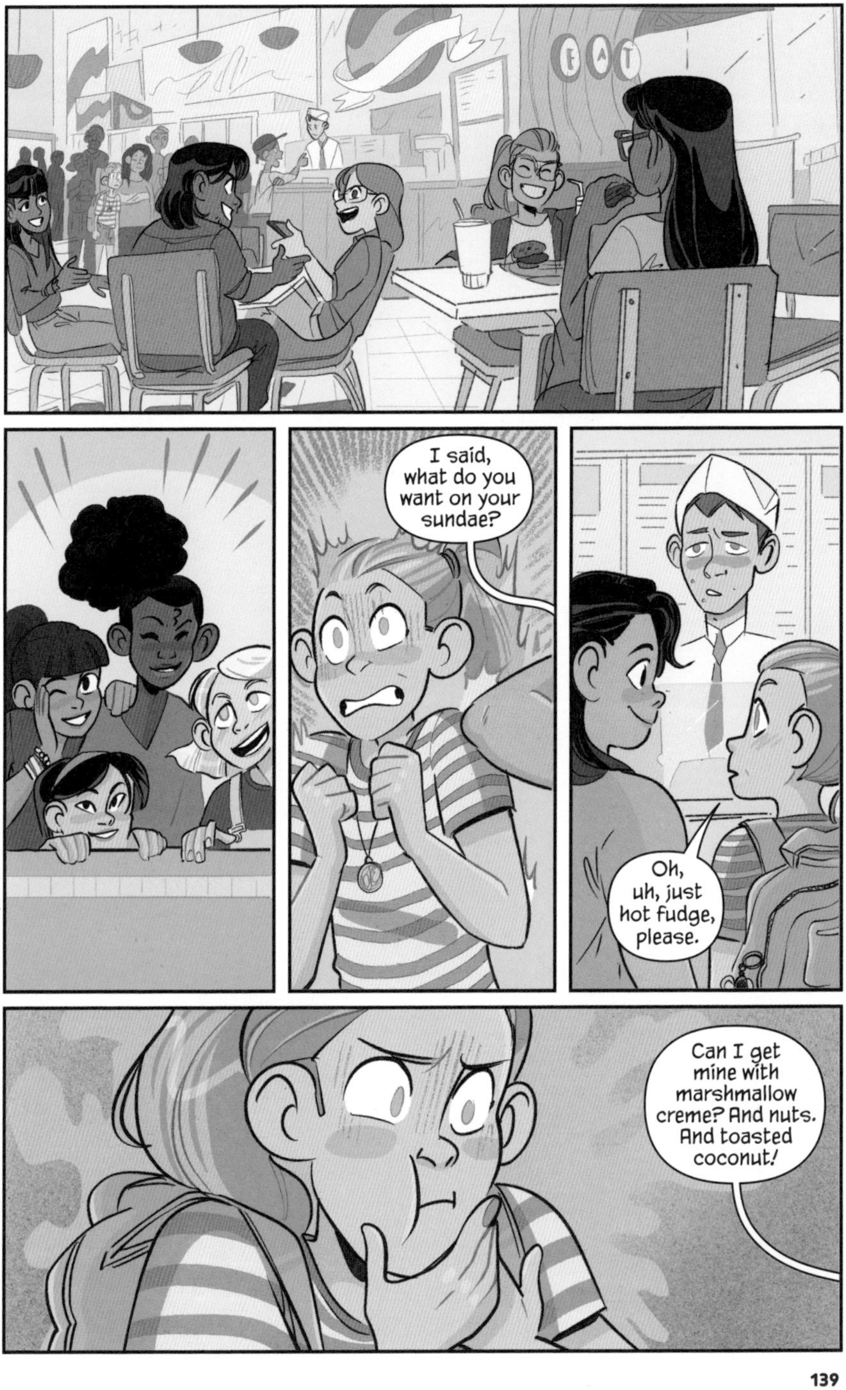
EAT
I said, what do you want on your sundae?
Oh, uh, just hot fudge, please.
Can I get mine with marshmallow creme? And nuts. And toasted coconut!

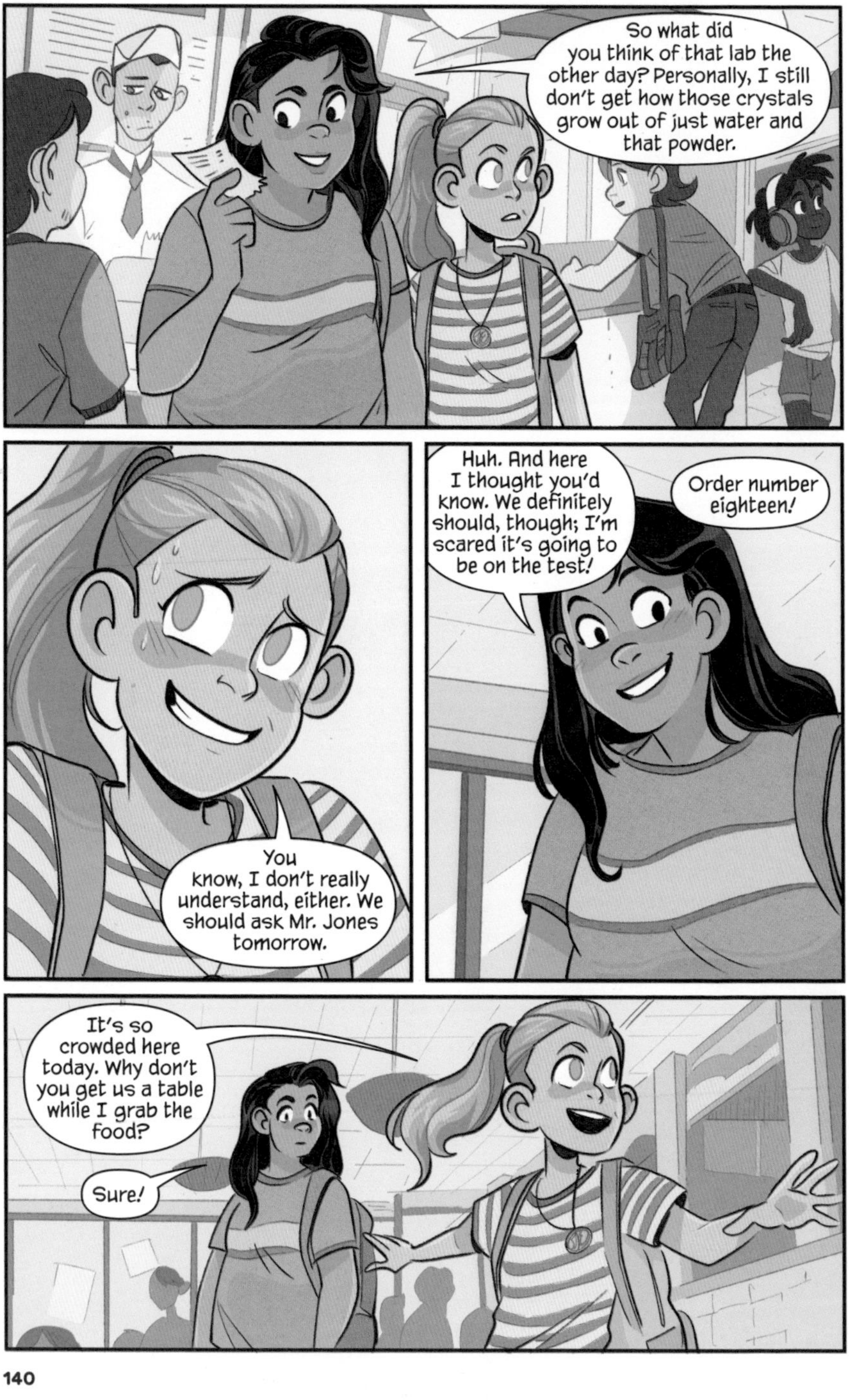

So what did you think of that lab the other day? Personally, I still don't get how those crystals grow out of just water and that powder.
You know, I don't really understand, either. We should ask Mr. Jones tomorrow.
Huh. And here I thought you'd know. We definitely should, though; I'm scared it's going to be on the test!
Order number eighteen!
It's so crowded here today. Why don't you get us a table while I grab the food?
Sure!

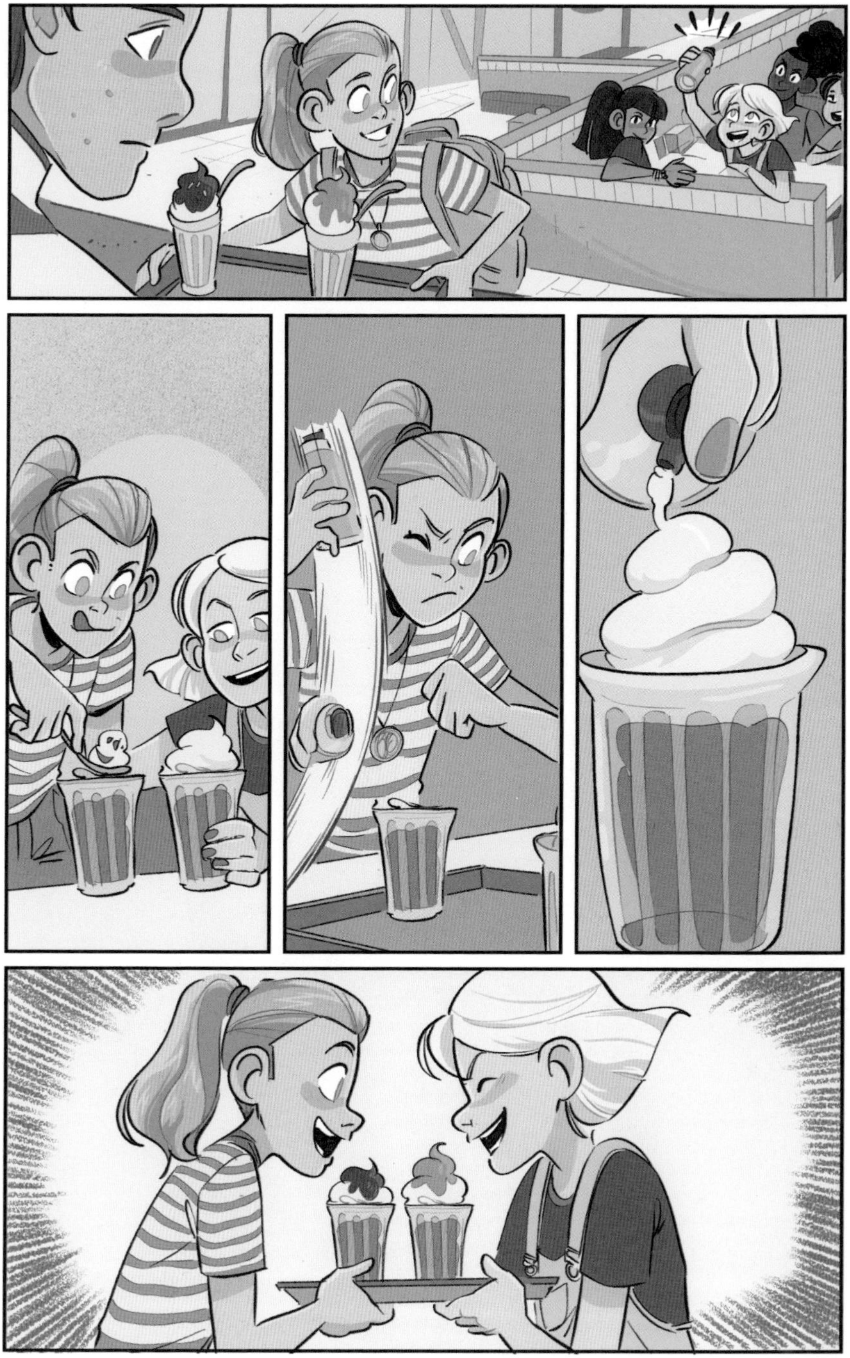

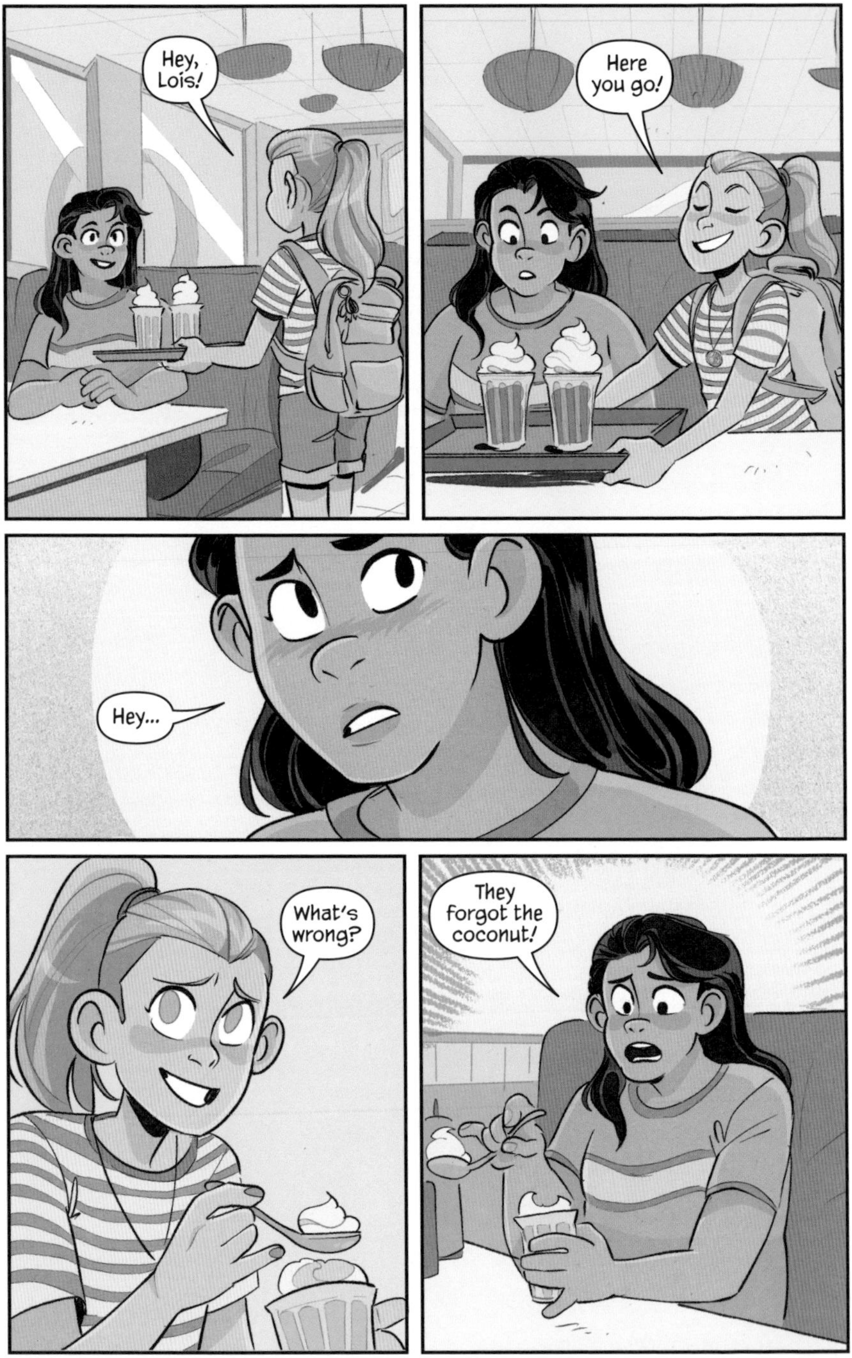
Hey, Lois!
Here you go!
Hey...
What's wrong?
They forgot the coconut!

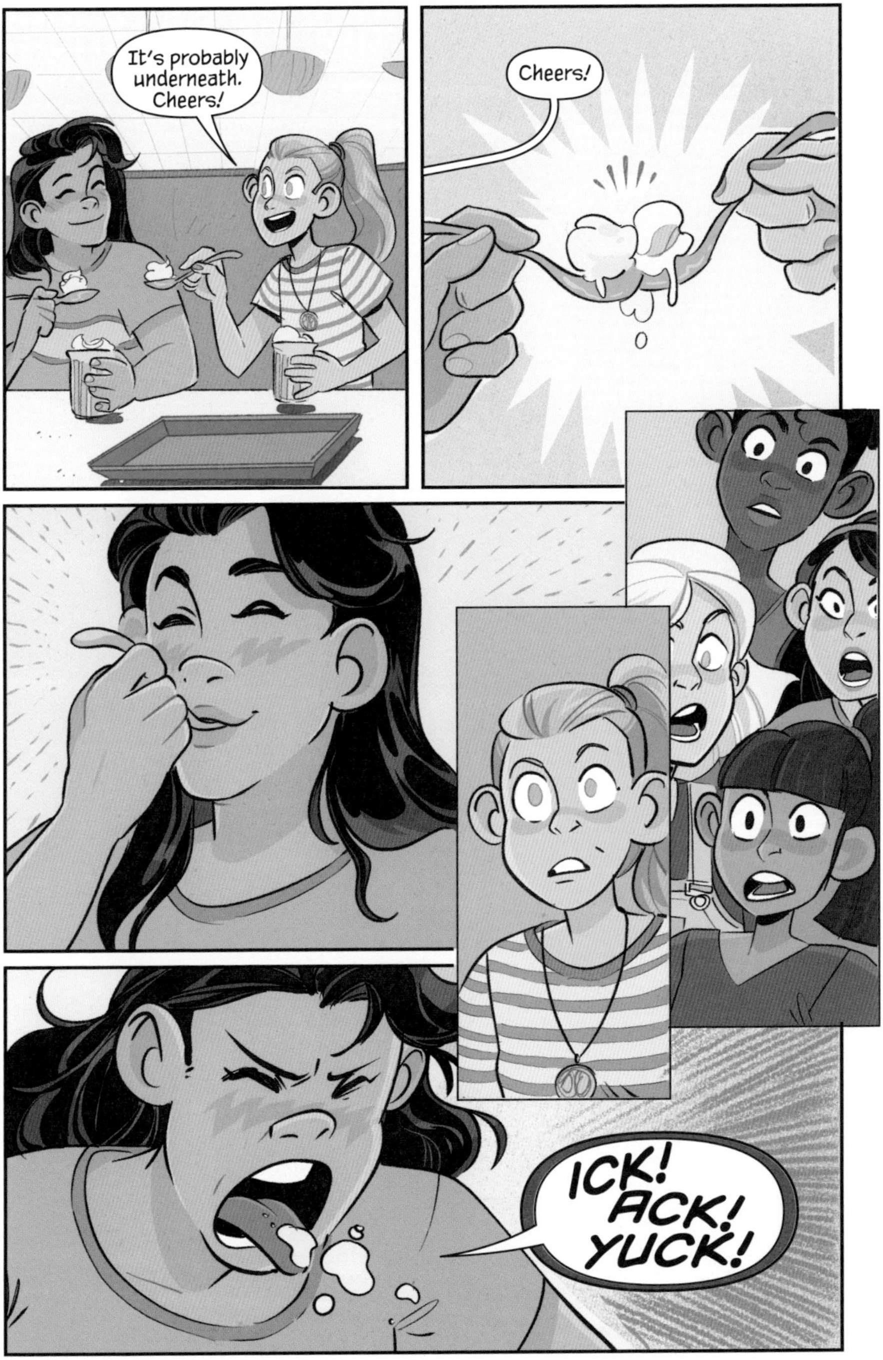
It's probably underneath. Cheers!
Cheers!
ICK! ACK! YUCK!

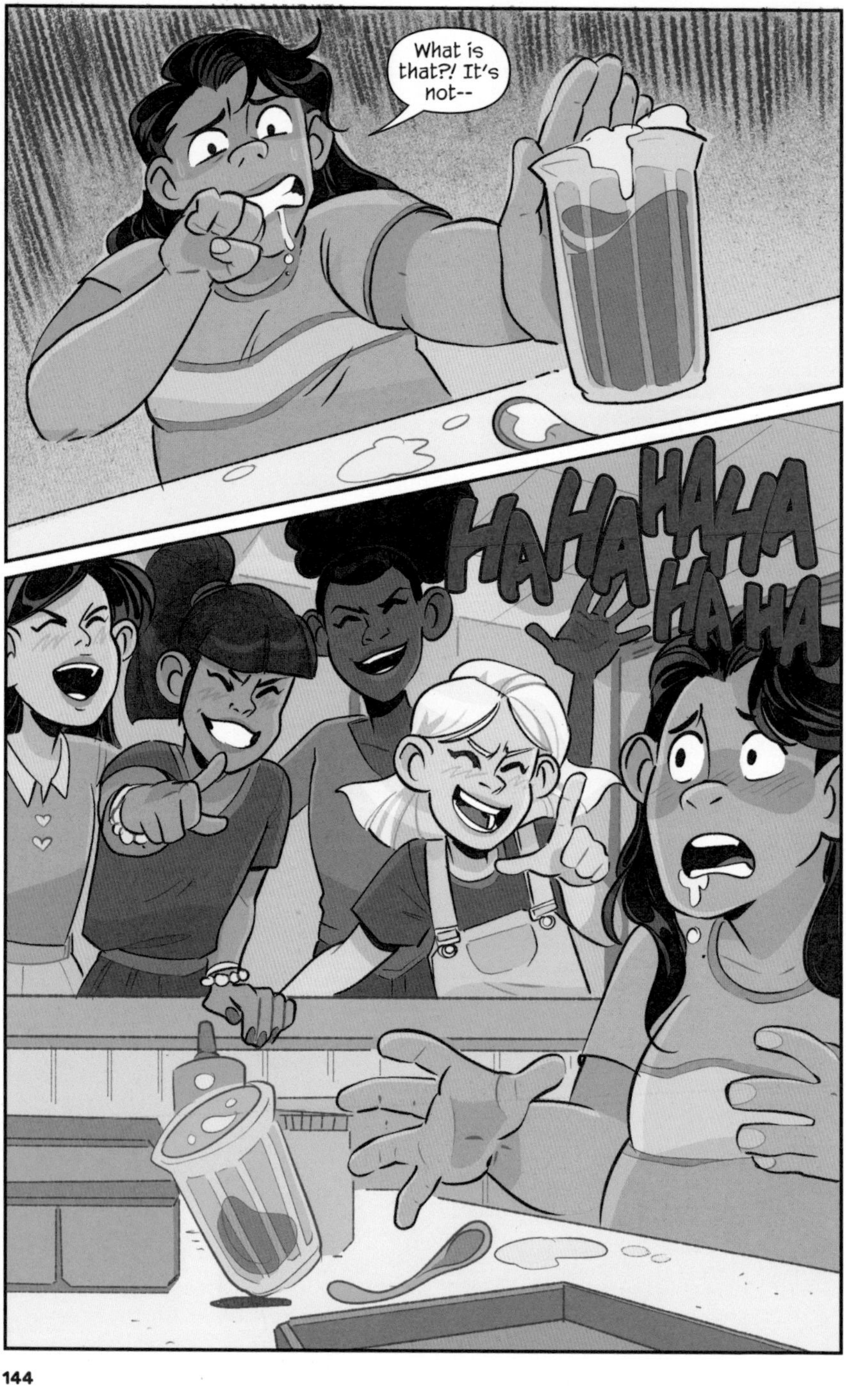
What is that?! It's not--
HAHAHAHA
HAHA
HAHA

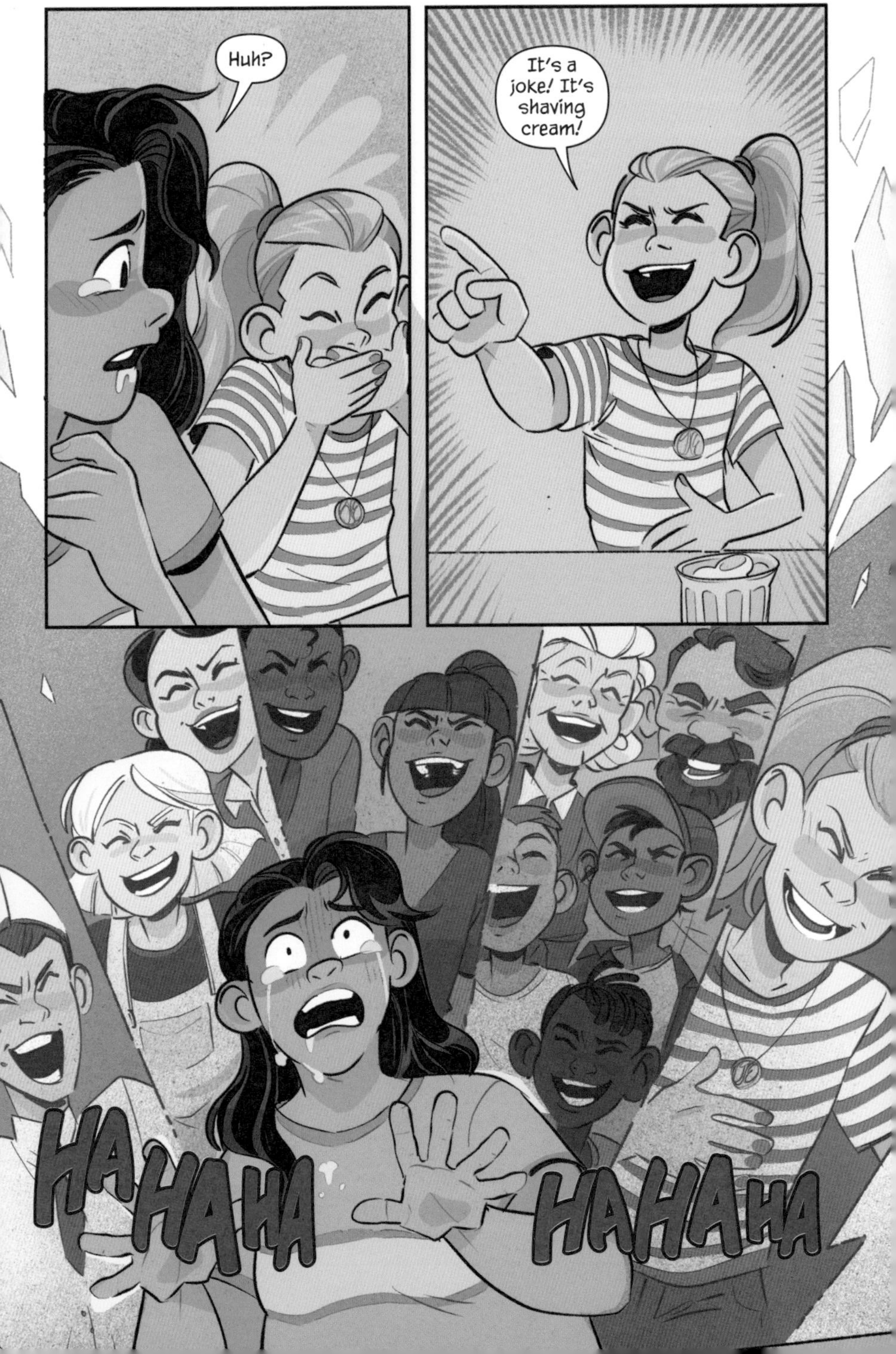
Huh?
It's a joke! It's shaving cream!
HA HA HAHA
HAHAHAHA

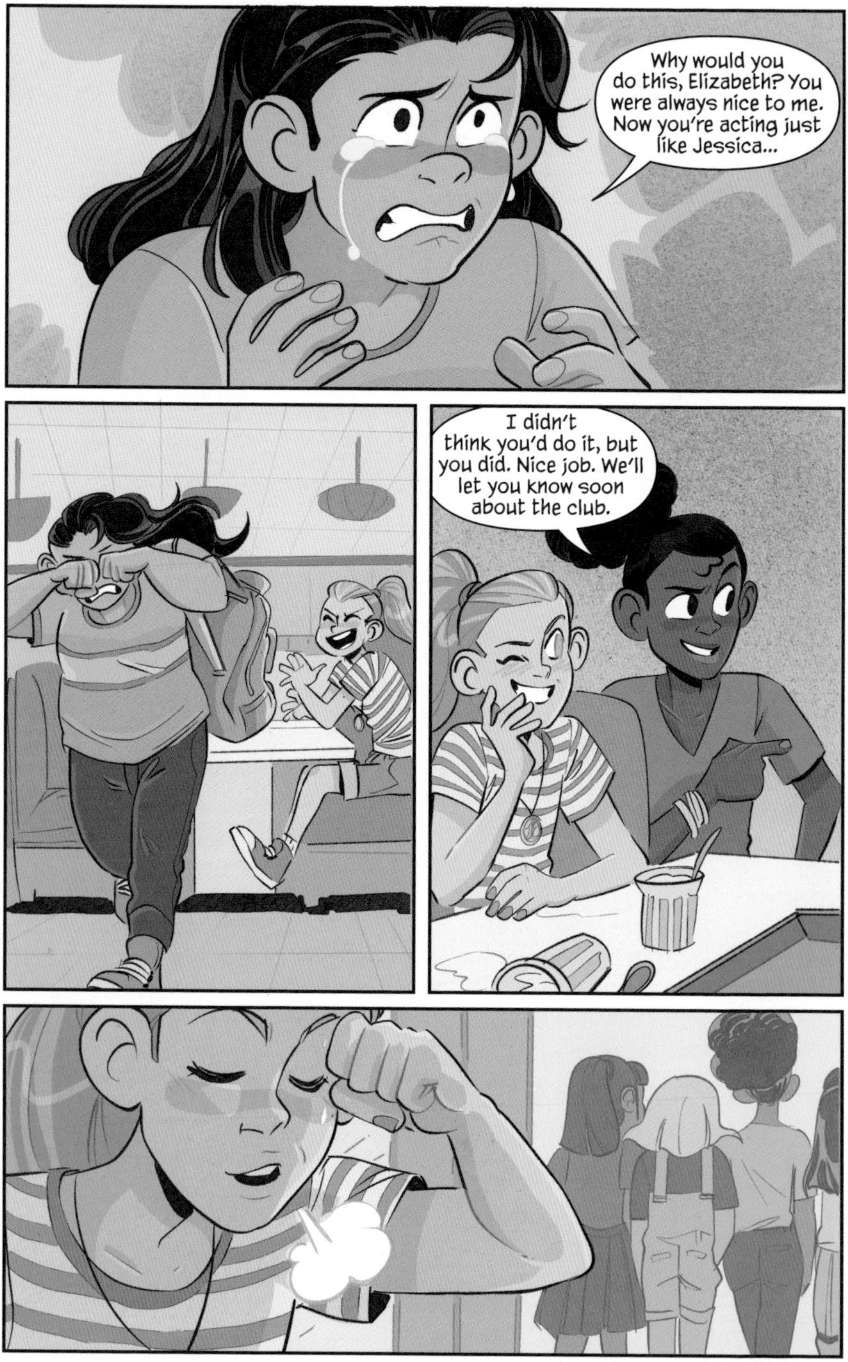
Why would you do this, Elizabeth? You were always nice to me. Now you're acting just like Jessica...
I didn't think you'd do it, but you did. Nice job. We'll let you know soon about the club.

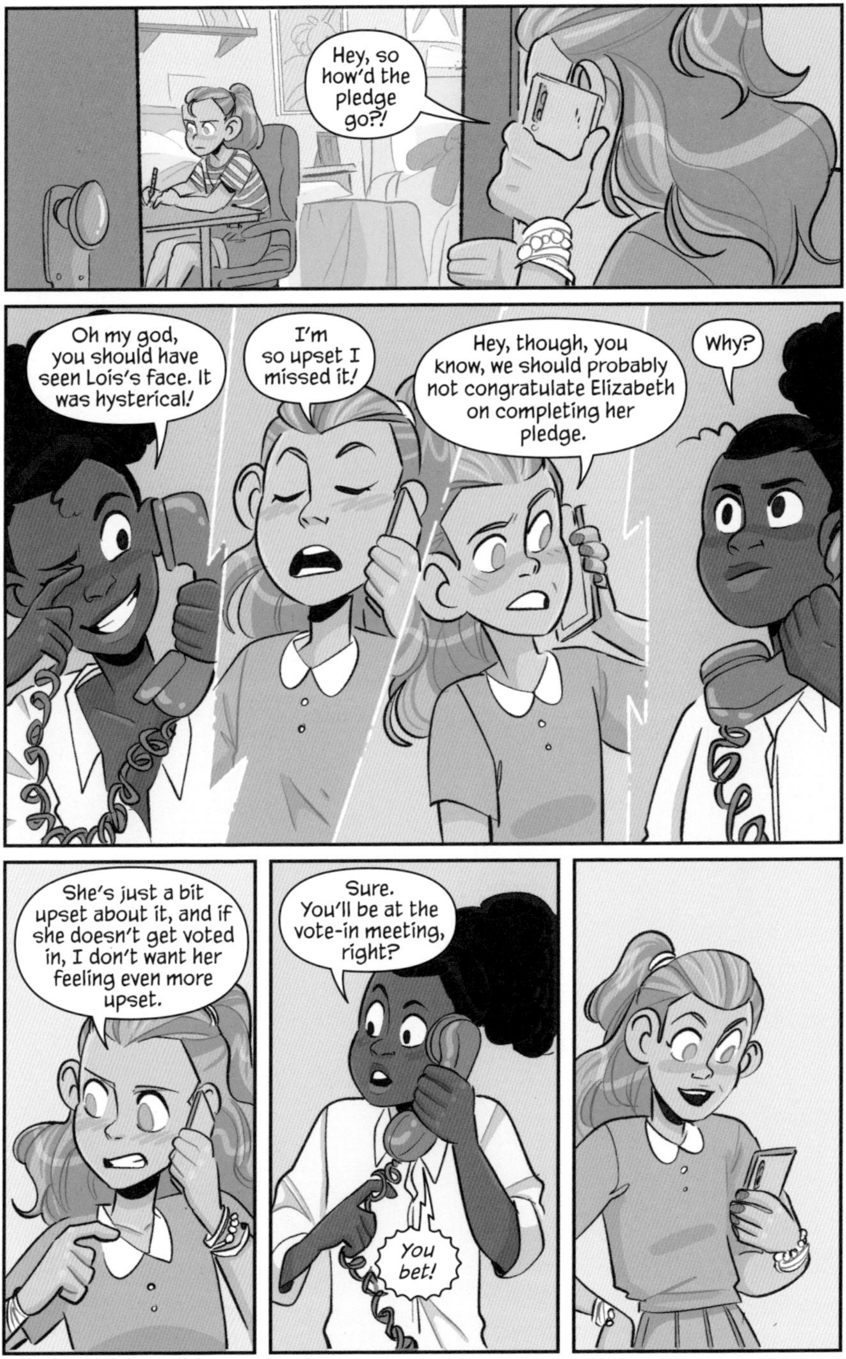

Hey, so how'd the pledge go?!
Oh my god, you should have seen Lois's face. It was hysterical!
I'm so upset I missed it!
Hey, though, you know, we should probably not congratulate Elizabeth on completing her pledge.
Why?
She's just a bit upset about it, and if she doesn't get voted in, I don't want her feeling even more upset.
Sure. You'll be at the vote-in meeting, right?
You bet!

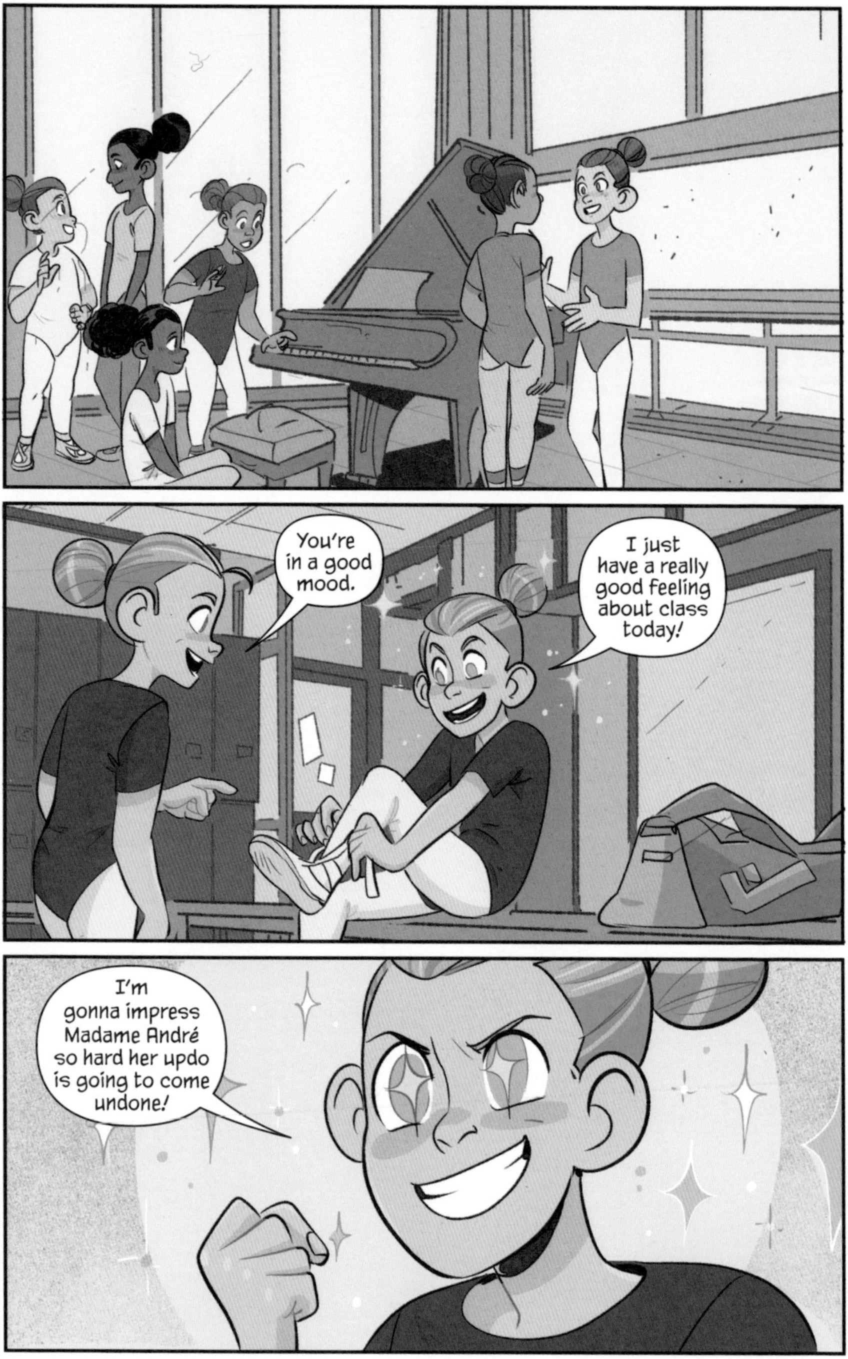
You're in a good mood.
I just have a really good feeling about class today!
I'm gonna impress Madame André so hard her updo is going to come undone!

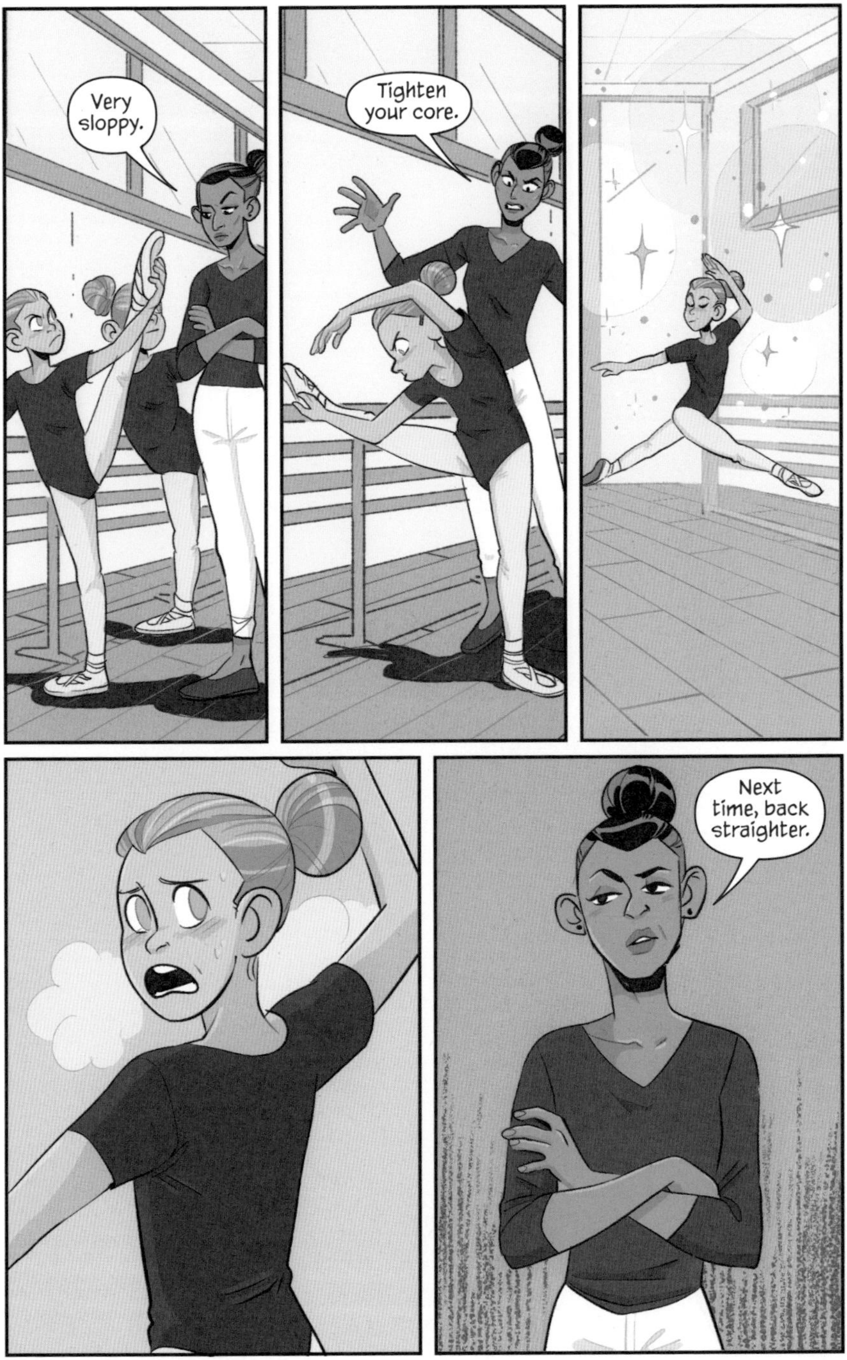

Very sloppy.
Tighten your core.
Next time, back straighter.

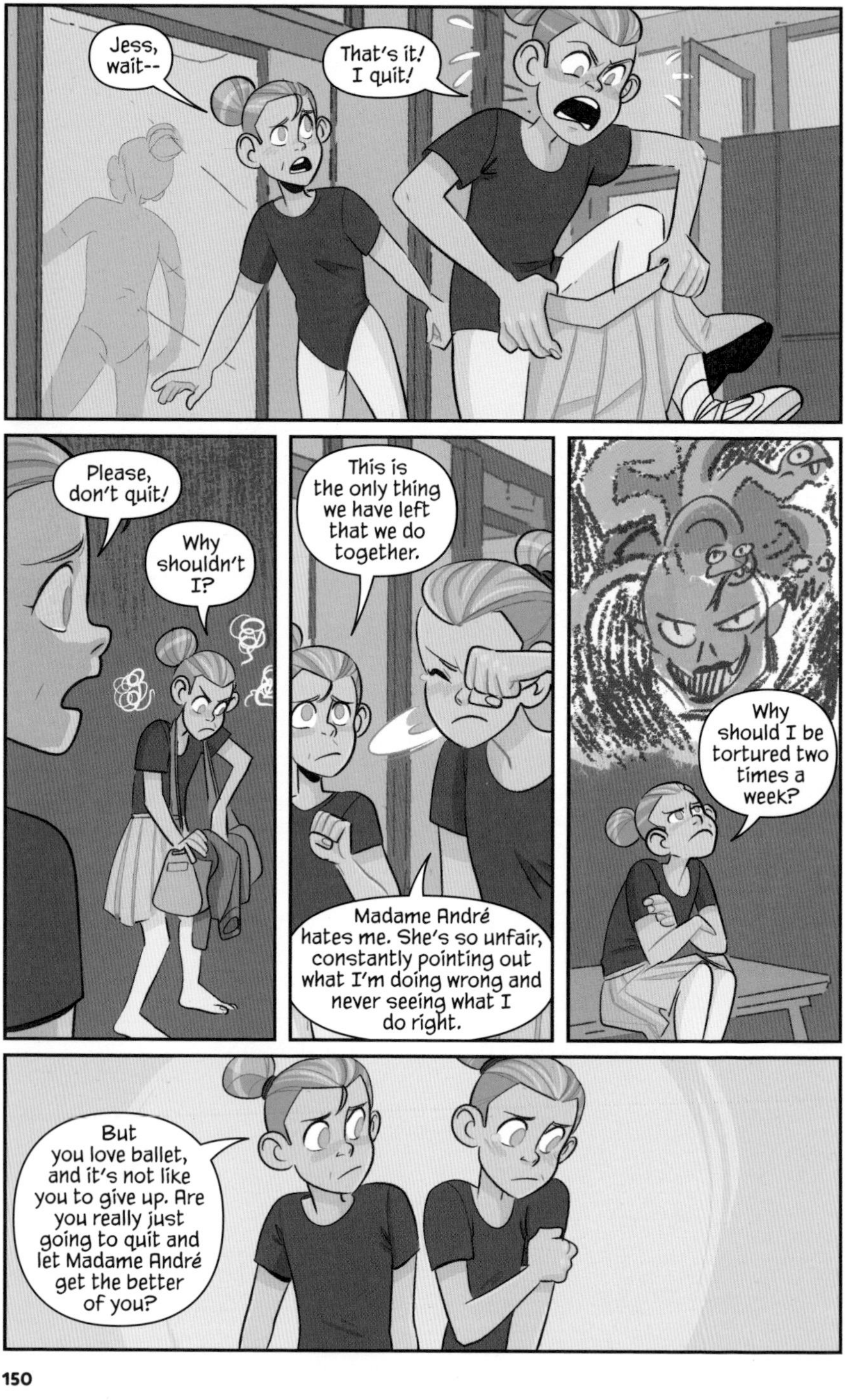

Jess, wait--
That's it! I quit!
Please, don't quit!
Why shouldn't I?
This is the only thing we have left that we do together.
Madame André hates me. She's so unfair, constantly pointing out what I'm doing wrong and never seeing what I do right.
Why should I be tortured two times a week?
But you love ballet, and it's not like you to give up. Are you really just going to quit and let Madame André get the better of you?

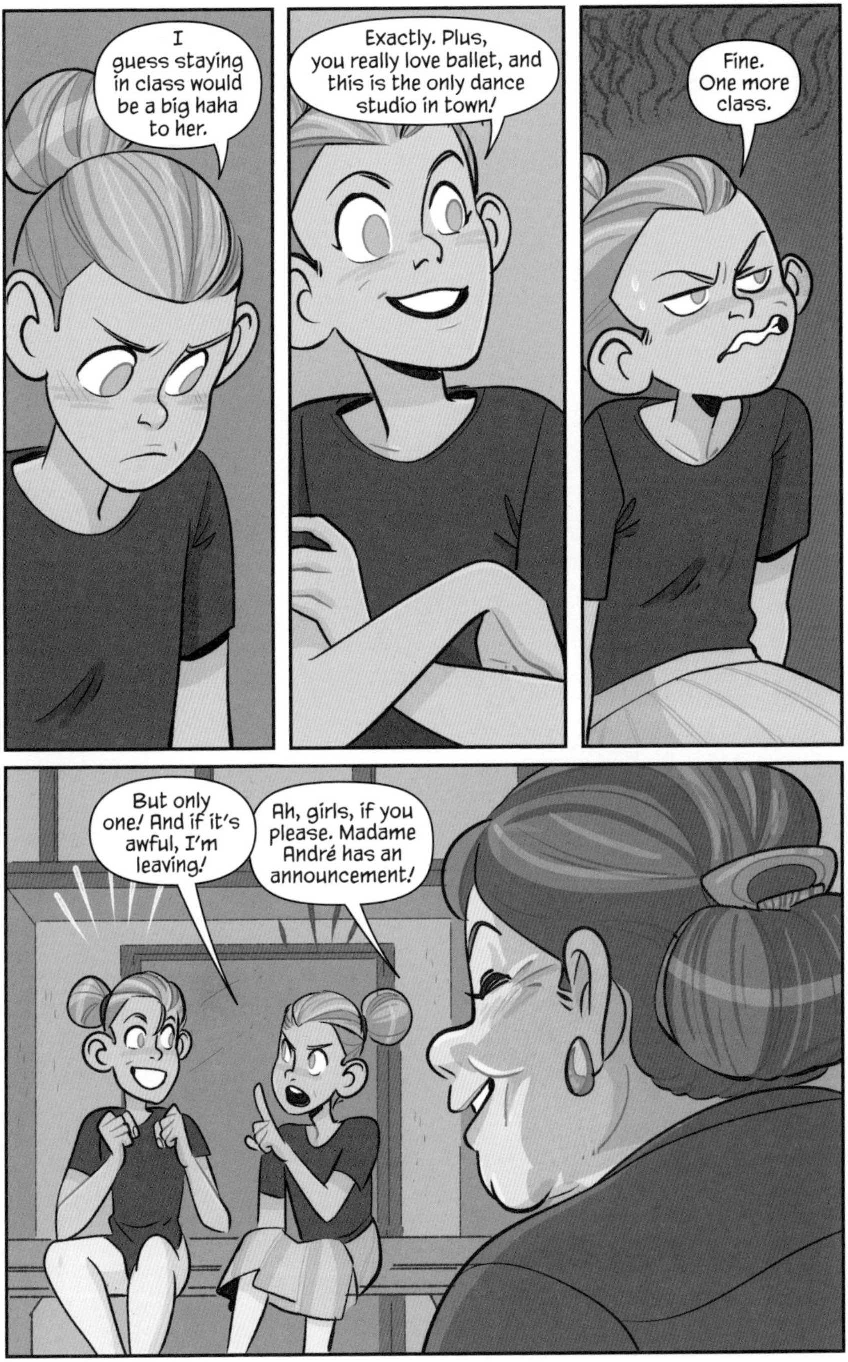

I guess staying in class would be a big haha to her.
Exactly. Plus, you really love ballet, and this is the only dance studio in town!
Fine. One more class.
But only one! And if it's awful, I'm leaving!
Ah, girls, if you please. Madame André has an announcement!

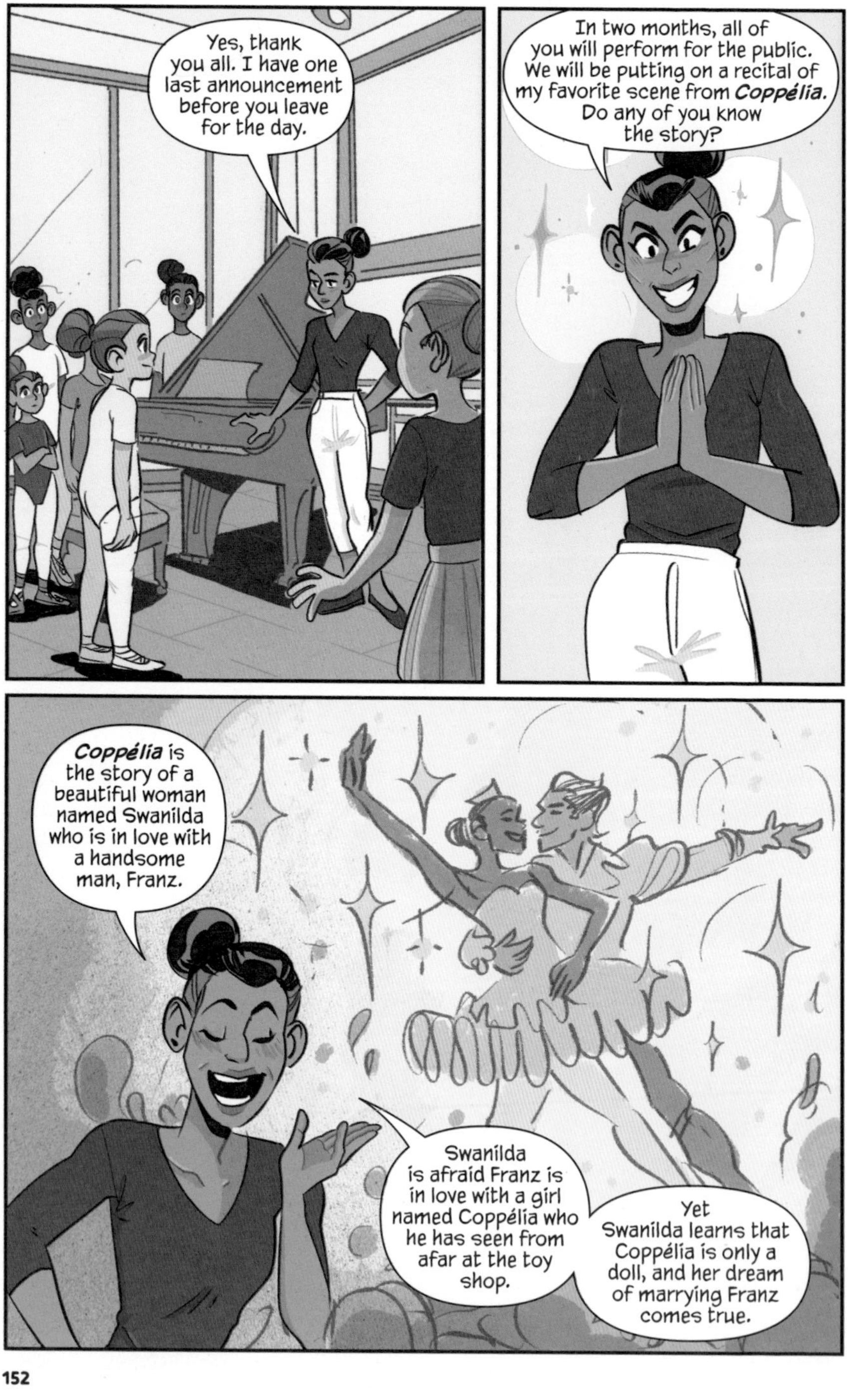
Yes, thank you all. I have one last announcement before you leave for the day.
In two months, all of you will perform for the public. We will be putting on a recital of my favorite scene from *Coppélia.* Do any of you know the story?
Coppélia is the story of a beautiful woman named Swanilda who is in love with a handsome man, Franz.
Swanilda is afraid Franz is in love with a girl named Coppélia who he has seen from afar at the toy shop.
Yet Swanilda learns that Coppélia is only a doll, and her dream of marrying Franz comes true.

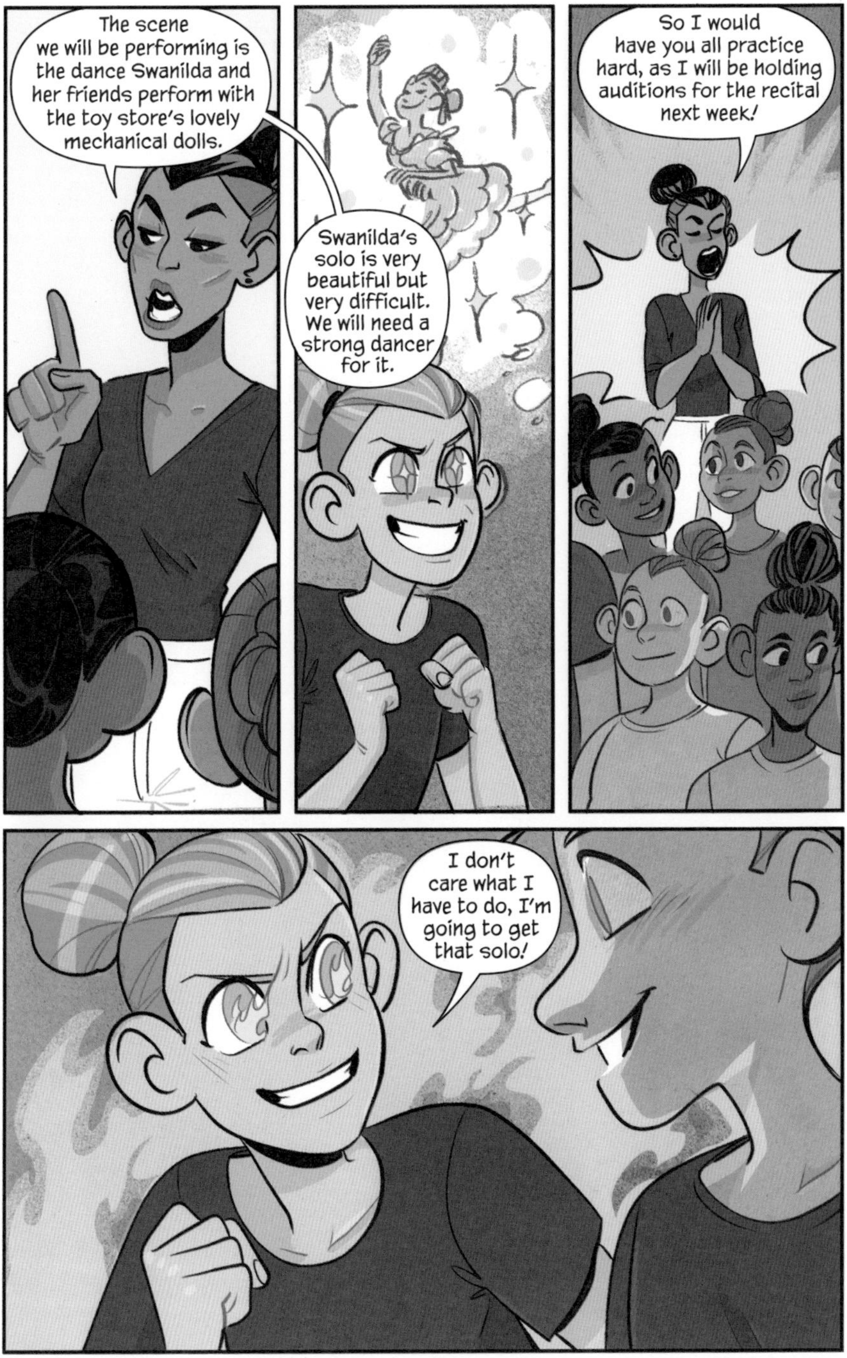
The scene we will be performing is the dance Swanilda and her friends perform with the toy store's lovely mechanical dolls.
Swanilda's solo is very beautiful but very difficult. We will need a strong dancer for it.
So I would have you all practice hard, as I will be holding auditions for the recital next week!
I don't care what I have to do, I'm going to get that solo!

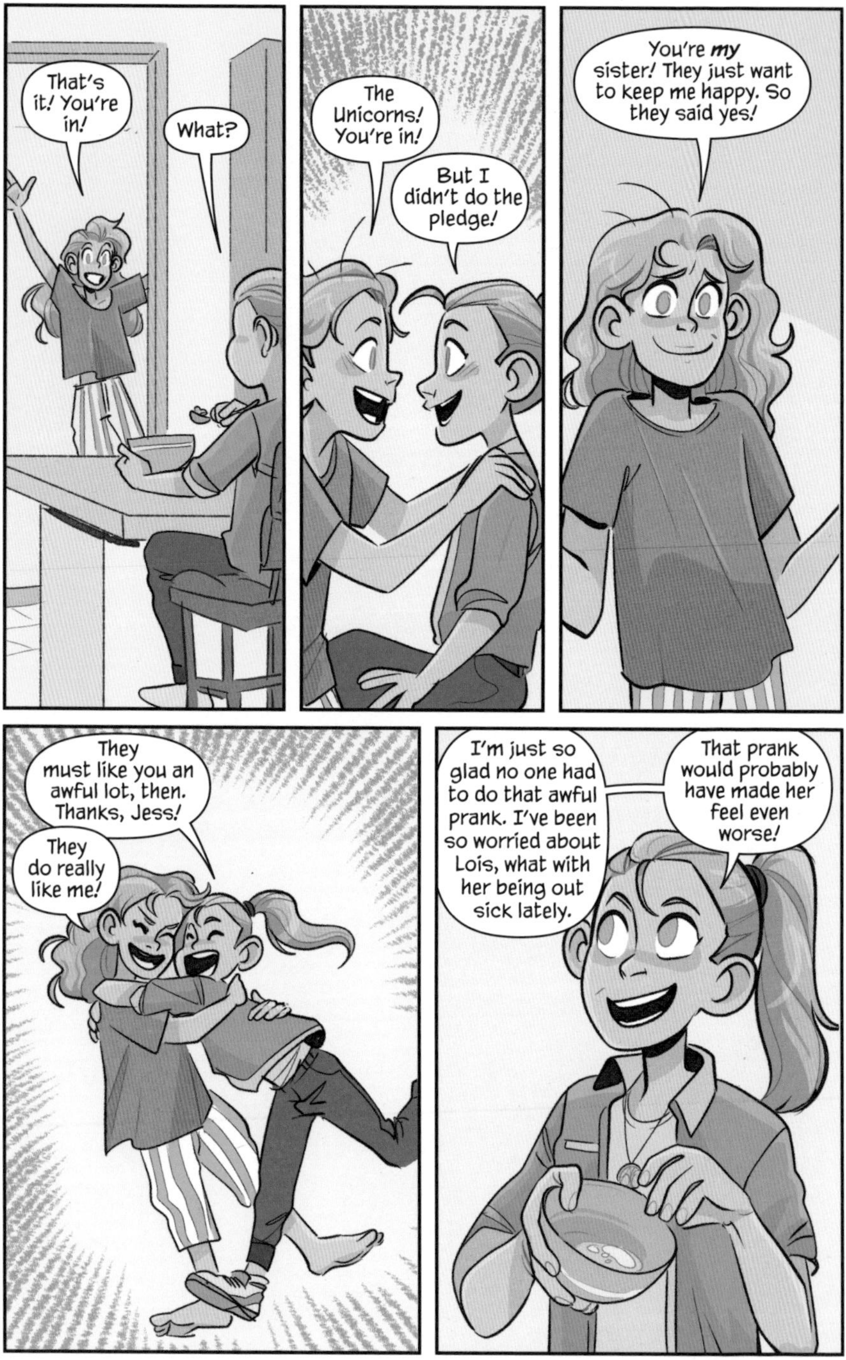
That's it! You're in!
What?
The Unicorns! You're in!
But I didn't do the pledge!
You're **my** sister! They just want to keep me happy. So they said yes!
They must like you an awful lot, then. Thanks, Jess!
They do really like me!
I'm just so glad no one had to do that awful prank. I've been so worried about Lois, what with her being out sick lately.
That prank would probably have made her feel even worse!

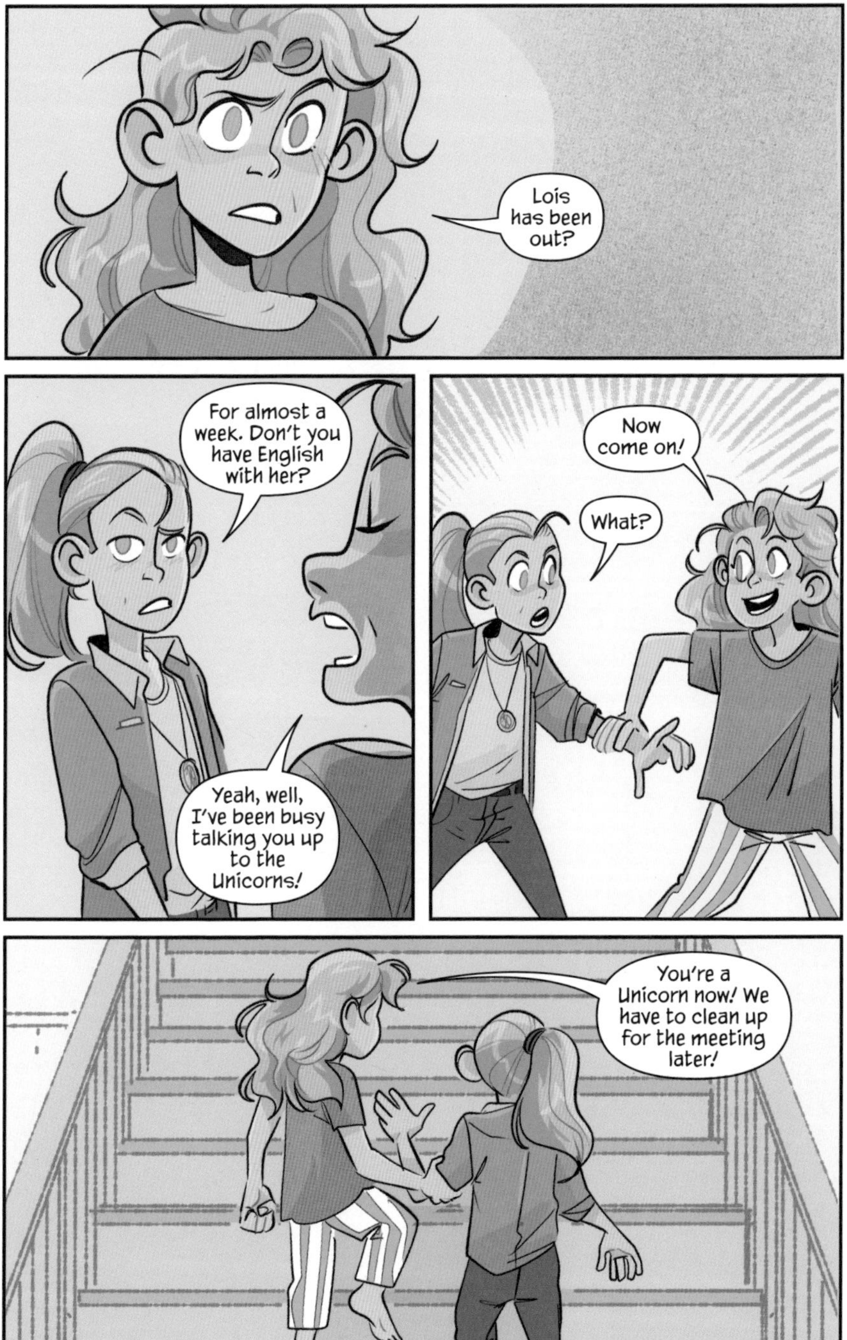
Lois has been out?
For almost a week. Don't you have English with her?
Yeah, well, I've been busy talking you up to the Unicorns!
Now come on!
What?
You're a Unicorn now! We have to clean up for the meeting later!

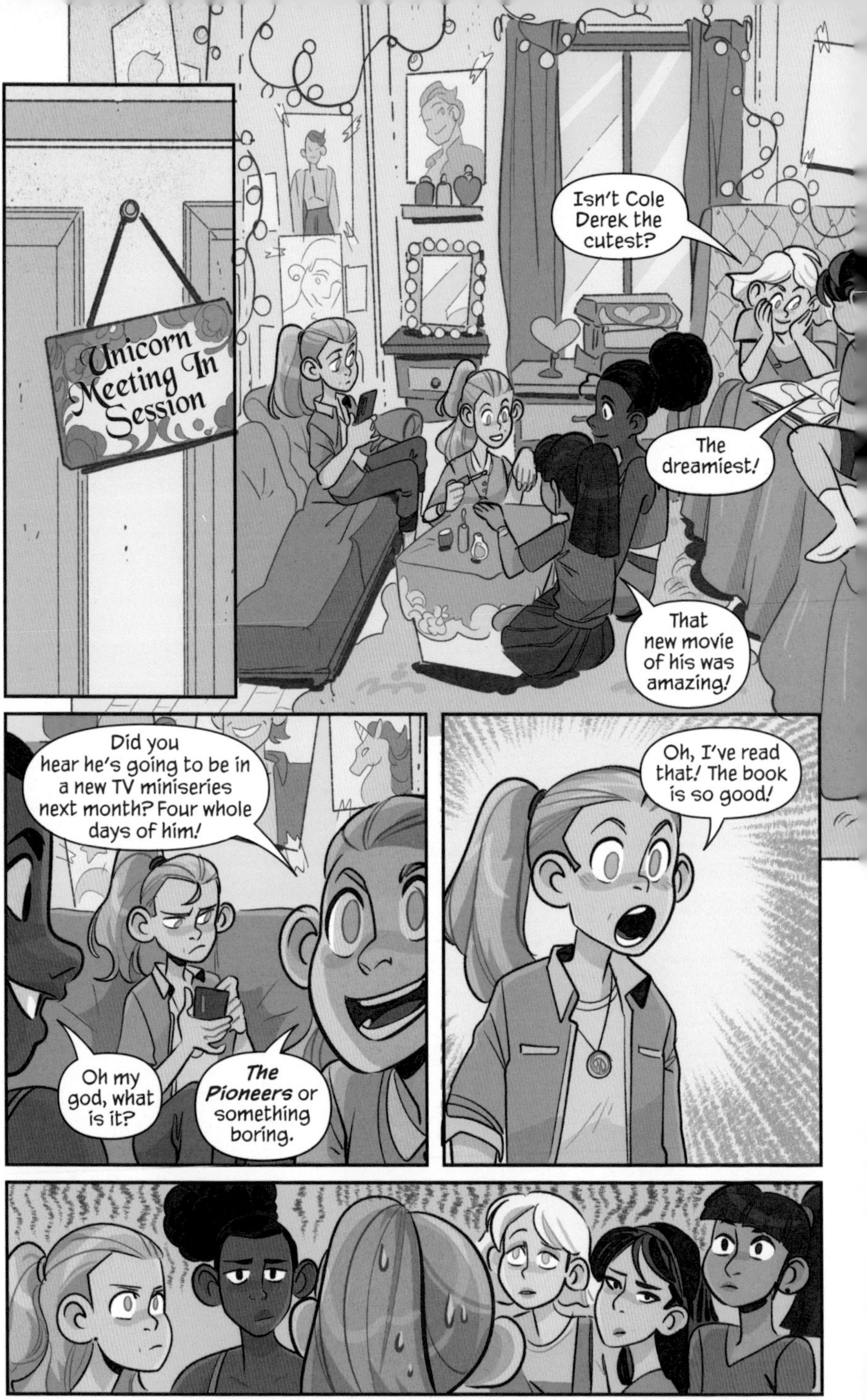
Unicorn Meeting In Session
Isn't Cole Derek the cutest?
The dreamiest!
That new movie of his was amazing!
Did you hear he's going to be in a new TV miniseries next month? Four whole days of him!
Oh my god, what is it?
The Pioneers or something boring.
Oh, I've read that! The book is so good!

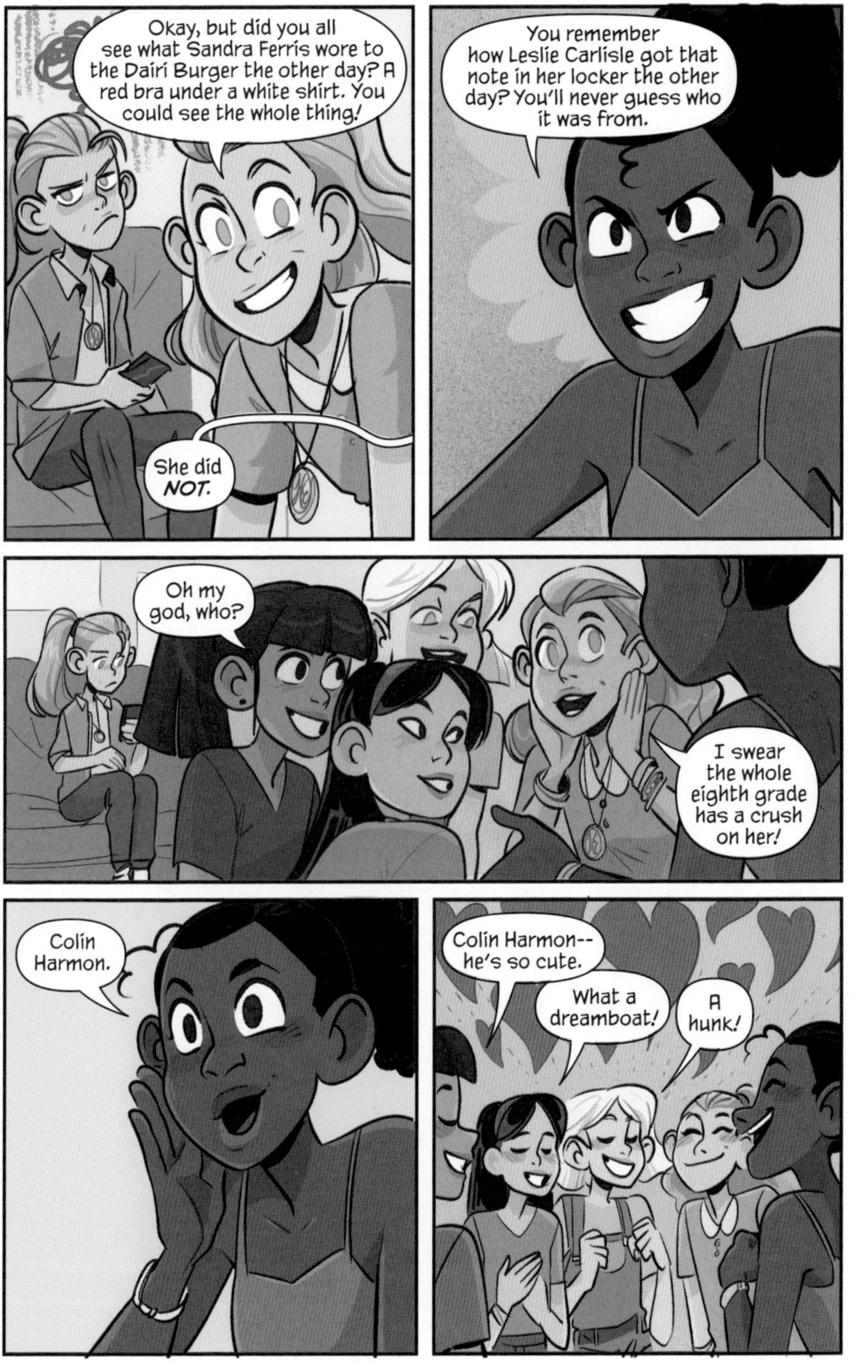

Okay, but did you all see what Sandra Ferris wore to the Dairi Burger the other day? A red bra under a white shirt. You could see the whole thing!
She did *NOT.*
You remember how Leslie Carlisle got that note in her locker the other day? You'll never guess who it was from.
Oh my god, who?
I swear the whole eighth grade has a crush on her!
Colin Harmon.
Colin Harmon-- he's so cute.
What a dreamboat!
A hunk!

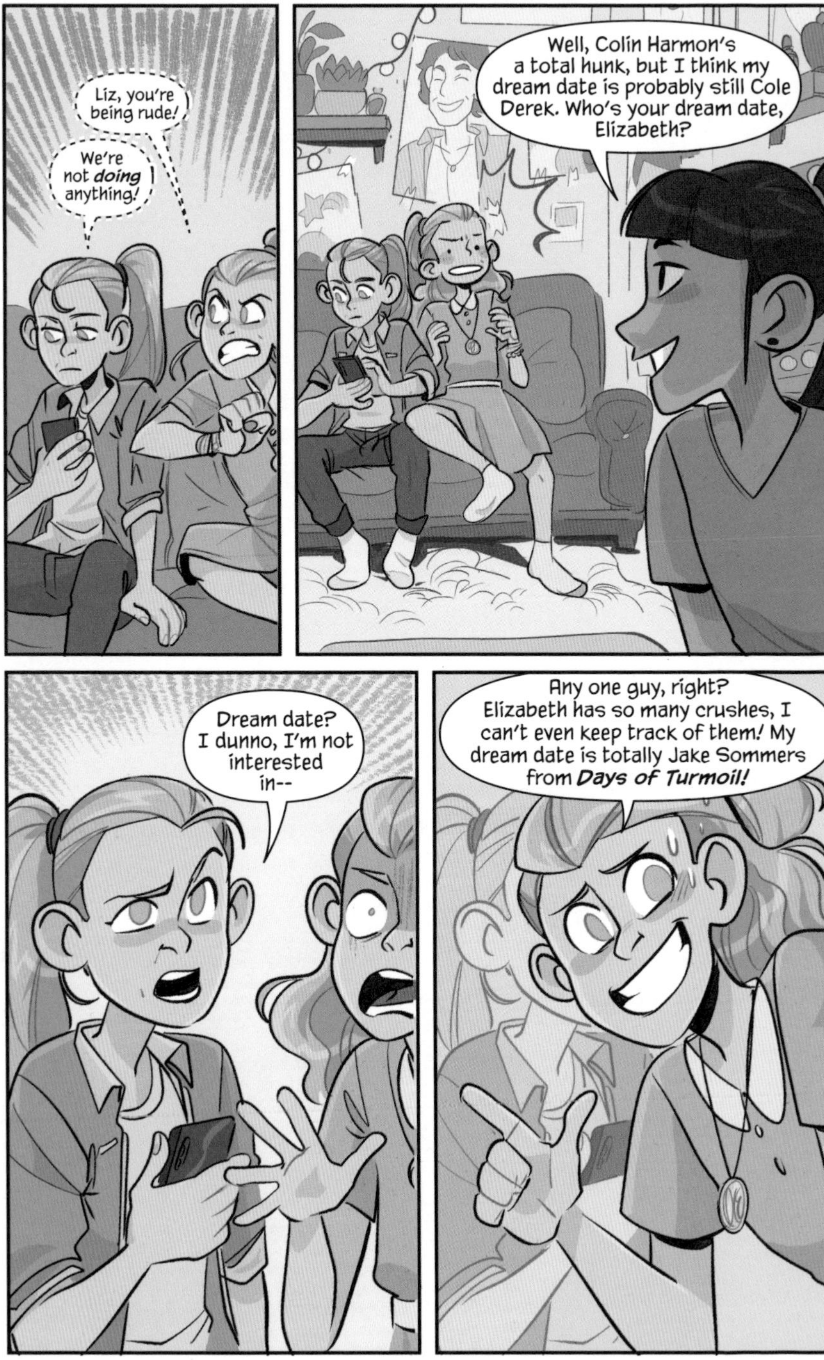
Liz, you're being rude!
We're not **doing** anything!
Well, Colin Harmon's a total hunk, but I think my dream date is probably still Cole Derek. Who's your dream date, Elizabeth?
Dream date? I dunno, I'm not interested in--
Any one guy, right? Elizabeth has so many crushes, I can't even keep track of them! My dream date is totally Jake Sommers from ***Days of Turmoil!***

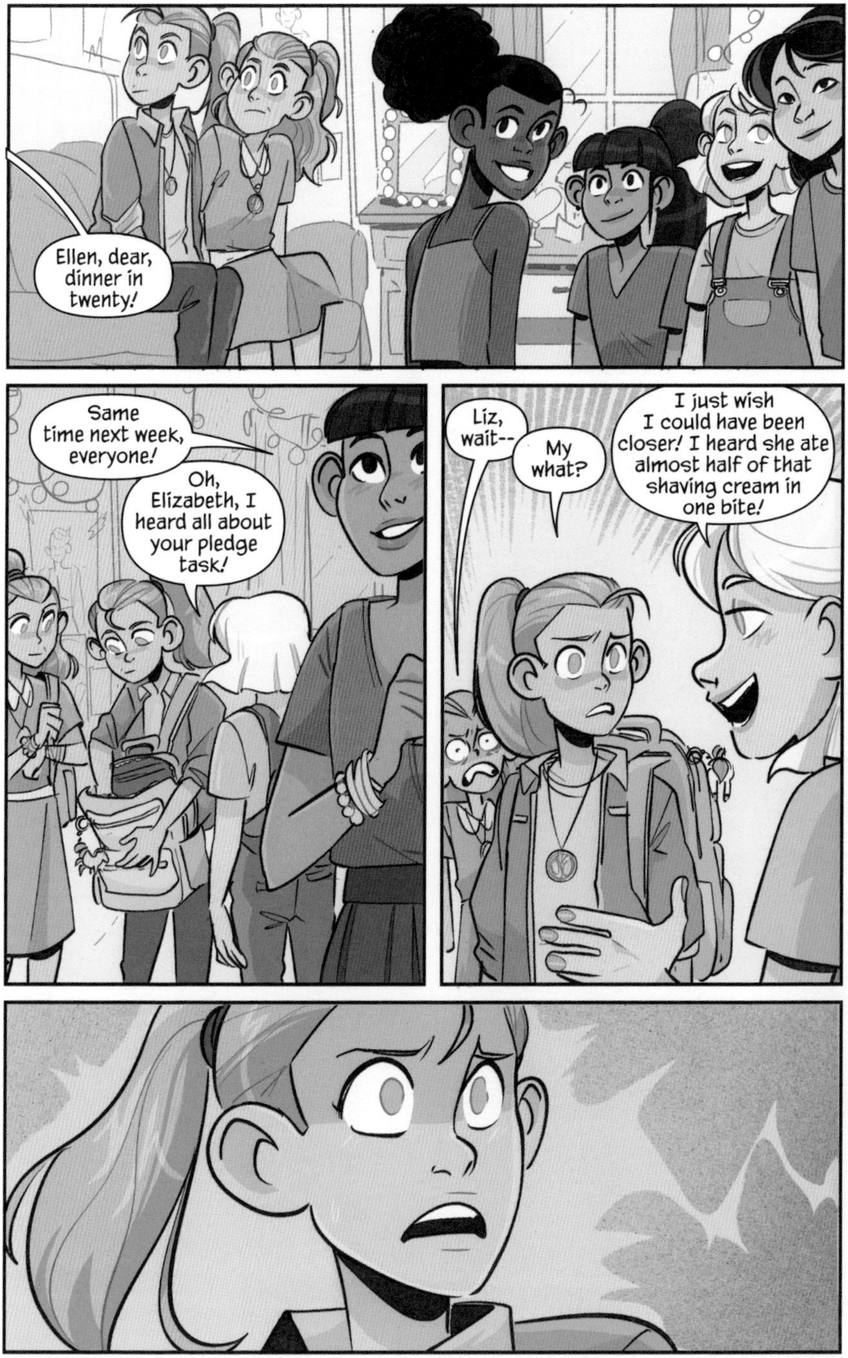
Ellen, dear, dinner in twenty!
Same time next week, everyone!
Oh, Elizabeth, I heard all about your pledge task!
Liz, wait--
My what?
I just wish I could have been closer! I heard she ate almost half of that shaving cream in one bite!

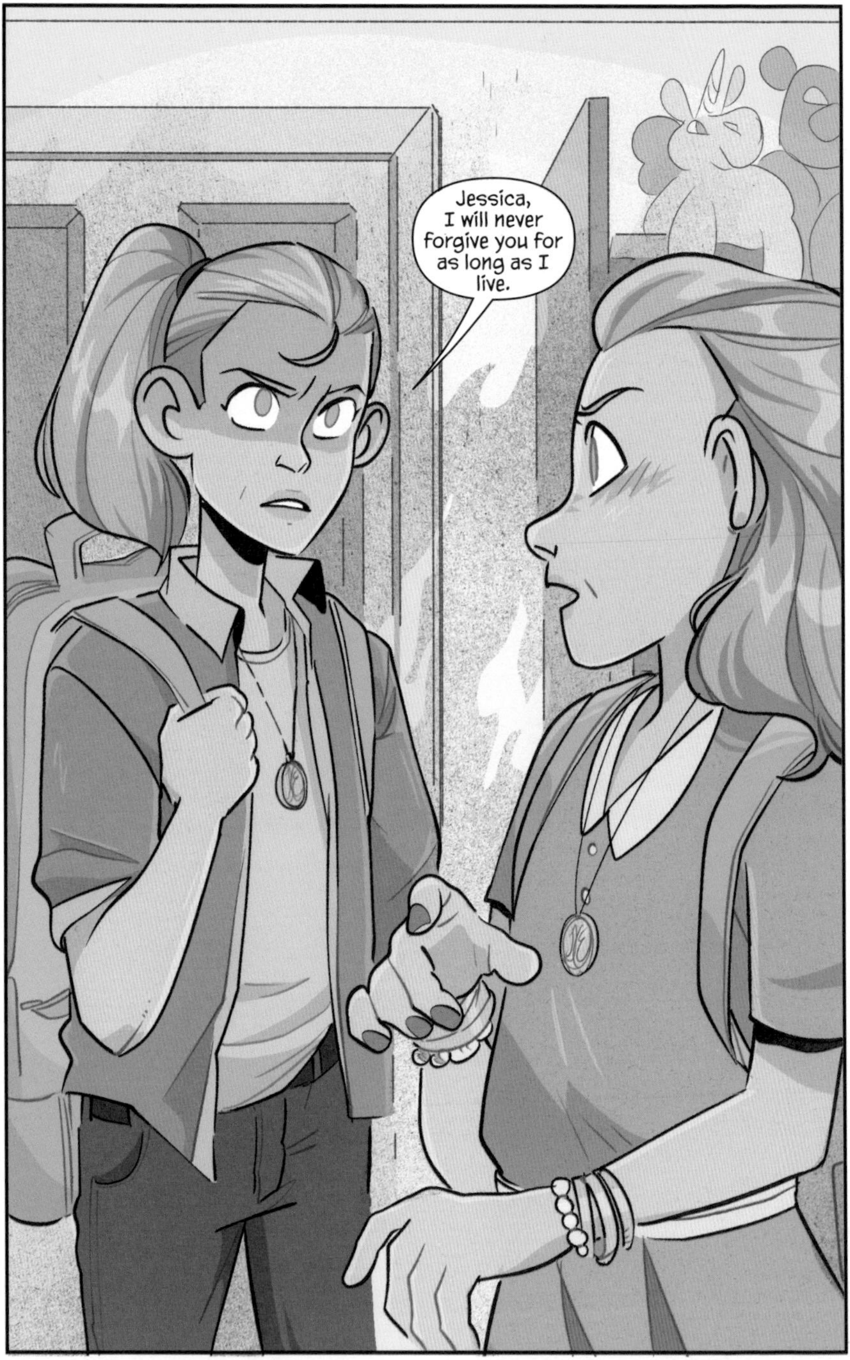
Jessica,
I will never
forgive you for
as long as I
live.

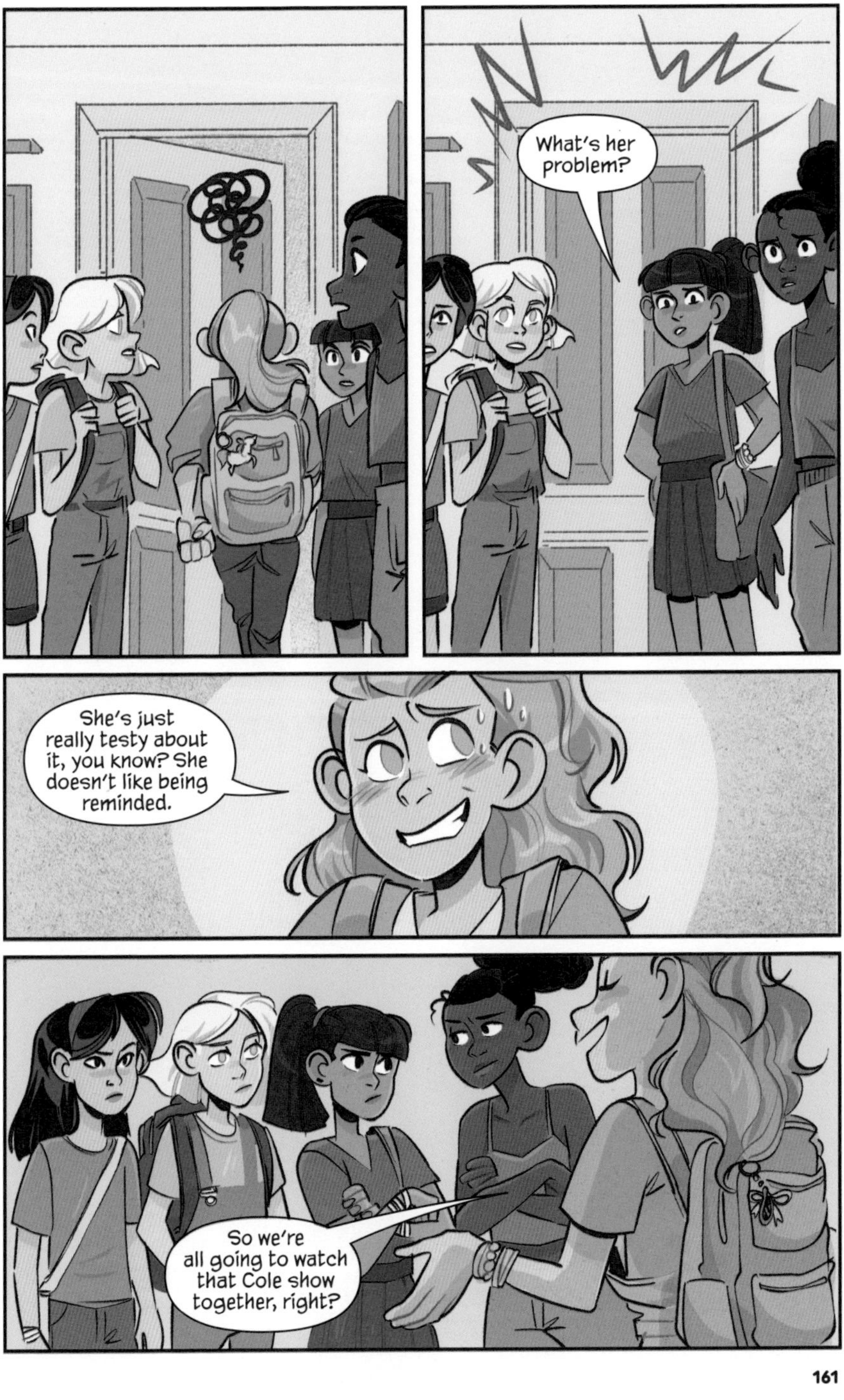
What's her problem?
She's just really testy about it, you know? She doesn't like being reminded.
So we're all going to watch that Cole show together, right?

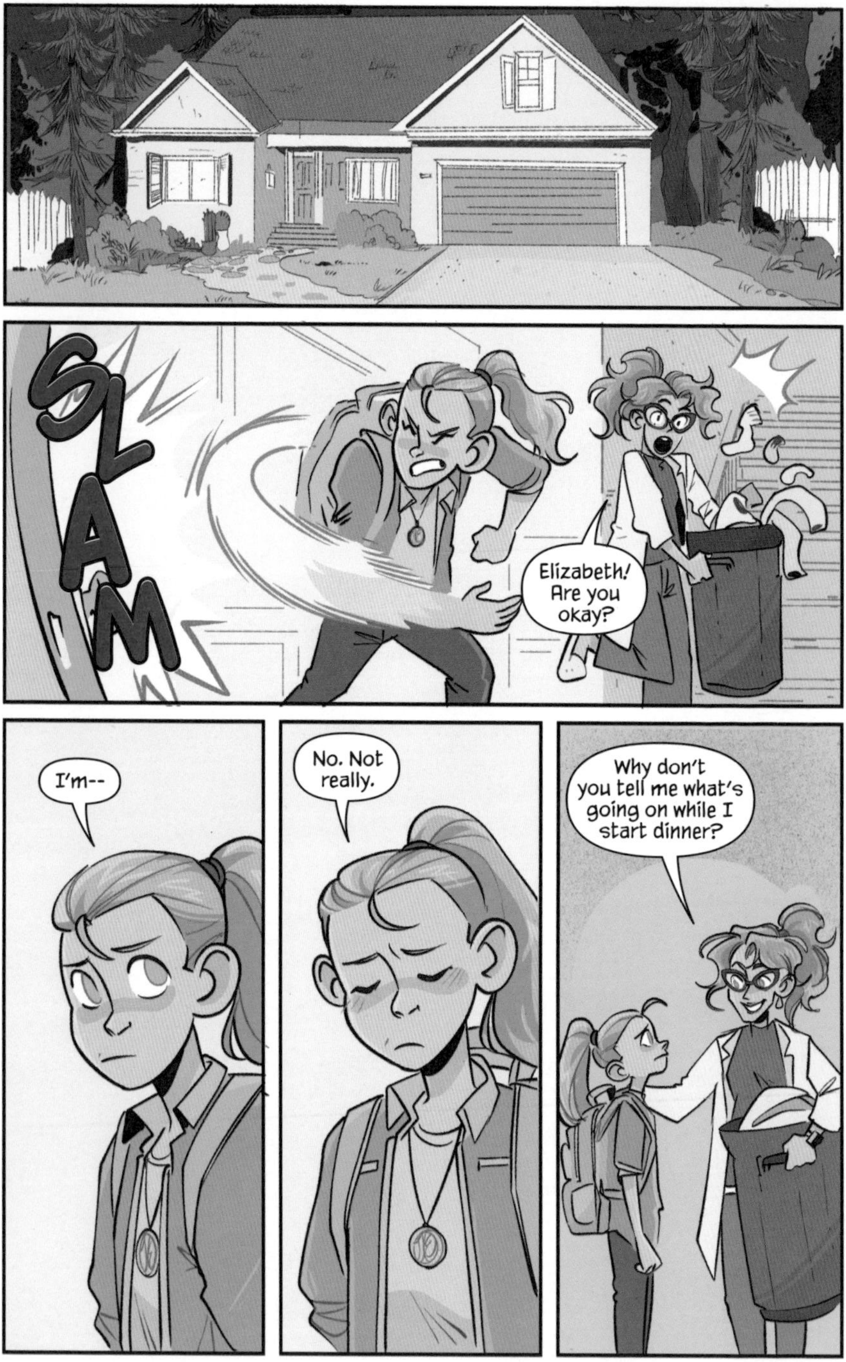
SLAM
Elizabeth! Are you okay?
I'm--
No. Not really.
Why don't you tell me what's going on while I start dinner?

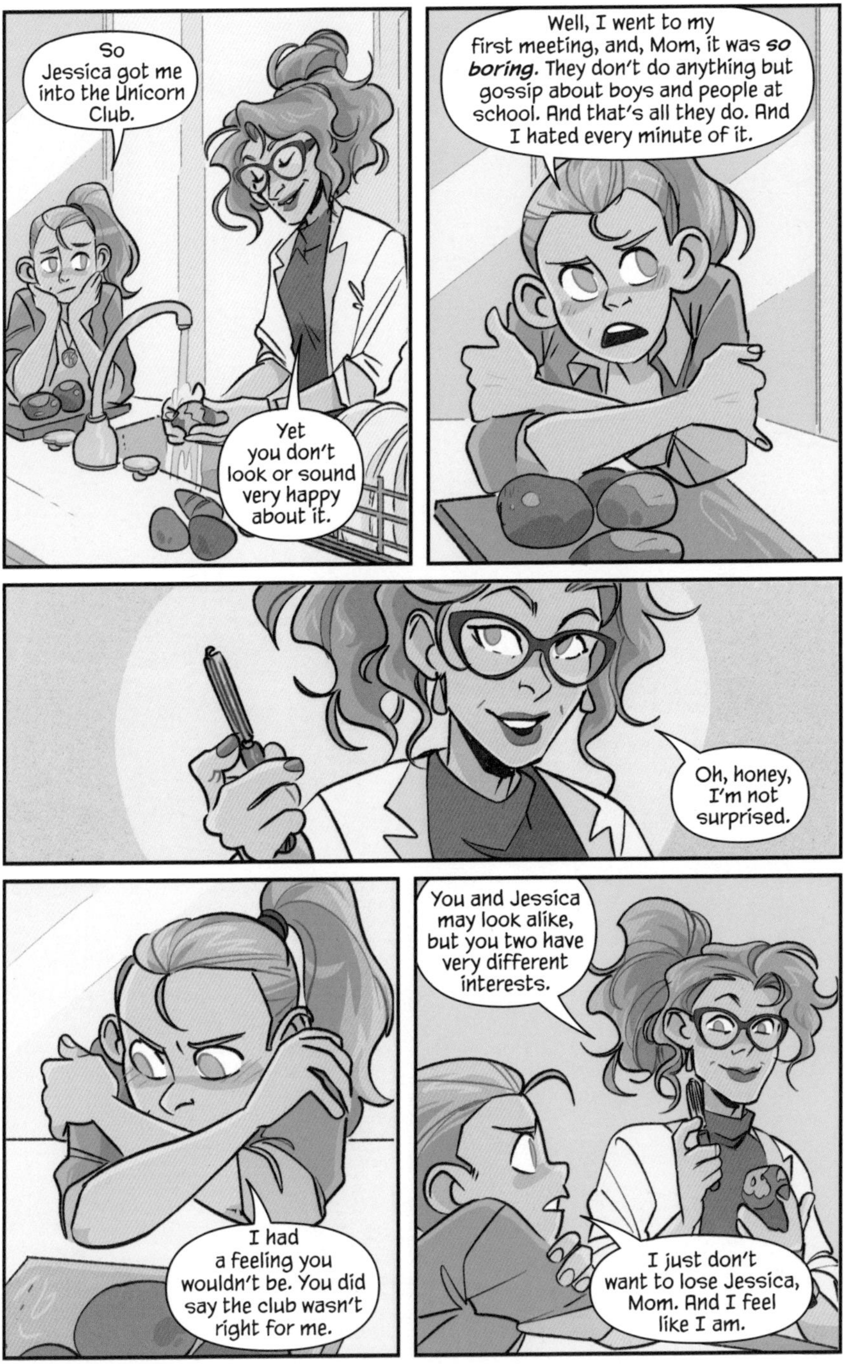
So Jessica got me into the Unicorn Club.
Yet you don't look or sound very happy about it.
Well, I went to my first meeting, and, Mom, it was ***so boring***. They don't do anything but gossip about boys and people at school. And that's all they do. And I hated every minute of it.
Oh, honey, I'm not surprised.
I had a feeling you wouldn't be. You did say the club wasn't right for me.
You and Jessica may look alike, but you two have very different interests.
I just don't want to lose Jessica, Mom. And I feel like I am.

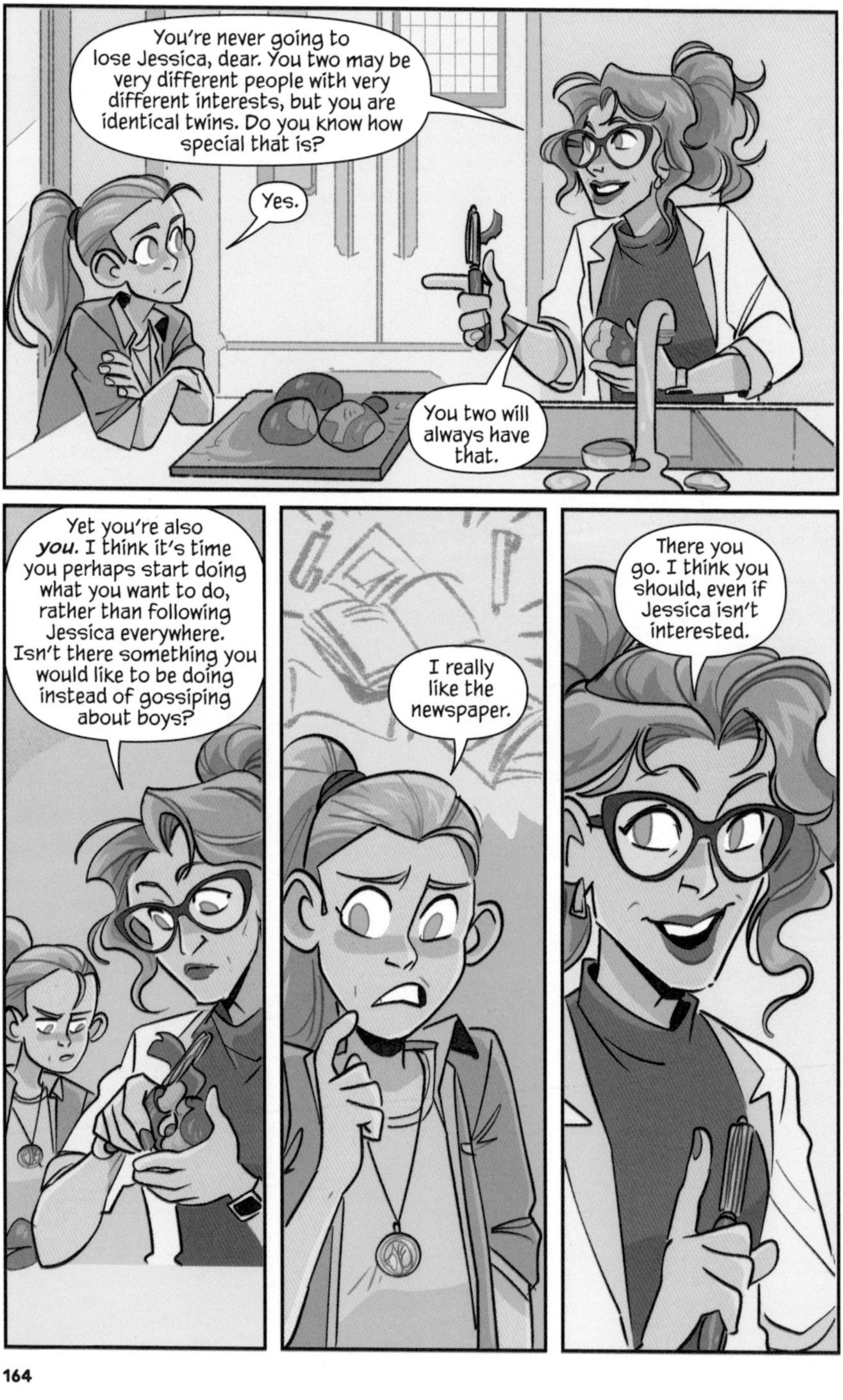
You're never going to lose Jessica, dear. You two may be very different people with very different interests, but you are identical twins. Do you know how special that is?
Yes.
You two will always have that.
Yet you're also *you*. I think it's time you perhaps start doing what you want to do, rather than following Jessica everywhere. Isn't there something you would like to be doing instead of gossiping about boys?
I really like the newspaper.
There you go. I think you should, even if Jessica isn't interested.

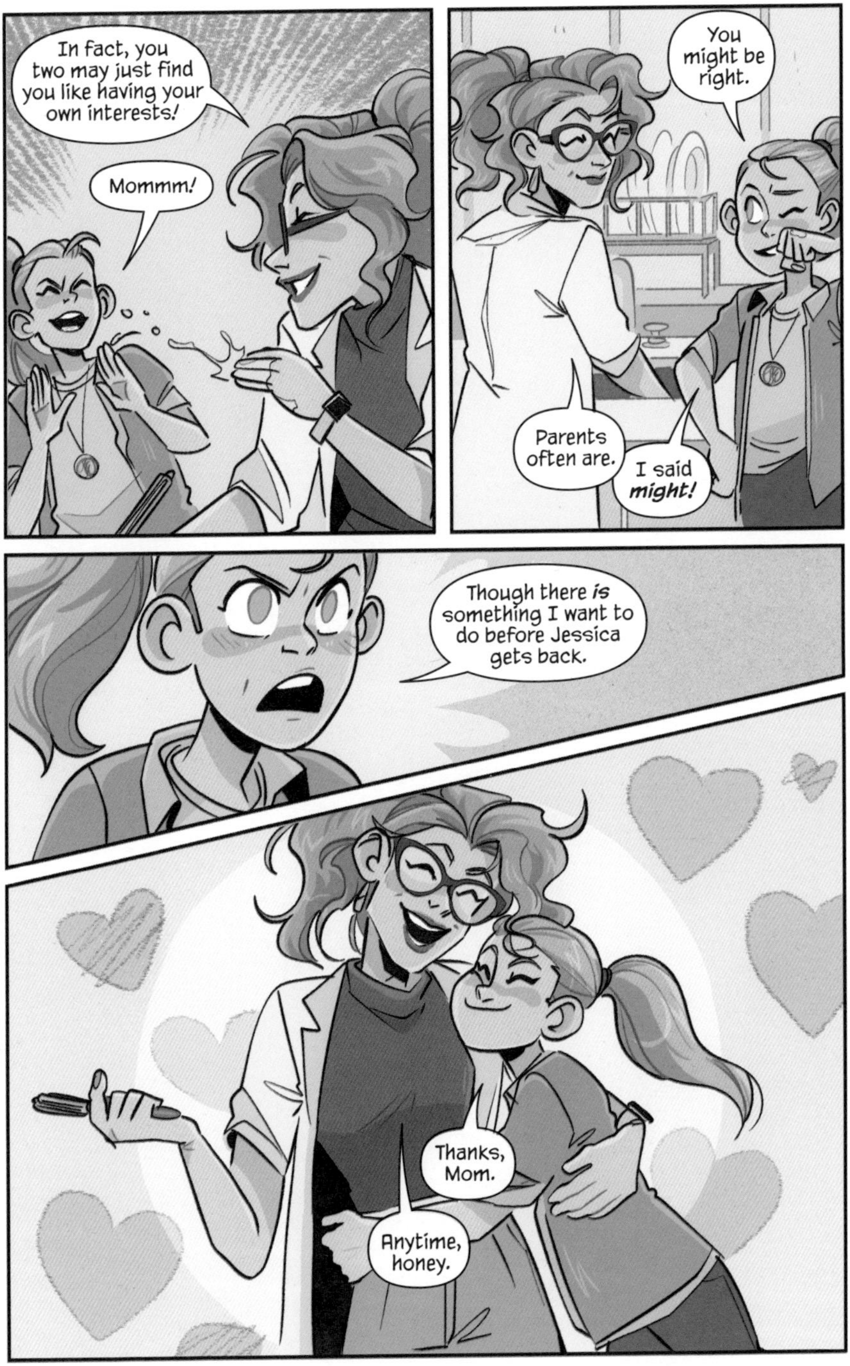
In fact, you two may just find you like having your own interests!
Mommm!
You might be right.
Parents often are.
I said *might!*
Though there *is* something I want to do before Jessica gets back.
Thanks, Mom.
Anytime, honey.

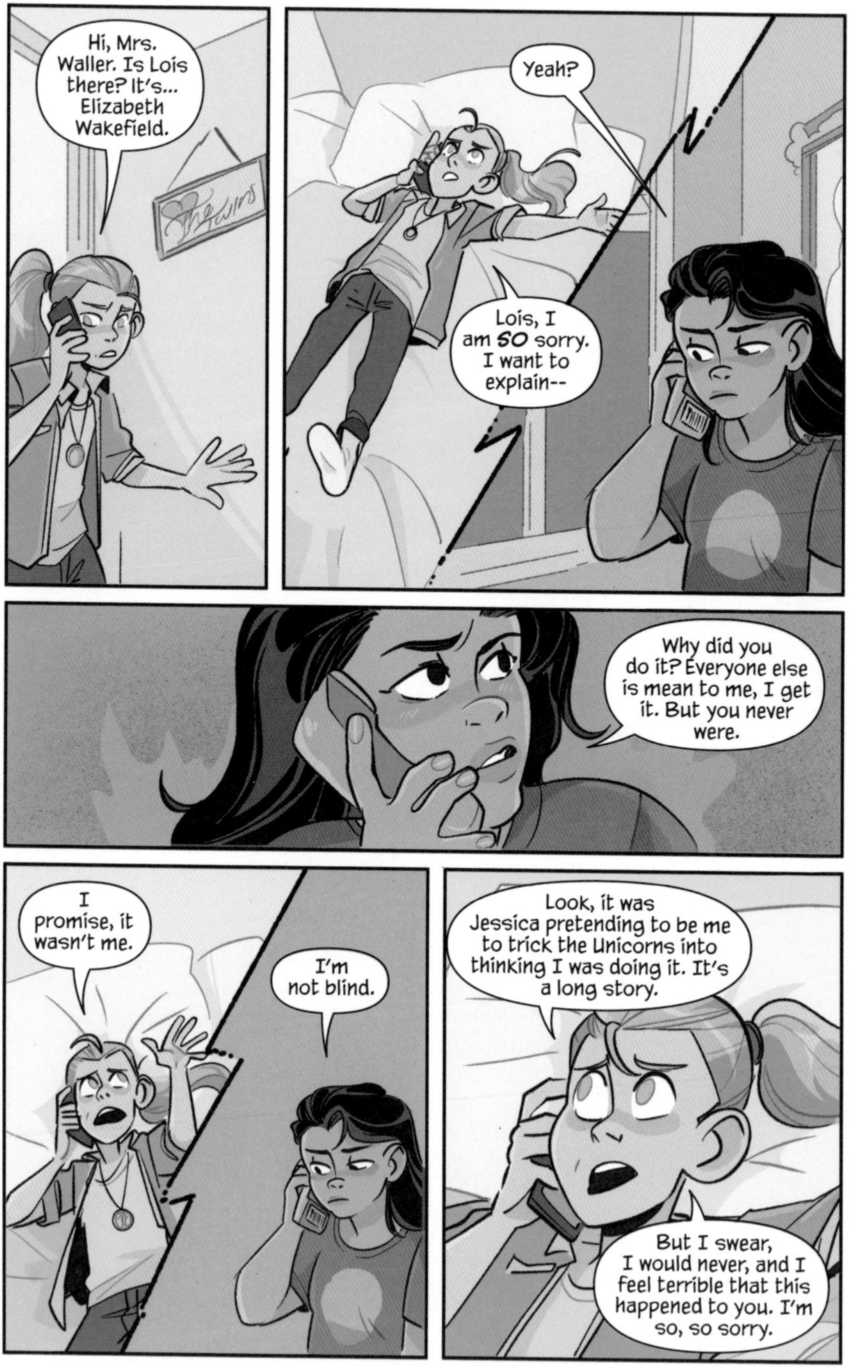
Hi, Mrs. Waller. Is Lois there? It's... Elizabeth Wakefield.
Yeah?
Lois, I am SO sorry. I want to explain--
Why did you do it? Everyone else is mean to me, I get it. But you never were.
I promise, it wasn't me.
I'm not blind.
Look, it was Jessica pretending to be me to trick the Unicorns into thinking I was doing it. It's a long story.
But I swear, I would never, and I feel terrible that this happened to you. I'm so, so sorry.

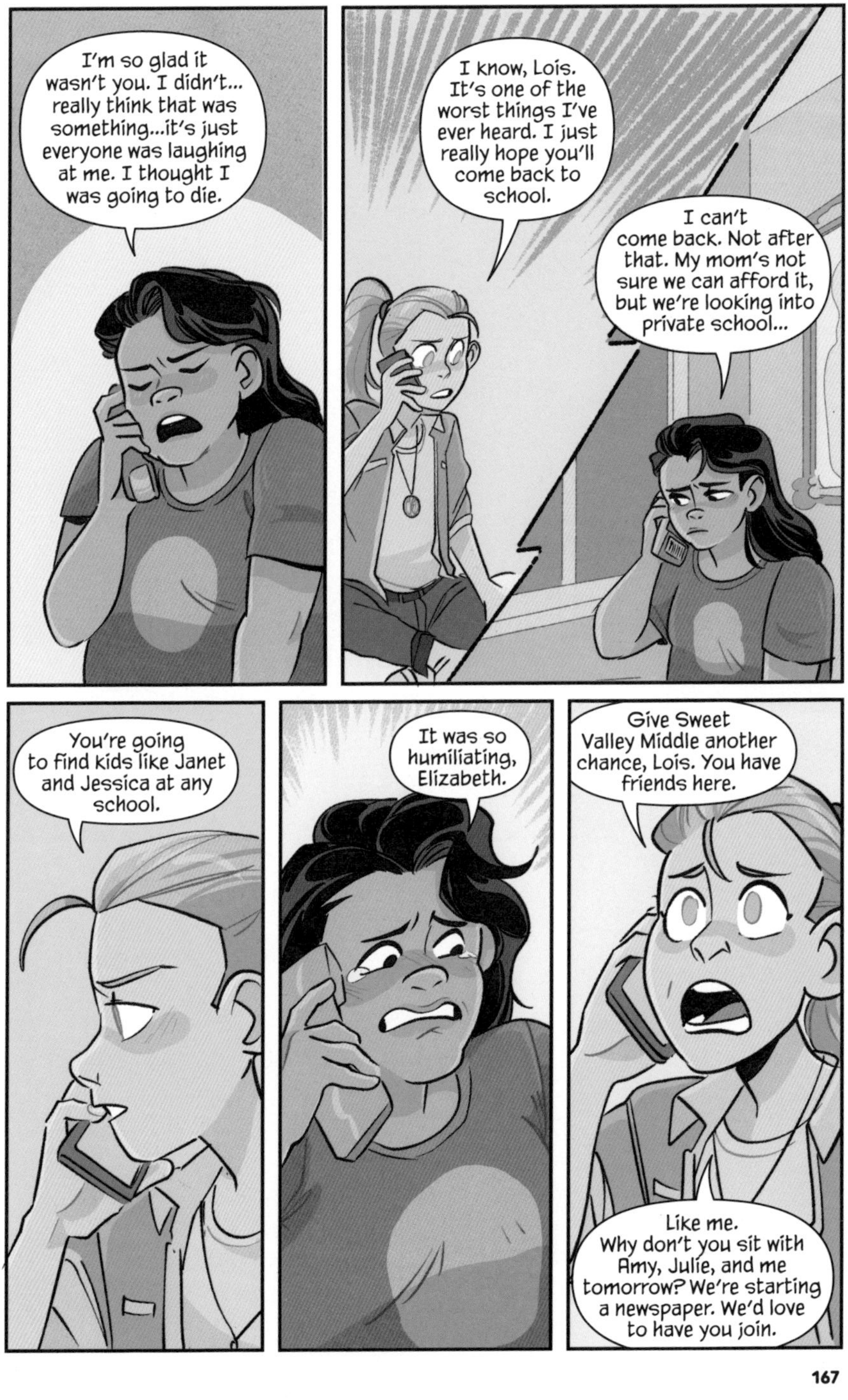
I'm so glad it wasn't you. I didn't... really think that was something...it's just everyone was laughing at me. I thought I was going to die.
I know, Lois. It's one of the worst things I've ever heard. I just really hope you'll come back to school.
I can't come back. Not after that. My mom's not sure we can afford it, but we're looking into private school...
You're going to find kids like Janet and Jessica at any school.
It was so humiliating, Elizabeth.
Give Sweet Valley Middle another chance, Lois. You have friends here.
Like me. Why don't you sit with Amy, Julie, and me tomorrow? We're starting a newspaper. We'd love to have you join.

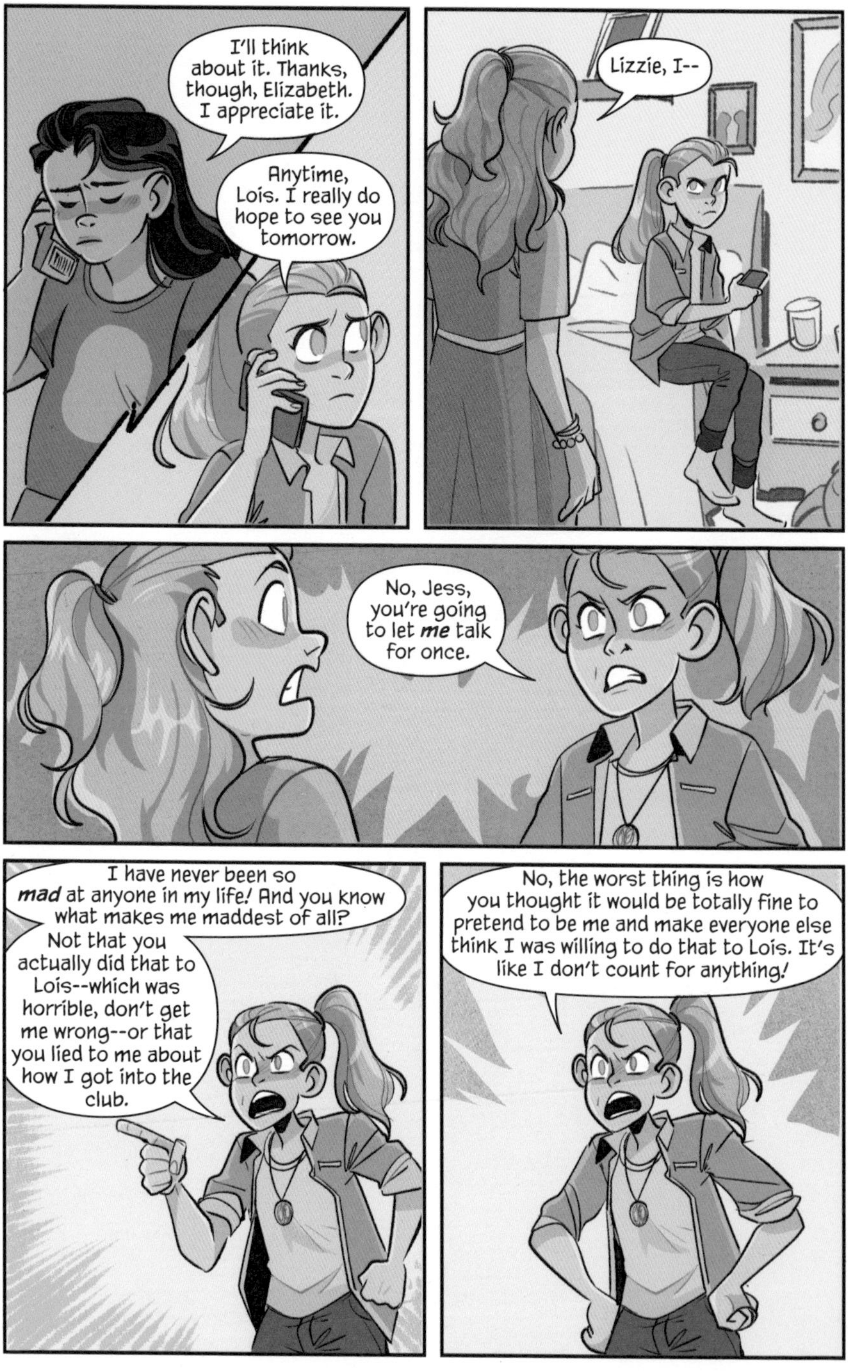
I'll think about it. Thanks, though, Elizabeth. I appreciate it.
Anytime, Lois. I really do hope to see you tomorrow.
Lizzie, I--
No, Jess, you're going to let *me* talk for once.
I have never been so *mad* at anyone in my life! And you know what makes me maddest of all?
Not that you actually did that to Lois--which was horrible, don't get me wrong--or that you lied to me about how I got into the club.
No, the worst thing is how you thought it would be totally fine to pretend to be me and make everyone else think I was willing to do that to Lois. It's like I don't count for anything!

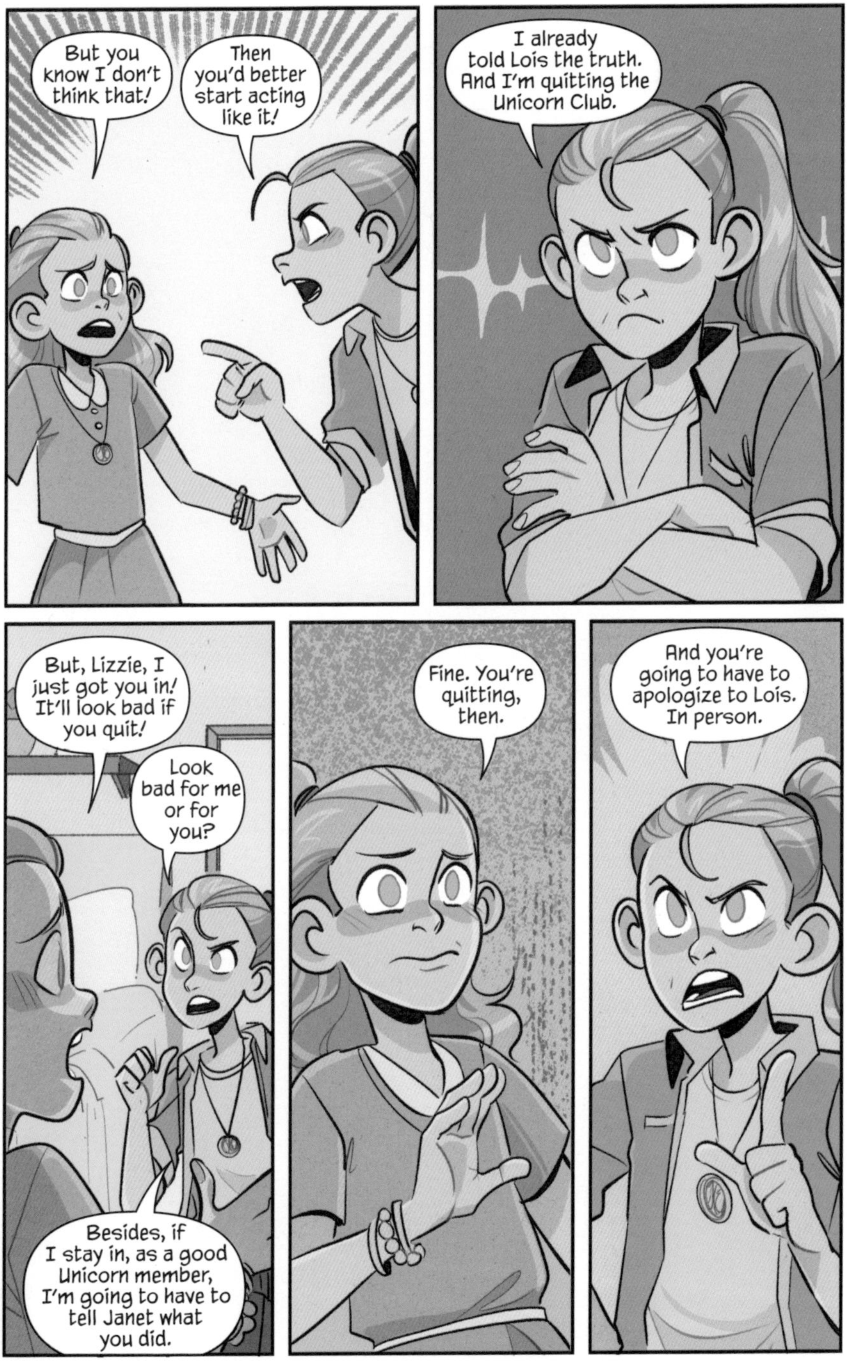
But you know I don't think that!
Then you'd better start acting like it!
I already told Lois the truth. And I'm quitting the Unicorn Club.
But, Lizzie, I just got you in! It'll look bad if you quit!
Look bad for me or for you?
Besides, if I stay in, as a good Unicorn member, I'm going to have to tell Janet what you did.
Fine. You're quitting, then.
And you're going to have to apologize to Lois. In person.

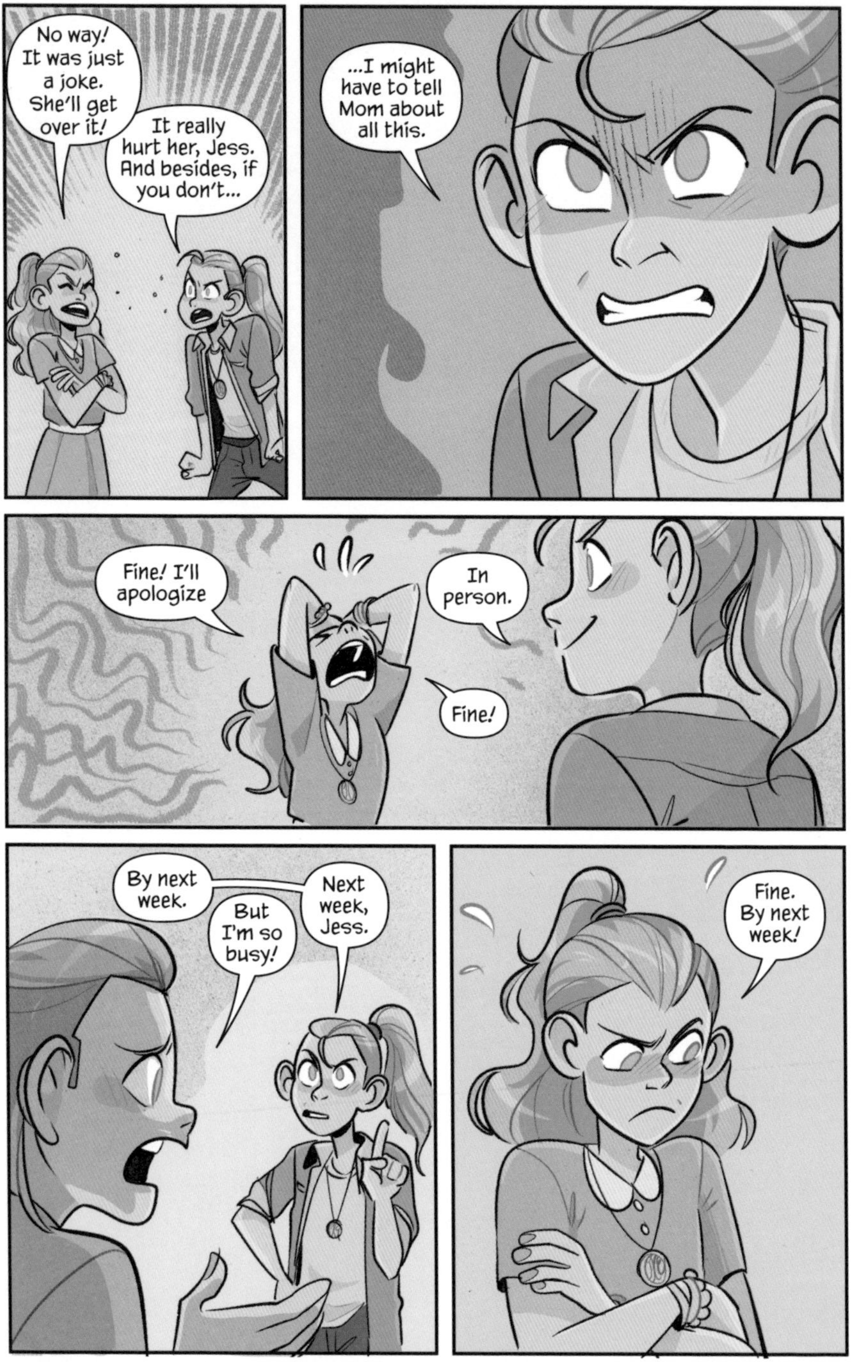
No way! It was just a joke. She'll get over it!
It really hurt her, Jess. And besides, if you don't...
...I might have to tell Mom about all this.
Fine! I'll apologize
In person.
Fine!
By next week.
But I'm so busy!
Next week, Jess.
Fine. By next week!

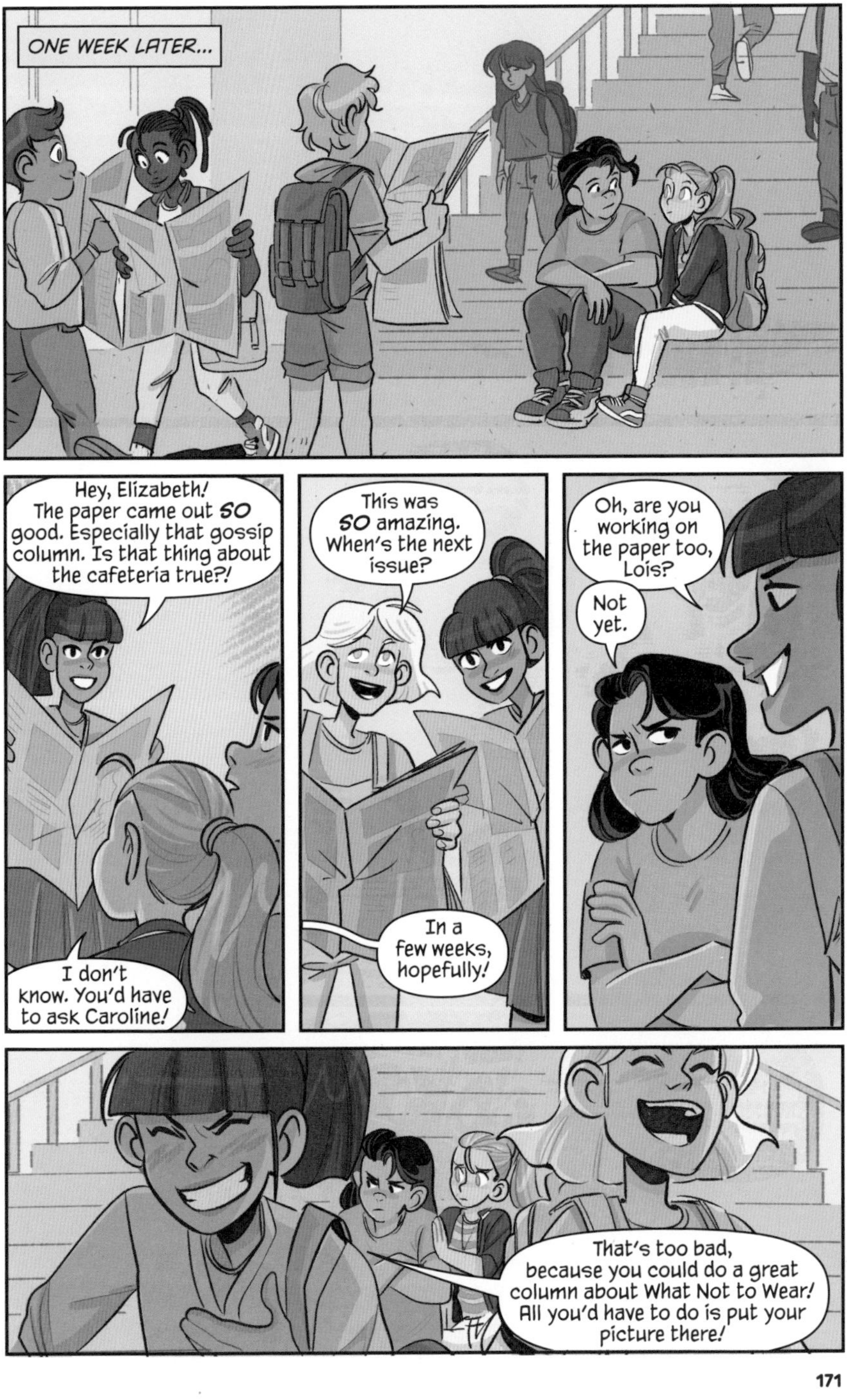
ONE WEEK LATER...
Hey, Elizabeth! The paper came out SO good. Especially that gossip column. Is that thing about the cafeteria true?!
I don't know. You'd have to ask Caroline!
This was SO amazing. When's the next issue?
In a few weeks, hopefully!
Oh, are you working on the paper too, Lois?
Not yet.
That's too bad, because you could do a great column about What Not to Wear! All you'd have to do is put your picture there!

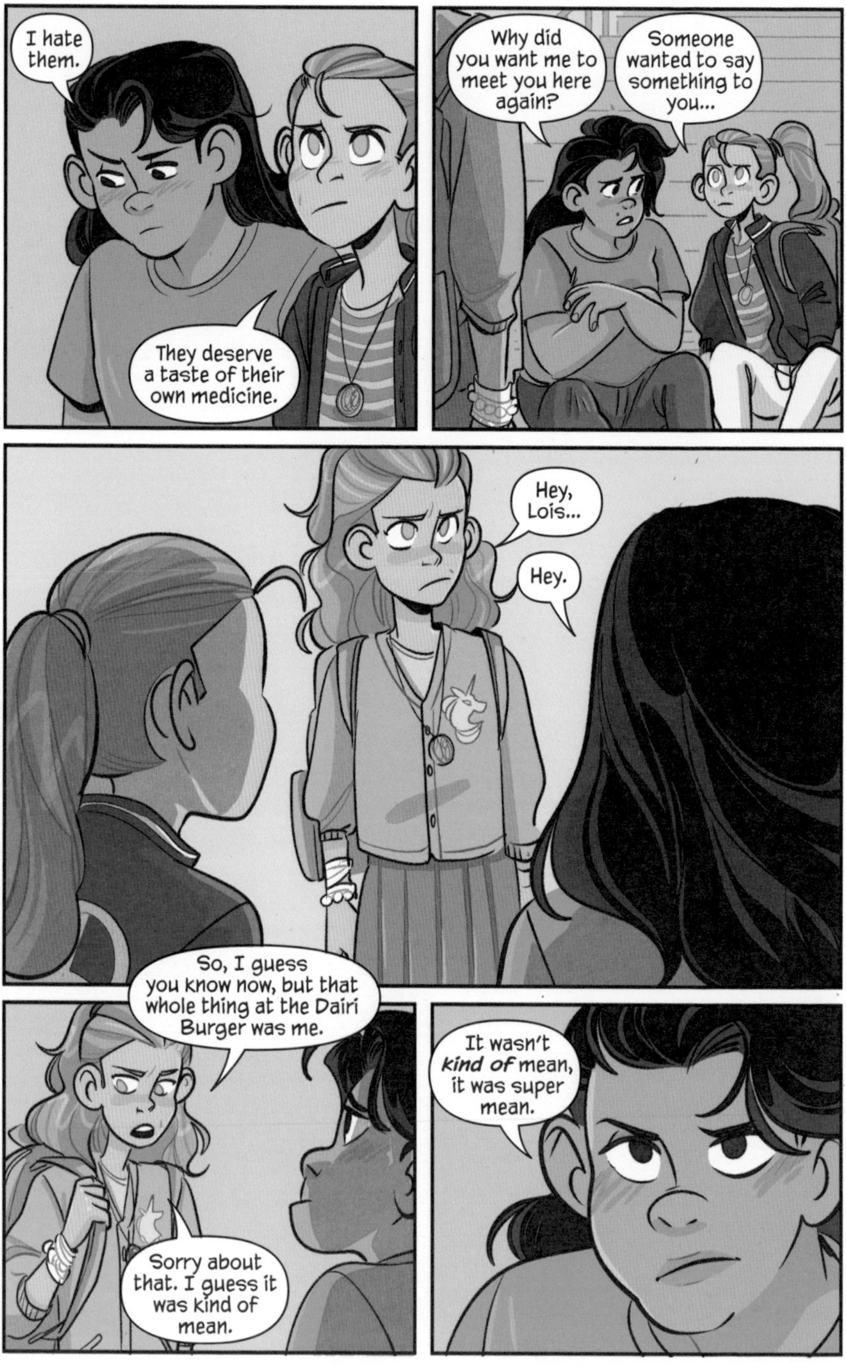
I hate them.
They deserve a taste of their own medicine.
Why did you want me to meet you here again?
Someone wanted to say something to you...
Hey, Lois...
Hey.
So, I guess you know now, but that whole thing at the Dairi Burger was me.
Sorry about that. I guess it was kind of mean.
It wasn't *kind of* mean, it was super mean.

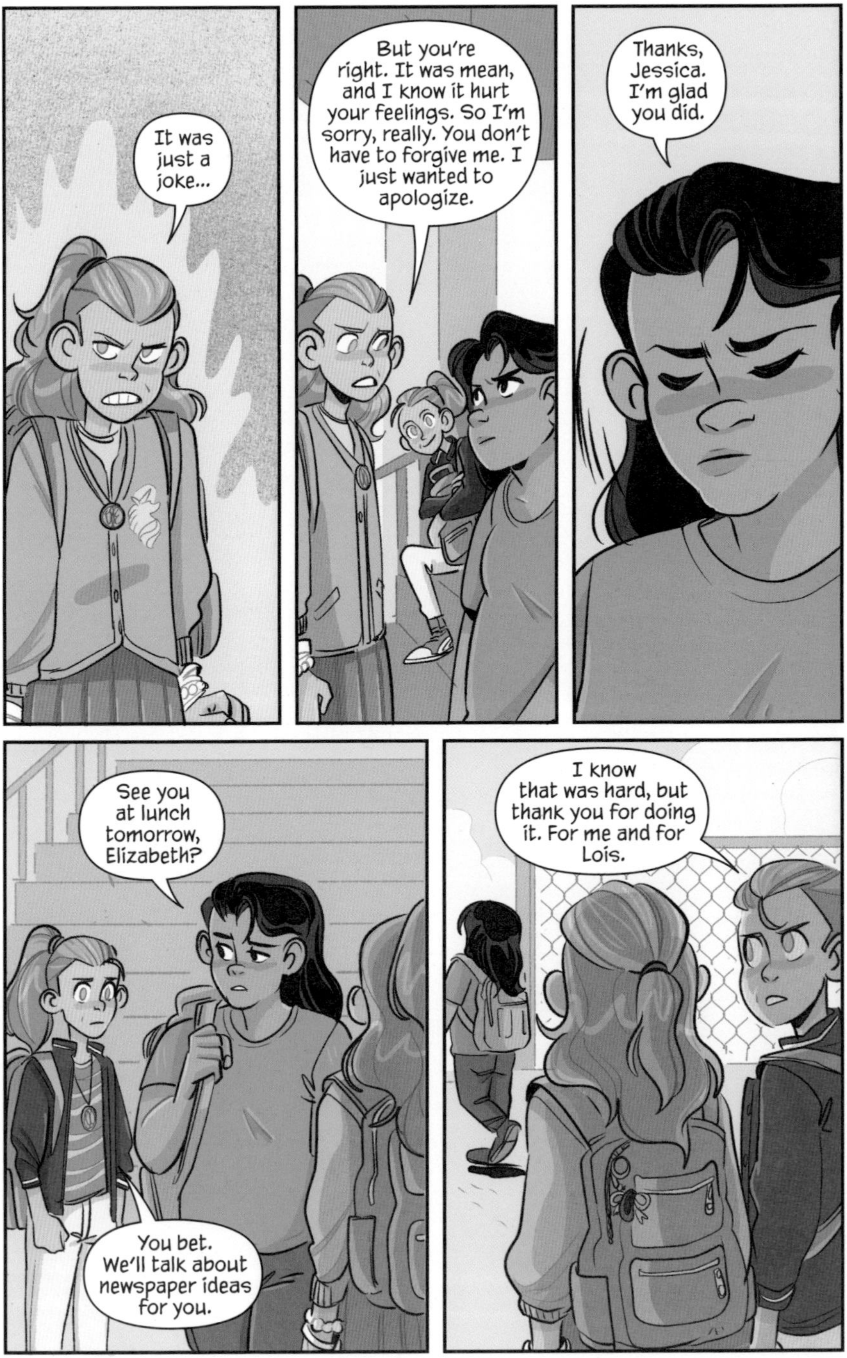
It was just a joke...
But you're right. It was mean, and I know it hurt your feelings. So I'm sorry, really. You don't have to forgive me. I just wanted to apologize.
Thanks, Jessica. I'm glad you did.
See you at lunch tomorrow, Elizabeth?
You bet. We'll talk about newspaper ideas for you.
I know that was hard, but thank you for doing it. For me and for Lois.

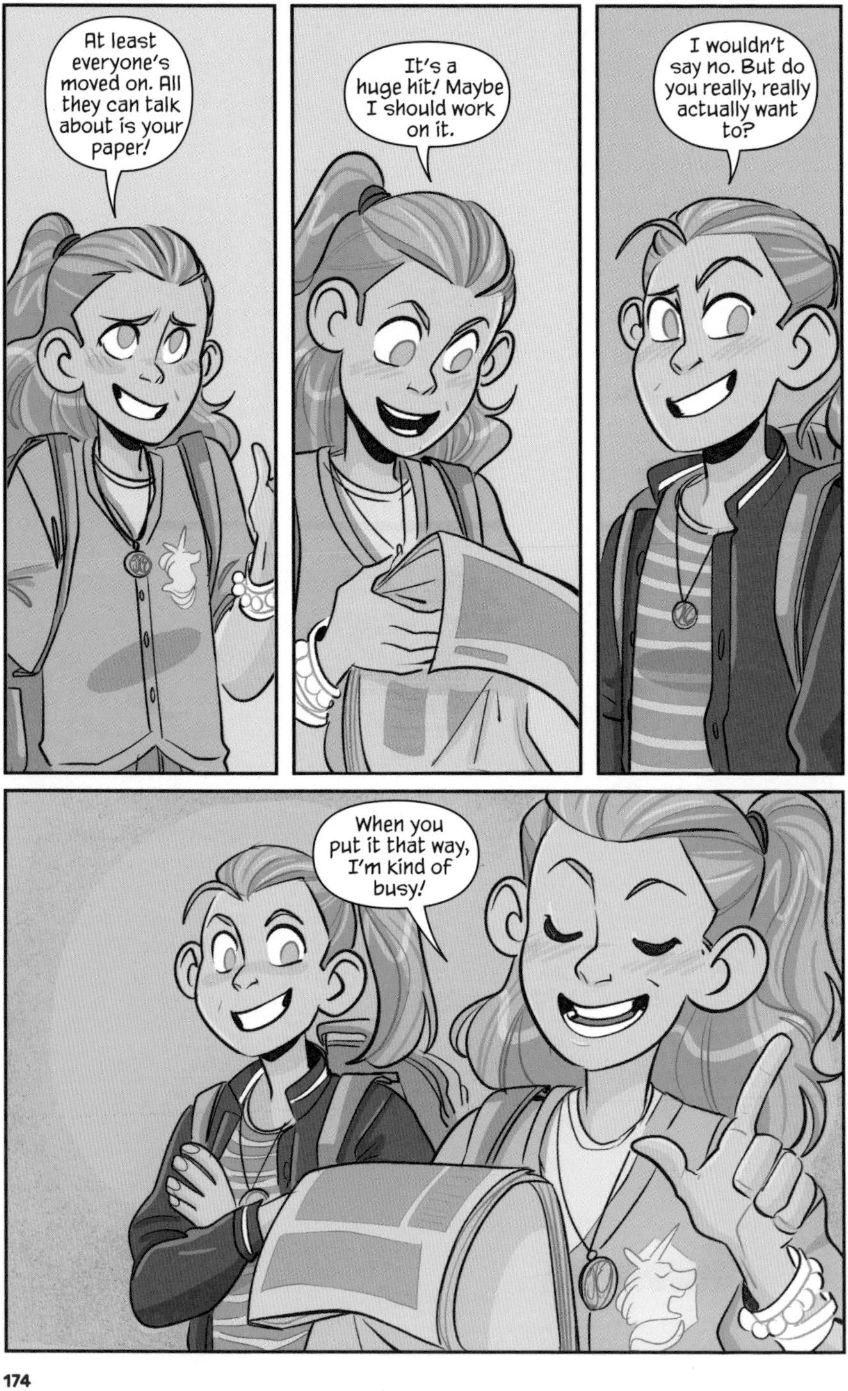
At least everyone's moved on. All they can talk about is your paper!
It's a huge hit! Maybe I should work on it.
I wouldn't say no. But do you really, really actually want to?
When you put it that way, I'm kind of busy!

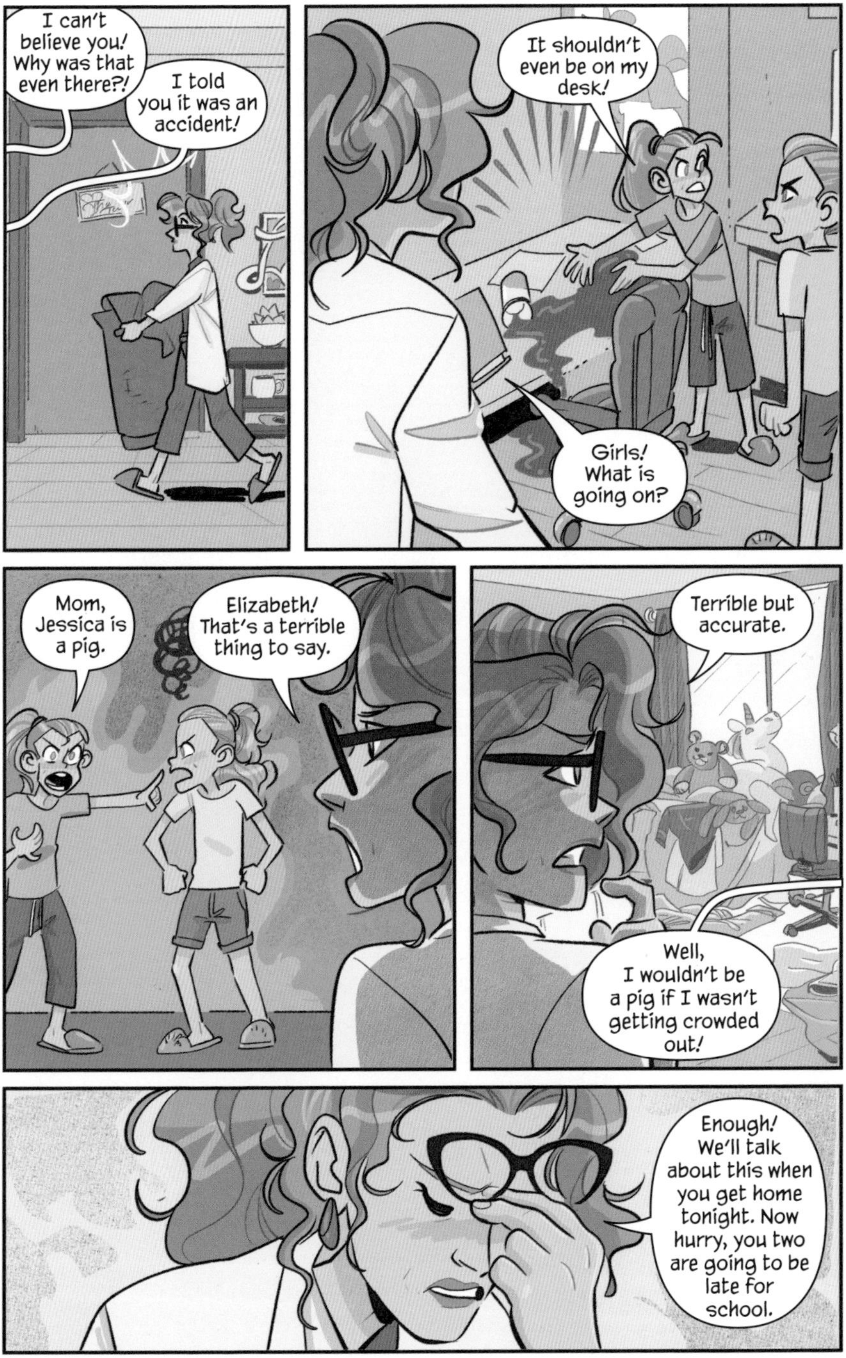
I can't believe you! Why was that even there?!
I told you it was an accident!
It shouldn't even be on my desk!
Girls! What is going on?
Mom, Jessica is a pig.
Elizabeth! That's a terrible thing to say.
Terrible but accurate.
Well, I wouldn't be a pig if I wasn't getting crowded out!
Enough! We'll talk about this when you get home tonight. Now hurry, you two are going to be late for school.

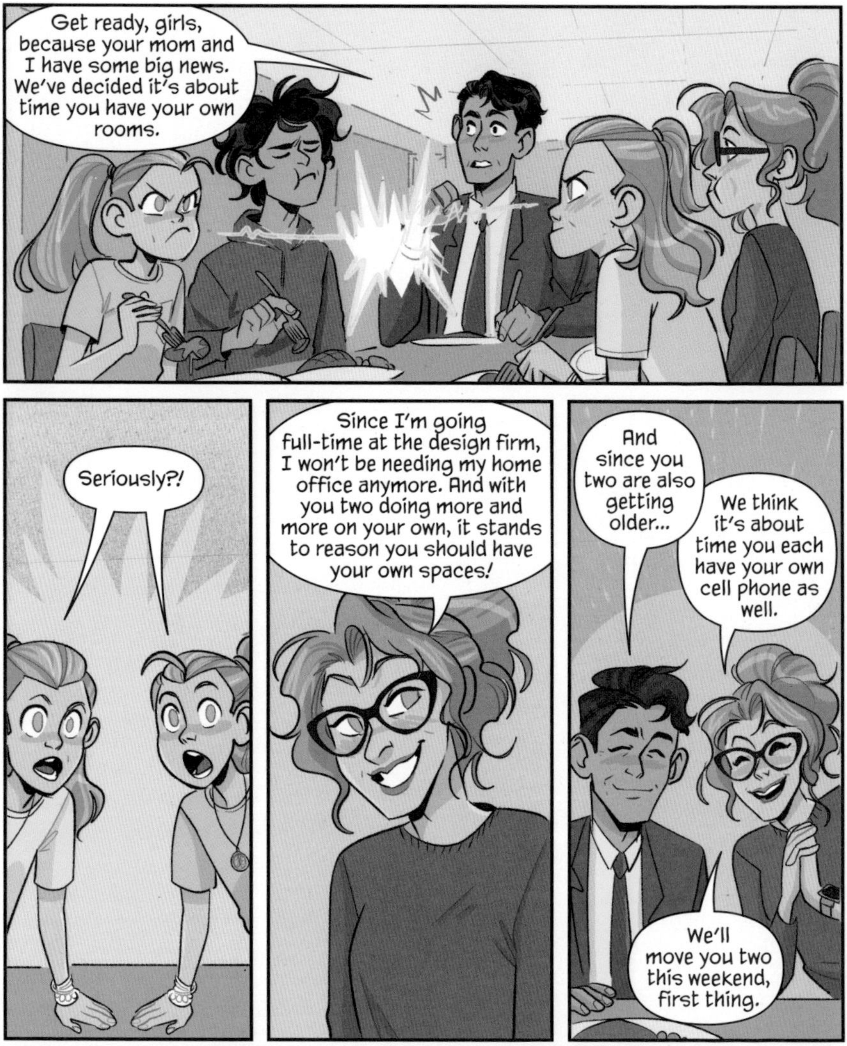
Get ready, girls, because your mom and I have some big news. We've decided it's about time you have your own rooms.
Seriously?!
Since I'm going full-time at the design firm, I won't be needing my home office anymore. And with you two doing more and more on your own, it stands to reason you should have your own spaces!
And since you two are also getting older...
We think it's about time you each have your own cell phone as well.
We'll move you two this weekend, first thing.
I know the exact phone case I want to get!
Wow. My own room!

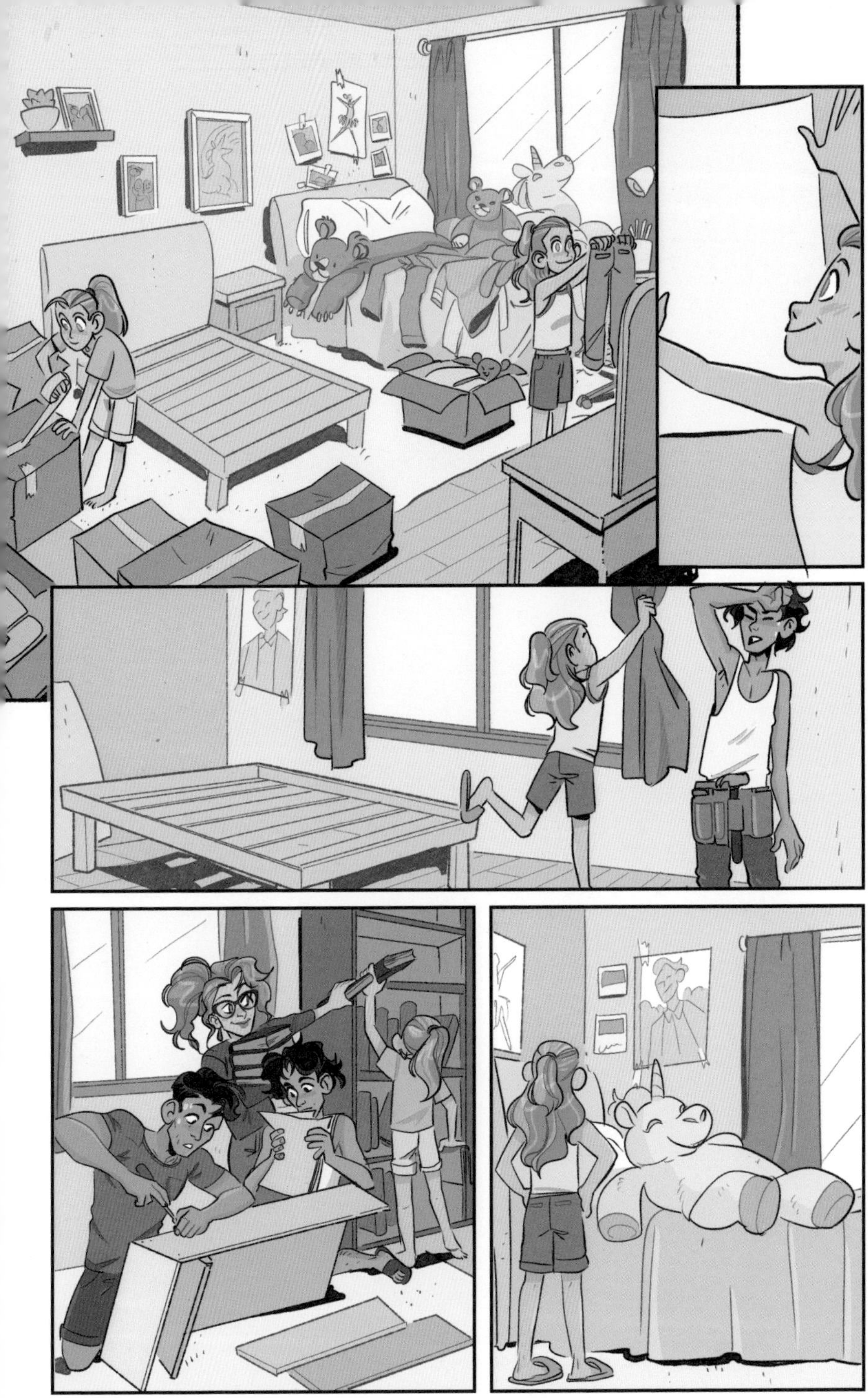

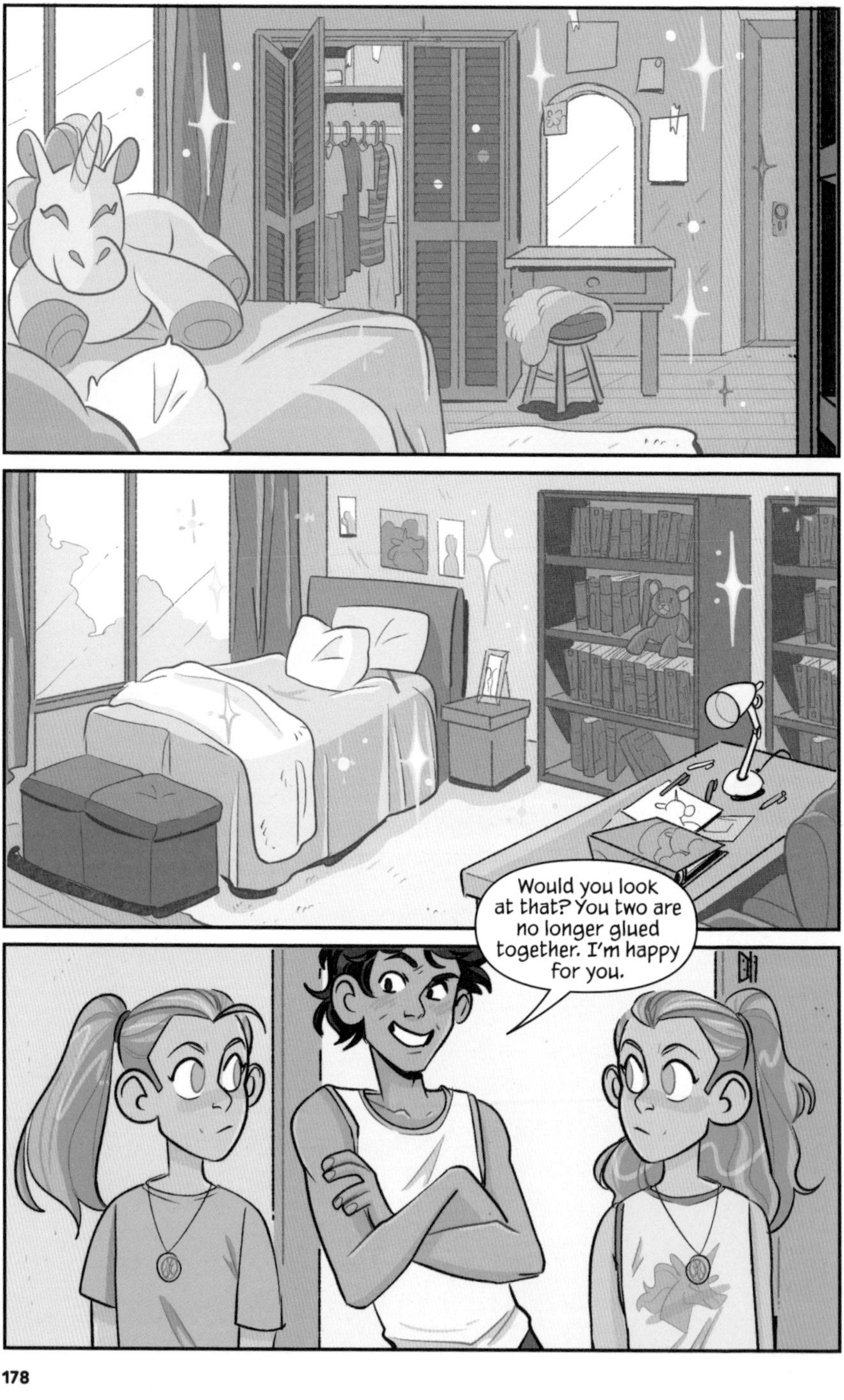
Would you look at that? You two are no longer glued together. I'm happy for you.

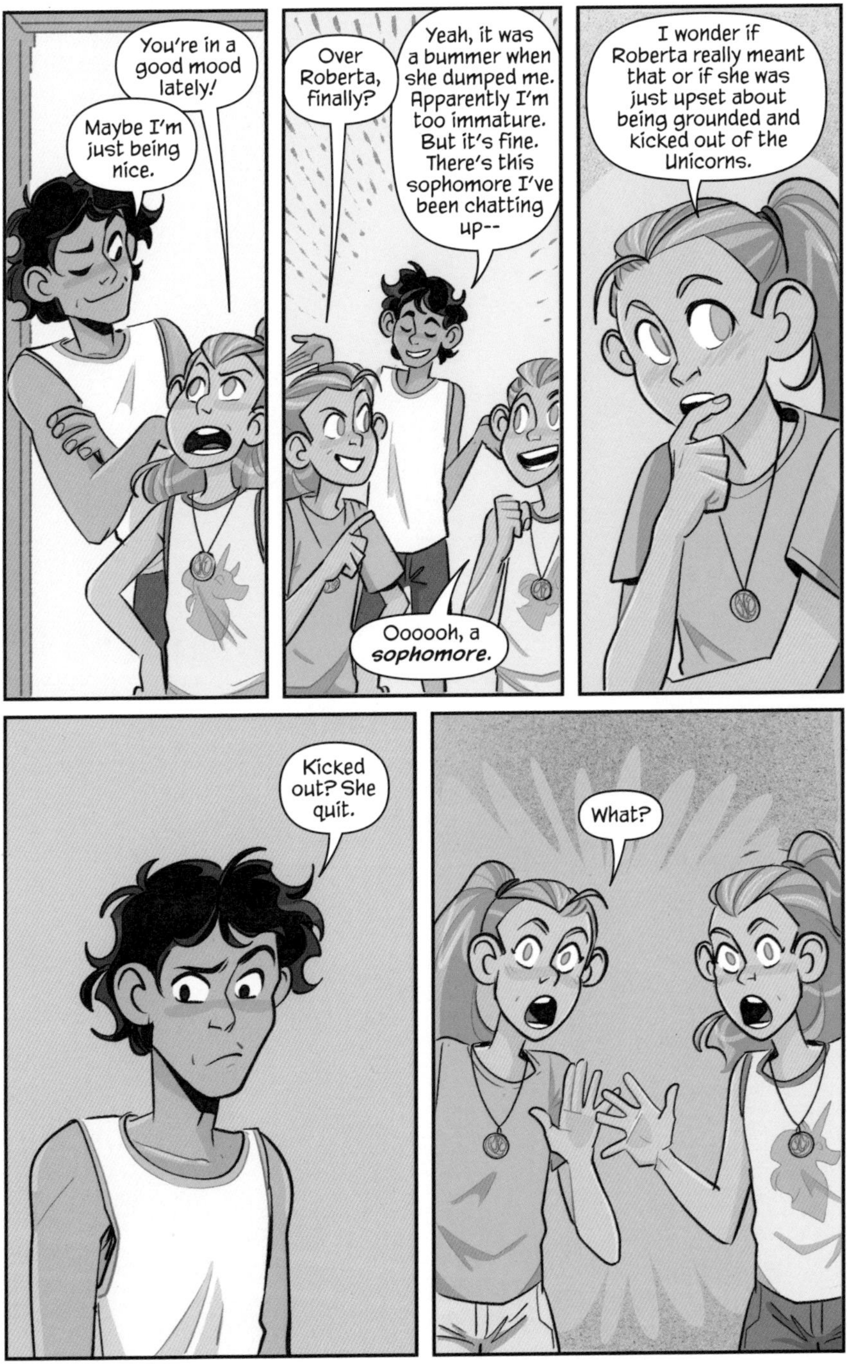
You're in a good mood lately!
Maybe I'm just being nice.
Over Roberta, finally?
Yeah, it was a bummer when she dumped me. Apparently I'm too immature. But it's fine. There's this sophomore I've been chatting up--
Oooooh, a *sophomore.*
I wonder if Roberta really meant that or if she was just upset about being grounded and kicked out of the Unicorns.
Kicked out? She quit.
What?

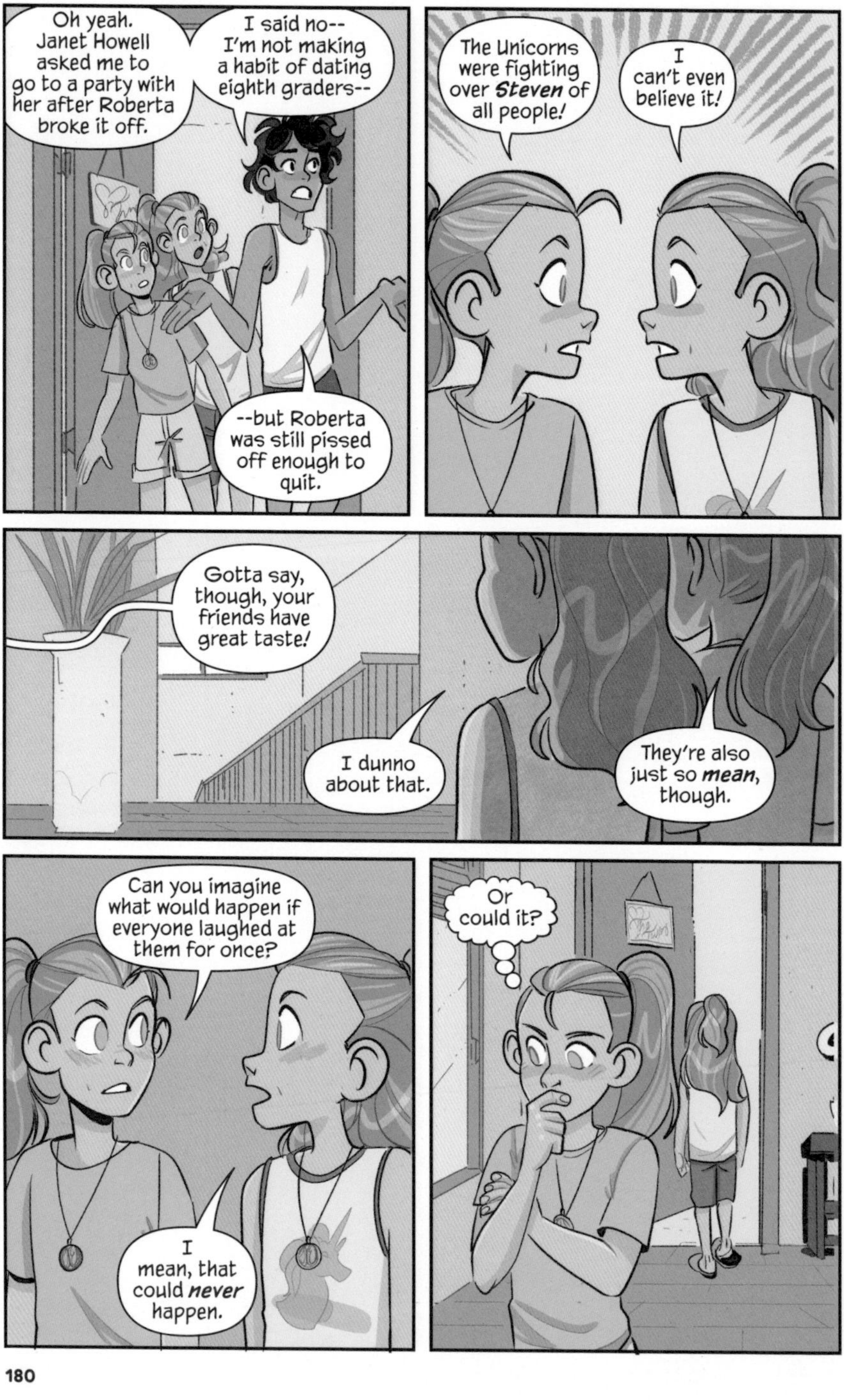

Oh yeah. Janet Howell asked me to go to a party with her after Roberta broke it off.
I said no-- I'm not making a habit of dating eighth graders--
--but Roberta was still pissed off enough to quit.
The Unicorns were fighting over *Steven* of all people!
I can't even believe it!
Gotta say, though, your friends have great taste!
I dunno about that.
They're also just so *mean*, though.
Can you imagine what would happen if everyone laughed at them for once?
I mean, that could *never* happen.
Or could it?

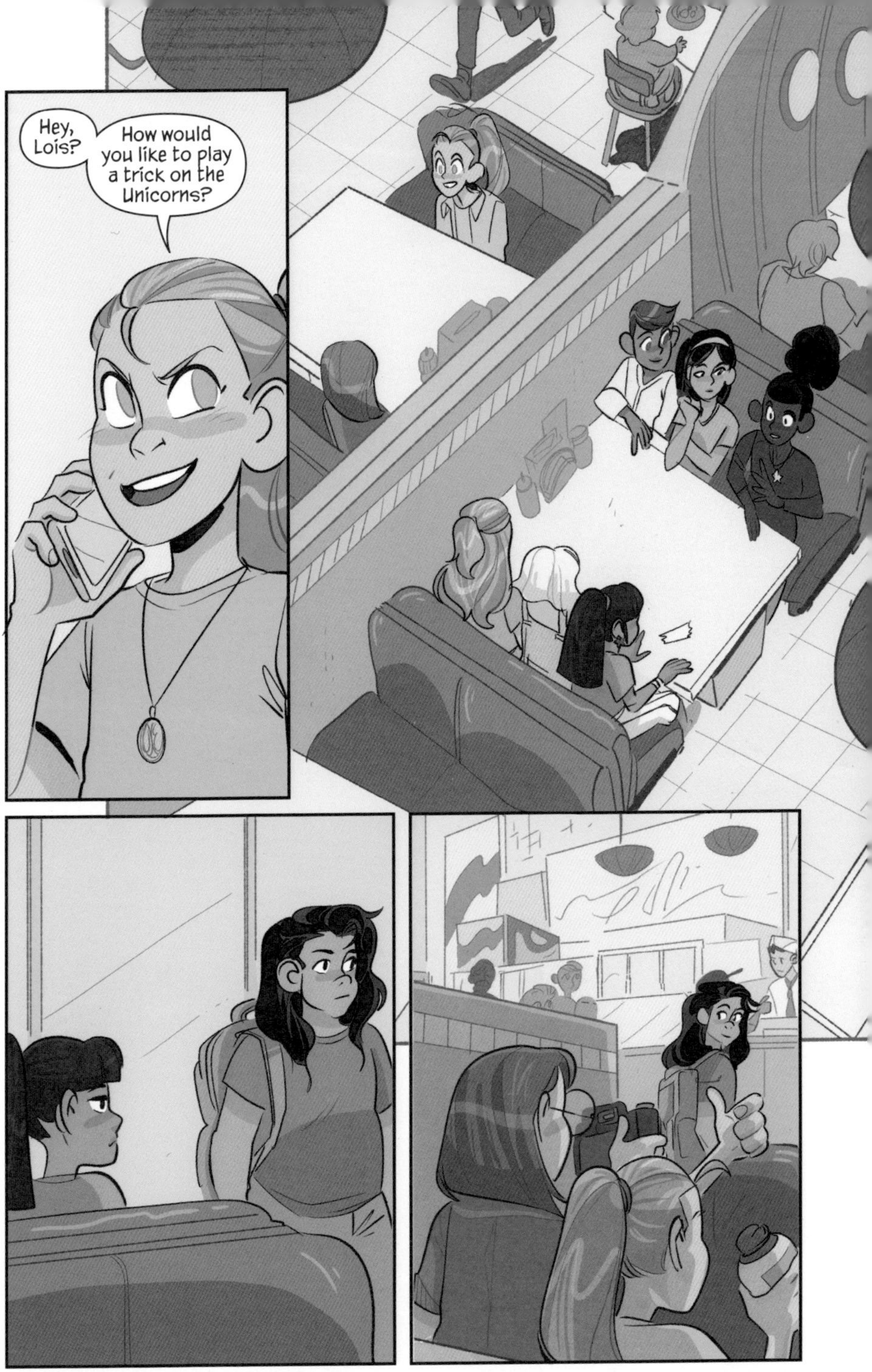
Hey, Lois?
How would you like to play a trick on the Unicorns?

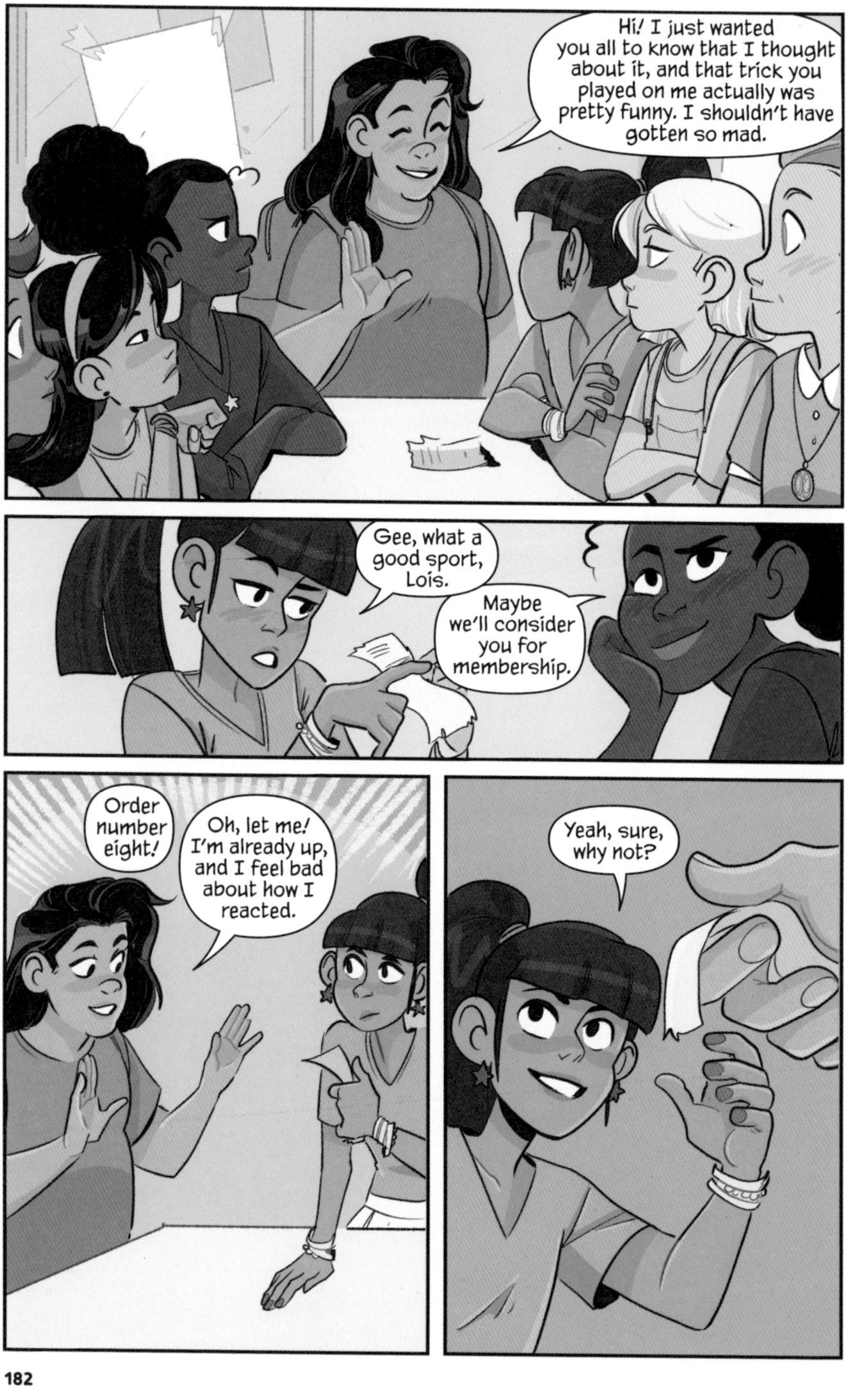
Hi! I just wanted you all to know that I thought about it, and that trick you played on me actually was pretty funny. I shouldn't have gotten so mad.
Gee, what a good sport, Lois.
Maybe we'll consider you for membership.
Order number eight!
Oh, let me! I'm already up, and I feel bad about how I reacted.
Yeah, sure, why not?

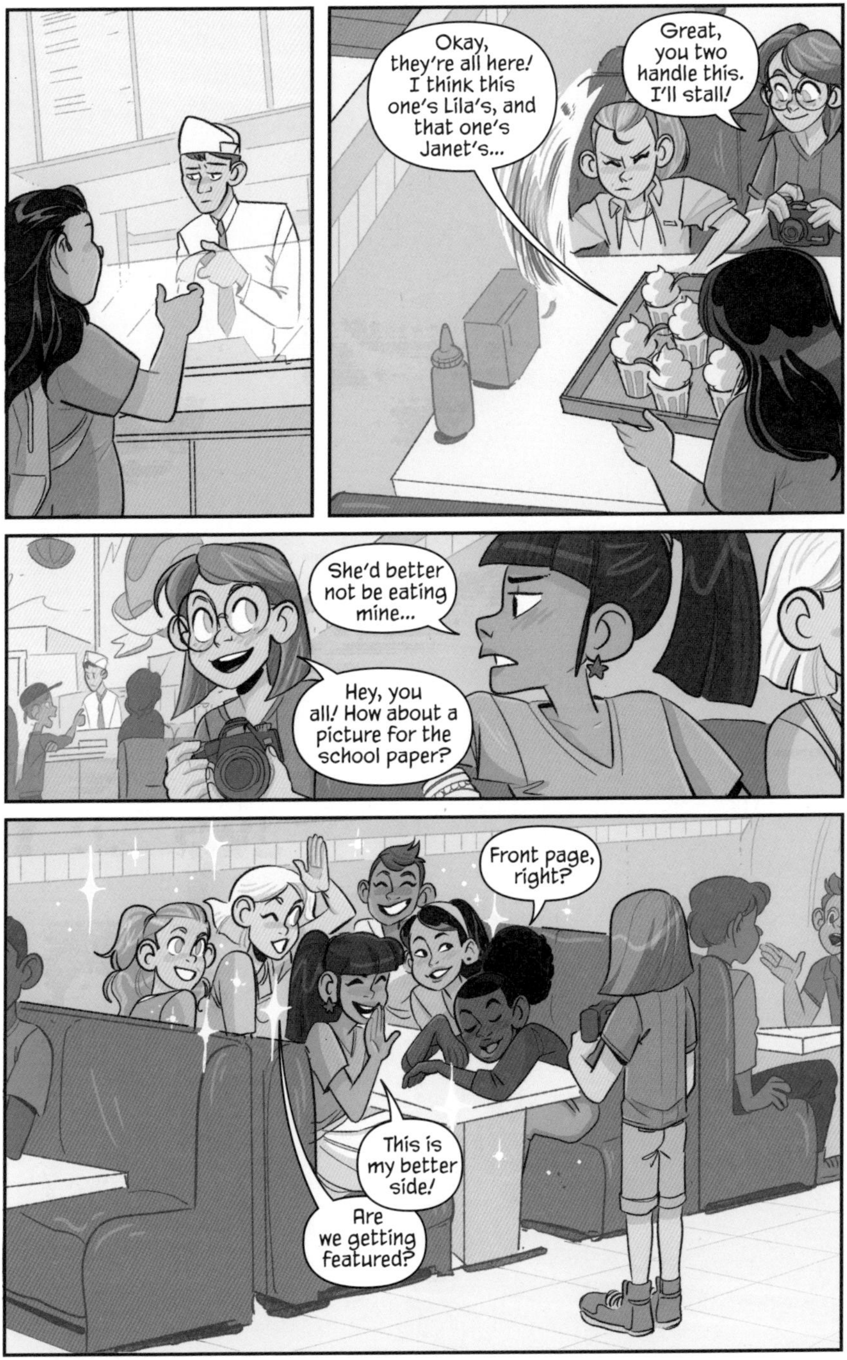
Okay, they're all here! I think this one's Lila's, and that one's Janet's...
Great, you two handle this. I'll stall!
She'd better not be eating mine...
Hey, you all! How about a picture for the school paper?
Front page, right?
This is my better side!
Are we getting featured?

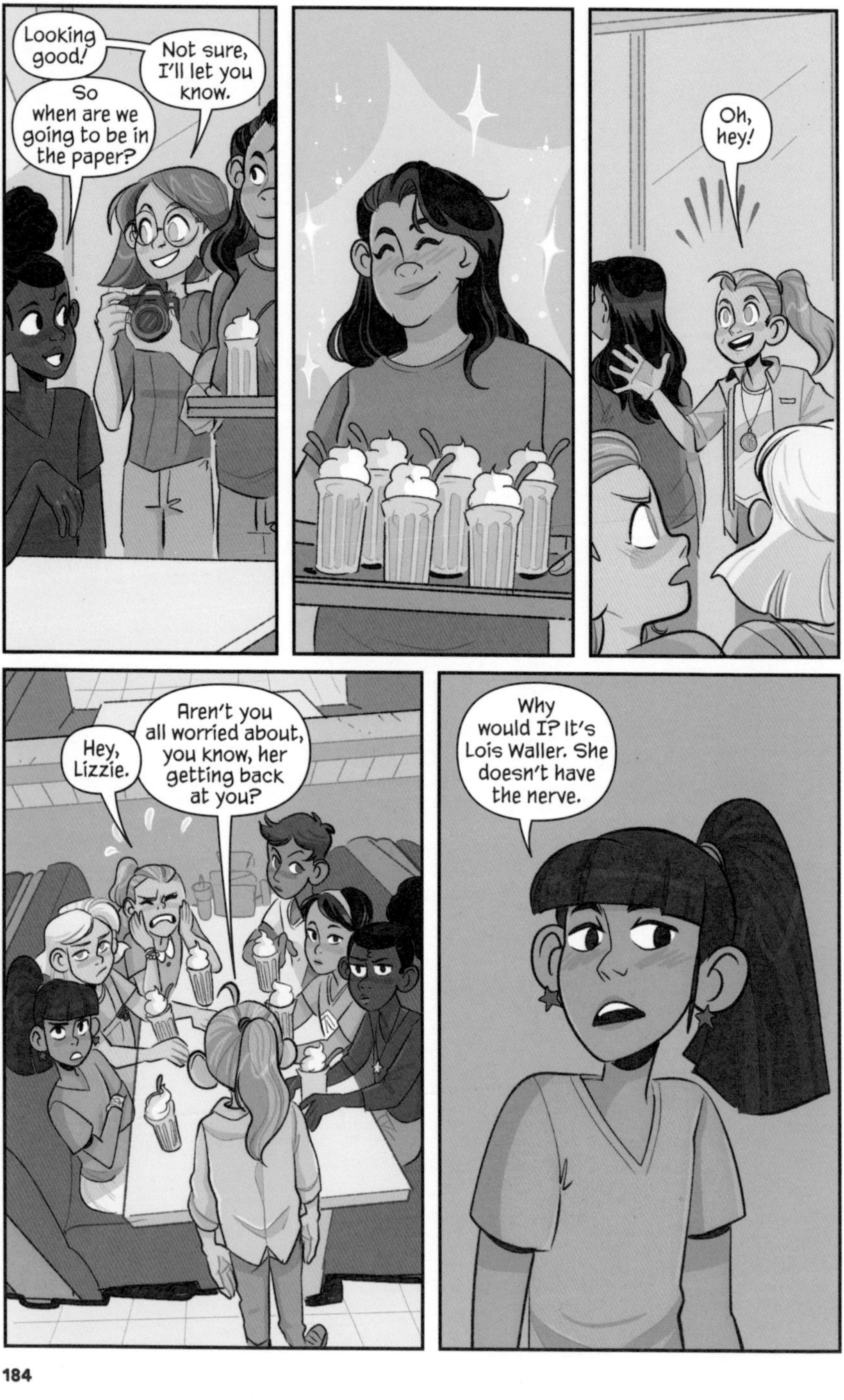
Looking good!
Not sure, I'll let you know.
So when are we going to be in the paper?
Oh, hey!
Hey, Lizzie.
Aren't you all worried about, you know, her getting back at you?
Why would I? It's Lois Waller. She doesn't have the nerve.

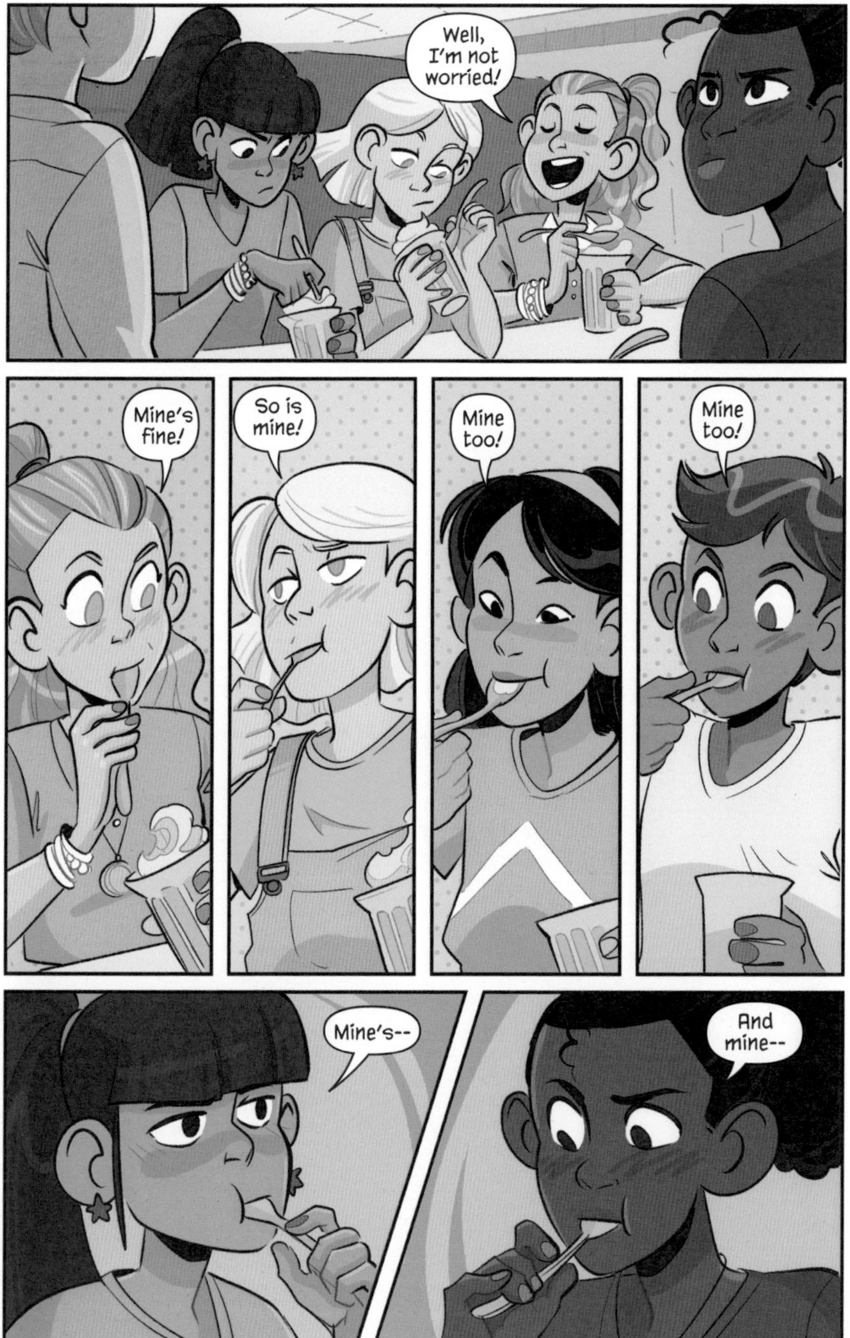
Well, I'm not worried!
Mine's fine!
So is mine!
Mine too!
Mine too!
Mine's--
And mine--

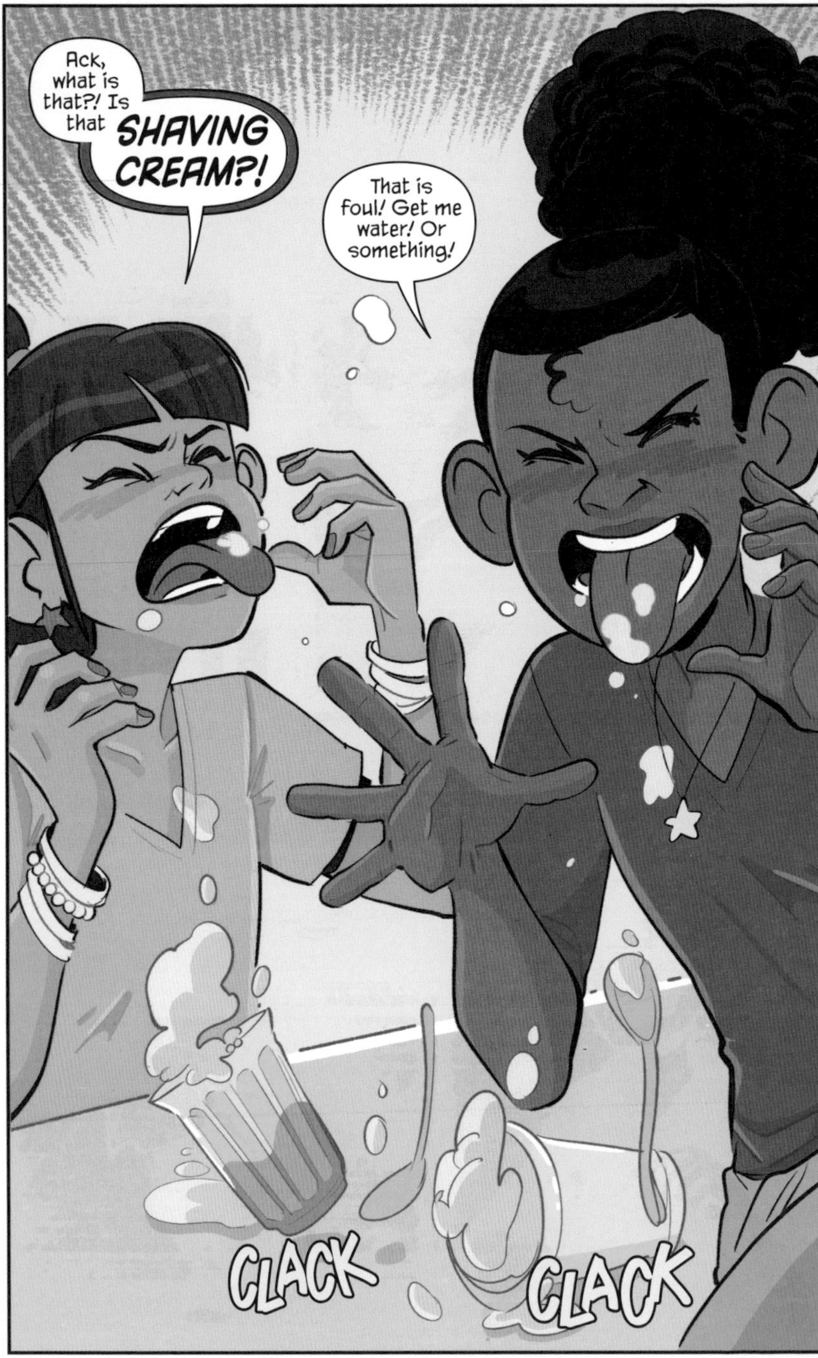
Ack, what is that?! Is that SHAVING CREAM?!
That is foul! Get me water! Or something!
CLACK
CLACK

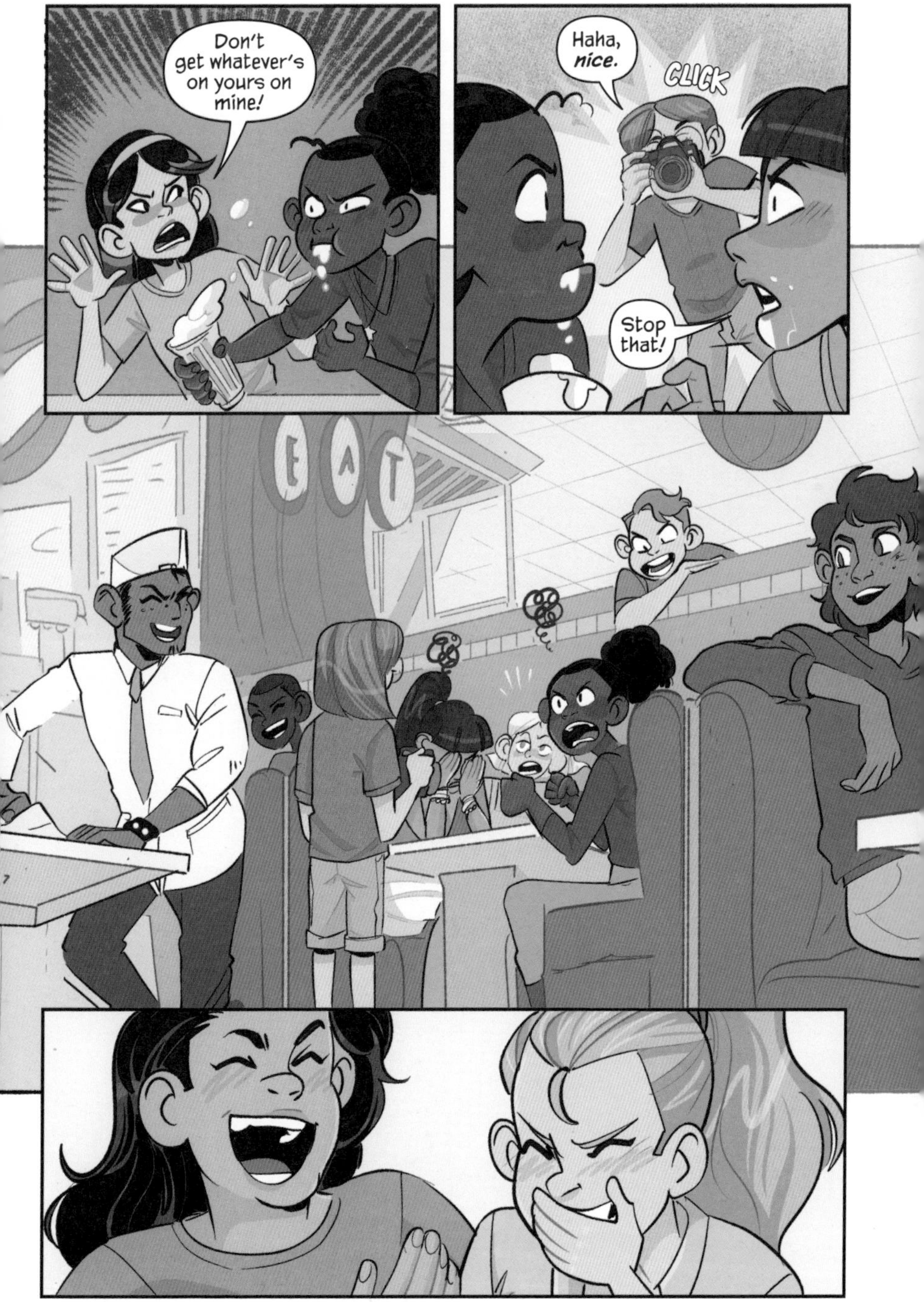
Don't get whatever's on yours on mine!
Haha, *nice*.
CLICK
Stop that!
EAT

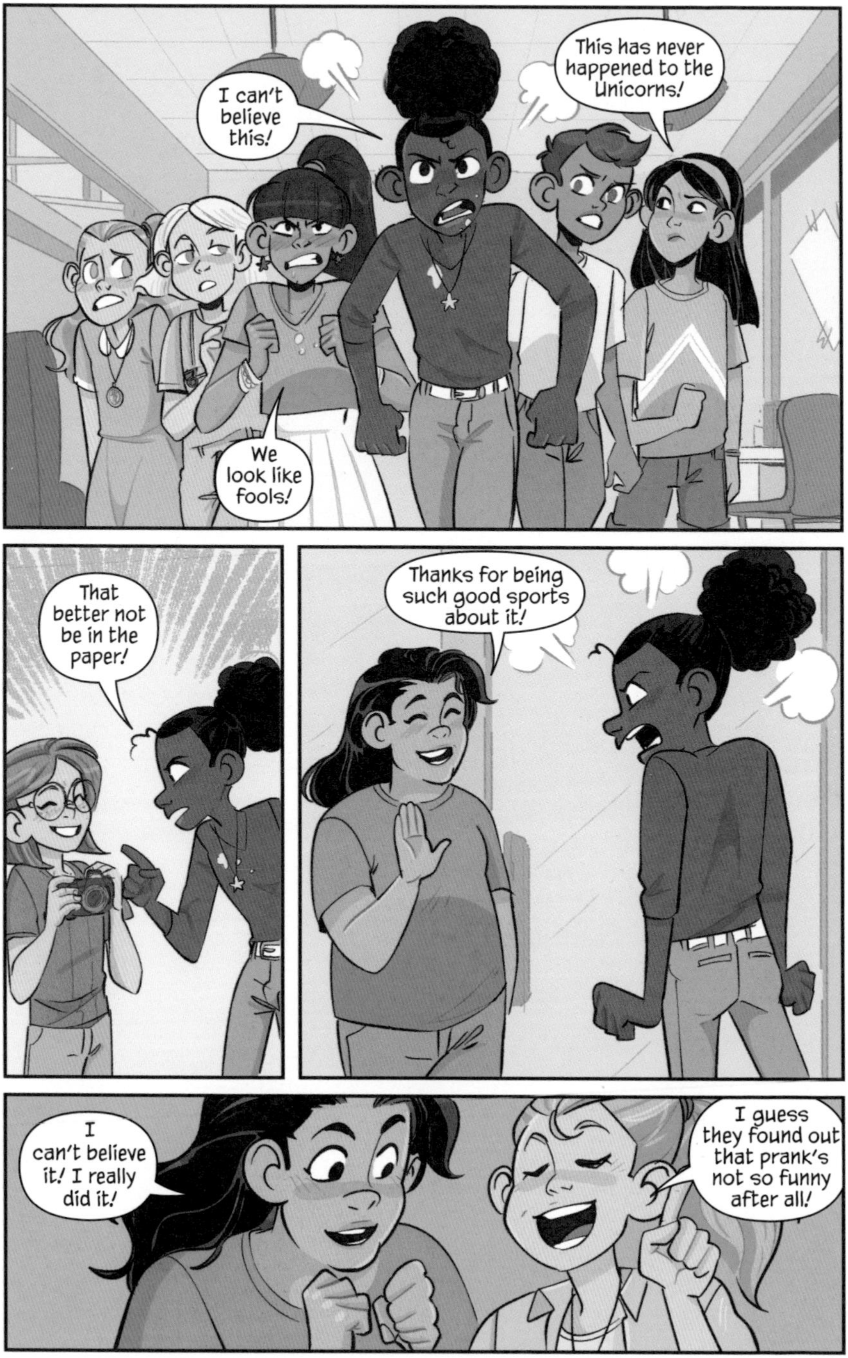
I can't believe this!
This has never happened to the Unicorns!
We look like fools!
That better not be in the paper!
Thanks for being such good sports about it!
I can't believe it! I really did it!
I guess they found out that prank's not so funny after all!

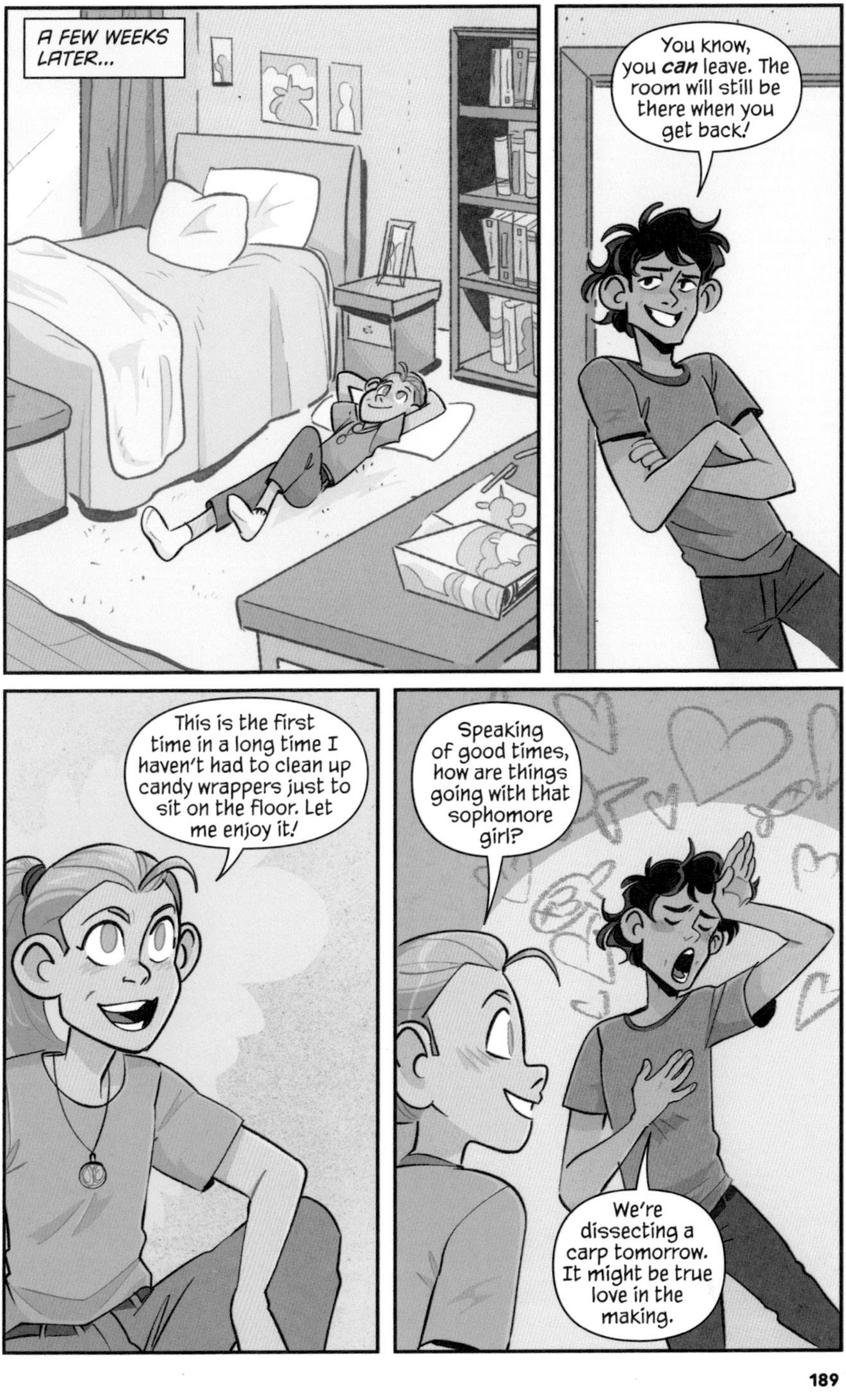
A FEW WEEKS LATER...
You know, you *can* leave. The room will still be there when you get back!
This is the first time in a long time I haven't had to clean up candy wrappers just to sit on the floor. Let me enjoy it!
Speaking of good times, how are things going with that sophomore girl?
We're dissecting a carp tomorrow. It might be true love in the making.

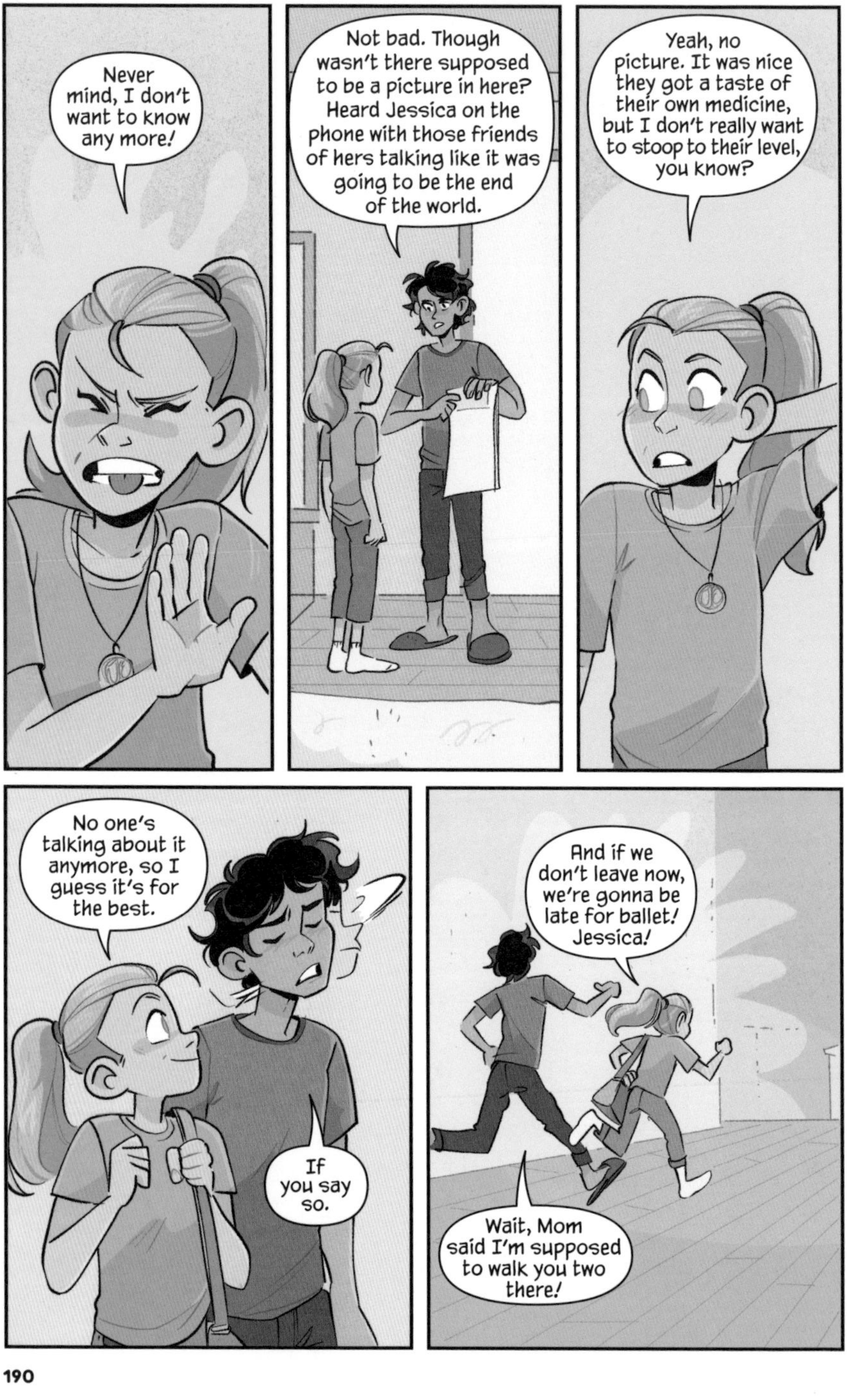

Never mind, I don't want to know any more!
Not bad. Though wasn't there supposed to be a picture in here? Heard Jessica on the phone with those friends of hers talking like it was going to be the end of the world.
Yeah, no picture. It was nice they got a taste of their own medicine, but I don't really want to stoop to their level, you know?
No one's talking about it anymore, so I guess it's for the best.
If you say so.
And if we don't leave now, we're gonna be late for ballet! Jessica!
Wait, Mom said I'm supposed to walk you two there!

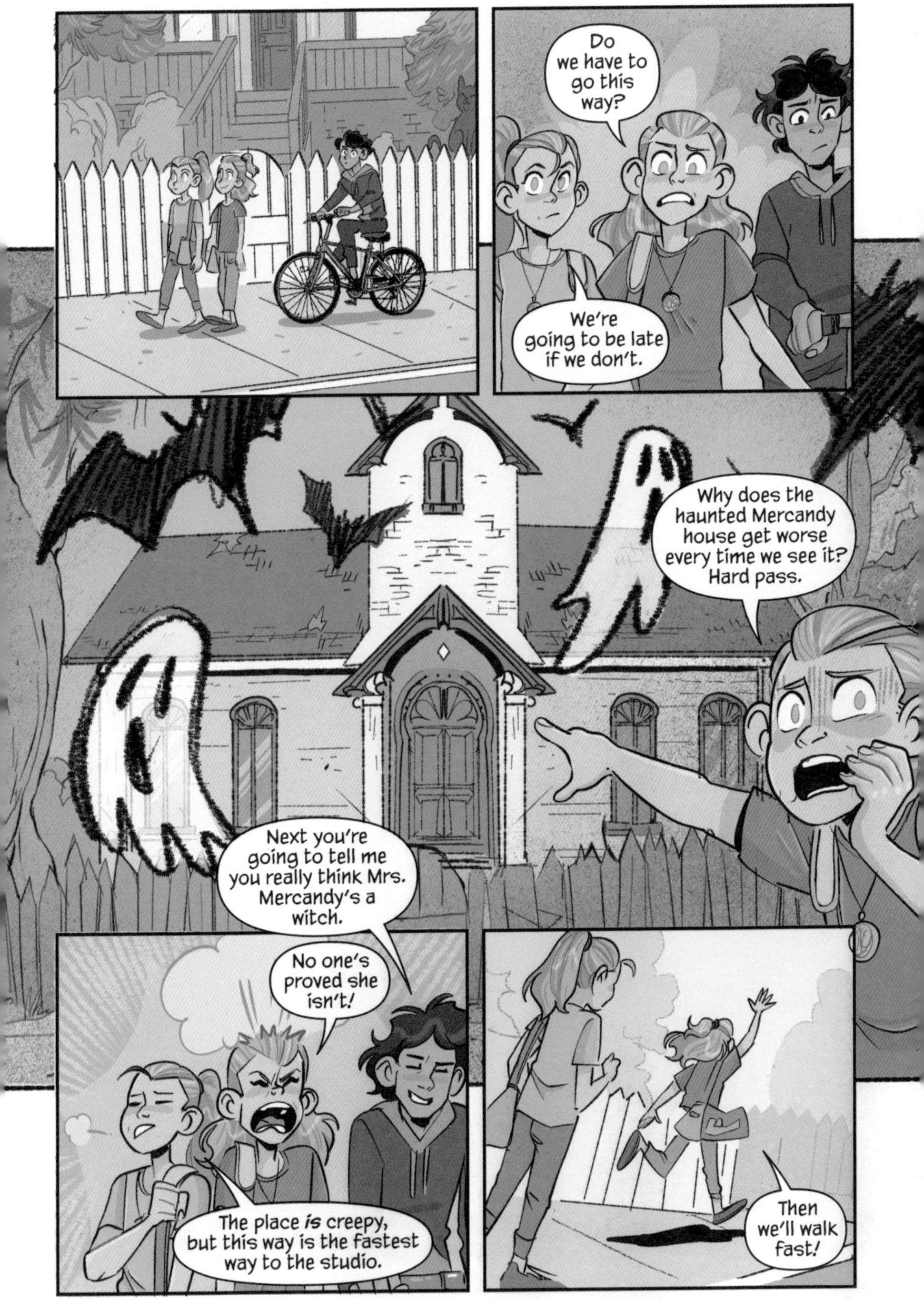
Do we have to go this way?
We're going to be late if we don't.
Why does the haunted Mercandy house get worse every time we see it? Hard pass.
Next you're going to tell me you really think Mrs. Mercandy's a witch.
No one's proved she isn't!
The place *is* creepy, but this way is the fastest way to the studio.
Then we'll walk fast!

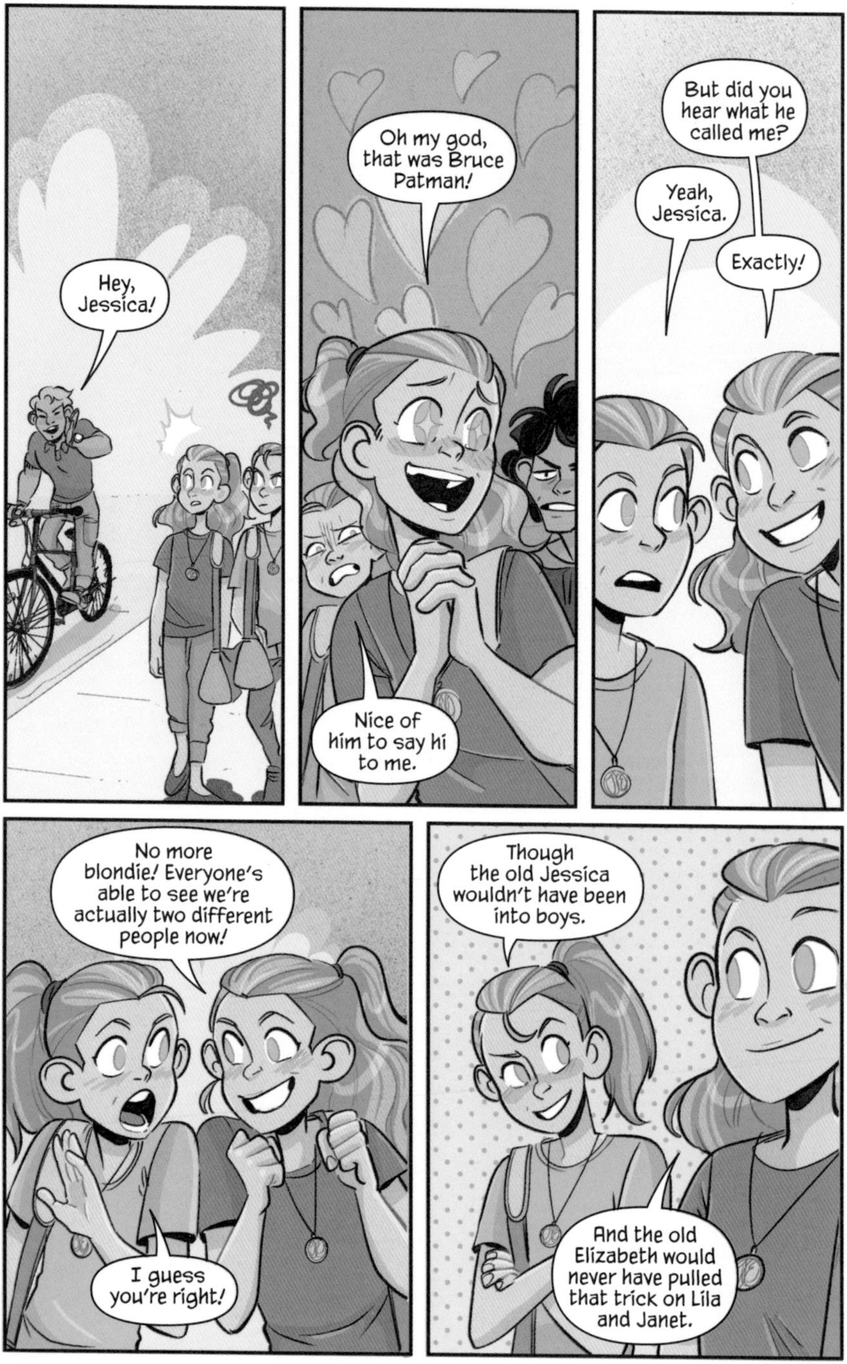
Hey, Jessica!
Oh my god, that was Bruce Patman!
Nice of him to say hi to me.
But did you hear what he called me?
Yeah, Jessica.
Exactly!
No more blondie! Everyone's able to see we're actually two different people now!
I guess you're right!
Though the old Jessica wouldn't have been into boys.
And the old Elizabeth would never have pulled that trick on Lila and Janet.

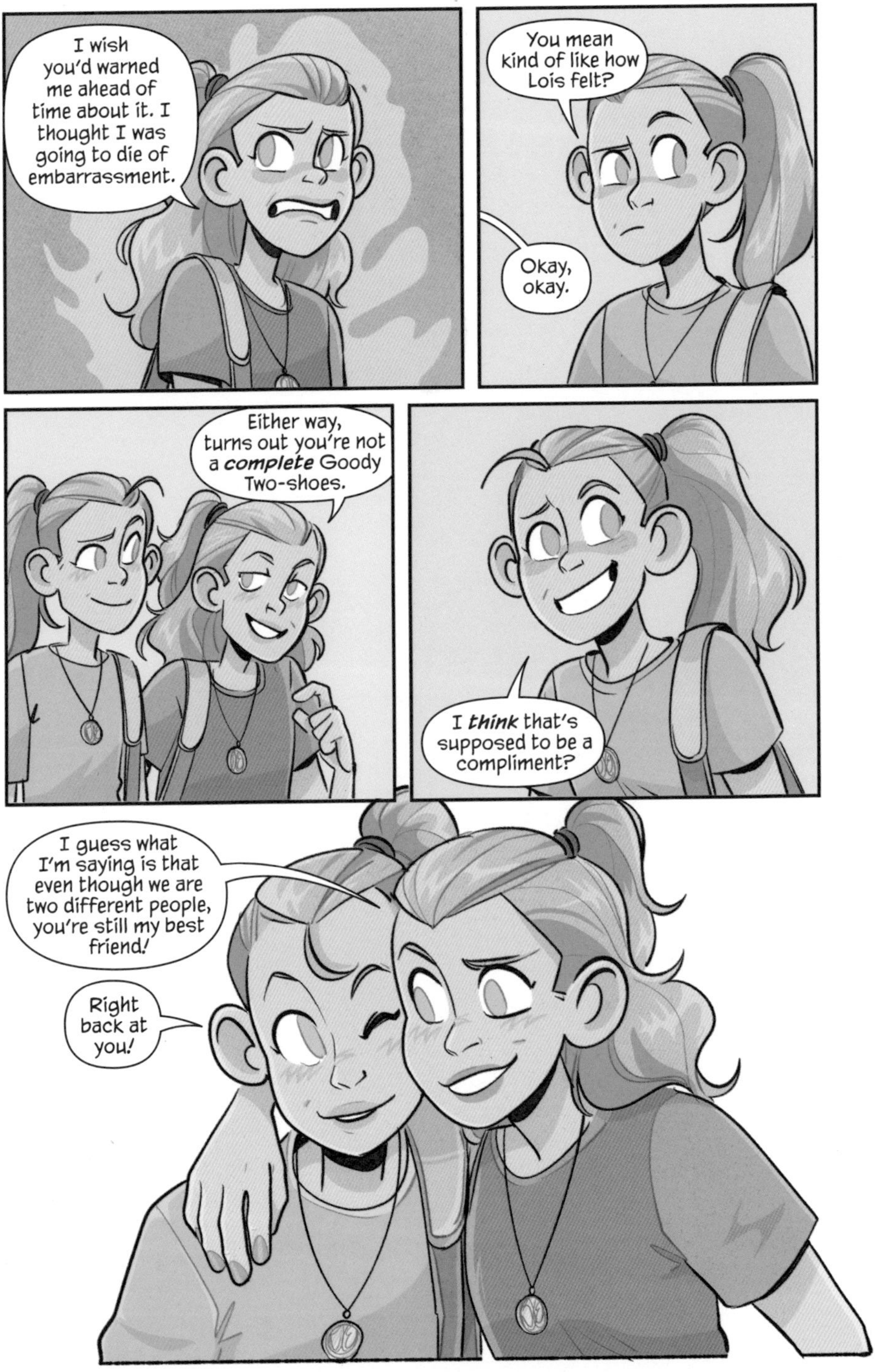
I wish you'd warned me ahead of time about it. I thought I was going to die of embarrassment.
You mean kind of like how Lois felt?
Okay, okay.
Either way, turns out you're not a ***complete*** Goody Two-shoes.
I ***think*** that's supposed to be a compliment?
I guess what I'm saying is that even though we are two different people, you're still my best friend!
Right back at you!

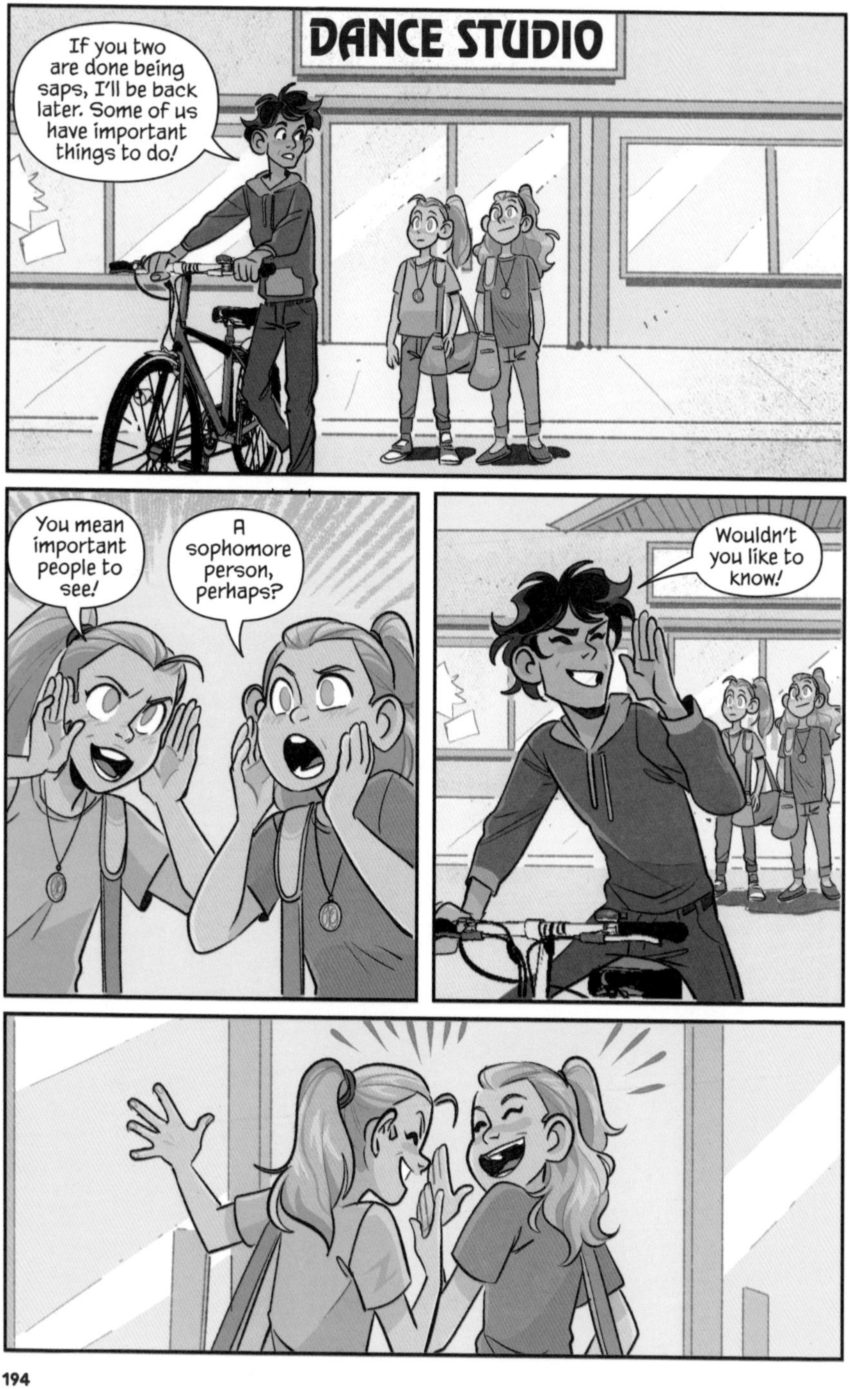
DANCE STUDIO
If you two are done being saps, I'll be back later. Some of us have important things to do!
You mean important people to see!
A sophomore person, perhaps?
Wouldn't you like to know!

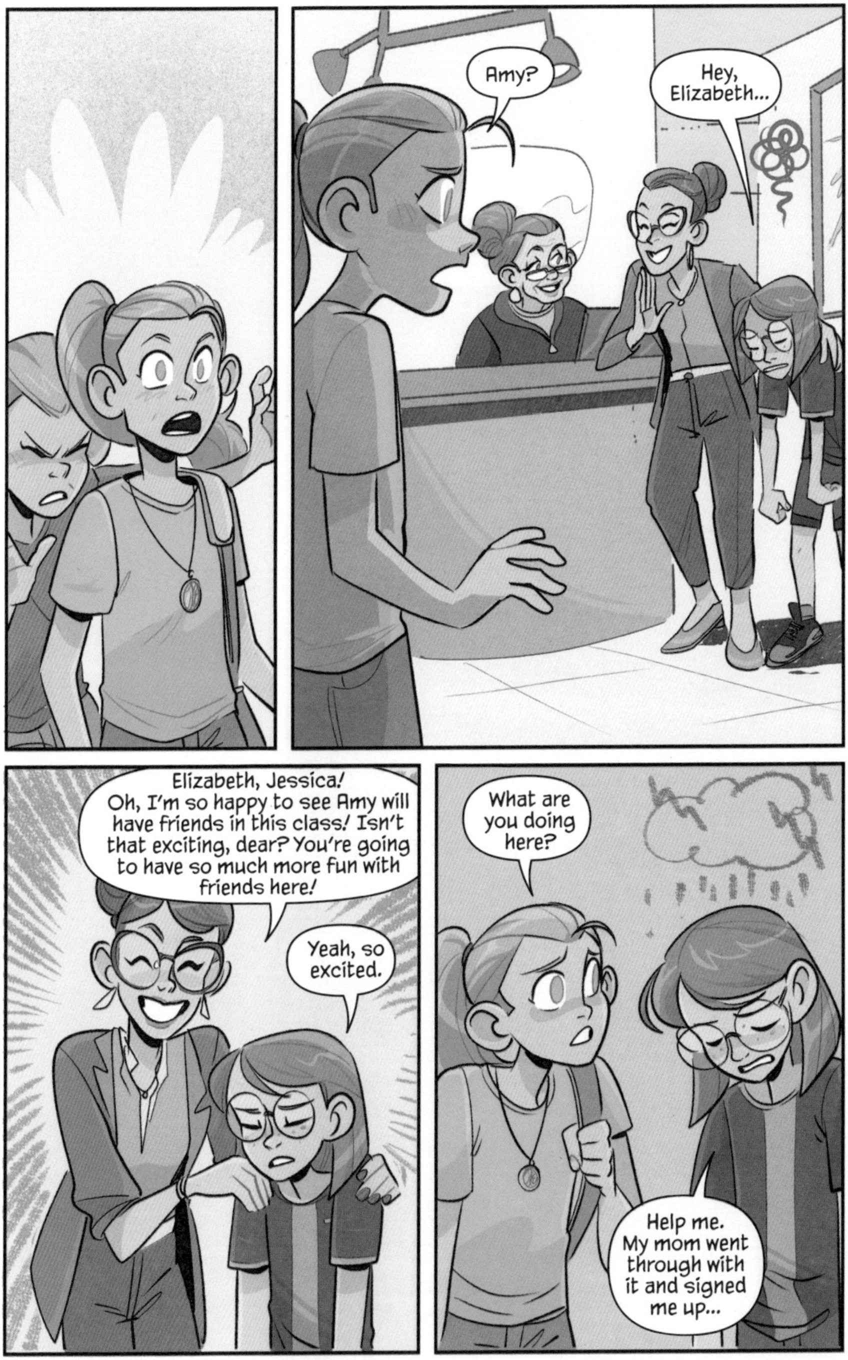
Amy?
Hey, Elizabeth...
Elizabeth, Jessica! Oh, I'm so happy to see Amy will have friends in this class! Isn't that exciting, dear? You're going to have so much more fun with friends here!
Yeah, so excited.
What are you doing here?
Help me. My mom went through with it and signed me up...

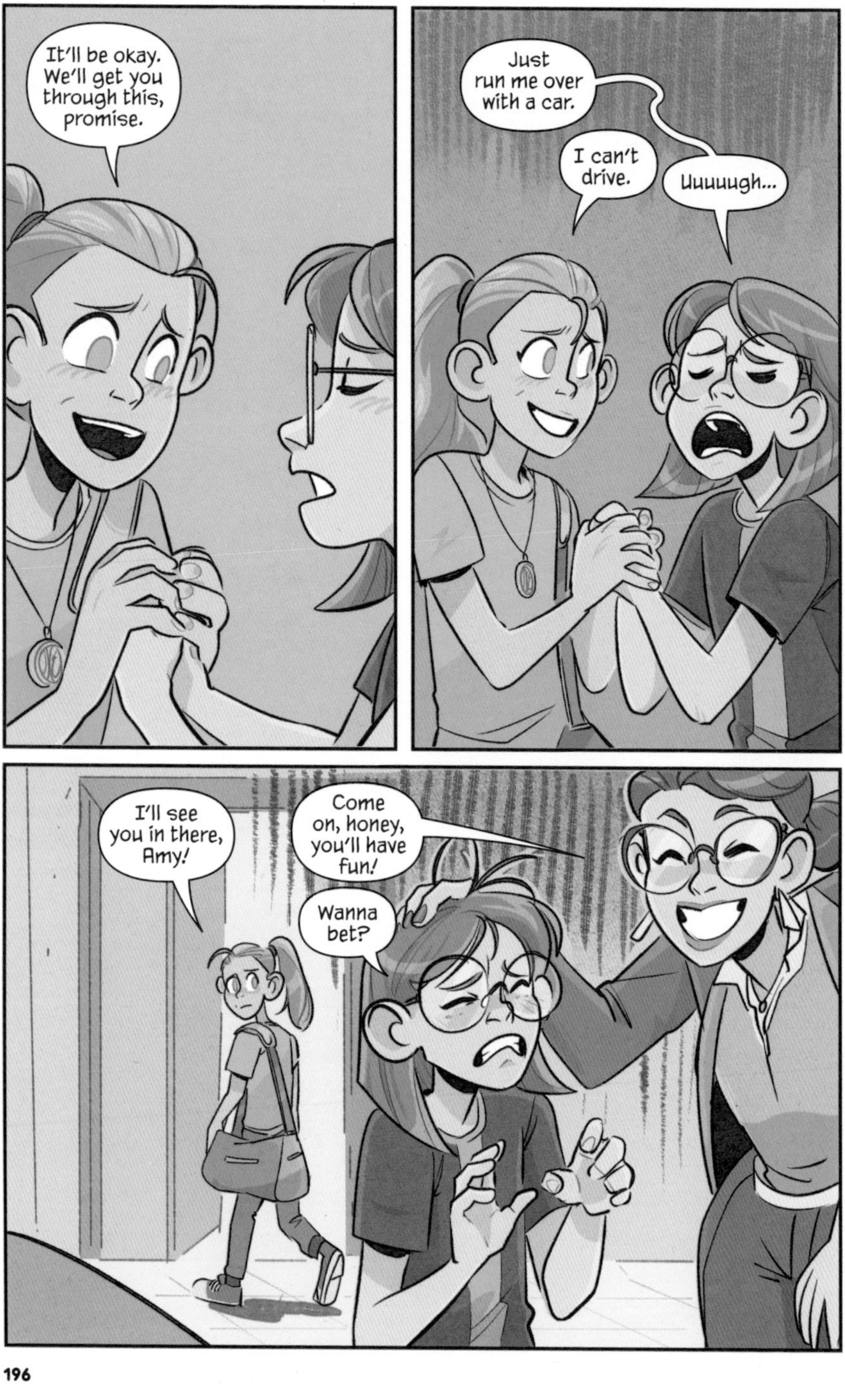
It'll be okay. We'll get you through this, promise.
Just run me over with a car.
I can't drive.
Uuuuugh...
I'll see you in there, Amy!
Come on, honey, you'll have fun!
Wanna bet?

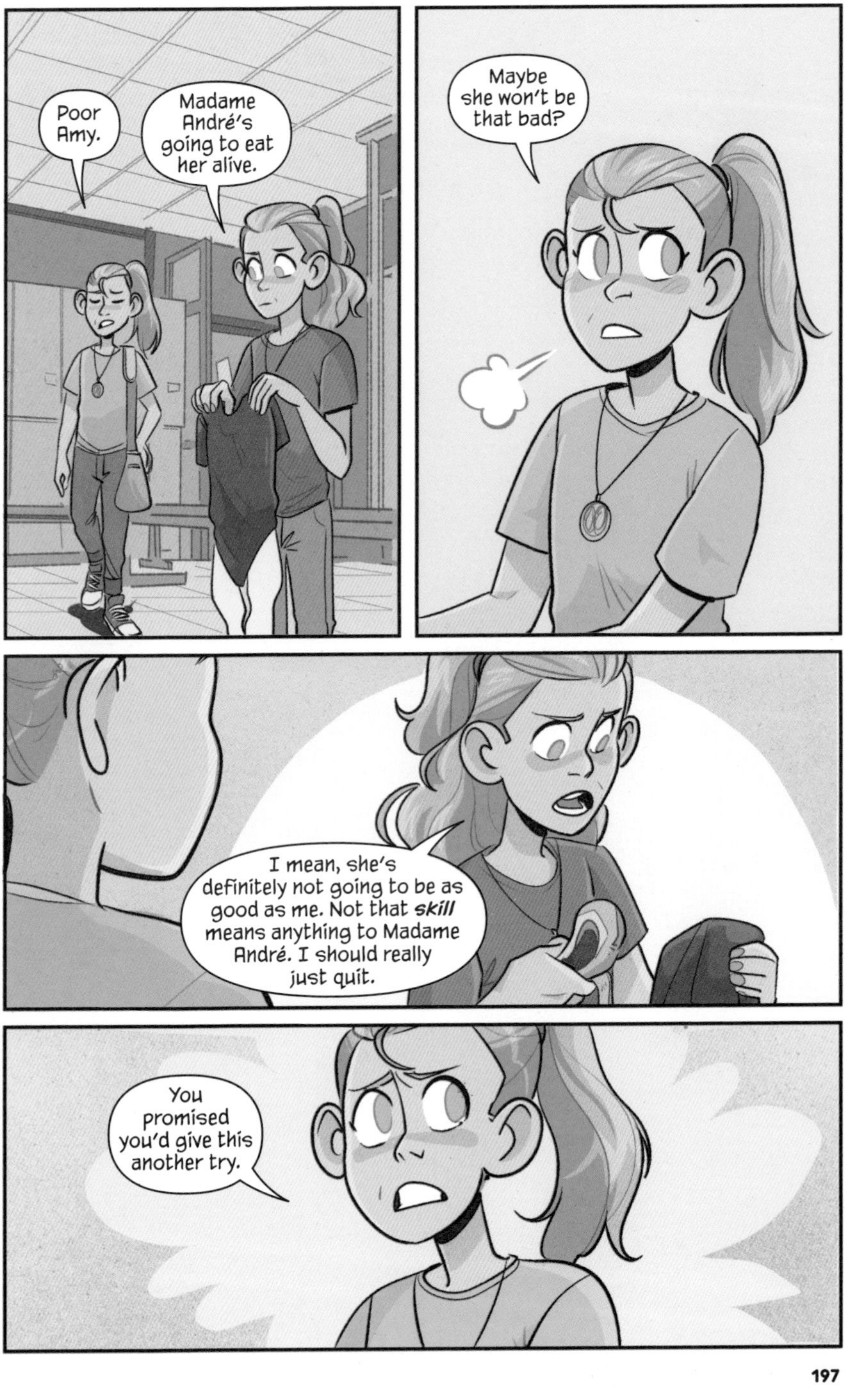
Poor Amy.
Madame André's going to eat her alive.
Maybe she won't be that bad?
I mean, she's definitely not going to be as good as me. Not that *skill* means anything to Madame André. I should really just quit.
You promised you'd give this another try.

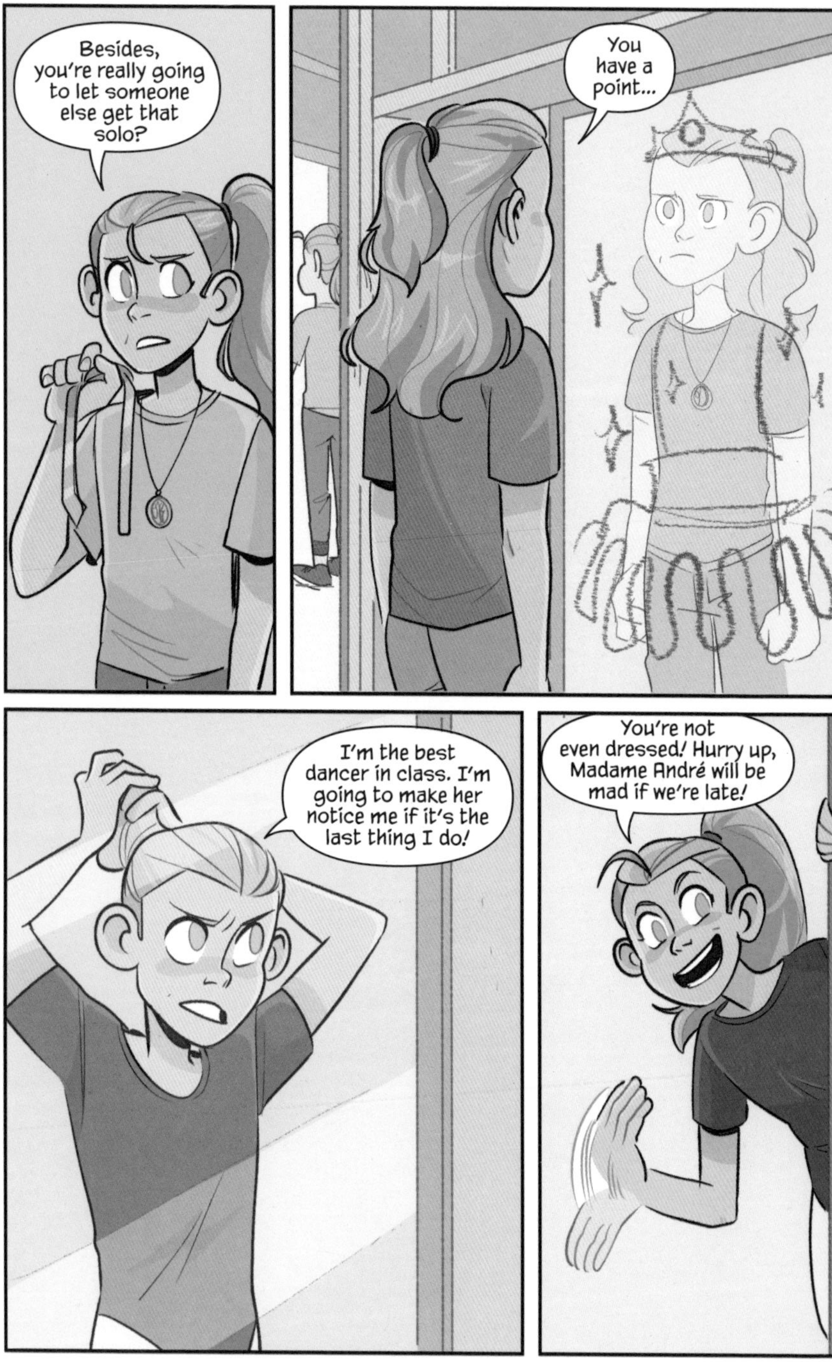
Besides, you're really going to let someone else get that solo?
You have a point...
I'm the best dancer in class. I'm going to make her notice me if it's the last thing I do!
You're not even dressed! Hurry up, Madame André will be mad if we're late!

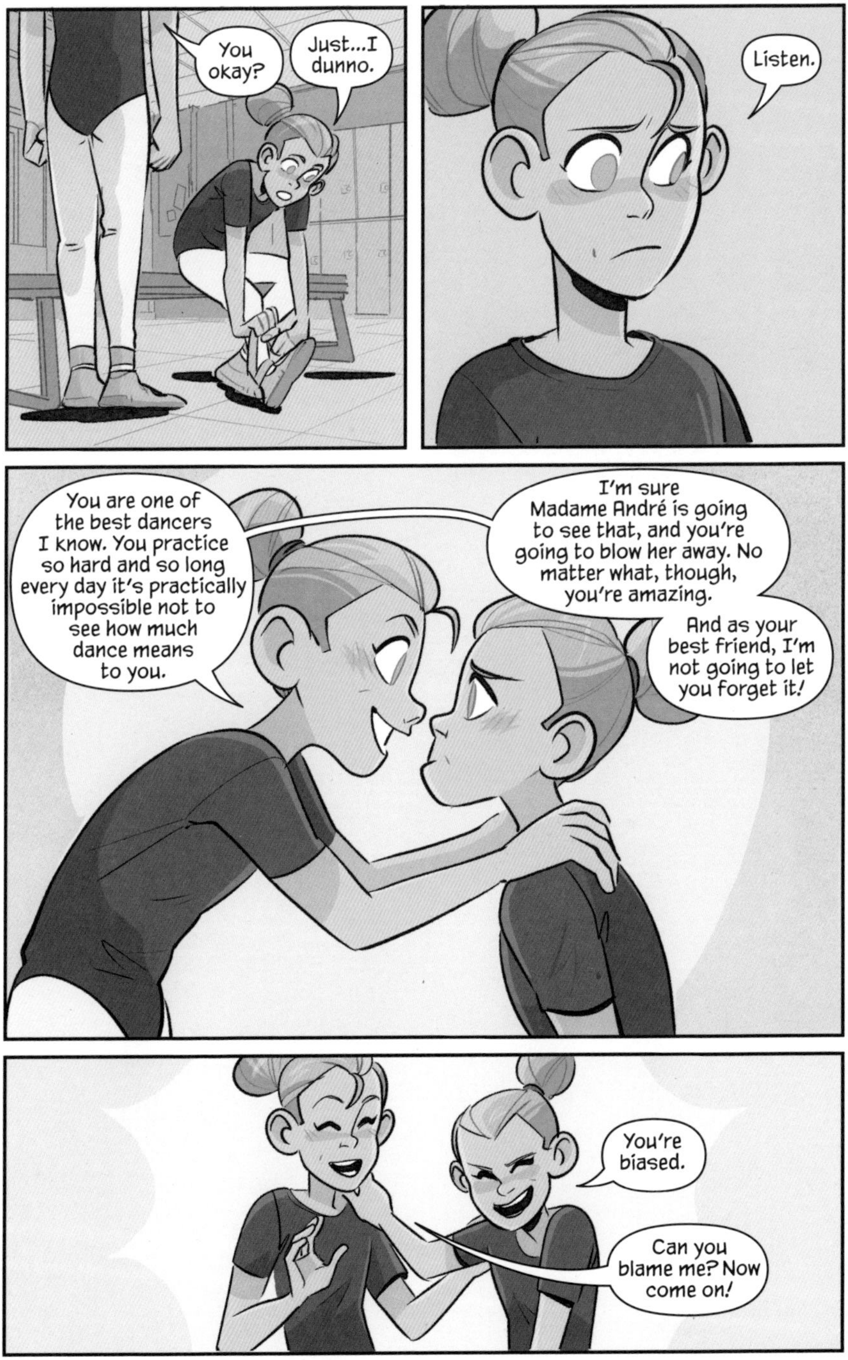
You okay?
Just...I dunno.
Listen.
You are one of the best dancers I know. You practice so hard and so long every day it's practically impossible not to see how much dance means to you.
I'm sure Madame André is going to see that, and you're going to blow her away. No matter what, though, you're amazing.
And as your best friend, I'm not going to let you forget it!
You're biased.
Can you blame me? Now come on!

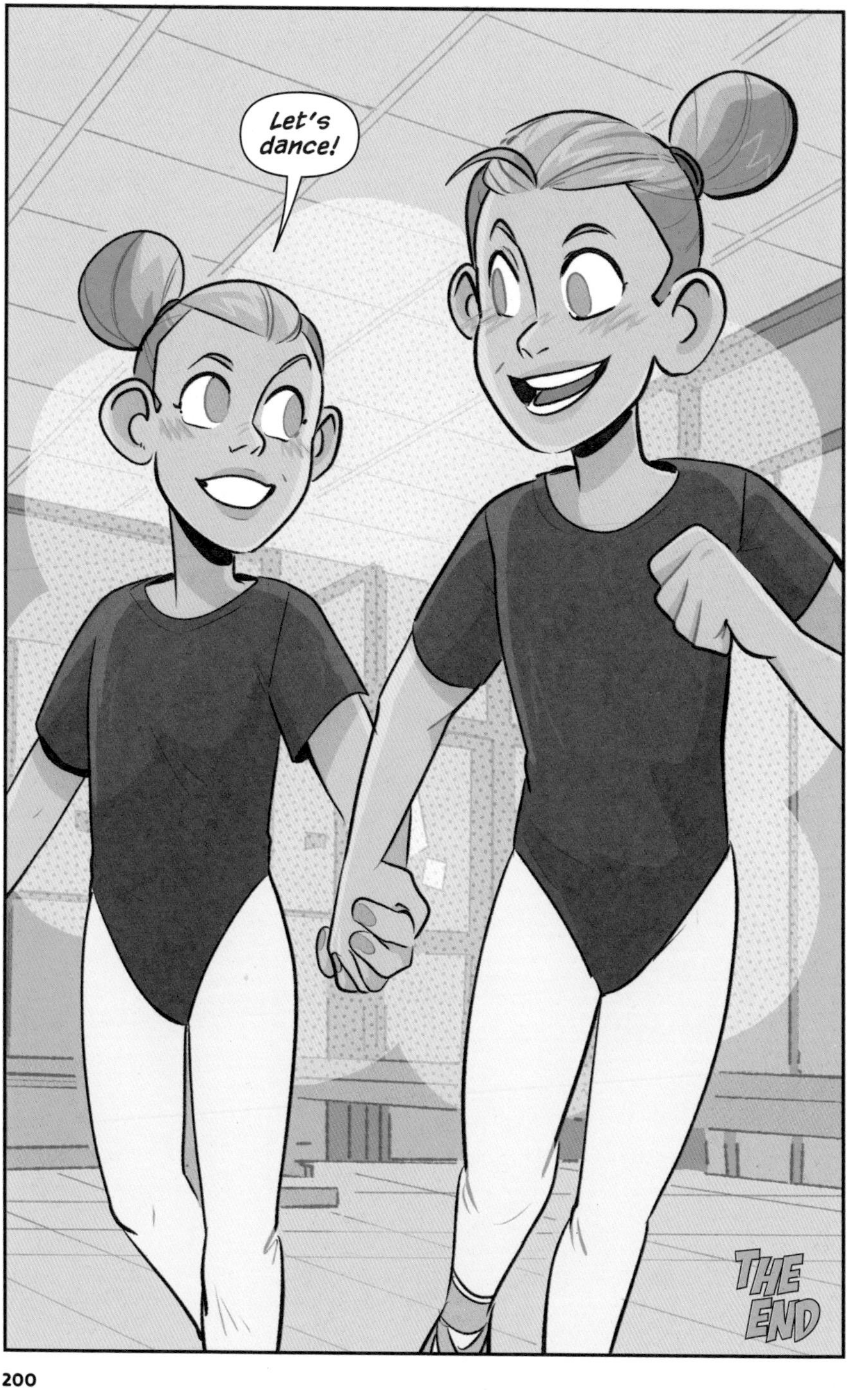
Let's dance!
THE END

Meet the fam!

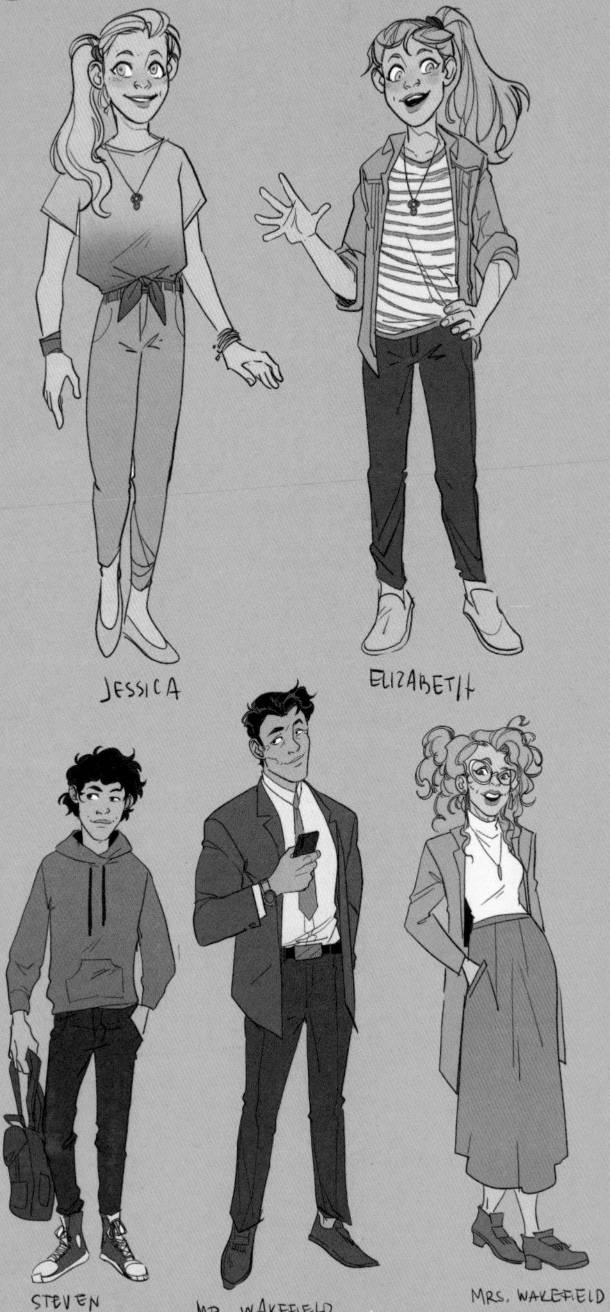
JESSICA
ELIZABETH
STEVEN
MR. WAKEFIELD
MRS. WAKEFIELD

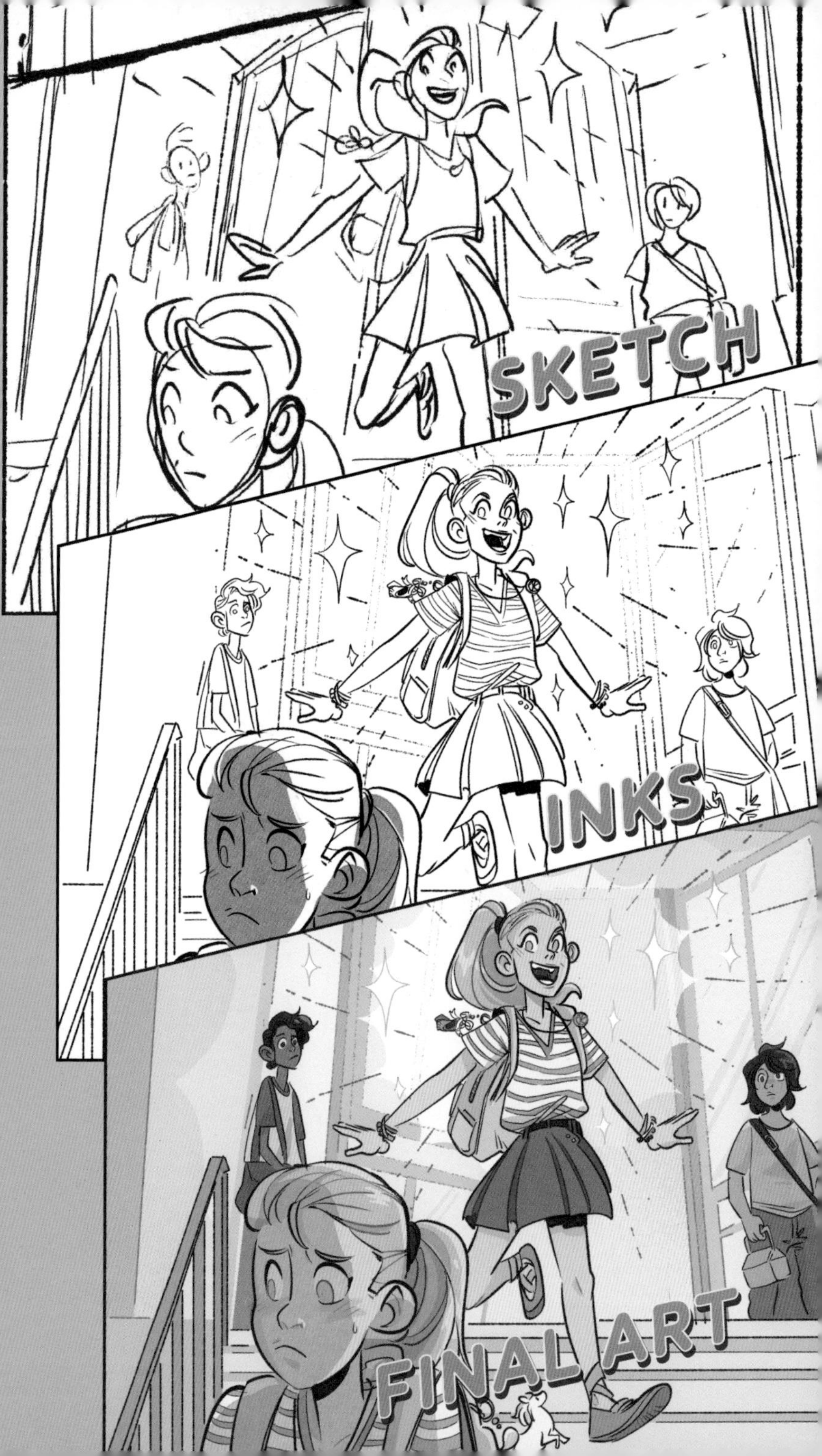
SKETCH
INKS
FINAL ART

JESSICA and
ELIZABETH
RETURN in

FRANCINE PASCAL'S

SWEET VALLEY

Twins

TEACHER'S PET

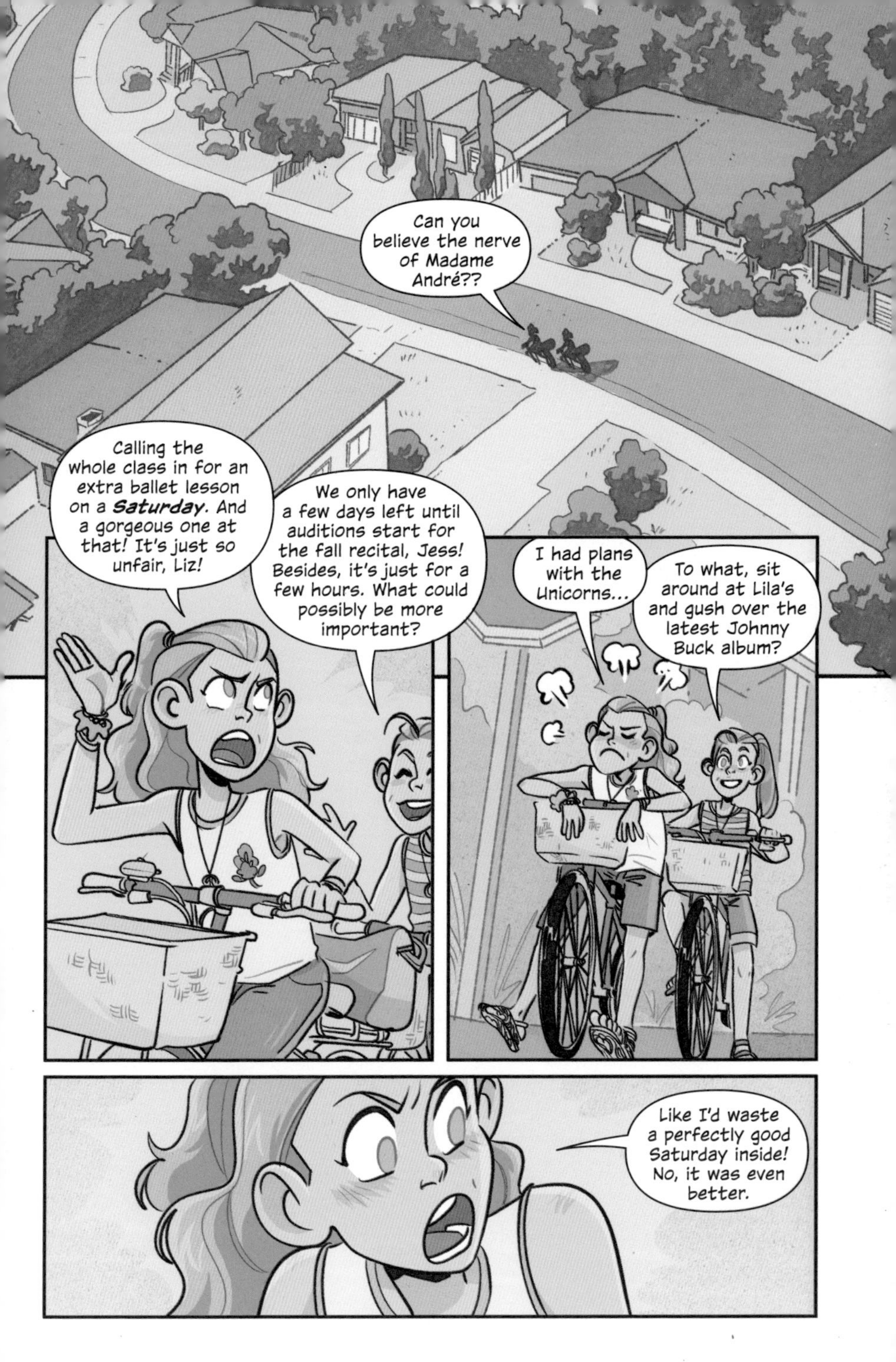
Can you believe the nerve of Madame André??
Calling the whole class in for an extra ballet lesson on a ***Saturday***. And a gorgeous one at that! It's just so unfair, Liz!
We only have a few days left until auditions start for the fall recital, Jess! Besides, it's just for a few hours. What could possibly be more important?
I had plans with the Unicorns...
To what, sit around at Lila's and gush over the latest Johnny Buck album?
Like I'd waste a perfectly good Saturday inside! No, it was even better.

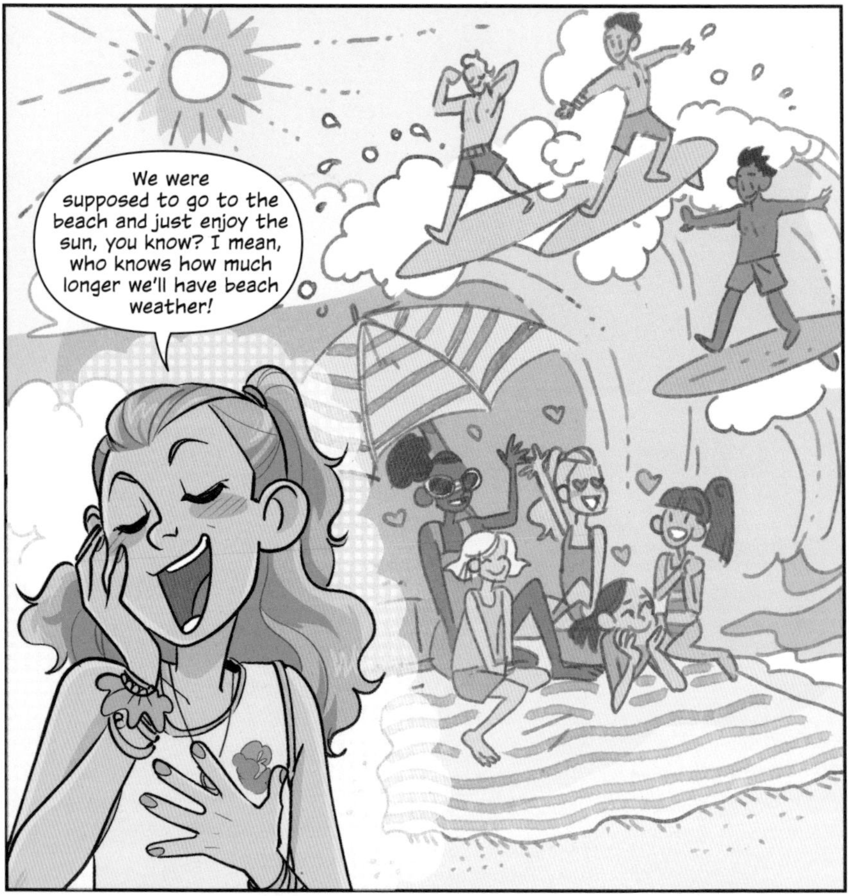
We were supposed to go to the beach and just enjoy the sun, you know? I mean, who knows how much longer we'll have beach weather!

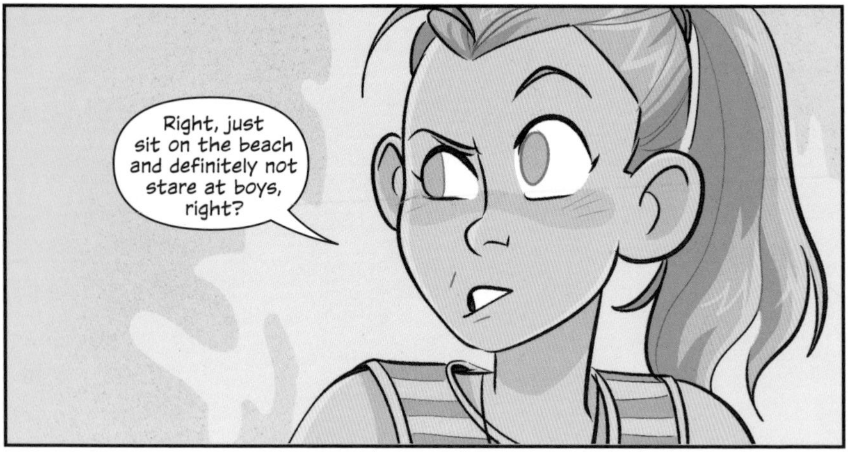
Right, just sit on the beach and definitely not stare at boys, right?

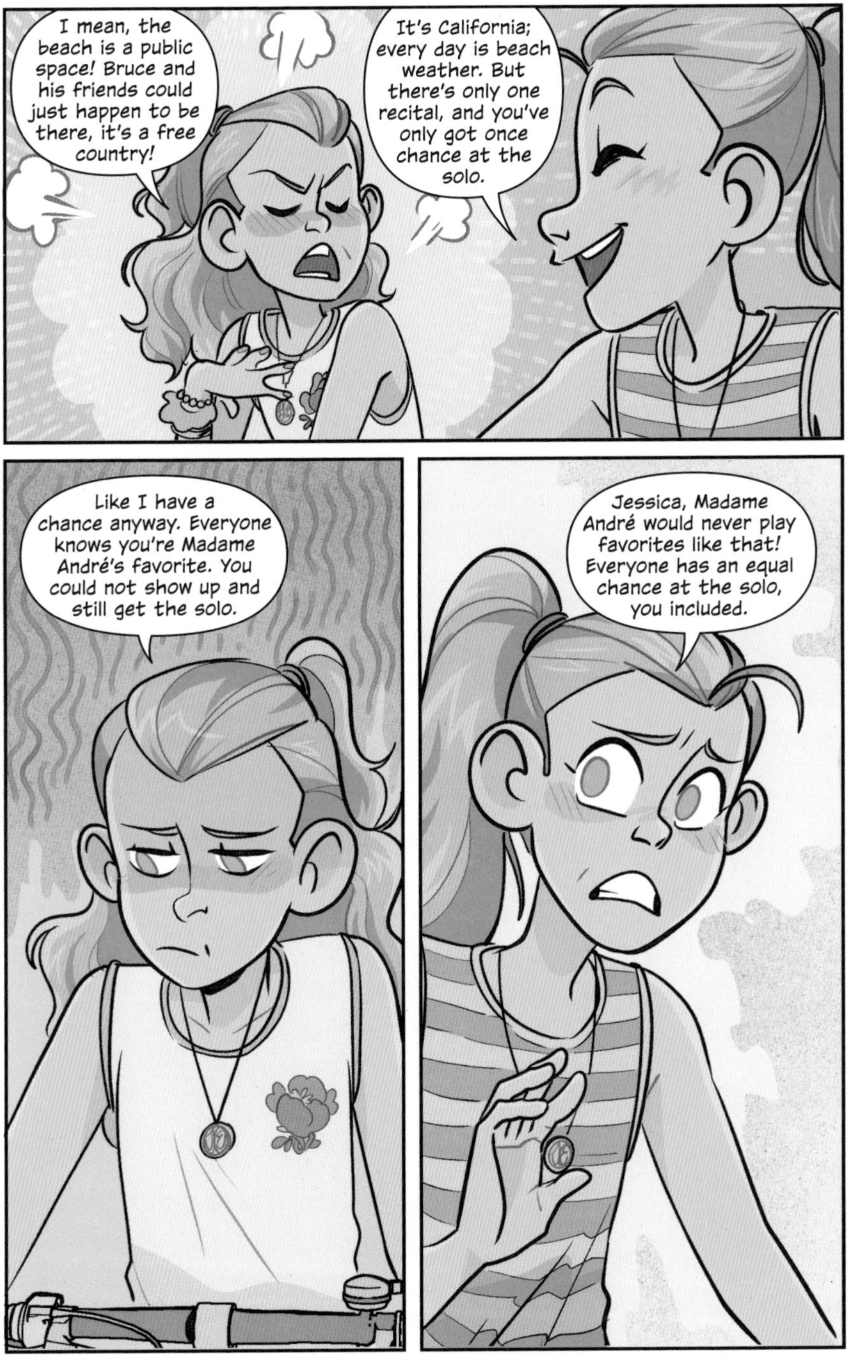
I mean, the beach is a public space! Bruce and his friends could just happen to be there, it's a free country!
It's California; every day is beach weather. But there's only one recital, and you've only got once chance at the solo.
Like I have a chance anyway. Everyone knows you're Madame André's favorite. You could not show up and still get the solo.
Jessica, Madame André would never play favorites like that! Everyone has an equal chance at the solo, you included.

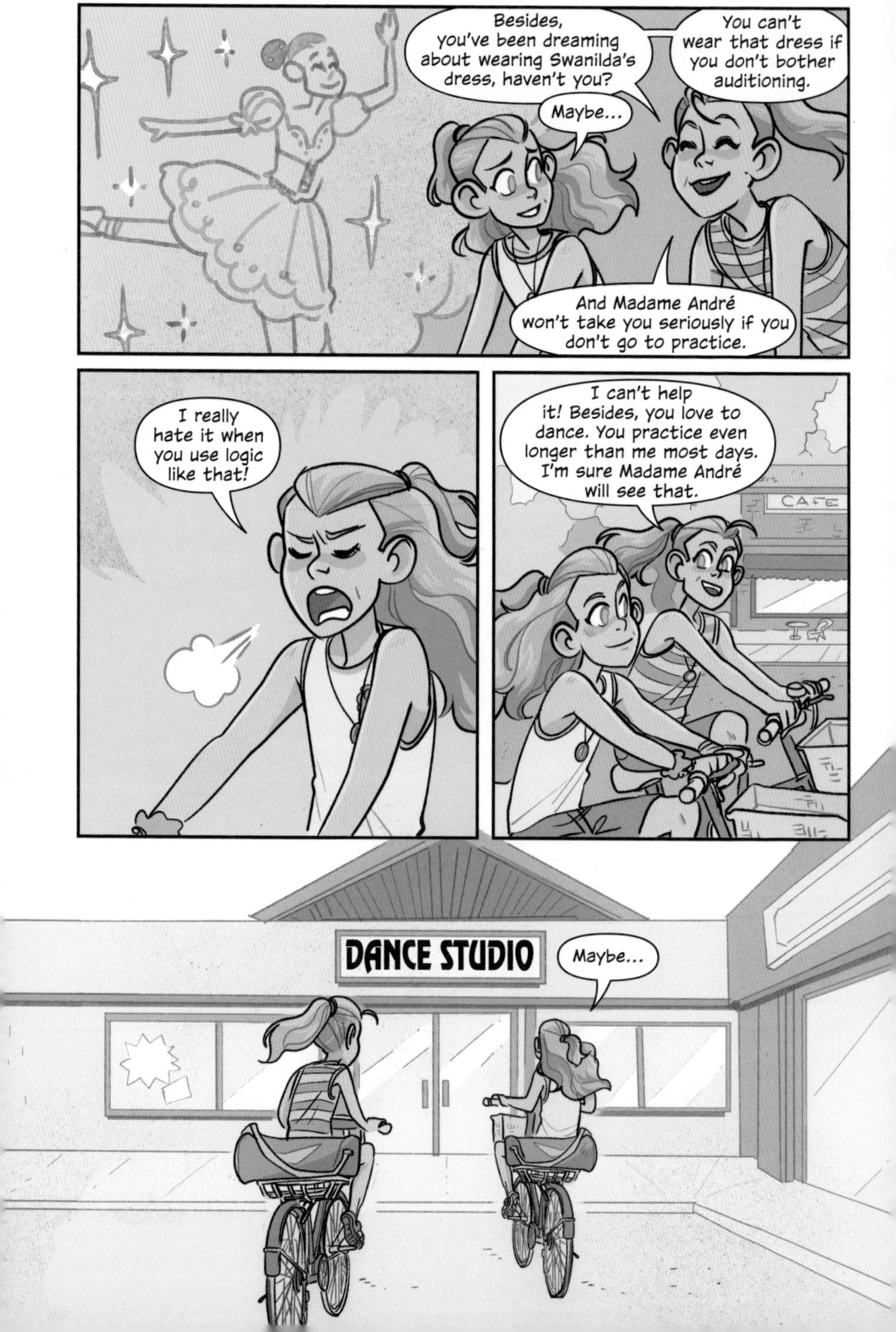
Besides, you've been dreaming about wearing Swanilda's dress, haven't you?
You can't wear that dress if you don't bother auditioning.
Maybe...
And Madame André won't take you seriously if you don't go to practice.
I really hate it when you use logic like that!
I can't help it! Besides, you love to dance. You practice even longer than me most days. I'm sure Madame André will see that.
CAFE
DANCE STUDIO
Maybe...

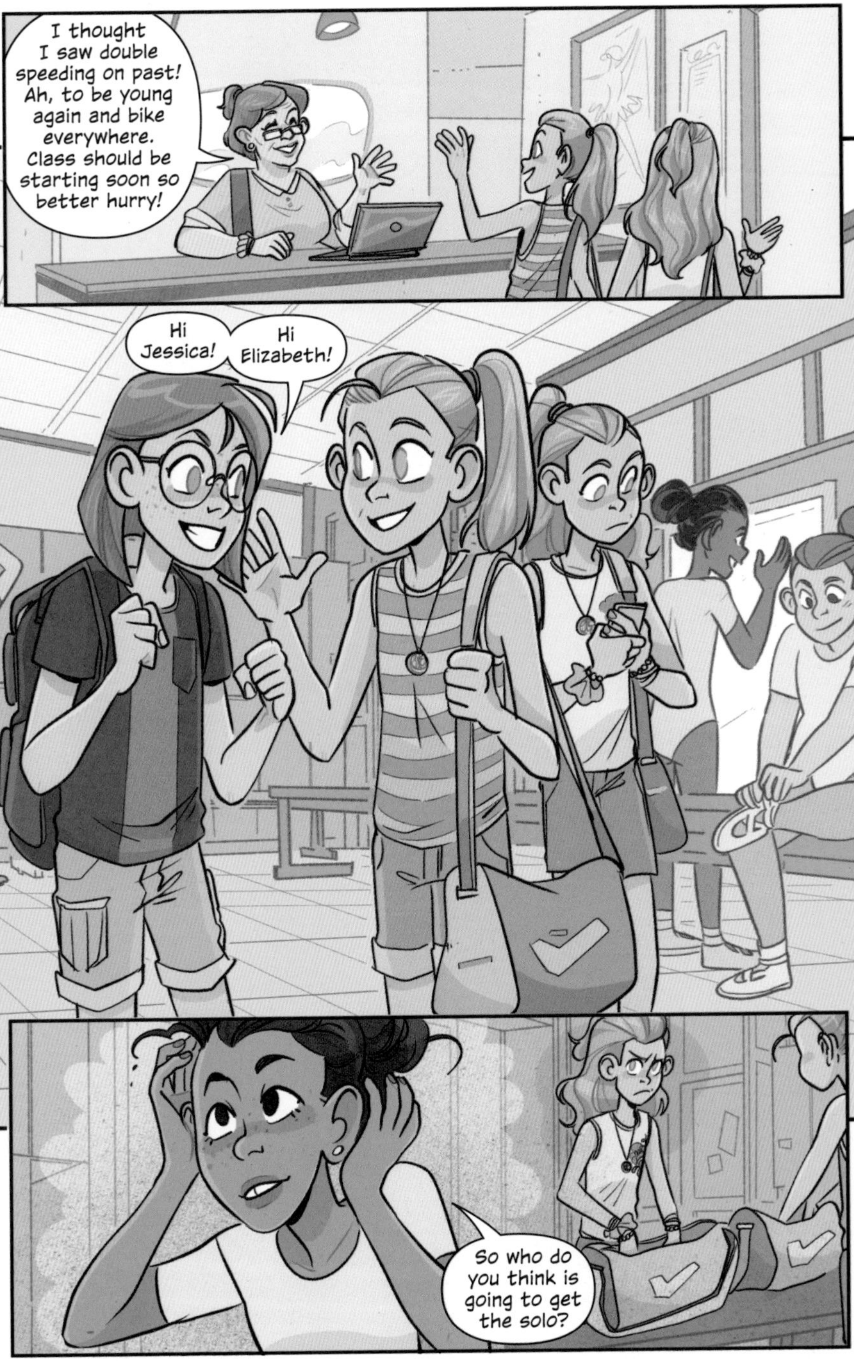
I thought I saw double speeding on past! Ah, to be young again and bike everywhere. Class should be starting soon so better hurry!
Hi Jessica!
Hi Elizabeth!
So who do you think is going to get the solo?

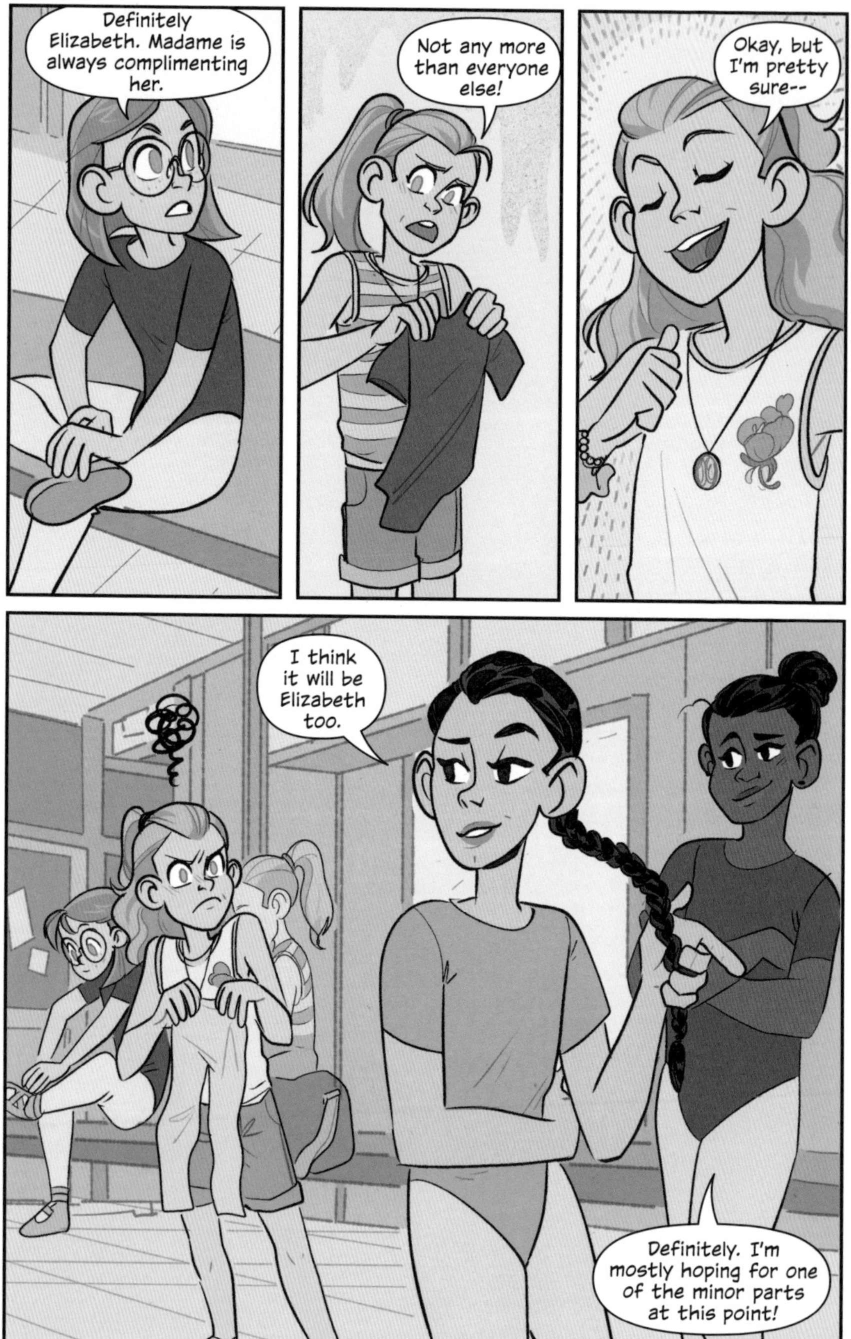
Definitely Elizabeth. Madame is always complimenting her.
Not any more than everyone else!
Okay, but I'm pretty sure--
I think it will be Elizabeth too.
Definitely. I'm mostly hoping for one of the minor parts at this point!

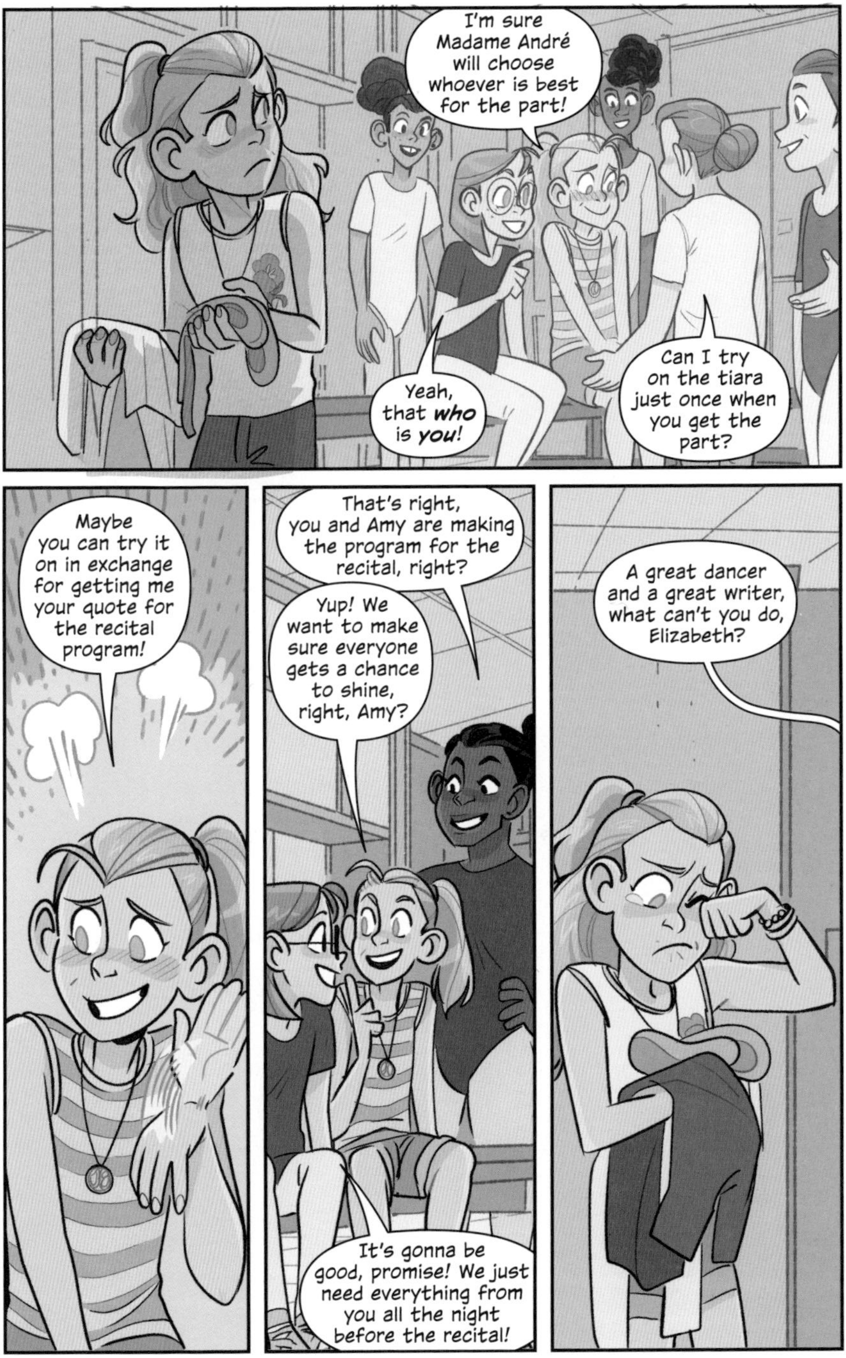
I'm sure Madame André will choose whoever is best for the part!
Yeah, that *who* is *you*!
Can I try on the tiara just once when you get the part?
Maybe you can try it on in exchange for getting me your quote for the recital program!
That's right, you and Amy are making the program for the recital, right?
Yup! We want to make sure everyone gets a chance to shine, right, Amy?
It's gonna be good, promise! We just need everything from you all the night before the recital!
A great dancer and a great writer, what can't you do, Elizabeth?

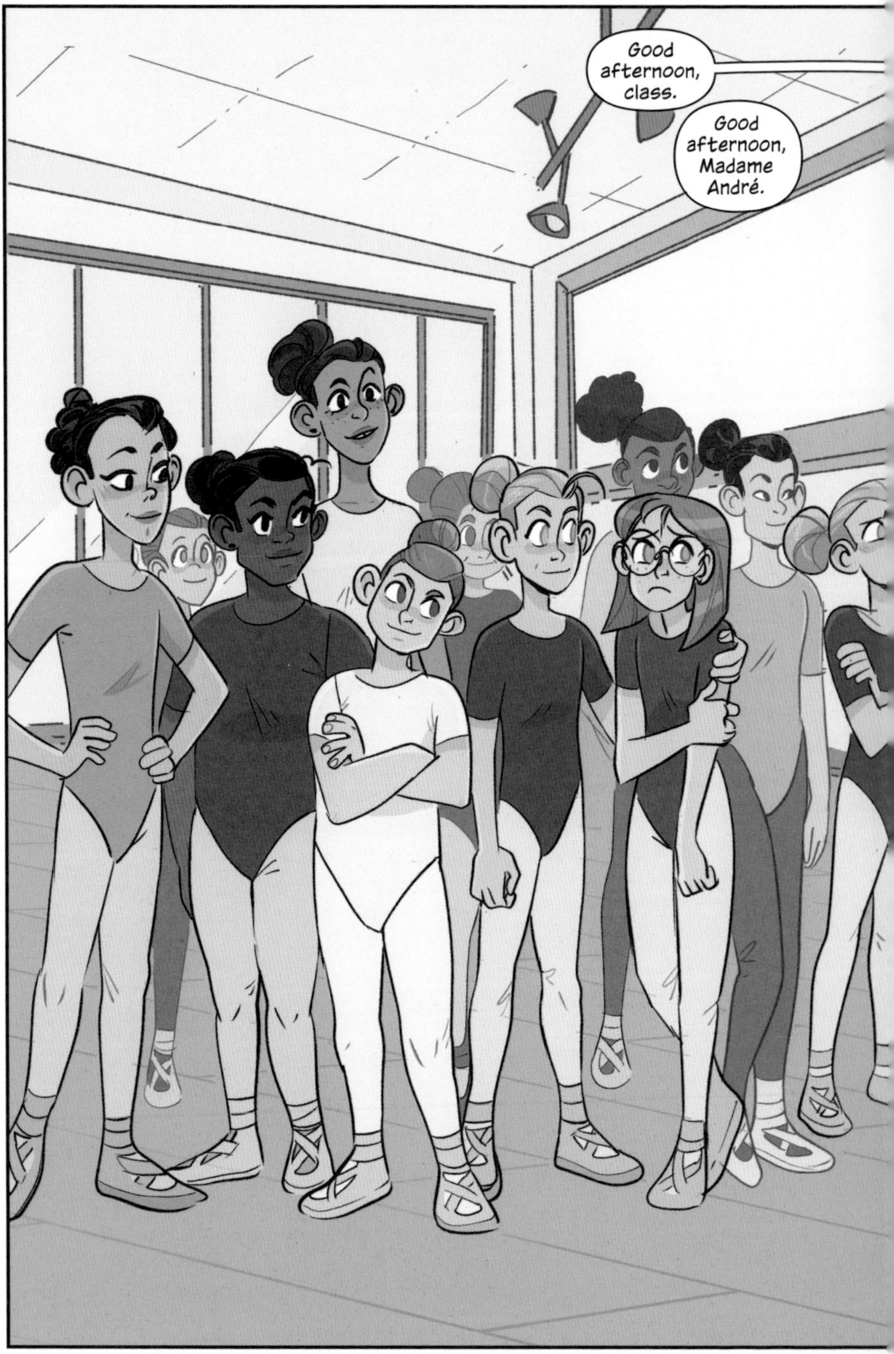
Good afternoon, class.
Good afternoon, Madame André.

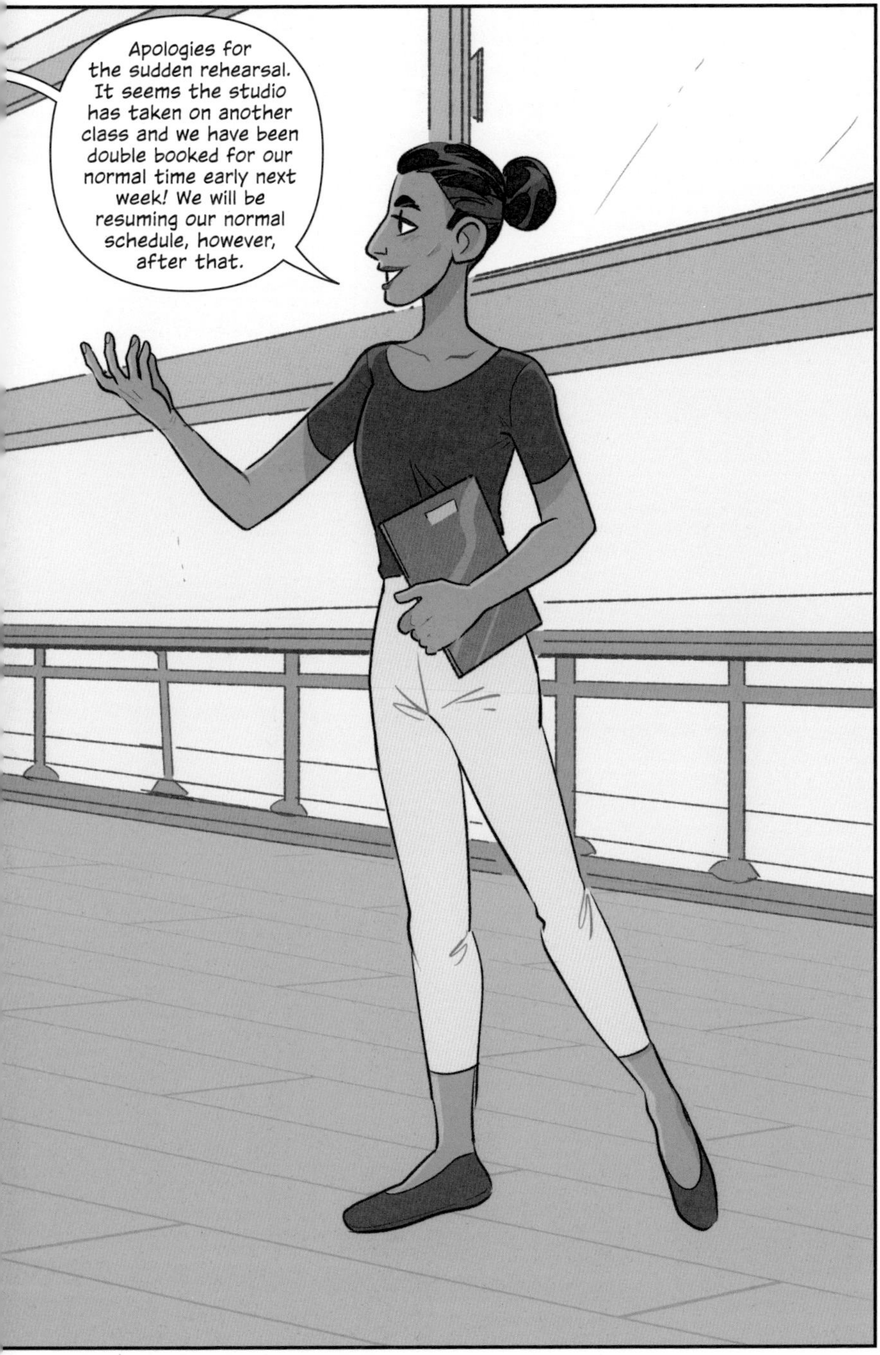
Apologies for the sudden rehearsal. It seems the studio has taken on another class and we have been double booked for our normal time early next week! We will be resuming our normal schedule, however, after that.

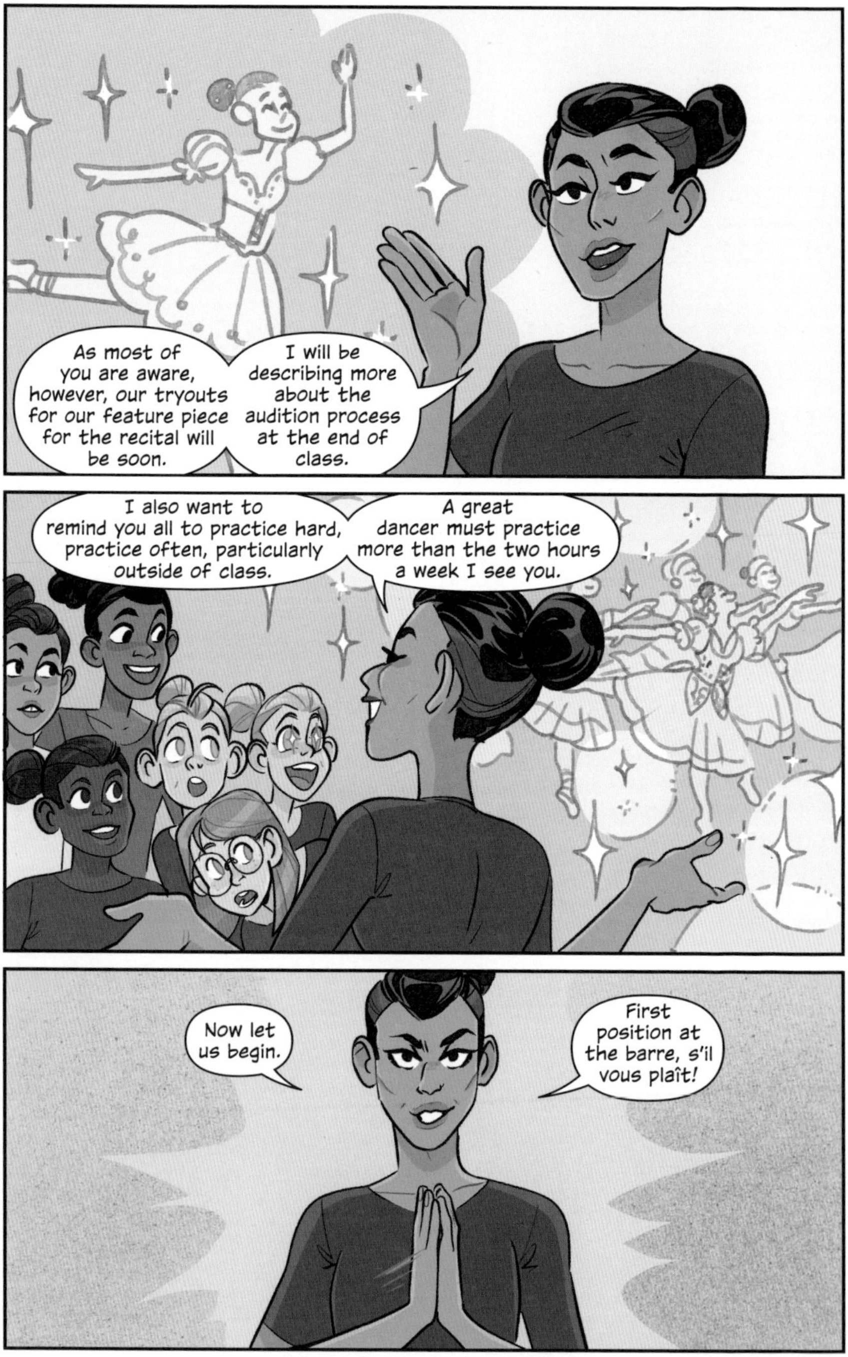

As most of you are aware, however, our tryouts for our feature piece for the recital will be soon.
I will be describing more about the audition process at the end of class.
I also want to remind you all to practice hard, practice often, particularly outside of class.
A great dancer must practice more than the two hours a week I see you.
Now let us begin.
First position at the barre, s'il vous plaît!

FRANCINE PASCAL

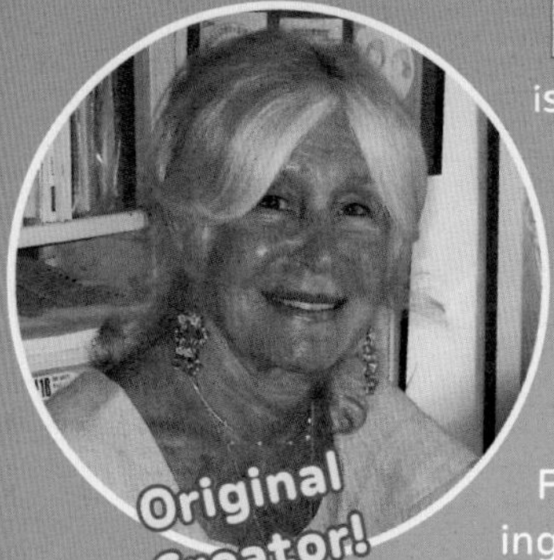
Original Creator!

is one of the world's most popular fiction writers for teenagers and is the creator of the Sweet Valley universe. This includes Sweet Valley Twins, Sweet Valley High, and Sweet Valley Unicorn Club. Over their lifetime, Sweet Valley books have sold millions of copies and have inspired board games, puzzles, and dolls. Francine is also the author of several bestselling novels, including *My Mother Was Never a Kid, My First Love and Other Disasters,* and the Fearless series. Her adult novels include *Save Johanna!* and *La Villa* and the nonfiction book *The Strange Case of Patty Hearst.* She has collaborated with Michael Stewart on the Broadway musical *George M!,* and with Jon Marans and Graham Lyle she has written the musical *The Fearless Girl.* She is on the advisory board of the American Theatre Wing. Her favorite sport is a monthly poker game. Francine lives in New York and the South of France.

@francinepascal_

NICOLE ANDELFINGER

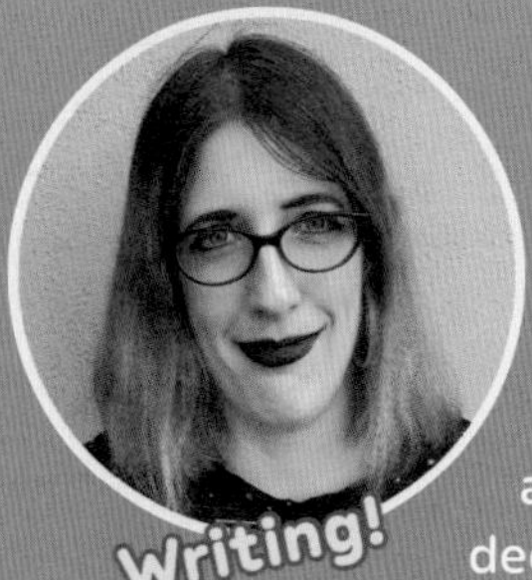
Writing!

was crafting stories as far back as when coloring in the squiggles on your composition book was considered cool. Since then, she's only continued to dwell in the realms of magic, monsters, and myth. She lives with her absolutely, most decidedly perfect cat in Los Angeles.

@nandelfinger

CLAUDIA AGUIRRE

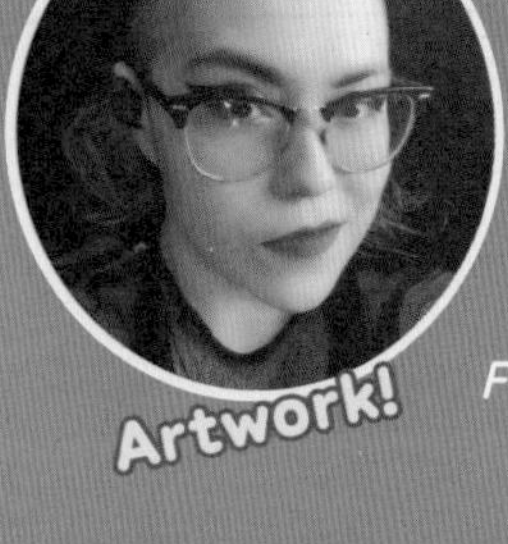
Artwork!

is a Mexican comic-book artist and writer. She is a cofounder of Boudika Comics, where she self-publishes comics, and is a GLAAD Media Award nominee and an Eisner Award nominee. Her comic works include *Lost on Planet Earth, Hotel Dare, Firebrand, Morning in America,* and *Kim & Kim.*

@claudiaguirre

Lettering!
WARREN MONTGOMERY

has been in comics for over thirty years and has lettered for publishers like Insight Editions, HarperCollins, and Boom! Studios. His work includes *Adventure Time*, *'Namwolf*, and *Over the Garden Wall*. He also self-publishes comics (Will Lill Comics) from his home base in Portland, Oregon.

🐦 @twm1962

Coloring!
SARA HAGSTROM

is a freelance illustrator and designer who loves nostalgia, trinkets, and all things narrative. Currently based in Baltimore, Sara also co-runs Lucky Pocket Press, a micropress that publishes comics and zines. Along with comics and coloring, Sara has done work for indie video games and taught as adjunct faculty at Maryland Institute College of Art.

🐦 @nucheki
sara-hagstrom.com

Coloring!
ANDREA BELL

is an illustrator, comic artist, and colorist living in Chicago, through the best and worst seasons. She has a BFA from Columbia College Chicago and began her comics career self-publishing, traveling throughout North America exhibiting her work. She has since gone on to illustrate the Diary of a 5th Grade Outlaw trilogy, *The Leak*, and *Maker Comics: Conduct a Science Experiment!* and provided coloring for *Twins*, *Wrapped Up*, *Cat Ninja*, *Sci-Fu 2*, and *Chunky*. When she's not drawing, Andrea enjoys long nature walks, curating playlists, and a warm meme on a cold day.

🐦 @andyharvestyeah
andreabelldraws.com

FIND YOUR VOICE
WITH ONE OF THESE EXCITING GRAPHIC NOVELS

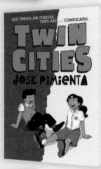

PRESENTED BY **RH** GRAPHIC

🐦 📷 @RHKIDSGRAPHIC

A GRAPHIC NOVEL ON EVERY BOOKSHELF